I0761673

Wandering WILD

Books by Lynette Noni

STANDALONE NOVELS

Wandering Wild

THE PRISON HEALER TRILOGY

The Prison Healer

The Gilded Cage

The Blood Traitor

THE MEDORAN CHRONICLES

Akarnae

Raelia

Draekora

Graevale

We Three Heroes

Vardaesia

Kaldoras

THE WHISPER DUOLOGY

Whisper

Weapon

LYNETTE NONI

Published in 2025 by Blackstone Publishing
Cover and book design by Larissa Ezell

Printed in the United States of America

First edition: 2025
ISBN 979-8-8748-1172-3
Young Adult Fiction / Romance / Contemporary

Version 1

Blackstone Publishing
31 Mistletoe Rd.
Ashland, OR 97520

www.BlackstonePublishing.com

This book is for anyone who has
stopped dreaming
stopped hoping
stopped believing
stopped ***living****.*

Dare to dream again.

♥

Dear Reader—

For the most part, this book is intended as a romantic (mis)adventure through the wilderness, but please be aware that it also contains themes regarding mental health and personal trauma that may be triggering for some readers.

PROLOGUE

I've never feared dying.

Maybe it's because I'm young, still a teenager, and in perfect health.

Maybe it's because I know death comes for everyone, and there's no point dreading the inevitable.

Or maybe it's simply because I've never given much thought to my own mortality, having always viewed it as something to contemplate in the distant future, perhaps during a midlife crisis or some other existential predicament.

Had I known I would soon be lost in the wilderness and freefalling down a colossal waterfall, about to meet my end, I might have given my life—and death—more consideration.

But it's too late for regrets.

It's too late for *anything.*

Because when I finally stop plummeting only to slam into the hard surface of the raging, icy river, I don't have time to be afraid of what's coming next. I don't even have time to mourn everything I'm about to lose, the life I could have had, the dreams I'll never see come true. All I have time for is a single thought, a single feeling, before everything goes black:

Pain.

Zander

The moment I step out of the elevator into my agent's high-rise office, the light streaming in through the floor-to-ceiling windows hits me like a slap in the face. I shield my eyes from the glittering Los Angeles skyline, hissing as my retinas sting in protest.

A *tsk* sound greets my ears, followed by a deep voice saying, "Your community service might be over, but you're still required to remain sober. Do you *want* to be sent back to rehab?"

I squint through the room until I find my agent, Gabriel King, reclining on his cream leather couch and watching me over the rim of his takeout coffee cup.

"I'm not hungover." The injustice of his assumption burns in my chest, compounded by guilt, shame, and—worst of all—grief, all of which I quickly stifle. "Your office might as well be on the sun. Haven't you heard of blinds?"

"Gotta get my Vitamin D," Gabe says, sliding one dark-skinned arm into a sunbeam. His sleeves are rolled up to his elbows, his starched collar unbuttoned, his general appearance more disheveled than usual. It doesn't bode well that he's called me to his office, since we usually talk over the phone—especially lately, with how much I've been trying to avoid the paparazzi.

Gabe waves to an identical cream couch opposite him. "Have a seat, Zander."

I head to where he indicated, trying to ignore the uneasy tension in my stomach. Gabe isn't just my agent, he's my friend. A father figure, almost. He's been championing me ever since I accepted a dare to audition for a film inspired by a popular children's book series and, without any experience or training, surprised everyone by being cast as the lead. *The Lost Heirs* franchise took off, resulting in four blockbuster movies—and overnight fame for me. A real-life Hollywood fairy tale, reporters say, whenever they reference my rise to stardom, and Gabe was with me through it all. Contracts, scripts, endorsements, interviews, fans, social media—I had no idea what I was doing until he swooped in and took control. I was barely twelve when I signed with him. I'm now eighteen, and I still have no idea what I'm doing. But it turns out that the one thing I do know is how to act. Even more, I enjoy it. When I sink into the mind of a character, from the moment the director calls "Action!" to when they announce "That's a wrap," I feel alive. I feel free. I'm one of the lucky few who has found their calling in life, and I can't imagine doing anything else.

Maybe that's why I'm so nervous as I take my seat opposite Gabe. Because there's a look on his face I've never seen before, a resigned set to his features, a depth of sadness in his eyes.

Sadness—*for me.*

"I'll get straight to it," Gabe says, not one to waste time. "The studio is threatening to find someone else to play Titan Wolfe."

A single sentence is all it takes for something precious inside me to wither and die.

"You were already labeled difficult after everything with Summer," Gabe continues, and when I open my mouth to object, he stops me with a look. "The truth doesn't matter, Zan. This is Hollywood." Despite his firm words, his tone is apologetic. "Lord knows you have the talent and the charisma and the—well, *everything*—but you also made an enemy out of one of the most powerful directors in the biz. Your reputation is mud. And we're in damage control." His dark eyes snare mine. "You already know how many favors I had to call in just to get you an audition for *Titan's War*. They saw your skill enough to cast you as the lead, but can you blame them for being wary now? Especially with the DUI charge on top of the rest? They're not out of line for citing breach of contract. I'm frankly surprised they're only threatening to replace you."

I clench my jaw and look out the window-wall, but then the last part of what he said sinks in.

"They're not—" My voice is hoarse, so I cough and try again. "They're only threatening? Does that mean they're not actually terminating?"

Gabe takes a long sip of his coffee. "Not yet."

A breath whooshes out of me, but my relief is short-lived.

"Things aren't looking good though, kid."

It's his gentle tone that really hits me, making me realize how serious this is. And it's because of that—and because of how much my career means to me—that I square my shoulders and ask, "How do I fix this?"

He could say anything and I would do it. Acting is all I have; losing it would be like losing myself.

Gabe sips his coffee again, before declaring, "We need to clean up your image."

I frown, since that much is obvious.

But then he continues, "And we only have two weeks to do it."

My heart skips a beat. "Two *weeks*?"

Gabe nods, then places his coffee on the small table between us, swapping it for his tablet. "Val tried appealing to the producers while you were away—"

He makes it sound as if I took a vacation, not like I was fulfilling my court-ordered rehab and community service hours—both of which were a slap on the wrist compared to what they could have been.

"—but they're eager to get the cameras rolling, which means if they have to recast, they needed to do it yesterday. A fortnight was the best she could manage, but she also warned that you're going to have to pull off a near miracle to convince them to keep you on."

I lean forward and rub a hand over my face. Valentina Martínez—the director of *Titan's War*—is one of my biggest advocates, and also one of the reasons why I won the lead in what is already being hailed by the media as a "movie of the decade" despite it only being in pre-production. Val doesn't care about gossip; she cares only about her creative vision. Apparently, she took one look at my audition and demanded that the casting director have me return for a chemistry read with the female romantic lead. I didn't know it at the time, but I was the only actor who Val personally requested for a callback. She envisioned me as Titan Wolfe from the beginning. If I end up losing the role, she'll be almost as devastated as me.

But only almost.

"Did they offer any suggestions for how I can . . . prove myself?" I ask Gabe, stumbling over the words. How can I show that I'm not the person they think I am, when the entire world believes it to be true?

"Nothing specific," he answers, swiping at his tablet. "But Val and I spoke at length about this and, well . . ." He taps the screen, before looking up at me again. "She has an idea."

At his prompting, I glance toward the side of his office where a television is mounted to the wall, the screensaver showing rolling waves breaking onto a sandy shore. Another tap of Gabe's finger and the waves are replaced by footage of a young teenager seated on a blue couch, laughing at something his interviewer is saying. The sound is muted, but I remember that day like it was yesterday.

The boy is me, four years ago, on the press tour promoting the second *Lost Heirs* movie. I'd just turned fourteen and, thanks to the success of the first film, all the major talk shows around the world had invited me in, mostly as an individual but sometimes with my castmates.

My gaze remains locked on the television as the interview continues playing. I find it hard to believe how innocent I seemed back then.

How . . . *wholesome*. It's strange watching myself; I almost have to think of the person on the screen as someone else. As a kid who wins the audience with a flick of his unusual silver hair and a well-timed wink of his startlingly blue eyes, aimed straight at the camera. I nearly snort at his attempts to charm the viewers, but I manage to resist. Partly because I'm aware of Gabe's intense focus on me, and partly because I'm too busy beating back all the emotions that are vying for my attention. It doesn't make sense that I'm envious of *myself*, but that's my predominant feeling right now.

"We need to get you back to that," Gabe says quietly. "Or an older, more seasoned version of it." He pauses the footage on my fourteen-year-old self grinning brightly enough to melt hearts all over the globe. "We need to recapture that human side of you. The innocence, the sincerity, the inherent goodness that made people fall in love with you. That's what we have to show everyone—we want them to see *you* again, not 'Zander Rune: Hollywood's Bad Boy.'"

The title has my hackles rising. "I'm not—"

"I *know*, Zan," Gabe cuts me off, losing patience. "But it's not me who you need to convince."

I blow out an aggravated breath, reminding myself that he's trying to help. "You said Val has an idea?" I wave to the television screen. "What does this have to do with it?"

Gabe shifts in his seat, a nervous movement that puts me on edge, and then he fast-forwards the footage. He pauses it again when the interviewer reveals a photograph of an even younger version of me, seven years old, standing shin-deep in a bubbling creek and holding a fishing rod. The camera had a timer function, so both my mom and dad made it into the shot, their arms wrapped around me, all three of us beaming.

I school my expression as I turn back to Gabe, knowing he's watching me carefully. I remember why the interviewer showed this particular photo, just as I remember every word of our conversation that came after it was shared with the world. What I don't understand is why Gabe has brought it up now.

"I lied before," he admits. "Technically, it's my idea, not Val's. But I did ask for her help since we're strapped for time and she has the contacts to make it happen. She's worked with his production team before, so she can cut through the red tape and get things moving before your fortnight is up."

Gabe stops speaking, as if waiting for my response, but all I can do is repeat, "*His* production team?" My confusion is clear. "*Whose* team? And for *what*?"

It takes a moment for Gabe to answer, during which time he sips the dregs of his coffee. "This idea . . . you're not going to like it."

The hesitation in his voice is enough for me to brace, especially when he sighs, long and loud, before continuing, "You're too talented as an actor for the studio—and the public—not to question if you're just faking your way back into their good graces, so that means we need someone else to bring out the 'you' they want to see. Someone who will remind them that you're still the same boy who made the world fall to its knees, and that your recent notoriety is nothing more than a passing blip. Someone who will help prove you're still worth their investment and adoration."

Every muscle in my body is tense. "When you say 'someone,' what does that mean?" I recall his mention of a production team and warily ask, "Who else have you suckered into this plan to redeem my image?"

Gabe's response is to offer a slow grin that sets off warning bells. "That's the brilliance of my idea." He begins tapping at his tablet again. "No one can say we rigged it, because no one will be 'suckered in' unless they choose to be. And as long as you keep your head together and offer your best manners for a few days, you'll be in the clear just in time for your end-of-fortnight deadline."

I'm more confused than ever, but at Gabe's look, I smother my questions and wait for him to explain. He doesn't use the main television to share from his tablet this time, keeping the photo from my family's one and only camping trip on the screen. I should have realized it was a forewarning, Gabe's way of softening the blow of what he was about to reveal, but there was no way I could have anticipated that it was his inspiration for saving my career. Instead, comprehension hits me like a freight train when he flips his tablet around so it's facing me.

My eyes travel over the drafted media announcement, and all I can do is utter a quiet expletive, knowing Gabe is right on two counts:

His idea *is* brilliant.

And I absolutely hate it.

Charlie

The soulful lyrics of Randy Newman's "You've Got a Friend in Me" wake me from the dead of sleep, the chorus growing incessantly louder until I roll over and fumble around on my bedside table for my phone. I don't have to look at the screen to know who's calling—that ringtone is only allocated to one person.

With my heart in my throat, I connect the call.

"Em?" I croak out. "Are you—"

Her high-pitched scream causes me to wince, though it also makes my unease vanish. Screaming is good. It's Ember's silence that I've learned to dread, rare as it is from my best friend these days—thank God. But despite my relief, when I glance blearily at the clock and see it reading past two a.m., I groan loud enough to interrupt her shrieks.

"It's the middle of the night," I rasp, my voice thick with sleep. "What the hell, Ember?"

"It's not in LA!" she cries nonsensically, her tone still pitched high enough for dogs in neighboring countries to hear. "Now get your butt over here—we need to submit our entries!"

She disconnects the call, leaving me blinking into the dark of my room. All I know is that I've been summoned, and if I don't crawl through her window within minutes, she'll attempt the reverse journey herself. So with another groan—this one resigned—I heave myself out of bed and use my phone's flashlight to search for my beloved pair of pink Uggs.

Cursing the day Ember Ashley moved in next door—and then cursing myself for such an uncharitable thought—I stumble toward my window and shove it open. The chill of the early September air hits me and I shiver, looking longingly back at my bed. But then I see Ember poke her head out of her own window, gesturing for me to hurry.

Grumbling about sleep-stealing best friends, I ease out over the ledge until I'm balanced on a thick gum-tree branch that offers a bridge between our two houses. The smell of eucalyptus provides a sensory kick to help energize me—combined with the two-story drop beneath my feet—and I spider-crawl my way from my window to Ember's, swinging into her warmly lit room.

"I hate you a little more each day," I tell her as I move straight to her bed and collapse on top of it.

"Thankfully, you also love me a lot, so it'll take you a while before you hate me completely," she returns, plonking down beside me.

I scowl at her, but I can't maintain my grumpy act for long in the face of her contagious happiness. I've never known anyone like Ember, someone who always manages to see the bright side of things regardless of what life brings. It's beautiful—and exhausting.

"There had better be a good reason for you dragging me over here at this hour," I warn, my glare bouncing off her like oil on water.

"Not just a good reason," she says, reaching for her laptop and opening the web browser. "The *best* reason."

While she waits for the page to load, I glance around her bedroom that is as familiar as my own, with very few differences between them. Her walls are painted light pink while mine are pale yellow, but both are plastered with photos of the ten years of memories we've shared.

The Ashleys relocated from New Zealand to Australia when Ember was a toddler, but they didn't move in next door until just before my eighth birthday, with them trading their big-city lives in Sydney for the peace and quiet of our small coastal town. I will never be able to thank them enough for that decision, since I can't imagine my life without Ember in it. The things we've been through together . . . I know neither of us would have survived this far, if not for each other.

Looking at my friend now, I ignore the dark memories trying to force their way into my thoughts, and instead focus on the excited gleam in her brown eyes. There's a rosy flush to her cheeks, and her short black hair is spiking out from beneath her hot-pink beanie, the sight of which warms me—the color is so perfectly Ember—while at the same time it brings a coil of remembered dread to my stomach. But I banish my fears, knowing they are nothing more than ghosts.

Shifting into a more comfortable position, I jolt slightly when I catch sight of my reflection in the mirror across from Ember's bed. It's not my sensible flannel pajamas that surprise me, nor my skin that's on the pale side from winter. No, the shock I get is something that has happened frequently over the last few days whenever I've seen myself—or rather, whenever I've seen my hair. "Galaxy," they call it: a mixture of blue, purple, and magenta. I thought I would hate it, but even if I did, it wouldn't matter, since I made a deal with Ember three years ago saying she could choose my hair color every time it's due for a trim. I've long since learned to relinquish my trepidation, especially given how much our deal meant to her at the time. And despite some truly outrageous hair adventures, she always manages to find something that flatters me. While my current look is painfully attention-grabbing, I can admit that it works magic on my eyes, making the dusky blue-gray shade appear almost ethereally violet.

Even so, it's going to take time for me to get used to it.

"Okay, so, don't freak out," Ember says, reclaiming my attention as the web page finally loads. Those five words are enough to have me sighing inwardly—and that sigh becomes audible when she shoves her laptop in my face and points to the screen.

On it is an image of someone who is all too familiar to me—and to the rest of the world. Impossibly blue eyes in a too-perfect face, frosted silver hair styled messily enough to look as if it's *not* styled, golden tanned skin, and a body that clearly has the benefit of numerous personal trainers.

Zander Rune: actor extraordinaire and unfairly gorgeous Hollywood bad boy.

I haven't seen a photo of him in three months, but those three months have only made him more attractive—as unfathomable as that is. Instead of acknowledging it, I repress my slowly simmering anger and say the first thing that comes to mind: "He always did look like an anime character, but now it's becoming ridiculous."

Ember was about to scroll down the page, but she's startled enough to choke on a laugh and halt her movement. "He looks like *what*?"

"Oh, please, as if you don't see it. His hair, his eyes, his"—I gesture to his face and body, not wanting to compliment him aloud—"*everything*. He doesn't look real."

Still laughing, Ember says, "You don't even watch anime."

"Doesn't matter. Google it," I challenge. I pull her laptop closer and open a new tab, typing *silver hair blue eyes anime male* into the search bar, letting out a triumphant sound when the results load. Zander could be likened to any one of them, but the perfect example jumps straight out at me. "There. Him. Satoru Gojo. I told you so."

Ember cocks her head to the side. "Why's he wearing a blindfold?"

"Just look at the images without the blindfold." I click on one to enlarge it. "He's the spitting image of Zander Rune."

"He's also extremely hot."

This time it's me who chokes. "He's an animated character."

Ember rolls her eyes. "As if you've never crushed on someone from Disney. Robin Hood? Simba? They weren't even *human* but you can't deny their hotness."

"It was their *personality*—"

"And don't get me started on Flynn Rider and Li Shang." She utters a dreamy sigh. "Total babes."

I send her a deadpan look. "I worry about you sometimes."

She grins and blows me a kiss, before scrolling through more of the images as she murmurs, "I really need to start watching anime, if the guys look like this." But then she sits up straight and frowns. "No, I won't be distracted. This is *important*."

Ember returns to the page that has the photo of Zander on it, but this time she scrolls far enough for me to see *why*. The text is in bold, a blaring declaration heralded across the entertainment website:

WIN AN ADVENTURE WITH ZANDER RUNE!

"You woke me up for *this*?"

Despite my annoyance, I'm not surprised. When it comes to Zander Rune, Ember is like most girls our age—and girls younger . . . and older . . . and many boys and genderqueer persons as well, for that matter. Zander is a Hollywood icon. Once upon a time, I was among the number who idolized him. I vividly recall being twelve years old and watching the first *Lost Heirs* movie at the cinema with Ember, and as soon as the credits began rolling, we sprinted back to the box office to purchase two more tickets so we could watch it all over again. Five years later, I can still remember every minute of that day—and the movie that left the world infatuated with the American heartthrob.

Until three months ago, I was one of Zander's biggest fans. But then he turned eighteen and made a series of choices that, in my mind, tarnished his image beyond repair. All the usual media scandals could be affixed to his name, but whether they were true or not, those weren't the things that turned me from my starstruck naivety. He was barely four months older than me, so I could easily relate to his teenage antics and had no grounds to cast judgment.

But then he wrapped his fancy car around a tree, and while he escaped miraculously unscathed, a routine test resulted in a DUI charge—and *that* was something I couldn't forgive. His actions had put others at risk, and yet, because of his celebrity, he was sentenced to only a few hours of community service and a short stint in rehab. Ever since that day, any infatuation I'd felt toward Zander Rune was gone. Forever.

Ember understood—more than anyone. And until tonight, she'd respected my unspoken wish to never talk about him again, even if she remained a not-so-secret fan. She's free to admire whoever she wants—of course she is—but this competition . . . This I don't understand. And my lack of understanding only grows as I begin reading the terms and conditions.

"You can't be serious," I say, my voice flat. She's practically bouncing beside me, her features aglow with excitement.

"Can you *imagine*?" she cries, flopping back onto her pillows. "Four days on vacation with Zander Rune."

"Vacation?" I point toward the fine print. "Did you read any of this?"

She ignores me and continues wistfully, "Him and me, alone, for ninety-six whole hours."

I snap my fingers in front of her glazed eyes. "Earth to Ember. Tell me you read this?"

She blinks herself back into the room and sits up again, nodding eagerly. "Every word."

Gathering my patience, I say, "Then you'll know that the winner *won't* be alone with Zander. And it's not promising a relaxing time—quite the opposite."

The competition grants not just an adventure with the actor, but also with Rykon Hawke, star of the reality survival show *Hawke's Wild World*. The man is a legend, having started his career as a park ranger in the Canadian Rockies before founding the first of many wilderness survival camps across the globe, most for rehabilitation programs, though plenty of schools and organizations use them as well. From there, he made the jump to television, where he quickly became a household name thanks to his ability to captivate audiences through various adventures—whether they be him climbing vertical cliffs with his bare hands, digging wind shelters into icy tundras, sprinting down volcanoes, staggering through deserts, or being stranded in the middle of the ocean. Each new episode sees Hawke taking viewers to an off-the-grid destination and surviving anything from a few days to weeks at a time. *Hawke's Wild World* is beyond extreme, and while I enjoy watching it, I can't help thinking that the man himself must be a little unhinged to dance with death so eagerly.

. . . And my best friend apparently wants to go on a trip with him and Zander freaking Rune.

"Not to point out the obvious here, but you and nature don't mix well," I say, subtlety be damned. "You couldn't even last the night camping in your own backyard for your thirteenth birthday party."

"There was a mosquito in the tent," she defends. "It had a vendetta against me."

Unless the winner of the competition is being sent to some ice-barren land, then they'll likely have to face *millions* of mosquitoes. But I don't bother saying that, instead continuing, "And this prize—if it can be called that—will send you out to the middle of nowhere for four days. Do you know what that means?"

Ember smiles widely. "Four days of Zander's entire focus, since there'll be no distractions?"

I shake my head, unsure if she's being deliberately obtuse or trying to rile me for the fun of it. "It means no indoor plumbing—no toilets, or showers, or running water. It means sleeping out in the open with all kinds of bugs crawling over you, rain, hail, or shine, and eating whatever Hawke says will keep your strength up—most likely something disgusting, like wriggling worms or dead birds or rabbit guts. Depending on the destination, you might even have to drink your own pee. And no matter where you end up, there'll be hours of hiking and climbing and living like you're lost in the wilderness, because that's exactly what you'll be: *Lost. In. The. Wilderness.*"

This time it's Ember who shakes her head. "Not *lost.* Just . . . wandering. With purpose." Her eyes glaze again. "And none of that matters because I'll be with Zander Rune."

God help me, I'm about to kill my best friend. "Snap out of it, Em, and think for a second. You can't possibly be considering this."

Finally, Ember comes back to herself. "Of course I'm not considering it."

The tightness eases from my shoulders. Until—

"I don't need to consider, because I've already entered. Now it's your turn. And after that, you can help me sign up for hundreds of fake new email addresses so we have more chances of winning."

I gape at her, then say, weakly, "Please tell me you're joking."

She pats me on the cheek. "Don't worry, Charlie Bear—if you win, I'll take your place, okay?"

Not okay. None of this is *okay*. And while I know Ember would skin me alive if I uttered my real argument against her taking off on some intrepid adventure—an argument that doesn't involve Zander at all, though he's definitely a good reason *not* to go—I still wish there was a way I could gently pull her back to reality. But looking at my friend and the light shining out of her, I just don't have it in me to remind her about all the reasons why she won't be able to go, even if she does miraculously win.

Instead, I dutifully fill out the online competition form, entering my personal details while making a mental note to unsubscribe from the spam that will flood my inbox later.

I then spend the next few hours yawning my way through the creation of fake email accounts, refilling the competition form over and over until neither Ember nor I can keep our eyes open a second longer.

As dawn touches the horizon, I crawl back to my own bedroom, barely having the energy to close the window before I topple into bed and fall soundly asleep. My last thought is to hope that when I wake up, the whole night will have been a dream, and one that I never have to think about again.

Zander

"Are you insane?"

I wince and cover my ears, but it does little good, since I can still hear every word my *Lost Heirs* co-star Summer West is screeching through my speakerphone.

"Four days stranded alone with a *fan*? You *are* insane!" she declares. The wind in the background reminds me that she's on vacation in the Maldives, and I consider how I might convince her to go back to relaxing, before realizing how futile any attempt would be. "They could be a psychopath! They probably *are* a psychopath!"

"Hawke will be there, too," I say, though I'm inwardly agreeing with her, and wondering for the millionth time why I agreed to this publicity farce. "Along with his production team."

"Not every moment," Summer argues, her heated tone not hiding her concern. "His crew will only be there for emergency support—that means it'll mostly be just you, him, and some potential stalker-fan. Four days means three full nights, Zan. Three full nights where this person could—"

"Summer, please," I cut her off with a groan, collapsing onto my couch and staring beyond the glass balcony of my beach house overlooking the Malibu coastline. "I really don't need whatever grisly image you're going to put in my head."

As expected, she ignores me and begins to share—in detail—all the things that could go wrong. I tune her out to keep my stomach from churning, focusing instead on the calming sight of the sun setting over the Pacific Ocean. But soon enough not even that helps.

"Summer, I beg you, please stop," I finally say, interrupting her recitation of a fan encounter one of our colleagues endured that resulted in a messy lawsuit and hundreds of hours of therapy. "I know it could backfire, but I don't have a choice. If I don't do something, I'll lose Titan. And if I lose Titan, I'll—" Emotion clogs my voice, keeping me from finishing.

There's a long pause on the other end of the line, until Summer whispers, her own voice equally full of feeling, "Oh, Zan. This is all my fault."

I sit bolt upright. "No," I say firmly. "Don't you dare."

"But I—"

"No, Summer." I tap my phone to activate the video feed, revealing my friend on the deck of her grandfather's yacht, backlit by the early-morning sun and surrounded by the pristine Indian Ocean. Her blond hair is tied in a loose bun with errant strands blowing into her jade-green eyes, and her peaches-and-cream skin has a light dusting of freckles across her nose that are usually hidden when she's in full make-up. It's barely seven a.m. where she is, so she's still wearing her pajamas, the *My Little Pony* branding nearly causing me to smile. But then I note the despair splashed across her features and any mirth I feel dissolves.

"If you hadn't—" she starts, but I don't let her finish.

"I did, and I'd do it again." I hold her eyes through the screen. "And again, and again." She bites her lip, uncertain, so I continue, "I mean it, Summer. I have no regrets, and the last thing I want is for you to carry the burden of my choices on top of everything else you're already shouldering. You promised me you would let it go."

"That's easier said than done when you almost lost your career because of me," she says quietly. "Hell, you still *might*."

"And what about you?" I return. "How many roles have you been offered in the last year?"

Summer looks out at the ocean, not answering.

I soften my voice. "You aren't responsible for my decisions, Sum. That's ridiculous, and you know it. I'll be okay—and you will, too. We just have to get through this rough patch. Both of us. Then we'll be golden."

I send her a confident smile, hoping it doesn't appear as forced as it feels. She doesn't look convinced, but she eventually nods, indicating that she'll at least try to accept what I said. I'm relieved, but that fades quickly when she returns to our previous topic, causing me to slump back into my cushions.

"I still don't understand why you had to bring Hawke into this competition thing," Summer says, tucking a wisp of hair behind her ear. "Can't you just take the winner to lunch? Or do literally anything else that doesn't involve a multiday camping trip?"

My heart warms, since I know why she's asking, and I love her for wanting to protect me. She was there during the interview four years ago, waiting to join me on the couch, so she had a front-row seat when the photo of me fishing with my parents was revealed. We'd known each other for two years by then and she'd become like a sister, so I'd already told her more than what I shared with millions of viewers that day—*much* more. Because of that, she knows *exactly* why this fan experience is going to be so difficult for me.

"Hawke's image is spotless, unlike mine," I answer, then move on swiftly so she doesn't return to blaming herself. "Gabe and Valentina are confident that spending a few days filming with him and the competition winner will improve the studio's view of me, in the time we need for it to happen."

"That's easy for them to say," Summer mutters, her frown visible through the screen. "They're not the ones who have to go and play *Hunt for the Wilderpeople* for four days."

That prompts a chuckle from me. "That was set in New Zealand. Hawke's taking us to Australia."

Her eyes flare with interest. "Australia? You didn't mention that before."

I grimace. "I'm trying not to think about it."

"Australia is amazing." Summer makes a wistful sound. "That'll be so much better than freezing your ass off in the Arctic Circle, or boiling in some African desert."

She has a point. But I still say, "I've heard everything in Australia wants to kill you."

Summer waves a dismissive hand. "The survival part isn't going to be your problem—you're unnaturally good at all that outdoorsy stuff. It's the fan aspect that's going to be your biggest challenge. And . . . you know . . ." She clears her throat. "The rest."

I deliberately ignore the last part of what she said, stretching my jeans-clad legs out as I share, "Did I tell you there's been over ten million entries since the comp went live three days ago? Thank God it closes tonight. I feel sick just thinking about why so many people have entered."

Summer's lips twitch and she relaxes against the railing behind her. "You do realize that at least nine-point-nine million of them want to win because they're hoping you'll fall madly in love with them, right?"

I pull a face. "And the remaining point-one mil?"

Her lip twitch grows into a full, wicked smirk. "They're hoping for something a lot less wholesome." Before I can reply—not that I even know what to say to that—she sobers and asks, "Have you spoken with your parents about this yet?"

"Yeah," I answer. "They're about as thrilled as you are." That's an understatement. But they also know how much the role of Titan means to me, and how far I'll go to keep it.

Carefully, Summer prompts, "And Maddox?"

My gut tightens. "He still won't take my calls."

There's a hesitant pause, before Summer says, "It's been three months."

I don't need the reminder. "You know how he feels about what happened that night."

Both of us fall silent, neither needing—or *wanting*—to talk about the night of my DUI. Maddox, especially, doesn't want to talk about it. My best friend is icing me out, and even though I understand why, I still hate it.

Compassion fills Summer's eyes, but I don't want to hear what she's about to say, so I jump in first to share, "Once the winner is notified—tomorrow, I think Gabe said—I'll be boarding a plane straight to Sydney, so I doubt we'll have another chance to talk until it's all over. But Hawke's team have pulled some strings and they've arranged to slot the episode into their current release schedule, so you'll at least get to witness my misery almost as soon as it happens."

"'Misery' is a strong word—let's stay positive here," Summer says, before catching my skeptical look and quickly moving on. "Do you know when the episode is dropping? And where?"

I rattle off the names of the streaming services, but as for the timing, I shake my head. "It depends on how good their editing team is, but Gabe said they're aiming to upload the full episode a day or so after we're done. It's pure luck that Hawke owed Valentina a favor and agreed to make this happen much faster than normal, otherwise there's no way it'd be ready within the time the studio gave me."

"Don't think about that now," Summer says soothingly. "Everything is falling into place, and it's all going to work out perfectly."

Her conviction has me arching an eyebrow. "I thought you said I was insane for doing this?"

She grins. "I stand by that. But I'll also be stocking up on popcorn since I'm in dire need of some quality entertainment, and you, my friend, are going to deliver. Four days in the wild with a crazy stalker-fan?" She snickers. "I can't wait to watch that. On repeat."

I glare at her. "You're awful."

Her grin widens. "Love you, too, Zan. Call me when you're back in civilization." She winks, before finishing, "And try not to fall in love with your stalker-fan, or I'll never let you live it down."

She air-kisses the screen and terminates our call, missing the eye roll I offer in response to her words.

Combing a hand through my hair, I glance out at my view once more, noting the swiftly darkening sky. I need to go for a run before dinner, but an impulse comes over me, and I tap my phone to activate a new call. As anticipated, it rings only twice before I'm sent to voicemail, like every other time I've tried in the last three months.

"Yo! You've reached Maddox. Leave a message."

When the beep sounds, I begin talking automatically, stumbling over the words. "Hey, it's me. Uh, Zander. I just . . . well, I wanted to let you know that I'm heading overseas for about a week. Not sure if you've seen the media blast, but Gabe's got me doing this competition thing to help with—" I break off quickly, careful not to bring up my public image problems to Maddox of all people.

"Listen," I say, quieter, "I get it, man. You know I do. But please . . . call me back." I pull out the big guns and add, "I have to go camping, Mox. Four days, with Rykon Hawke and a fan. And I just . . . after everything that happened . . ." I pause, take a breath, then finish weakly, "I'd feel a lot better if I could talk to you before I leave."

I hang up without saying goodbye, already knowing Maddox isn't going to return my call. No amount of pleading over the last three months has moved him to communicate with me, and any attempts I've made to visit him in person have led to him closing the door in my face—the first time—or not opening it at all—every time since then.

I miss my best friend. Now, more than ever.

But I also know there's nothing else I can do. He'll talk to me when he's ready. I just wish he would hurry up and *be* ready.

Placing a hand over my aching heart, I allow myself a moment to grieve, before finally rising to my feet. My phone begins to ring, causing my pulse to leap with hope, but it's not Maddox's name on the screen.

It's Gabe's.

Dread and anticipation fill me as I accept the connection, both growing exponentially when his deep voice comes clearly through the speaker:

"We've drawn the winner. Are you ready for your adventure?"

Charlie

"Miss Hart! Mickey dropped my snowflake crown in the hot fudge!"

I dash forward to hand the birthday girl a spare, saying, "Luckily I saved the best one for last." Her bright smile takes the sting out of her making my seventeen years seem ancient by calling me "Miss Hart." But then again, on days like today, I *feel* ancient, supervising a group of hyperactive seven-year-olds and ensuring they have the time of their lives.

When I started working at Sandy's Scoops and Sprinkles two years ago, it was a fun way to earn some extra cash after school and on weekends. It was the best casual job I could imagine, but then the owner, Sandy, expanded their business from a normal ice-creamery to one that offers parties for children. They renovated the tasteful pink-and-cream-colored space to add a separate event room—a rainbow-walled monstrosity—so regular customers can sit and eat peacefully in the parlor, while sugar-high kids enjoy hours of uninterrupted glee.

When Sandy first asked me to oversee the weekend parties, I nearly quit, but they convinced me to give it a go, and it turned out they were right—I really do love helping kids make chaotic ice-cream cakes covered in every topping imaginable. The only downside is that I'm required to wear a costume inspired by the party's theme, often sacrificing my dignity in the process. Today I'm dressed as Elsa from *Frozen*, which isn't terrible, but at least once a month I have to don my Bluey onesie, tail and all.

"Miss Hart! Ellie won't share the edible glitter!"

I hurry over to the end of the bench, arriving just as a small girl tosses the sparkling pot in the air, scattering it all over the table and the floor. And *me*.

Repressing a sigh, I separate the troublemakers and distract them with gummy bears and whipped cream, before shaking the glitter from my hair and checking on the birthday girl. She's absorbed in decorating her Olaf-shaped ice-cream cake—at least, I think that's what it is—and the rest of her friends are equally content. Even so, relief hits me when I see there are only a few minutes left of the party.

"Time for your finishing touches," I announce. The kids respond with sad noises, but they help me pack their creations into insulated bags, then skip off to show their loved ones what they made. My role is over once they leave the rainbow room, and I hear Sandy's bright voice in the parlor *ooh*ing and *ahh*ing while deftly encouraging the partygoers and guardians out of the store.

"All clear," Sandy finally calls, followed by the sound of the front door locking and the *closed* sign being flipped over.

When I enter the calming pastel parlor, Sandy does a double take, their purple-lipsticked mouth stretching into a grin. "Aren't you sparkly."

I dust glitter off my shoulders. "Anything is better than last week's honey and raspberry-sauce disaster. I'll never be able to wear my Tigger costume again without looking like a crime scene."

Sandy laughs, their short, bleached mohawk jostling with the movement, before they look toward the party room. "On a scale of one to ten, what's the damage?"

"A solid six," I answer. "It's not too bad. I should be done within the hour."

Usually Sandy helps me close on Saturdays, with them seeing to the parlor while I tidy the party room, but it's their date night and I know they're keen to get home.

"Are you sure you're—"

"I'm sure." I shoo them toward the door. "Go celebrate being flirty and free, thirty-three."

"You'll have to come up with a new rhyme after my next birthday," Sandy says, scrunching their nose. "Let's hope it's not 'single and poor, thirty-four.'"

I snort. "Don't even try that on me—I've seen your annual turnover. And we both know Xin's obsessed with you. You'd be walking down the aisle tomorrow if only you'd say yes."

"I'm too young to get married."

I raise an eyebrow.

Sandy frowns and amends, "Too young at heart."

It's an argument we've had many times, so I just say, "Go, or *I'll* leave and you can clean."

Their face softens into a smile. "You're too good to me, Charlie. Best employee I've ever had."

"Feel free to give me a raise," I suggest, only half joking.

They chuckle and unlock the door to leave, but then they turn back, eyes serious. "One of these days we're going to talk about you finally quitting so you can go forth and conquer the world. You can't stay here forever, cherub. I won't let you."

Before I can tell them how much I'm looking forward to that *super fun* chat, they disappear out the door, leaving me standing there with my insides roiling.

I know Sandy means well, but I don't like being pushed to think about my future. Once upon a time, I'd had it all mapped out, how I'd graduate from high school and spend a year backpacking with Ember before we left our small coastal town for the big city—Sydney, Melbourne, or Brisbane were our top picks. She would major in drama and I in whatever course I could get into, and we would live together and enjoy every aspect of the college lifestyle, after which we would, as Sandy aptly said, go forth and conquer the world.

But then life happened, derailing our perfect plans, creating an imperfect reality.

First, it was Ember's circumstances that halted our futures.

Then it was mine.

We still both took a gap year after graduating at the end of last year, but instead of traveling, I've been scooping ice-cream and trying to glue the broken pieces of myself back together, while Ember has been completing a bridging course to catch up on all the school she missed. There are only three months left of the year and I know I need to make decisions about the future, but I just can't bring myself to do it yet.

Because that would mean I'm ready to move on, when I'm not.

And right now, I can't imagine how I ever will be.

It's on that pitiful thought that I hear tapping at the front door, and I look to see my best friend waving through the glass. Even when Sandy closes with me, Ember often joins us, talking Sandy's ears off and taste-testing new flavors. She never helps with the cleaning, but she keeps herself entertained by sitting at the counter and encouraging me to tidy faster—bless her cotton socks.

I don't mind, since it makes the time pass quickly. And she usually has some upbeat story to share about her day, even if it's as mundane as her search for a missing hair tie.

Today, however, there's a look on her face that I haven't seen in a long time—sadness mixed with resignation, combined with a heavy dose of determination—and it causes me enough alarm that I nearly trip over a stool as I scramble to open the door.

"What's happened?" I ask. "What's wrong?"

I catalog her appearance as she walks in and slumps onto the nearest stool, noting that she's not tired or pale, and her eyes are bright and healthy despite the emotion in them.

Last time I saw her this despondent, it was on the worst day of her life, and the second-worst of mine: the day when Ember was told she had leukemia. We were fourteen years old, with no one certain if she would ever reach fifteen.

But she did.

Then sixteen, seventeen, and, two weeks ago, eighteen.

My friend isn't a survivor—she's a warrior. She faced the hardest battle of her life, and not only did she conquer it, she did so while keeping a smile on her face. To anyone else, it might have seemed easy.

It wasn't.

It took years of agonizing treatments, with Ember in and out of hospital, seeing small victories and terrifying setbacks, before she finally entered remission at the beginning of this year. We had two beautiful months of celebrating . . . and then my world fell apart all over again, in a different—and even more devastating—way.

I don't think I can handle anything else going wrong so soon.

No—I *know* I can't handle anything else going wrong so soon.

And I definitely can't handle hearing that my best friend's cancer has returned. I was able to remain strong for Ember and her parents during the three years of her treatments, holding her hand through every moment, but now . . . I'm not sure I have anything left in me to give, not when she's the only thing that's been keeping me together for the last six months.

Looking at her, I wonder if I'm going to be sick all over Sandy's pink tiles. I can feel it burning in my stomach, the absolute terror of what I'm about to hear. But I swallow it back, praying I'm wrong.

"I have something to tell you," Ember finally says, causing ice to flood my veins.

She glances up for the first time since entering the store, and whatever she sees in my expression causes her to visibly startle.

"God, Charlie, I'm so sorry—that was stupid of me." She jumps off her stool and pulls my trembling body in for a tight embrace. "Nothing's wrong. I'm not sick—it's nothing like that. I'm perfectly healthy. I promise. I'm fine. Everyone's fine."

It takes a second for the words to process, but when they do, the tension leaves my body in a heady rush that causes me to sway into her.

"I didn't think," Ember says, still holding me close. She then repeats, her voice full of remorse, "I'm so sorry."

"It's okay," I say shakily. "You just scared me."

We break apart, and Ember sends me a sheepish smile. "I guess a bonus of that little misstep is that you won't think what I'm about to tell you is anywhere near as bad as it could be."

Nothing could be as bad as what I'd feared she was going to say, so she's right about that.

"Even so," she says, guiding me to the seat beside hers, "you should sit down for this."

I'm still trembling enough that I yield limply when she pushes on my shoulders, and I crumple onto the chair. She sits much more gracefully, her years of dance classes making her move fluidly even when she's not trying.

"I want you to take a deep breath," Ember instructs, "and think calming, tranquil thoughts."

I shake off the last of my fear and pin my eyes on my friend, her words bringing a new kind of alarm to me, especially coupled with the look on her face. Because now the sadness and resignation are gone, and in their place is apology—and guilt.

The determination, however, is stronger than ever.

"What have you done this time?" I ask with a sigh.

Ever since entering remission, Ember has been all about living life to the fullest. I love that for her, I really do. But my friend also follows the better-to-ask-forgiveness-than-seek-permission mentality, and it frequently lands her in trouble. I only hope she hasn't "borrowed" our neighbor's dog again, since last time it took two gift vouchers and a homemade pavlova to stop old Mrs. Kirby from reporting the dognapping to the police. Admittedly, Ember's claim of "But Buddy loves me more!" didn't do her any favors.

"I'm just going to rip the bandaid off," she says. "So keep breathing and hold onto those tranquil thoughts."

I frown at her, getting worried now. "Em, what—"

She talks over me, her words blending together in her rush to get them out. "*IwontheZanderRunecompetition.*"

I blink twice and lean back in my seat, certain I must have misheard. *Praying* I misheard. "Say it again, minus the chipmunk speed?"

Ember bites her lip, likely noting my rapidly paling features, then repeats, "I, uh, well . . . I won the, um, the Zander Rune competition. The one with Rykon Hawke. They called me this afternoon." She utters a nervous laugh and tugs at her hair. The strands are growing back thick now that her treatments are over, but the length is still short enough that she can't get a good grip. "I thought it was a scammer or someone else messing with me, but turns out it's legit. I won. And not even on any of the fake entries—on my real entry."

I stare at her in horror, lost for a response.

"They said millions of people applied," Ember goes on, rambling now to fill my silence. "Even with our dummy email addresses, the odds of either of us winning were basically zero. Can you believe that?"

When I continue to remain mute, she bites her lip again, the look in her eyes warning me to brace.

"The thing is," she says slowly, fiddling with the buttons on her denim jacket, "there's a slight hiccup. You know how I had that chest infection last month?" She doesn't wait for me to answer. "Well, I called Dr. Gibbons after I got the news about winning, and he said that since I've only just finished the second course of antibiotics, he's worried about my immunity being compromised. And given, you know, my history"—she says this fast, as if what she went through was nothing, when we both know she's buried her trauma deep beneath her smiles—"he's strongly advised against me being out in the elements for a multiday survival situation right now."

I could kiss Dr. Gibbons. In fact, the next time I see the grandfatherly hematologist, I plan to do exactly that.

"I'm sorry, Em," I say, patting her leg. I know how much she wants this, but I'm also knee-weakeningly relieved that she's smart enough to listen to her doctor—just as I'm glad it wasn't me who had to make her see reason, which is what I'd feared most upon us entering the competition. At least this way, I'm not the one crushing her dreams.

I expect to see devastation in her features, maybe tears. But all I can see is that apologetic-yet-determined look, even fiercer than before.

A slow sense of dread builds in me when she takes my hand, as if to keep me from running away.

"Remember those tranquil thoughts?" Ember asks, her fingers tightening. "This is the part where you're going to need them."

Through stiff lips, I ask, "What did you *do*?"

She winces, then pulls her phone from her pocket to open her social media. Every part of me solidifies when she flips the screen around for me to see.

Her hand still holding mine gives a squeeze. "Please don't hate me."

I open my mouth and shut it again, unable to form speech, my eyes locked on the media blast:

SMALL-TOWN AUSSIE TEENAGER CHARLIE HART WINS SURVIVAL TRIP OF A LIFETIME WITH ZANDER RUNE AND RYKON HAWKE!

There's even a picture of me, a horrendous image from what has to be at least three years ago, since I have a mouth full of metal braces, my face is covered in acne, and my hair is a shocking shade of orange—the only poor choice Ember ever made for me.

An unintelligible sound leaves my throat when the post doesn't magically vanish, nor does my supposed best friend burst into laughter and confess that it's a fake announcement she mocked up herself.

Instead, Ember says, her voice quiet, "Say something, Charlie Bear."

I settle on the first coherent sentence I can form, snatching my hand from hers as I screech, "*What the hell, Ember?*"

She jumps slightly, then adopts a soothing tone as she explains, "When I called the competition people back after speaking with Dr. Gibbons, they said I could transfer the prize to someone else. I didn't—I just—" She clears her throat. "I know you hate Zander. And I understand why. But Hawke . . ." She leans toward me, her next words prompting a sharp, unexpected pain in my chest. "Your mum was obsessed with him, Charlie. *Obsessed.* She watched every episode he ever filmed, and I swear she ran some of those fan accounts dedicated to him—that's how much she loved him. So this prize . . . she'd be the first person shoving you out the door to meet him."

Ember wasn't wrong. "Obsessed" didn't come close to describing how my mother felt about Rykon Hawke. She used to watch anything he was in—not only *Hawke's Wild World*, but interviews, cameo appearances, everything. She donated to his rehabilitation camps, sponsored kids to go to them, read his books, listened to his podcasts, even bought survival merchandise with his branding despite having no use for most of it. If Andrea Hart hadn't been so well adjusted in every other area of her life, and if she hadn't beamed joyfully every time she saw photos of Hawke alongside his husband, I would have been concerned by my mother's near-stalkerish fixation on the man.

"She would want you to do this, Charlie," my friend says quietly. "And not just so you can meet Hawke. She'd want more than *this* for you." Ember waves her hand around the ice-cream store. "She'd want you to get out and see the world, to go on adventures, just like this one."

At my incredulous look, Ember quickly amends, "Okay, maybe not *just* like this one. I doubt even your mother could have imagined you'd go camping with two of the most famous people in existence. But you get my point. She wouldn't want you missing out on any amazing opportunities in life—and you can't deny that this is one hell of an opportunity."

That may be so, but I'm still about to tell her there's zero chance of me ever agreeing to it. She, however, isn't finished.

"Since you're not eighteen until next month, I've already spoken with Jerry and he's happy to sign the paperwork they need," Ember shares cheerfully, as if she's done me a favor. "He's totally fine with you going."

"Of course he is," I mumble, unable to keep the hurt from my voice.

"He'll do anything to avoid being near me, even ship me off into a wilderness nightmare without caring who I'm going with."

Compassion floods Ember's face. "That's not true. Your stepdad loves you."

"I know he does." Softly, I add, "But I also know the very sight of me brings him to tears, so he hasn't looked at me properly in six months."

My friend has no rebuttal since she's witnessed his avoidance firsthand, and while she maintains I just need to give him time, I don't know how much longer I can keep tiptoeing around my own house. Jerry is the only father I've ever known, with him having married my mother when I was five years old. He loves me beyond reason, and the feeling is mutual—which is why it hurts so much to have such distance between us now, even if I understand his struggles. I feel them myself every time I look in a mirror.

"Forget about Jerry," Ember says, rallying. "Be thankful instead, because other people's parents might have concerns about signing whatever liability forms Hawke's legal team is sending through."

"I can't imagine why." My tone is as dry as the desert Hawke likely intends to take his victims to. "Who *wouldn't* want their underage daughter to head into a survival situation with two men she's never met and the entire world watching?"

Ember grins widely. "See, you sound sarcastic, but I'm sensing there's already a bit of excitement building in you."

The look I send her speaks volumes. "You're sensing wrong."

She pouts. "Come on, Charlie Bear, the headline says it all." She waves her phone at me again. "This is the trip of a *lifetime.* You *have* to do it."

"I don't *have* to do anything." I cross my arms. "And in this case, I'm definitely *not* doing it. I'd rather stick bamboo shoots down my fingernails. Hell, I'd even rather—"

I cut myself off when tears fill her eyes. They're not fake; Ember's dream is to be an actress, but she's incapable of crying on command.

"Sorry," she mumbles, swiping at her cheeks and looking away in embarrassment. "I just—no, never mind. You're right, it was a stupid idea. If you don't want to do it, of course you shouldn't. It'd probably be awful anyway, everything you said the other night—rain and bugs and drinking your own pee. Plus, even Zander Rune would reek after four days without a shower. That's gross. There's nothing attractive about BO."

She's on a roll, so I don't tell her that there are other ways to bathe in nature, or that Zander likely owns a good deodorant. I also don't mention that I doubt Hawke would make someone as famous as Zander drink his own urine, and therefore the winner wouldn't have to, either.

"No one in their right mind would sign up for any of that," Ember goes on, sniffing. "I don't know what I was thinking, telling them you'd go in my place. I guess I hoped . . ." She looks up at me, her brown eyes full of remorse, but it's the despair in them that feels like a punch to my gut, especially when she says, "I guess I just thought that if *I* couldn't go, then at least I'd get to live vicariously through you. Plus, this way I'd still get to meet Zander, since the competition people said I could accompany you to the drop-off location. They even offered to put me up in a hotel for the four days you'd be out adventuring, so I'd be there to meet you when you were done."

She turns away again, wiping her face once more. "But I get it. Even without your feelings toward Zander, I can see why you wouldn't want to do this. I know you're not allergic to camping like I am, and you actually enjoy being in nature like some kind of weirdo"—she wrinkles her nose at the thought—"not to mention, you were blessed by the fitness gods, so you'd have no trouble with the hiking and all the rest . . . But if you're uncomfortable, then you're uncomfortable, and that's that. So I'll—I'll call them as soon as I get home and—and tell them to pick a new winner."

If I didn't love my best friend so much, I would loathe her for the emotional manipulation, because she knows—*she knows*—I can't stand to disappoint her. It was one thing when I thought it was only me who would have to go on this ridiculous trip. *That* I could turn down, no problem. But if they truly have offered for Ember to meet Zander, how can I say no to that?

I groan and drop my arms onto a sticky, yet-to-be-cleaned table, lowering my head until it's pillowed in the crook of my elbow. "I despise you," I mutter into the blue sleeve of my Elsa dress. "Not a little. A lot."

There's a beat of silence as Ember processes what I said, but then a high-pitched squeal leaves her, and a moment later she's hauling me up for a jumping hug.

"I love you, I love you, I looooove you!" she screams into my ear, before repeating my own words. "Not a little. A lot!"

"You'd better," I say grouchily, unable to muster the same level of enthusiasm. Or *any* enthusiasm. But then I exhale deeply and return her embrace, knowing how much this means to her. It's four days of misery and discomfort for me, but I can suffer through that for my best friend.

Ember finally releases me, though she clasps both of my hands and says, "I know you're not super excited about this, but just remember, I'll be with you the whole time." She pauses. "Except for when I'm not."

I look at her flatly. "Real comforting. Thanks, Em."

She grins back at me. "This is going to be *the best*. You'll see."

I try to dredge up a smile for her sake, but then a thought hits me. "My passport is expired. Will I have enough time to renew it?"

Ember waves an unconcerned hand. "Zander and Hawke are flying here. Well, not *here*-here"—she gestures out the store's windows to indicate our hometown—"but here as in Australia. So you won't need your passport at all, since we're only taking a domestic flight to Sydney and then a train into the mountains. Or maybe a car." Her brow furrows in thought, until she shrugs and finishes, "All I know is that someone will collect us from the airport and take us where we need to go."

A nervous thrill runs through me at this news. I consider what I know of the geography near Sydney and guess, "The Blue Mountains?" At Ember's confirmation, I ask, "When?"

My friend scratches her cheek and looks anywhere but at me, prompting new alarm bells to ring in my ears.

"*When*, Ember?"

She murmurs the answer too low for me to hear, but when I arch my eyebrow in question, she sighs and says, louder, "The trip starts on Tuesday."

When she doesn't offer a date, I splutter out, "Wait—*this* Tuesday? As in *three days away*?"

She nods reluctantly, then shares, "We'll fly out on Monday morning, head straight to Katoomba, go sightseeing for a few hours that afternoon, and then spend the night in a hotel before meeting up with Zander and Hawke first thing on Tuesday." Her eyes lose focus and a dopey smile touches her lips. "Can you believe I just said that? We get to meet *Zander* and *Hawke.* Dreams really do come true."

I want to conk her over the head with the nearest ice-cream cone. She must see that on my face, since her own sobers.

"I know this is a lot, and it's happening fast."

"It's not fast," I grit out, "it's *lightning speed.*"

"That's good, though, right?" she asks tentatively. "This time next week, you'll be back here doing another birthday party, dressed as Shrek or Princess Leia or Thor or whoever else, and life will go on. You might be more tanned and maybe have a mosquito bite or five hundred, but otherwise, it'll be like it never happened. You don't have to dread it for weeks; you can just get it over with fast. Kind of like a bikini wax." Seeing my grimace, she quickly adds, "But with less pain."

I'm not sure she's right about that, but despite my trepidation—and against my better judgment—I've already committed to seeing this madness through.

"I need to check with Sandy," I say, resigned. "They'll have to ask someone to cover my shifts."

I don't bother stating the obvious—that Sandy will be so excited that they'll likely offer to pack my bags and drive me straight to the airport.

Ember knows this, so she says nothing as I collect a cloth and start wiping down the tables, my movements hurried now that I have a checklist of things to do before leaving on Monday. Even knowing how happy it'll make her, I can't believe I'm doing this; that I'll be spending four days in the wilderness with someone I despise. The mere thought of Zander's too-perfect face has me burning with anger—and flooding with heartache. But at least Hawke will be there as a buffer. I'll never be completely alone with Zander, and during the time we're stuck near each other, I'll find a way to tolerate him, for Ember's sake.

And then, as soon as our four days are up, I won't have to think about him again.

"There's still one very serious thing we need to discuss," Ember says as I move between the tables.

My pulse spikes. "There is?"

Her smile is pure sunshine as she answers, "I have a fashion emergency. You have to help me figure out what to wear on Tuesday, since I want to look *perfect* when I meet my favorite actor of all time."

I consider throwing my cloth at her, but resist when she sighs contentedly and finishes, "I sense good things ahead, Charlie Bear. This is one adventure you're going to thank me for. Just wait—you'll see."

I will see. And so will the entire world. Because in three days, I'll be hiking through the Blue Mountains with two of the most famous people alive, our every word and action recorded and watched by millions.

My insides lurch, but I paste a smile on my face and reply, "We could both use some good things ahead, so here's hoping you're right."

She's not, but that doesn't matter, because it's only four days.

It'll be awful, but I've been through worse.

Much worse.

Compared to the last six months, this will be nothing.

I've got this, I tell myself over and over, scrubbing with renewed vigor. *It'll be fine.*

But no amount of mental repetition helps me believe it.

Zander

"Don't be nervous," Gabe tells me, swatting at a bee buzzing near his face.

"I'm not nervous." I cover a yawn. "I'm jet-lagged."

"You look nervous. You keep rubbing your forehead and shuffling your feet."

"That's because I have a headache, and I'm trying to stay awake." I look straight at my agent, who decided to accompany me on my Australian trip like an overprotective babysitter, and reiterate, "Because I'm *jet-lagged*."

After fifteen hours cramped inside a plane from LAX to Sydney, and then another ninety minutes driving to Katoomba, the only thing I want right now is to fall into bed. But that will have to wait, since Gabe has organized for us to meet the competition winner a day early to get a feel for her personality under the guise of us playing tourist together. It's not ideal timing, but the alternative is meeting her tomorrow when Hawke's cameras might already be rolling, so at least here we can get any overenthusiastic reactions out of the way. Or overcome any shyness, if she's the kind of fan who is unable to speak in my presence. Having seen an image of her—a young teenage girl, maybe thirteen or so, with obscenely orange hair that's sure to scare off any wildlife within a hundred miles—I'm hoping for the latter. Starstruck into silence is always preferable to overexuberant with no boundaries.

I'll know one way or another soon enough, but until then, all I can do is lean against the railing at Echo Point Lookout, waiting for her to appear.

The view, at least, is diverting, offering a stunning panorama over the Blue Mountains National Park and a postcard-perfect look at what the plaque beside me calls the Three Sisters—three iconic sandstone peaks formed by erosion millennia ago. I could lose time marveling at their beauty, but I cast my gaze beyond them to the forested mountains and valleys stretching further than I can see. The sight is as humbling as it is daunting, and I shiver at the knowledge that, come tomorrow morning, I'll be somewhere out there, doing everything I can to save my career.

I've got this, I tell myself. *It'll be fine.*

I've repeated the same inner mantra for days, but now that I'm about to meet the winner, trepidation fills me. Gabe is right—I *am* nervous. So much is riding on this. I *need* this fan to help change the world's opinion of me. Because if the plan fails and I return home without improving my public image, then—

I don't let myself finish the thought, and instead pull my baseball cap lower and push my sunglasses up my nose when a group of kids heads my way. I brace for their ambush, but like all the other tourists on the crowded viewing platform, they don't spare me a second glance, their eyes on the plaque and the view as they talk animatedly among themselves. I remind myself that unless someone looks closely, they won't recognize me, and I don't have to be on guard for paparazzi because no one knows I'm here. News of the competition and the winner spread widely, but the location where Hawke is taking us will remain secret until the show airs. That means, for this afternoon, I can just be a regular guy, seeing the sights and enjoying myself like any normal person.

"Here she comes," Gabe says, straightening beside me.

My stomach sinks as I remember that what I'm about to do *isn't* normal and I likely *won't* enjoy it, but I brush my hands down the front of my long-sleeved white shirt and over the top of my jeans, then adopt a friendly smile as I turn in the direction Gabe is facing. The crowd around us has cleared slightly, but I can't see a young teenager with bright orange hair anywhere. I do, however, notice two girls around my age, one with short black hair who seems about to burst from happiness, and the other with pale, rosy skin and hair an interesting mix of blue and purple, her striking violet eyes looking everywhere but at me.

"Omigosh, omigosh, *omigosh*, I can't believe it's really you," the dark-haired girl breathes, stopping before me and rocking on the balls of her feet as if considering whether or not to launch herself full-body into my arms. "I'm your biggest fan. Like, *biggest*."

I should have known someone would eventually spot me, even with my hat and shades. I'm about to offer her a selfie and hope she'll move on quickly so Gabe and I can give our attention to the competition winner—who I still can't see anywhere—but I freeze when my agent reaches out his hand for her to shake.

"You must be Ember," he says warmly. "Congratulations on winning the competition."

A beaming smile lights up her whole face. "Thank you so much! I can't tell you what a dream this is."

I blink between them, using all my acting skills to hide my confusion.

"And this, I assume, is Charlie," Gabe says, turning to the blue-haired girl.

My body locks, since "Charlie" is the name of the person reported as the winner. But this young woman looks nothing like the gangly, prepubescent teen from the photos.

"Yes, this is Charlie," Ember confirms. "She's my best friend, the one taking my place on the trip."

I flick a startled glance toward Gabe, but he shows no reaction, indicating he was already aware of the switch.

Questions flood me, but I hold my tongue—for now—and mask

my surprise, turning back to Ember to find her watching me closely. A knowing smirk plays at her lips, proof that she didn't miss my initial response to seeing the non-orange real-life version of Charlie.

Somewhat slyly, Ember says, "The media did her dirty with the photo they used. It was from years ago, back in her awkward pre-glow-up stage. Clearly."

Clearly, indeed.

I'm careful to keep my eyes from drifting to Charlie again, even when she clears her throat in embarrassment, since Ember is still watching me—and not like when she first arrived and wanted to fangirl out on me. There's a different light in her gaze now, something worryingly similar to how Summer looks whenever she wants to play matchmaker.

I cover my apprehension—and my confusion about Ember winning but Charlie taking her place—by stepping forward until I'm beside Gabe, adopting my smoothest voice to say, "It's a pleasure to meet you both."

Ember's grin becomes blinding, but Charlie remains oddly expressionless. She still hasn't looked my way, her gaze moving from her feet to the view, to Gabe and to Ember, but never settling on me. I assume she must fall under the "shy, nervous fan" category, and in an effort to help her, I ask, "Are you excited for tomorrow, Charlie?"

Finally, her attention comes to me, her eyes flashing with an unreadable emotion before they flit away again almost immediately, and she mumbles a sarcastic, "Can't wait."

My eyebrows shoot upward, and even Gabe seems taken aback, but Ember elbows her friend and leans in to whisper something, causing Charlie's shoulders to slump. She sighs and turns to me again, holding my gaze this time as she says, "Sorry. Jet lag."

I'm about to assure her that I can relate, but then I recall hearing that the winner lives in a coastal town only a short flight from Sydney. My eyes narrow at her lie, but she just peers steadily back at me, as if daring me to call her on it.

Gabe wades in to break up our stare-down, saying, "We're so pleased you two were able to meet us today, especially since this introduction wasn't on the itinerary. But I thought, since we're all here, it might be nice if we get to know each other a little before tomorrow." He gestures between them both. "Are you hungry? Shall we grab a late lunch, then stretch our legs on a short bushwalk? That could be fun."

"So much fun," Charlie says. Her smile doesn't come close to being genuine.

"We could go on the cable car," Ember says enthusiastically, as if trying to cover for her friend's inexplicable attitude. She points beyond the lookout's railing. "Or whatever that terrifying thing is."

I follow her finger to see the glass-bottomed Scenic Skyway ambling across wires high above the valley. The hotel concierge said it's different from the cable car, though both offer views of the rainforest canopy, ancient ravines, and waterfalls. I grin at Ember, causing her to blush as I cast my vote with hers. "That sounds good to me."

She looks like she's going to faint from joy—and Gabe looks like he's going to faint from something else entirely. He's never been comfortable with heights, despite having a high-rise office, which he claims is different. A quick glance at Charlie, and I can't tell how she feels about riding the Skyway. All I know is that, given her disposition toward me so far, it doesn't take a genius to realize she might not be here of her own will.

Anxiety grips me, since not once did I consider that the person accompanying me on tomorrow's adventure might not actually *be* a fan. Ember won the competition, and it's clear she is, but Charlie . . .

If I can't get her to like me, or at least play along while the cameras are rolling, then there's no way I'll convince the studio that I'm worth keeping around. My career—my *life*—is in her hands, and she doesn't even know it.

Worse, I have a feeling that if she did, she wouldn't care.

My palms turn clammy, but I keep my features carefree as Gabe suggests we find a place to eat, prompting Charlie to look at her friend and confirm she's happy to leave. Seeing that, a plan forms in my mind. Charlie is obviously here because of Ember, so the best way to sway her into liking me—or at least losing the passive-aggressive vibes—is *through*

Ember. Thankfully, unlike Charlie, Ember doesn't seem inclined to push me over the side of the lookout, so I step closer to her and, in a dorky move that I'll have embarrassed flashbacks to later, I bow at the waist before offering her my arm.

"My lady, let us be away to the feast," I say, in for a penny, in for a pound.

A startled giggle leaves her. "Why, thank you, kind sir," she says with a curtsy.

As Ember wraps her fingers around my elbow, I sneak a look at Charlie and see her face soften at her friend's clear delight. Feeling more confident in my plan, I continue lavishing attention on Ember as I escort her away from the lookout and along the street. Even after we step into a quiet cafe and place our orders, I keep asking questions about her life, learning how her family immigrated to Australia when she was little, and then how she and Charlie became neighbors ten years ago and have been inseparable ever since. Nostalgia hits me as I think about my own best friend, and it quickly turns to melancholy as I remember that Maddox never responded to the voicemail I sent before I left. This time hurts more than all the other unanswered messages combined, given what he knows of my past, and what I'm walking into tomorrow.

I shake myself back to the present when our meals arrive, taking a bite of my burger and listening as Ember talks about her many childhood adventures with Charlie. My eyes shift frequently to the blue-haired girl sitting opposite me, but she mostly lets her friend speak and focuses on eating her own lunch—at least until Ember reaches their teenage years and stops abruptly, seeming uncomfortable for the first time since we met. She turns to Charlie with a strange, almost pleading look, and Charlie jumps to her rescue.

"This must be so boring, hearing about our lives," Charlie says, faking a laugh and fiddling with her napkin. "I'm sure there are a million other things we should be talking about." She nudges her empty plate. "Sidenote: is it just me, or was that the best burger you've ever tasted?"

It's clearly a ploy to distract us from whatever caused Ember to freeze, but since I'm eager for any points I can get with Charlie, I nod eagerly and say, "The pineapple really kicked it up a notch."

"Yuck." Ember pulls a face. "Hot pineapple is a crime against nature. No one can convince me otherwise, not even my favorite actor of all time."

It was a throwaway comment, but her praise still makes me flush with pleasure.

"Charlie's right, actually," Gabe interjects, leaning forward beside me. "There are things we should discuss about the next few days."

"We read the info you sent," Ember says, wiping condensation from her glass. "It was pretty vague."

"That's by design, I'm afraid," Gabe says. "Hawke's team likes to surprise his guests, so the details we have are sparse." He turns to Charlie and me. "I do know you'll be collected from the hotel lobby at six a.m. and taken to a rendezvous point where you'll meet the executive producer, Scarlett Quinn, as well as Hawke himself. Then after a quick photo op, you'll be away on your adventure."

I wonder if I'm imagining the look of dread on Charlie's face, or if I'm just projecting my own feelings. She can't know—*no one can know*—how much this trip is going to require of me, mentally and emotionally. The only people who *do* know are Summer and Maddox, and only one of them seems to give a damn about me anymore.

I grit my teeth against a stab of heartache, but at the prickling sensation of someone watching me, I turn to find Charlie's eyes. The curiosity in her gaze worries me, so even though I'm grateful that she's not emanating belligerence right now, I still wish she hadn't caught me in such an unguarded moment. I force myself to relax, casting all thoughts of my best friend aside so I can refocus on the conversation.

"Can I go with Charlie to meet Hawke in the morning?" Ember asks.

Gabe scratches his jaw. "I assume we can both accompany them to the rendezvous point, but I'll call Scarlett tonight to make sure."

Ember looks pleased—and excited—and I wonder again why she's not the one joining me.

"Now," Gabe continues, speaking once more to Charlie and me, "Hawke's team will outfit you both with all the gear you need, partly to keep their branding in the spotlight, but also because they know exactly what you'll require. You sent through your sizes, yes?"

I don't answer since Gabe sent mine, but I'm amused when Ember chirps out a "Sure did!" and Charlie looks surprised before frowning, as if wondering what else Ember might have done behind her back.

"Excellent," Gabe says. "So just wear your hiking boots and something comfortable in the morning, and everything else will be given to you." He grins and adds, "Assuming you're still standing when you return on Friday afternoon, we should indulge in a celebratory 'You survived!' meal that night before we all depart on Saturday. Sound good?"

"Sounds *amazing*," Ember says, turning to her friend. "Right, Charlie Bear?"

Charlie doesn't blink at the cute nickname, though her voice is strained as she replies, "It sure does."

"We have a plan, then." Gabe claps his hands together. "With that done, shall we go see the sights?" He indicates beyond the cafe's windows. "We could walk to the falls? I hear they're impressive. Or perhaps—"

"Let's do the flying sky-car thing!" Ember interrupts gleefully.

Gabe pales. "Oh, erm, yes." He coughs. "Of course."

My lips twitch but I suppress my smile, only to find Charlie doing the same. We share a moment of camaraderie before her expression shutters, as if she suddenly remembered that—for whatever reason—she hates me. I can't explain it, and I have no clue what might have caused it, but her antagonism toward me is impossible to miss. She's keeping it mostly in check, but I fear that's only for Ember's sake, which means that, come tomorrow when we're alone with Hawke, I have no idea what's going to happen.

I need to know why she's here, since maybe that will give me answers as to why she doesn't *want* to be here. But I also can't just blurt out the question. I'll have to wait until I'm alone with Gabe again. He knew about Ember transferring the competition to Charlie, so hopefully he'll be able to tell me what I need to know in order to make this work.

Because if I can't, then that's it for me, my dreams over and done.

I don't get a chance to interrogate Gabe until we separate from Charlie and Ember at the hotel later that night, after hours spent riding the Skyway over the valley and walking to Katoomba Falls. Aside from Charlie's continued coolness, the afternoon was nice. Fun, even. Ember reminds me a lot of Summer—if Summer didn't have the weight of the world on her shoulders—and I enjoyed hearing about her application to a prestigious drama school and her hopes of becoming an actress. She didn't badger me for advice or ask for help reaching her goals; instead, she stated upfront that she wants to make her own way, even—and especially—knowing all the hard work it will require. I can't help respecting her for that.

Charlie, however, remained a locked vault during our hours together, and I feel as if I know *less* about her now than I did upon meeting her. My frustration only grows when we finally say goodnight to the girls, since all Gabe can tell me is that Ember won the competition, but she's recovering from a chest infection and her doctor advised her not to risk being out in the elements just yet. Because of that, I'm stuck with her best friend, who spends half her time ignoring me, and the other half looking like she wants to spit on me.

"You've got your work cut out for you," Gabe warns as we walk down the homey-feeling hotel corridor toward our rooms. "If I'd known Charlie would be an issue, I would have organized a redraw."

My ears perk up. "Can we do that? Postpone for a few days and—" I stop, knowing it's useless. Hawke's team are already here and ready to go.

"You'll find a way," Gabe says, patting my shoulder. "You're Zander Rune. No one can resist you."

I wish I had his confidence. All I can think about are Charlie's cold, violet eyes flashing with resentment whenever she looks at me.

We halt outside Gabe's door, and his serious gaze locks on mine. "Whatever it takes, you need to get through to her. Because if you don't . . ."

He doesn't finish, but he also doesn't need to.

My throat is dry when I respond, "See you in the morning."

He takes the hint, nodding once and vanishing into his room.

I continue along the hall until I enter my own suite, barely taking in the dimly lit space. It's still early, but I want a good night's sleep before my morning departure, so I prepare for bed. The problem is, when I burrow beneath my blankets, I can't get my brain to shut down. I keep replaying every interaction with Charlie, wondering why she dislikes me so intensely. Apparently she was once a huge fan of the *Lost Heirs* franchise—which means she was once a fan of *me*—so I can only assume her current prejudice comes from what she's heard in the media. If I didn't need her help improving my image, then her unfair judgment wouldn't matter so much, but I can't deny that it hurts.

I sigh and roll over, trying to silence my thoughts, but sleep continues to elude me. I finally admit defeat around midnight and push back my covers, deciding I need some fresh mountain air. I don't have a balcony, and I can't get my windows to open, so I tug on a hoodie and sweatpants and leave my room.

The hotel is unnaturally quiet as I walk along the carpeted hallway toward the elevator, reminding me that Katoomba is a small country town, and tourists come for the scenery, not the nightlife. Even when I step into the lobby, the only person I see is a middle-aged man dozing behind the concierge desk, and I slip past him, heading for the glass doors at the rear of the building.

Outside, the crisp September air is colder than I anticipated—just forty-five degrees according to my weather app, or seven in the local Celsius metric. Until now, I haven't given much thought to what physical challenges this trip will bring, but as I stroll down the cobblestone path toward the hotel's private tea garden, I wonder about Hawke's plans for Charlie and me. While I'm not worried about the adrenaline side of things, or even the general discomforts of camping, I'm definitely apprehensive about the quiet moments, since Hawke often uses them to ask his guests prying questions. His wilderness camps are known to offer counseling sessions as part of their programs—or the rehab ones, at least—and while he's not a trained therapist, he's learned a thing or two from his employees about how to get people to open up. It's why Gabe and Valentina want me on his show—to have those vulnerable conversations that remind viewers I'm a real person—but knowing it's a PR strategy doesn't lessen my unease about airing my private life so publicly.

Reluctant but resigned, I continue walking until I reach the small garden illuminated by fairy lights. It ends at a glass railing atop a cliff, overlooking the shadowy outlines of the Blue Mountains beneath the moonlight. I shiver at the beauty of the misted peaks and take a moment to just stand there, marveling at the sight. But then a shuffling sound causes me to whip around, only to find Charlie sitting on a wooden bench, staring at me.

Unsure of my welcome, I consider leaving her to her thoughts, but change my mind at the last second and hesitantly ask, "Can't sleep?"

I half expect her to ignore me, but she surprises me by answering, "Ember snores like a bear with a sinus infection. It's astounding how someone so small can make such a loud sound."

I chuckle, partly from what she said, but mostly because I'm relieved she's not scowling at me. "My friend Summer is the same."

Charlie tilts her head, causing her fleecy blue pajamas to shimmer under the fairy lights. "Summer West?"

I nod, then share, "My co-stars and I used to nap on set, but if Summer fell asleep first, no one else was able to. She also sleeps like the dead, so whenever her snoring kept the rest of us awake, there may have been a few, uh, retaliating pranks."

Curiosity touches Charlie's face. "What kinds of pranks?"

Eager to capitalize on her non-hostile mood, I send a mental apology to Summer and offer the first example that comes to mind. "Did you ever see that movie *The Parent Trap*?" At Charlie's confirmation, I go on, "We were shooting the third *Lost Heirs* film on location, doing the lake scene over and over until we were all exhausted. But the moment Summer dozed off, no one else stood a chance at sleeping, so we found an inflatable mattress and let her enjoy her own version of a waterbed." I adopt a suitably chastised look. "She ended up drifting so far out that we needed a boat to bring her back in."

Miracle of miracles, a smile quirks at Charlie's lips. "And she's still your friend after that?"

"Amazing, isn't it?" I grin. "She tells me it's because I'm irresistible."

I know immediately it was the wrong thing to say, since Charlie's face turns to stone. Since I can't take the words back, I rush to add, "Like a sad little puppy dog. Her words."

I'm unsure if I helped myself or made it worse.

"Why are you here, Zander?" Charlie asks, covering her hands with her sleeves to ward off the cold.

"It's the time difference," I say, unwilling to admit that she's the reason I can't sleep. "It's just after seven a.m. back home, so my body thinks—"

"Not here as in why you're awake," Charlie cuts me off with an exasperated look. "Here as in"—she waves toward the moonlit mountains—"*here.* Australia. Doing this competition. And don't feed me some line about it being fan service. I want the truth."

To delay answering, I ask, "May I sit?"

She deliberates for a moment, then slides over on the bench, hissing quietly and grumbling, "You're lucky I warmed that spot up for you."

I press my lips together to keep from laughing, a near-impossible task when she wiggles her backside to heat her seat faster.

"Thanks," I say as I drop down beside her. And then I proceed to lie through my teeth. "I'm here because I thought it might be a fun thing to do before I start shooting my next film. I've always admired Hawke's show, and I love being in nature, so—"

"Cut the bull," Charlie interrupts, her eyes slitted. "I saw your face when you met Ember and me earlier today and realized I'm not some starry-eyed fan. You looked about two seconds away from full-blown panic."

I swallow, before murmuring, "I thought I hid my reaction pretty well."

"Then you're not as good an actor as you think you are."

Ouch.

I don't reveal how much that stings, and instead lean in close as if to share a secret. "Has anyone ever told you that actors are terribly insecure?"

She cocks an eyebrow. "You don't seem the type to be insecure about anything."

Our gazes lock as I reply, pointedly, "Guess I'm not such a bad actor after all."

To my relief, an amused light enters her eyes. I make a snap decision, knowing Gabe will murder me if he finds out, but also aware that it might be the only way to do as he instructed and get through to Charlie.

I tell her the truth.

"You're right," I say, straightening on the bench. "Your first words to me made it clear you weren't a fan, and I did have a moment of panic."

"But *why*?"

"Because I need you."

Her body turns rigid. "Excuse me?"

I stretch my legs out on the grass, casting my gaze over the darkened view. "From the way you act, I'm guessing you've seen the negative media reports about me."

"You mean like how you were charged with a DUI?" Her tone is like acid. "Yeah, I'm aware."

Her sudden hostility makes me long to defend myself, but I stay on track. "That—and a few other things—have meant that the next movie I'm meant to be shooting—"

"*Titan's War*?"

"That's the one. The studio has threatened to cut me from the lead if I don't clean up my public image. They've given me a fortnight." I pause. "Less now."

There's a beat of silence, before a sound of bitter amusement leaves Charlie. "So the competition is a PR stunt. You need a fan to help make you shine; something genuine and not scripted."

"Yes," I confirm, impressed by how quickly she put it together. "I need the studio—and the world—to see I'm not just a bad boy with an image problem."

Her brow furrows as she looks away from me and into the garden. "Does this have anything to do with what happened to Summer last year, and how you—"

This time it's me who interrupts her. "Not directly, but that's certainly made things difficult for me, and it's part of the reason why I don't want to lose this movie. Well, that, plus it's a kickass role, and I'll be devastated if Titan goes to someone else."

"And humiliated."

I jolt. "Pardon?"

"It was announced months ago that you're playing Titan Wolfe," Charlie says. "If they cut you, it'll be pretty obvious why. The gossip sites will have a field day."

Now I'm the one looking out at the garden. "Thanks for the reminder."

There's another pause, before she says, quieter, "Sorry. I didn't mean—"

"It's fine." My voice is harsher than I intended. "It's not as if I'm oblivious to how it would play out. That's why I'm here, after all. To try to keep that from happening."

"Which leaves you with a problem," Charlie says. "Me."

"You," I agree. With a rueful smile, I add, "Here I was, worried about surviving four days with a stalker-fan, only to discover I'll be with someone who is the complete opposite. I never imagined that could be worse."

"Gee, I'm flattered."

I nearly backpedal, but then I see the reluctant humor in her gaze. An idea comes to me—it's a risk, but at this stage, I have nothing to lose. But first, I have to make sure I'm right about her motives.

"I answered your question, now it's your turn—why are *you* here?" I shift into a more relaxed position. "You're clearly not thrilled about any of this, so why did you agree to take Ember's place?"

Charlie uncrosses her legs only to cross them again, her own stalling tactic. "She's my best friend. I'd do anything for her."

"Seems a bit of an extreme 'anything.'"

There's silence for a moment, before Charlie says, "I don't know how much your people told you, but Ember was sick."

"Gabe mentioned she had a chest infection. I'm glad she's—"

"No." Charlie shakes her head. "She was sick, as in *sick*. For years." Her throat bobs, and a haunted look comes to her features. "She was diagnosed with leukemia when we were fourteen."

My stomach pitches. I can't reconcile the thought of the bubbly, effervescent girl I met today with someone who had to endure that kind of nightmare at such a young age.

"It was—I can't explain what it was like. For her. For her parents. For me."

Charlie's voice cracks on the final word, and I fight the overwhelming urge to comfort her.

Pulling herself together, she continues, "She entered remission earlier this year, and she's doing well now, but this recent infection hit her hard. When she won the competition, she learned she could still meet you if she transferred the prize to someone else." Charlie blows out an aggravated breath. "So, yes, it's an extreme 'anything,' but after everything she's been through, and how much she's been there for—" She breaks off quickly, before changing direction to finish, "She's my best friend, and meeting you has always been her dream, so of course I agreed to do this trip in her place."

"Even though you don't want to be here?"

"Even though I *really* don't want to be here."

I hold her eyes. "And why is that?"

"A lot of reasons." She looks past my shoulder. "This may come as a shock, but you're not as irresistible as Summer West claims."

I wince, wishing I could turn back time and retract that statement.

"You don't like me," I say, a statement, not a question.

Charlie rolls her eyes. "At least your observational skills are better than your acting abilities."

Ouch, again.

"Since you're deflecting," I say, "I assume you're not going to share *why* you have a problem with me, despite never having met me before today?"

"And he's smart, too," Charlie murmurs, plucking at a thread on her pajamas.

It takes effort to keep from reacting. Instead, I implement my idea. "Then in that case, I propose we make a deal."

That brings her eyes back to me. "A deal?"

"You help me with my image problem," I tell her, "and I'll give you something in exchange."

Charlie snorts. "You don't have anything I want."

"You said you'd do anything for Ember. You also said Ember's dream was to meet me, but that's not entirely true, is it? Because Ember told me today that her dream is to become an actress." I fortify myself against the way Charlie stills in the moonlight, and continue, "You might not think I'm much of an actor, but most of Hollywood *does*, which means I have the contacts to help Ember get a foot in the door."

Charlie shakes her head. "She doesn't want help."

"She told me that as well, and I admire her immensely for it. But she'd also be a fool to turn down any advantage she can get, especially from someone like me"—just saying that makes me want to punch myself in the face—"and deep down she has to know it. As, I'm sure, do you."

When Charlie looks torn, I go in for the kill: "I'll put in a good word for her at the drama school she's applied to, and if they offer her a place, or even if they don't, I'll talk to Gabe about getting her some auditions. We can connect her with local agents, or ones abroad, if that's her desire. Whatever she wants, I'll do what I can to open doors for her." I drive my point home by finishing, "As unfair as it is, in this industry, it's as much who you know as it is what you know. And I happen to be someone worth knowing."

Charlie's skepticism is clear. "With all the bad press you've had lately, how can you help her, when you can't even help yourself?"

"That's where our deal comes in," I say. "It's mutually beneficial. Once my public image is back to where it should be, I'll be better able to help Ember reach her dreams."

I can see Charlie struggling with this, her love for her friend warring against whatever problem she has with me. But, finally, she grits out, "What would I have to do?"

Hope blossoms within me. "Not much. You'd just have to rein in the attitude a little."

She splutters. "*Attitude?*"

I send her a look. "What would you call it?" When she says nothing, I continue, "You don't have to act all fangirl-obsessed, but it'd help if you didn't glare daggers at me while the cameras are rolling. No sarcastic comments, no passive-aggressive remarks, no ignoring me. Treat me like . . . like . . ." I think quickly, and settle on, "Hawke. Treat me like you'll treat him."

"I *like* Hawke," Charlie says.

"Exactly." Under my breath, I add, "Though, I find it supremely unfair that you haven't cast judgment on him like you did me."

"Hawke didn't give me a reason to hate him," Charlie states.

"And I did?"

Her eyes are flinty. "Yes."

"But you still won't tell me that reason?"

She turns away from me. "It doesn't matter. After this week, we'll never see each other again."

There's a strange burning in my chest, as if her words pain me, but that doesn't make sense, since I'm just as eager to be rid of her as she is me.

"Do we have a deal?" I ask.

"Of course we do," Charlie says, huffily. "I'm already stuck with you. I might as well get something out of it."

"Technically, what you got was Ember meeting me today."

"And now that that's happened, what's to stop me from flying home tomorrow?"

I freeze, realizing she's right—there's nothing stopping her. She and Ember could vanish in the night and I wouldn't know until we're due to meet Hawke's producer.

"Relax, Zander," Charlie drawls. It's the first time she's said my name, and a different kind of warmth fills me, making even less sense than the earlier burning sensation. "I might not want to be within a thousand kilometers of you, but I agreed to see this through, so you can lose the look of fear—I'll still be here in the morning." She sighs, then forces herself to say, "And I'll try my best to make you look good. At least while the cameras are rolling. I can't promise about the rest of the time."

Relief slams into me, and I send her a wide, grateful smile that makes her breath hitch, before she blinks and looks away, frowning.

"Thank you, Charlie," I say, with genuine feeling. "And, hey, you never know, maybe we'll manage to have some fun over the next few days."

She stands up and dusts the seat of her pajama pants. "That depends on your definition of fun."

"Okay," I amend, rising as well, "maybe we'll manage to resist pushing each other off a mountain over the next few days."

A hint of a smile touches her lips. "That sounds more plausible. Still not guaranteed, though."

Recalling her modification to our deal, I say, "I'll be sure to watch my back when the cameras are off."

Her eyes dance in the moonlight. "I did say you were smart."

"I have to be, since apparently I'm a bad actor."

She looks down at the ground, and I know it's to hide her amusement. I just don't know *why* she's not allowing herself to be amused. But I have four days to figure it out, and while earlier tonight that thought filled me with dread, I'm now looking forward to it.

What I'm *not* looking forward to is being awake and ready to leave in five hours, so I gesture toward the path and say, "Do you think Ember will have stopped snoring by now?"

"If she hasn't, she'll get a pillow in her face."

Her dark tone nearly makes me laugh, but my mirth turns into something softer when she asks, hesitantly, "Will you be able to fall asleep this time?"

The warm feeling from earlier intensifies. "Yeah, my mind is a lot calmer now."

"I've been told I have that effect on people."

This time I do laugh, but I stifle it fast when she glowers at me. She can't hold the expression though, her own features still working to hide her humor.

A few hours ago, I was cursing the effect jet lag had on my body. Now I'm grateful for it. Because it led me out to this garden and to Charlie, and for the first time in a long time, I feel hopeful about the future.

I wish Summer was here so I could talk to her about everything that happened today. I wish Maddox was here to tease me about fumbling my way through tonight's conversation. I wish both of them were joining me on tomorrow's survival trip, if only so I wouldn't have to face the ghosts of my past alone. But I learned long ago that wishes are nothing more than wasted words, and to place hope in them only results in heartache.

"Zander?"

I jump at Charlie's voice. "Yeah?"

She looks closely at me. "You okay?"

I cover my discomfort quickly. "Just ready to crash. You may not have heard, but I'm a high-maintenance actor and I need my beauty sleep."

She doesn't believe me, but goes along with it anyway. "Time for bed, then."

Together we head back up the path to the hotel, neither of us saying anything as we part ways, both knowing we'll see each other again in a few short hours.

And then the real acting will begin.

Charlie

I'm still half asleep when Ember and I meet Zander and Gabe in the lobby at the crack of dawn and follow them into a waiting van, the few hours of restless dozing I stole after midnight doing little to ease my nerves about today.

In a way I'm glad Ember's wake-the-dead snoring led me to the garden last night, since it was good to speak candidly to Zander. We know where we stand now, with each of us holding the cards to what the other wants: me, his career, and him, Ember's dreams.

I haven't told her about the deal I made, and I don't intend to, just in case I can't keep my side of the bargain. But I'm willing to try, since Zander wasn't lying about the doors he could open for her. It's worth putting up with him for a few days, especially since, as much as I loathe to admit it, he's not entirely awful to be around.

I'd hoped he would be a troll. A miserable ogre who offered smiles when on camera but was haughty and vain in person. He's . . . not. But I don't want to think about what he is—how he gave Ember the best day of her life yesterday, how he didn't lose patience with me no matter how intolerable I was, how he was kind and compassionate and even funny—because if I do, then I might forget what he's done. I might forget why I hate him.

Deep down, I know I'm being irrational. But irrationality isn't something I can simply wish away. Nor can I wish Zander away—as much as I might want to.

"We're nearly there."

I look out the tinted window of the van. Ember is beside me, Gabe and Zander behind us, and there's a driver up front. I can barely recall leaving the hotel, but as our chauffeur's words penetrate, I pinch myself awake and focus on the forested landscape passing by, searching for a hint of our destination.

My stomach dips when we turn down a gravel driveway and the dense trees disappear, revealing a grassy clearing—never a good sign in *Hawke's Wild World*, since it almost always means a dramatic aerial departure. For the millionth time in the last few days, I wonder what I've gotten myself into, and whether it's too late to back out.

But then I feel Ember jiggling with excitement and I remember that whatever is ahead, I can handle it, for her.

We drive until we reach the far side of the clearing and stop at a cluster of large shed-like buildings. People are moving around in the misty early-morning light, hauling gear between vehicles and checking camera equipment. Their confident actions imply they've done this many times before, and that helps ease something within me. Slightly.

When our driver opens the side door, Ember leaps out, and I follow more sedately with Zander and Gabe at my heels. Now that we're here and this trip is imminent, adrenaline begins to flood my veins. Despite myself, I'm looking forward to meeting Rykon Hawke—I just wish my mother could have been here with me.

That, however, is an impossible wish.

Even having my stepdad here would be a comfort—and a less impossible wish—but Jerry had only mumbled a quick "Stay safe" after confirming he signed the liability forms, and that was the last I saw of him before Ember and I had to catch our flight to Sydney. I learned six months ago that I can't count on him in challenging times, but that doesn't stop it from hurting all the same.

"Zombie-Charlie, are you awake?"

I jerk backward when Ember waves a hand in front of my face, nearly clipping my nose.

"If I wasn't, I am now," I say. "But feel free to tell me I'm still asleep and this is all a dream." More like a nightmare, I add to myself.

Ember links her elbow with mine as our driver beckons us toward the nearest shed-building, his suit contrasting starkly with the casual wear of everyone else in sight.

"It *is* a dream," Ember says over the sound of frosted grass crunching beneath our feet. "The kind that happens while you're awake." She squeezes my arm. "You're going to have the *best* time. I'm so jealous!"

I bite back my retort, since I know she's telling the truth. She would swap places with me in a heartbeat if she could—and I would *absolutely* let her.

"In here, if you please," the driver says, opening a door built into the side of the shed, revealing a small, dusty office. "Ms. Quinn will be with you momentarily."

The man vanishes, leaving Zander, Gabe, Ember, and me alone for all of three seconds before the door reopens and a woman walks through. She has a solid figure and short auburn hair, with both her puffer vest and beanie featuring a front-facing hawk in flight—the logo on all of Hawke's survival merchandise.

"Gabriel, lovely to meet you in person," she says with a hint of a South African accent, offering Gabe her hand, before introducing herself to the rest of us. "I'm Scarlett Quinn, EP of *Hawke's Wild World*. We're so thrilled to have you here."

"We're just as thrilled to be here," Gabe says with a smile.

It takes everything in me to hold my tongue, since it's not *him* who has to go without basic amenities for the next few days. I make the mistake of looking at Zander and find him already watching me, a sparkle in his unnaturally blue eyes as he reads me like a book.

"Rykon's a few minutes away," Scarlett says, moving toward the nearest desk and wiping it with her sleeve. "Once he's here, we'll film some sound bites and take a couple of photos, but we're on the clock so we'll keep things brief." She winks at Zander and me and adds, "Don't worry, you'll be out in the wild starting your adventure soon enough."

The word "wild" echoes in my ears, along with all that it means. I remind myself that it won't make for good television if any of us die on this trip, and that Hawke's team is too experienced to let it come close to that, anyway. My confidence takes a hit, however, when Scarlett places a tablet on the desk and declares, "Time to sign your lives away."

Ember chokes beside me. I can't tell if it's the sound of laughter or—no, it's definitely laughter.

"I'm not eighteen until next month," I say when Scarlett nudges the tablet my way. "My stepdad already signed your forms."

"You still need to confirm your consent to be filmed, and for the footage to be shared publicly," Scarlett explains. "You too, Zander."

He looks at Gabe, as if waiting for him to object, but his agent just says, "I've already read it all and made the necessary amendments. You're good to sign."

I wish I had someone to tell *me* that, since when I open the digital document, I have to scroll and scroll and *scroll* before I reach the last page where Jerry has already filled in his guardian part, and a space remains for me.

"It's going to take forever to read this," I say. "At least three years." I'm exaggerating, but not by much.

"Unfortunately, we don't have that long," Scarlett says, looking out the window at a large black vehicle pulling up. "Rykon's just arrived, and he'll want to get things moving fast."

"I don't care if the King of England just arrived," I return, crossing my arms. "I know better than to sign anything without reading it first."

"Charlie, I assure you it's fine," Gabe says placatingly. "I read it thoroughly and—"

"No offense," I cut him off, "but you're not *my* agent. You might have Zander's best interests at heart, but I could be signing away my firstborn child for all I know."

Scarlett laughs and jumps in to say, "I promise we don't want your children, firstborn or otherwise." Her features soften with understanding. "You're smart to be careful, but don't you think your stepdad would have done his due diligence?" She taps Jerry's name, and I realize she's right. His mother was a lawyer, so he knows not to mess around with contracts, nor would he sign anything without reading every single word.

Ember shifts closer, as if she's preparing to have my back should I refuse to cooperate, and that alone gives me the courage to mutter, "Fine," before I autograph it with a flourish.

"Your turn, Zan," Gabe says.

There's a crease in Zander's brow as he copies my actions and scrolls, scrolls, *scrolls*, but then he too gives in and signs the last page.

"Wonderful," Scarlett says, reclaiming the tablet. "With that done, let's go introduce you to Rykon."

Butterflies swarm in my stomach as we follow her back out into the crisp morning air. My nerves don't make sense, since it's not as if *I'm* a superfan of Hawke's—but then I realize they're likely covering the deeper heartache I'm feeling at being so close to someone who my mum would have given anything to meet.

I swallow and shove that thought away, burying it with all the emotions I've locked deep inside for the last six months.

"I'm so excited I can barely *breathe*," Ember says as we walk toward the second shed-like building, this one bustling with the most activity.

"I take it you're a Hawke fan?" Zander asks, matching his pace to ours.

"Don't worry." Ember grins at him. "You're still my favorite."

His eyes are bright as they catch mine. "At least someone likes me."

"You're hardly short on admirers," I reply. "One person not falling at your feet is good for you. Keeps your ego in check."

"Are you saying I should thank you?"

"No." I smirk. "But you're welcome."

Right then, as we're looking at each other, a flash goes off.

"Perfection, my sweetlings!" crows the man holding the camera as I blink away stars. He's slender and has wavy brown hair, and I'm instantly envious of his eyeliner skills. "Now let's try again, but this time smile at each other."

"Give us a minute, Ollie," Scarlett cuts in. "I want them to meet Rykon first. Then they're all yours."

The photographer—Ollie—nods, but continues taking candid shots as we step through the open entrance to the shed-building. It's large enough to be an aircraft hangar, but there are no planes in sight, only a small fleet of vehicles all with the hawk logo on the side.

Another flash of Ollie's camera has me rubbing my arms self-consciously as I realize this is going to be my life for the next four days, my every move recorded. There will be times when physical exertion will leave me red-faced and sweaty, moments when my unfiltered words could be misinterpreted, camera angles showing unflattering bulges and make-up-free skin and—

"Rykon! Over here!" Scarlett calls across the hangar, yanking me from my inner spiraling.

I take a deep breath and remember that even if I end up publicly humiliated, it'll hardly be the worst thing that's ever happened to me. And when Ember is a big-time movie star thanks to the opportunities Zander creates for her, she can pay for any therapy I need resulting from this trip.

Resolved not to dwell on what's ahead, I watch as the survivalist legend breaks away from a group of people loading gear into a vehicle and strides our way.

Rykon Hawke is even more impressive in real life than he is onscreen. My mum once described him as "the epitome of masculinity" and I can see why. Standing at well over six feet, with dark skin and hair, coupled with an easy smile behind a neatly trimmed beard, everything about Hawke exudes warmth and kindness. But it's the muscles rippling along his arms and shoulders that emphasize his strength and remind me of just how long he's been in the physically demanding survival business, going all the way back to his park ranger years. Seeing him in person, any lingering fears I have for the next few days dissolve, since it's impossible not to feel safe in his presence.

"These must be my VIP guests," Hawke says once he reaches us.

"Ryk, this is Zander Rune and Charlie Hart," Scarlett introduces.

"Zander, love your work," Hawke says, shaking the actor's hand.

"Right back at you." Zander seems almost embarrassed by Hawke's praise, though I'm sure I'm imagining his humble reaction.

"And Charlie, a pleasure," Hawke tells me.

"You too," I say, before adding, somewhat stupidly, "You're taller than I thought you'd be."

Hawke's smile returns. "My father always said, 'Eat your greens if you want to grow up tall and strong.' I guess he was right."

Before I can say anything more embarrassing, like how he must have existed solely on leafy vegetables during his formative years, Scarlett thankfully continues her introductions. "And this is Zander's agent, Gabriel, and Charlie's best friend, Ember."

Hawke offers handshakes to them both, holding Ember's the longest, but only because she grips him like a monkey and breathes, "I freaking love you."

A chuckle leaves Hawke and he moves his free hand to clasp hers gently between both of his. "That's very kind of you. It's always nice to meet a fan."

I step closer to Ember just in case I need to catch her when she melts into a puddle at our feet.

"Rykon, we're so grateful for you agreeing to this competition on such short notice," Gabe says.

The survivalist waves off Gabe's gratitude. "Not at all. I was already planning to film this episode here, so my team only needed to make a few adjustments for a guest to join me. Or guests, in this case." He winks at me, and I wonder if Ember will have to catch me instead. It's easy to see why my mum was obsessed with him. There's something so endearingly charming about him, from his handsome features to his Canadian accent to his overall physicality.

"As much as I'd love to get to know you all better, you two especially," Hawke says, indicating Zander and me, "we need to leave soon to make the most of the daylight."

"Ryk, don't forget, we need some photos and—"

Scarlett is interrupted when someone calls Hawke's name, and he glances across the hangar, dipping his chin at them before turning back and saying, "We can spare ten minutes for promo once they're dressed—will that be enough?"

Scarlett looks to Ollie, who has been taking surreptitious shots the whole time we've been talking.

"I can make that work," the photographer says.

Hawke claps Ollie on the shoulder. "Good man." With a polite nod to the rest of us, he adds, "See you soon," and walks purposefully away.

Scarlett immediately leads us toward a table holding an array of survival paraphernalia, some of which—like the grappling hooks and carabiners—cause a cold sweat to break out on my skin. Scarlett, however, ignores those items and gestures to the rack standing beside the table.

"These are your clothes." She hands garment bags to Zander and me. "The base layers are a moisture-wicking merino blend, and the outer layers will keep you warm and dry without making you overheat. We pride ourselves on the quality of our *Wild World* apparel, so rest assured that you'll be as comfortable as possible over the next few days." She points to a door in the hangar's wall. "Bathrooms for changing are over there."

Ember gives me a "Go on" nudge and turns her attention to the table, asking Scarlett about the climbing equipment. Since I'd prefer to remain in denial about why it's there, I hurry after Zander, lock myself in my half of the bathroom, and unzip my bag. The attire is simple—gray hiking pants that brush my boots, a white long-sleeved thermal shirt, and a fleecy lilac pullover, all featuring the small front-facing hawk logo. There's also a cream-colored waterproof down jacket, but as soon as I put it on, I have to take it off again, since the pullover is already plenty warm.

I step back into the hangar at the same time as Zander, and come to an abrupt halt at the sight of him. While my clothes are pale, pretty colors, his are darker, his hiking pants a deep navy and his pullover a royal blue that—God, how is it possible for his eyes to be brighter than before? Worse, how can *everything* about him be even *more* attractive than when he was in normal clothes?

I hate the betraying flush I feel staining my cheeks, and cover it by scowling and demanding, "Why did I get the girly clothes? You look like you're about to James Bond your way into a high-security vault, while I look ready to jump on a unicorn and go frolicking over a rainbow. Sexist, much?"

His stupidly, *stupidly* blue eyes flash with mirth. "I've never heard 'James Bond' used as a verb before."

My scowl deepens, but before I can reply, Ember skips toward us and says, "It's my fault. They asked for your color preferences when I gave them your sizes. You look *amazing*, Charlie Bear. I did good, if I do say so myself." She dusts her hands together, clearly proud, before her gaze flicks to Zander. "You, of course, look ridiculous. In the best possible way."

His mouth curls upward as he folds his waterproof jacket—black, naturally—over his arm. "Thanks, Ember." To me, he says, "She's right, you look great. Any unicorn would be honored to go frolicking with you."

The teasing glint in his eyes only makes my indignation grow, but I bite my tongue, partly because Ember is so pleased with herself, but also because I don't actually have a problem with my clothes. It's not the attire that has me so flustered—it's Zander. On an intellectual level, I can acknowledge that he's good-looking, but I didn't expect to be so . . . *affected* by him. It's infuriating that my hormones are going rogue, and I yank them firmly into line.

Blessed distraction comes when Ollie's flash goes off—reminding me that I need to heed caution with everything I do and say from here on out—and a moment later Scarlett calls us back to the table. Gabe is a short distance away talking on his phone, but his eyes are on us as Scarlett hands Zander and me identical wristwatches. I strap mine on, noting the analog face, compass, and light.

"Keep these on at all times," Scarlett instructs us. "We're experimenting with next-gen nano drones this trip—cameras unobtrusive enough that you won't know they're following you."

She pulls a small silver box off the table and opens it to reveal what appears to be a set of metallic winged insects no larger than her fingernail.

"The technology is military-grade and scarily impressive," Scarlett continues, "but while they can film in crystal clear HD, their audio strength is limited." She taps Zander's watch. "That's where these babies come in, since they'll act as your microphones. They sync up to the drones via GPS and work in tandem with them, so we can still record what you hear and say without the cameras flying in your faces."

Zander peers at his wrist with renewed interest. "I'm not a fan of cameras in my face."

Scarlett chuckles. "I figured you'd be on board with this tech. Our aim is to one day use the nano drones exclusively on these trips, but since they're still in the prototype stage, you'll have a cameraman with you on the ground capturing everything as a backup. And speaking of . . ." She waves to a cute, nerdy-looking man heading our way, someone I've seen in numerous photos and videos standing beside Hawke. His light brown hair is tousled and his black-framed glasses sit in front of warm chocolate eyes, his skin as pale as Hawke's is dark.

"Everyone, this is Rykon's husband, Bentley," Scarlett says, before turning to Zander and me. "He's our lead cameraman—he'll be with you the whole time you're gone, but he'll also remain mostly silent to keep the focus on you two and Hawke." She then adds, "We try not to have too many people tailing you and ruining the authenticity of the experience, so outside of regular support check-ins, it'll just be the four of you alone together."

I'm thrilled by this news, since it means there will be another buffer between Zander and me. The more the merrier, as far as I'm concerned.

"Delighted to make your acquaintance," Bentley says in a lush British accent, his tone as friendly as his husband's. He indicates the camera already in his hands, then taps a smaller GoPro version strapped to his shoulder. "I'll do my best to catch your good angles, but no promises. In the wild, anything goes."

"That should be your company slogan," Ember quips.

"I've tried to make it happen," Bentley says with a conspiratorial grin. "Along with many others. Alas, Rykon is set on *Live now, not later.*"

I've seen those words accompanying the flying hawk logo, so they're not new to me, but hearing them spoken yields a gravitas that I wasn't anticipating. *Live now, not later*—the phrase calls to me, prompting both guilt and longing.

"Are we all set?" Gabe asks, re-joining our group and quickly introducing himself to Bentley.

"Pretty much," Scarlett says, inspecting Zander and me. Satisfied, she tells us, "We have backpacks for you both with spare clothes and other essentials, but we'll get those to you right before you leave. For now . . . Ollie, are you ready for them?"

"Sure am," the photographer says, beaming. "We just need Hawke."

"I'll get him," Scarlett says, glancing over to where the survivalist is standing with a group of black-clad crew members studying a map spread across the hood of a vehicle. "Start with Charlie and Zander, and I'll bring Ryk to you in a few minutes."

She and Bentley move off together, leaving us with the still-beaming Ollie.

"This way, my darlings," he says, ushering us toward the hangar's exit. "I didn't introduce myself before, but I'm Oliver Arton: creative genius and content manager for *Hawke's Wild World*. I normally work behind a screen, but I pulled rank to be here with you two cuties today. You have *no idea* how excited I am."

Once outside, he guides us to a quiet spot away from the flurry of last-minute gear checks, gesturing for Zander and me to stop beside the hangar's corrugated iron wall while Ember and Gabe watch on.

"The lighting here is *perfect*," Ollie gushes. "I've got some nice candid snaps already, so these are for the posed media blasts. Try to look natural. Relax. *Smile.* You're excited about your upcoming adventure, remember? Share everything you're feeling with your new BFF Ollie."

Given my tumultuous emotions, it's not the best suggestion. But I have a bargain to uphold, so when Ollie asks me to step closer to Zander, I do so with a big, fake smile over my gritted teeth.

"Gorgeous!—Amazing!—Spectacular!" Ollie's praise is as constant as the photos he's taking. "Zander, can you put your arm around Charlie's shoulders? And Charlie, can yours circle his waist? Then lock eyes and smile like you're sharing a secret. Nice and intimate—our viewers will eat it up!"

I tense as Zander moves to follow Ollie's instructions, but his arm doesn't leave his side. In a voice meant only for me, he asks, "Is this okay? If you're uncomfortable, we can—"

"It's fine," I say, staunchly ignoring the warmth his concern prompts, and once again wishing he was a heartless ogre, since it would make it so much easier to keep my resolve around him.

"You don't look like it's fine," Zander says, though he hesitantly wraps his arm around me. I curl mine around his waist, touching him as little as possible. "You look like you're about to face a mountain lion." His eyes widen in alarm and shoot toward the distant mountains. "You don't have those here, do you?"

Something in me eases at the panicked look on his face—or perhaps it's because I know it's not real, and he's only trying to keep me from thinking about how we're practically half-hugging. "They're not native," I answer, "but I wouldn't be surprised if Hawke's team brought one along for the sake of entertainment."

"In that case, survival rules apply from here on out," Zander says, dead serious.

"Survival rules?"

A mischievous grin tugs at his lips. "Surely you've heard the saying, 'You don't need to run the fastest, as long as you're not the slowest'? My legs are at least fifteen times longer than yours, so I'm thinking you're fresh out of luck when it comes to carnivorous felines."

I play along, making a *pfft* sound. "Oh please, we all know Hawke will be the first to get eaten. He's obviously just a poster boy for the company, with zero survival skills."

"Per-*fection*, my lovelies! Absolutely *flawless*!" Ollie cries, breaking the spell between us. It's only then that I see we're doing exactly what he asked for: locking eyes and smiling, with our arms around each other. I hadn't even noticed, wholly caught up in our banter.

Zander, however, has a satisfied look on his face as he drops his arm and steps away, making me realize he was fully aware the whole time. The warm feeling in me intensifies, since instead of ignoring my discomfort or reminding me to act like an enamored fan, he did what he could to distract me. And it worked.

"I have everything I need from you two as a couple," Ollie says, squinting at his camera screen and therefore missing my knee-jerk reaction to the word "couple." Zander doesn't miss it though, and chuckles softly under his breath. So does Ember—but not as softly.

"Sounds like my timing is perfect," says Hawke as he strides into view. Bentley and Scarlett are with him, and they halt beside Ember and Gabe while Hawke joins us at the corrugated wall.

Ollie takes more photos, then finally waves Bentley over to film some short Q and As. I get asked everything from how excited I am about the adventure—"*Sooooo* excited! I can't *believe* I get to spend *four days* with *Zander Rune*!"—to what I'm going to miss most while I'm away from civilization—"Absolutely *nothing*, because I'll be with *Zander*! What more could I *need*?"

My answers make Ember choke on confused laughter and Zander look at me with enough exasperation that I dial it back a notch for Ollie's next question.

"It's obvious that you're a big fan of Zander's," he says, laughing, and I somehow manage to keep my fake smile in place, "but what about Hawke? Have you seen his show?"

I'm acutely aware of the camera recording my answer, but even so, I can't stop my smile from slipping. "I have, actually. Not every episode, but a lot of them." I hesitate a beat before sharing, "My mum was a huge fan of Hawke's, so he's been a staple in my home ever since the pilot of *Hawke's Wild World.*"

"'Was'?" Ollie repeats. "She's not a fan anymore?"

My mouth is suddenly too dry for me to speak. Ollie doesn't press and jumps straight onward, asking what food I'll eat first after we get back, and continuing with a barrage of non-invasive getting-to-know-you questions.

"We likely won't use them all," he says as an aside, "but it's better to have too much material than not enough."

When Ollie is finished with me, he turns to Zander, and I listen as he answers similar questions, plus others about the competition and his inspiration for it. There's no mention of his tarnished reputation, only his love for his fans, his true motives hidden behind gracious words and wholesome smiles.

I lied to his face last night when I said he's not a good actor. He is. One of the best. On-screen and—clearly—off.

Once both of us are done, Ollie's attention moves to Hawke, but he only asks a few things before saying he has all he needs.

"You two lovelies are going to shine like diamonds," Ollie tells Zander and me. "I can't wait to watch you over the next few days—this is going to be the best episode *ever.*"

With that, he blows air kisses and walks away, his thumbs moving at lightning speed over his phone keyboard.

"No matter how many times I have to do that," Hawke says, his eyes on Ollie's retreating back, "I will never, ever enjoy it."

His weary sigh has me biting back a laugh and realizing he's perhaps more of a kindred spirit than I thought.

"But at least now we can finally get to the good part," he continues, causing my humor to die a fast death. "Zander, I hear you trained with Fredrik Haas when you were filming in Austria, is that right?"

For some unknown reason, Zander turns to me with a look that's crossed between apprehension and anticipation, before he slowly answers, "I did."

"Excellent," Hawke says. "Come with me." To the rest of us, he adds, "We'll be back shortly. Charlie, time to say your goodbyes."

I wish he'd tacked on a "for now" or similar, since it would help lessen the fear rising in me as Zander follows him back into the hangar. I waste precious seconds wondering what they're up to before deciding to let it go, knowing the answers will come soon enough. Instead, I turn to Ember, seeing Gabe, Scarlett, and Bentley conversing a short distance away, giving us some privacy.

"So, you're suddenly Zander's biggest fan, huh?" Ember says, referencing my embarrassing promo clips, her lips quirking. "And here I thought I owned that title."

I'm still reluctant to tell her about the bargain, so I just say, "We've agreed to get along for the sake of the cameras."

She raises a dark brow. "Since he doesn't have a problem with you, I assume you mean that you've agreed not to hiss at him like a stray cat while the whole world is watching?"

I pluck at my sleeve. "I prefer my wording."

Ember grins. "I'm sure you do." She then sobers and steps closer, her voice low. "You can still back out. It means so much to me that we're here, but now that my excitement has faded, I feel really bad about putting you in this position, especially knowing—"

"Hey, stop," I say, placing my hand on her shoulder. "I'm a big girl and I made my own decision to come here."

"You did it for *me*."

"And I'd do it again," I say firmly.

"Tell me that in four days when you're miserable from chafing and bug bites and blisters," Ember says, before woefully adding, "I'm a horrible friend!"

"Maybe," I say, "but I still love you. And I'm not going anywhere. So give me a hug and tell me something encouraging so I don't throw up from nerves the moment Hawke and Zander return."

Ember doesn't delay in flinging her arms around me. "I love you, Charlie Bear. To the sun and moon and back again until forever."

My throat closes at the phrase we've shared a million times since we were kids, and I realize it's all the encouragement I need.

But Ember isn't done, since she whispers in my ear, "You're the best person I've ever known, and you're stronger than you think. The last few months have been . . ." She can't find an adequate word, so she settles on, "really, *really* awful, but you've made it this far, which means you can make it through the next four days, easy. Just try to remember that this trip isn't only about survival. Because life isn't about survival—life is beautiful, and it's meant to be *lived*." She swallows, then tentatively says, "Your mum would be so happy you're here, and if she were standing with us now, she'd tell you to enjoy every second."

I feel my eyes misting, but then Ember's voice lightens as she finishes, "Or she would, but only *after* she took three thousand photos with Hawke and begged him to leave Bentley and run away with her."

A surprised chuckle leaves me, the sound pained but genuine. "Try four thousand. Or more."

Ember pulls back, a soft smile on her face. "You're right. Definitely more." She takes my hands in hers. "You sure you're ready for this?"

I inhale deeply and nod. "As ready as I'll ever be."

"And you're feeling brave? Courageous? Daring?"

Warily, I ask, "Why are you using synonyms?"

She bites her lip and looks into the distance. "You know how I've always had a heightened sense of hearing?"

Her tone has enough warning in it that I follow her gaze, vaguely noting Scarlett, Gabe, and Bentley moving our way, the latter holding a camera pointed at me. "Yeah?"

"Well, I think I know how your trip is going to start," she says. "And you're going to need all the fearless synonyms you can get."

Within seconds, I hear it: the *whup-whup-whup* sound of rotating blades cutting through the air.

My insides churn as the helicopter comes into view, the noise growing uncomfortably louder as it approaches. But that's not the only reason for my twisting stomach, because Zander and Hawke have reappeared from within the hangar, both wearing harnesses and backpacks that I instinctively know aren't carrying our spare clothes and essential items.

The helicopter lands just as Hawke and Zander reach our group, the engine powering down and leaving me able to hear my own thoughts again. I'm unsure if that's a good thing, given my growing state of dread.

"As you can see, our ride is here," Hawke tells me with a grin, holding out a spare harness. "You're going to need this."

I take it from him automatically, watching as he passes a second harness to Bentley, who steps into it while keeping a steady grip on the camera he's using to film us.

Hawke helps me do the same, adjusting the straps until they're snug against my body.

"No questions?" he asks as he tugs and tightens everything. "You're not wondering why you're wearing this?"

"I'm actually freaking out enough that I figure it's best to keep my mouth shut so I don't vomit all over you."

Hawke throws back his head and laughs, his teeth bright against his dark skin. "We're going to have a great time over the next few days, Charlie. I can tell."

For obvious reasons, I don't believe him. "Your version of a great time is likely very different to mine."

He's still chuckling as he steps away and says, "You're all set." He then calls Zander over, and tells us both, "The starting point of our hike is too deep in the mountains for us to get there easily on foot, so we're flying in." A devious look accompanies his next words. "And by flying, I mean falling." He turns to me. "Charlie, keep thinking non-vomiting thoughts, or you won't be Zander's favorite person, since you're jumping tandem with him."

My mind short-circuits. "I'm *what*?"

"He's fully accredited," Hawke assures me. "Fredrik Haas is one of the most experienced instructors in the world, and he trained Zander personally. You couldn't be in better hands."

I'm too horrified to form a solid argument, so I just splutter, "Why can't I go with you?" If I have to plummet to the earth like a dead weight, I'd feel *much* safer doing it with Hawke at my back.

Bentley raises his free hand. "I'm afraid that's my fault," he says sheepishly. "I have a slight skydiving phobia, so Rykon and I have a long-standing agreement that the only way I'll ever do it is when I'm strapped to him. That way, if we perish, at least we'll be together."

"That's so romantic," Ember coos from my side. But I barely hear her.

"Oh my *God*," I breathe, my eyes wide. "I'm going to die. This is it. This is my end."

"You're not going to die, Charlie," Zander says, fighting a grin. "I've done this plenty of times. All those dragon battle scenes in the movies? Every time I fell through the air? That wasn't CGI. We had to do what felt like a million takes for some of those shots, and each one required me jumping out of a plane or helicopter." He lessens the distance between us, his voice quieting. "I won't let anything happen to you. I promise."

It's the earnest look on his face that stops me from accepting Ember's offer to run while I still can. But even so, I ask him, "How much do you value your life?"

He blinks. "Pardon?"

"On a scale of one to ten," I press. "How much do you enjoy living? Anything less than eight, and I'm staying put."

He finally understands, mirth filling his eyes, before an unexpected sense of grief shadows his features. But he shakes it off and says, "I assure you that I have plenty to live for—and no plans for that to change anytime soon."

Ember brushes her shoulder against mine, silently saying we can leave. But in doing so, she reminds me of all the reasons I agreed to this madness in the first place. So I exhale shakily and look Zander straight in his ridiculously blue eyes as I say, "Please don't make me regret trusting you."

There's a heaviness to my plea that he can't—and doesn't—miss.

Nodding solemnly, he replies, "You have my word."

"Wonderful," Scarlett says, clapping her hands together. "Let's get this show on the road."

Hearing that, Ember gives me a final rib-crushing embrace and whispers in my ear, "You've got this, Charlie Bear. I'll see you on Friday, and miss you every second until then."

She releases me and steps back just as Gabe finishes his own farewell with Zander. The two of them then wave cheerily as Hawke leads us toward the helicopter, his fingers curled around my elbow as if he expects me to run—or faint.

"Deep breaths," Hawke tells me with an encouraging smile as he slides open the rear door and shimmies across to the far side, followed by Bentley and Zander, then finally, me.

I hover uncertainly when I see how tight the space is, awkwardness replacing my fear as I watch Bentley sit in between Hawke's legs and realize I have to do the same with my own tandem partner.

Zander notices my hesitation and pats his lap. "Just act as if I'm Santa and you're making a Christmas wish." He immediately cringes. "Wow, that sounded a lot worse than I intended, but I figured 'I don't bite' was too clichéd."

I don't have a chance to respond before the pilot slides the door shut behind me and returns to the cockpit, with Scarlett settling into the copilot's seat. A moment later, the engine starts up, the sound thunderous in the cabin.

Since my desire to be sitting when we lift off is stronger than my aversion to being in direct physical contact with Zander, I lower myself unceremoniously onto his lap. He says something, but even with his mouth at my ear, I can't hear the words. The next second, however, his arms come around me, and my breath catches as I'm enveloped by all that is him. The scent of mint hits my nose, mixed with something earthy and undeniably pleasant, but I force those thoughts away and am about to yank myself out of his hold when I realize—with some humiliation—that he's not trying to cop a feel, but rather, he's connecting our harnesses in preparation for our jump. That must have been what he tried to tell me, his words drowned out by the roaring of the rotor blades.

I'm relieved he can't see my face right now, but I'm even more relieved when Scarlett turns around and hands out some aviation headsets. The instant I place mine over my ears, the deafening sound is muted, and this time I hear Zander clearly when he speaks into his microphone and asks, "All good?"

My voice only slightly betrays my anxiety when I answer, "Just peachy."

I can hear the humor in his tone as he warns, "I have to tighten everything, so this may feel a little uncomfortable. But we don't want any space between us when we jump."

For the sake of my sanity, I don't question the reason for that, and rest stiffly against him as he tugs at the joints between our harnesses. I turn to see Hawke doing the same with Bentley, though I also notice that Bentley has a large pack strapped to his front that he wasn't wearing before. He also still has his camera out, filming everything happening in the cabin.

"Everyone set?" Scarlett asks.

Hawke leans across to double-check Zander's work, then gives Scarlett the thumbs-up sign. A moment later, a subtle lightheadedness hits me as we rise swiftly upward.

"A few important things," Hawke says over the muffled sounds of flight.

My gaze is out the window as we soar away from the airfield and over the tops of trees, gaining height with every second, but I pull my attention back to him at the seriousness of his tone.

"Charlie," he says, "keep your arms up against your chest when you jump, right here." He taps the shoulder straps of my harness. "Somersaulting is normal, so don't panic, and trust Zander to control your fall.

When you're coming in to land, lift your legs, and let Zander do all the work. All you have to do is relax and enjoy the ride."

I hate how much I have to trust Zander in every aspect of our jump, but I find comfort in knowing he's not going to jeopardize his mission to save his public image by squashing us like pancakes against the earth.

That image hits me hard, making me loathe my overactive imagination, but I swallow my nausea and keep listening as Hawke goes on, "We've found a small ledge partway up the mountain range that's clear enough for us to use as a drop zone." He offers instructions to Zander that I can't begin to understand, but words like "trees" and "cliff" and "watch out for" have my heart feeling like it's going to beat out of my chest. The only reassurance I have—and I use that term loosely—is how calm and steady Zander is in his replies. Despite my doubts, he at least *seems* to know what he's doing. I try to channel his zen, but that becomes impossible when the pilot's voice crackles in our ears.

"ETA five minutes. Final checks, everyone."

"Goggles on," Hawke says, handing out protective glasses. "Any questions before we do this? You feeling okay about it all, Charlie?"

"No, and *absolutely no*," I answer, after which I actually *feel* Zander shake with silent laughter behind me. "But you said I don't need to do anything, so I'm holding you to that."

"Just enjoy the ride," Hawke confirms, repeating his earlier words. "And remember to breathe."

With no further warning, he leans across us to reopen the side door, causing wind to gust in with enough force that I would have flown straight back into Zander if I wasn't already plastered to him.

A garbled sound of fear leaves me, and I expect to feel Zander laughing again, but he just wraps his hands soothingly around my upper arms and says, "Don't worry, I won't let you go."

I nearly remind him that we're strapped together so he literally *can't*, but I'm incapable of forming intelligent words right now, my body quaking as I see how far down the Blue Mountains are beneath us.

I can't do this, I want to scream—but I don't. Because as scared as I am, there's another part of me, a small, long-buried part, that's whispering words of encouragement. It's reminding me that this is what living is meant to be: taking risks, embracing challenges, doing things that are as exciting as they are terrifying. It's been months since I've felt even a fraction of what I'm experiencing now, so while my instinct is to run from it, to hide from it, to avoid it, for the first time in a long time, I don't do that.

Instead, I shift my weight across the bench at Hawke's instruction, letting Zander do most of the maneuvering, until suddenly we're seated at the edge of the opening, our legs dangling above the skids and into nothing.

"You two are jumping first," Hawke yells over the raging wind, "but we'll be close enough behind for Ben to film you on the way down, just in case the nano drones miss anything."

I jolt at the reminder of the bug-sized cameras and look around the cabin, amazed anew that their diminutive size makes it impossible for me to spot them spying on us. But then my attention is diverted when our speed slows down, before we stop altogether, hovering in place.

Real panic slams into me now that our jump is imminent, and that feeling only grows when Hawke points out the door and tells Zander, "See the ledge about halfway up that peak? That's our drop zone."

I can see nothing but forest and mountains and jagged, *deadly* cliffs, but Zander offers a confident, "Got it."

"On your count, then," Hawke says, making my pulse skyrocket.

Scarlett turns around in her seat again, smiling widely as she says, "I'll see you all a bit later when ground support catches up to you. Take care, and have a great time!"

I'm increasingly doubtful about the last part, especially as we remove our aviation headsets and the roaring of the blades smacks into my eardrums all over again.

I only hear Zander because he's yelling straight into my ear now as he bellows, "On three!" He presses his hand to my brow, drawing my head back until it's supported against his shoulder, holding it in place long enough for me to know to leave it there.

"One!"

Everything buzzes within me, a previously unknown cocktail of numbness and adrenaline—

"Two!"

—mixed with exhilaration and terror—

"Three!"

—and then the only thing I'm feeling is weightless, because Zander has flung us out of the helicopter, and we're freefalling through the sky.

A scream erupts from my mouth, drowned out by the thunder of air pummeling me as we spin and twist uncontrollably. Everything is a blur of blue and green and blue and green and blue and—

Suddenly, we're not flipping anymore. We're still freefalling, but the ground is beneath us now, the sky above us, and Zander's hands are loosening the death grip I have on my harness so he can stretch our arms out to the side. The moment I capitulate, I feel like I'm flying; like I'm Superman soaring through the air. It's as if I'm on the world's scariest rollercoaster and I've finally let go of the safety railing, yielding my fear to embrace the thrill.

I feel . . .

I feel . . .

I feel *alive.*

Tears hit my eyes behind my goggles, but I blink them back, since I don't want to miss a moment of this.

And then, just as I begin to worry about how quickly the forested mountains are approaching, a violent tug yanks us upward as the parachute catches.

At first, the only thing I feel is overwhelming, immeasurable relief. But then I hear it: absolutely nothing.

The silence is unlike anything I've ever known. It's as if I'm alone in the world—*we're* alone in the world—and an unexpected peace settles upon me as we glide slowly downward.

"Wow," I whisper, feeling strangely humbled as I marvel at the view, realizing how small and insignificant I am against the vast sense of . . . of *life* stretching out before me.

"It's incredible, isn't it?" Zander's voice is soft, reverent, as if he's caught in the same spell. "Up here, there's nothing but freedom."

Freedom. It's the perfect word, and it causes my eyes to prickle again. My throat is clogged enough that I can't reply, but I don't think he expects me to. It's almost like he was saying it to himself, like he's feeling everything I am, like he *understands*—though I can't imagine how that might be true.

We say nothing as we glide down to the earth, silently agreeing to experience the journey without distraction. Hawke and Bentley soar near us, the latter pointing a small camera in our direction, but I choose to ignore him—and whoever might end up watching this—to instead sink into the moment.

All too soon, we approach our drop zone, and I see that Hawke's "ledge" is even narrower than I feared, bordered on one side by a rising, tree-covered mountain, and on the other by a plunging cliff steep enough to steal my breath. If Zander's steering is off by just a little, if the air currents from the mountain range cause an unexpected updraft, if we overshoot or undershoot or—

"Legs up," Zander tells me, his confident tone yanking me from my escalating dread.

I lift my lower half as high as I can, praying we're not about to go tumbling off the side of the mountain, our adventure ending before it begins.

But I needn't have worried, because from one minute to the next, we're landing on the rocky shelf, crumpling to the ground as gravity takes effect, with me once again in Zander's lap.

"We're alive," I gasp, somewhat stunned, as Hawke and Bentley land gracefully a few feet away.

Zander's laugh tickles my ear. "I promised I wouldn't let anything happen to you."

"That doesn't mean I *believed* you."

His reply is soft, meaningful, and causes a shiver to travel down my spine. "Now you know better."

Zander

The adrenaline from our skydive stays with me as I unclip our harnesses and help Charlie to her feet. There's a flush in her cheeks, and her eyes are bright, indicating she feels the same lingering exhilaration that I do.

I still can't believe she trusted me with her life. If our roles were reversed, I doubt I could have placed that kind of faith in someone I barely know. Or in Charlie's case, someone she loathes. Her acting skills are impressive; I have to keep reminding myself that her behavior is only a guise for the cameras, and that in reality, she can't wait for this trip to be over—mostly so she can be rid of me.

I wish I knew the reason for her antipathy, whether it's based solely on the "bad boy" gossip or if it's something else entirely. But with Bentley's cameras and the nano drones now on us twenty-four seven, I can't ask her without the world hearing, which would only risk what we're trying to achieve here. Not that I think she'd answer me, anyway.

Resigned to us both having to keep up appearances for the next four days, I follow Hawke's instructions to fold the parachute back into its pack, listening as he explains how it'll provide an effective shelter when we make camp tonight. I know he's speaking for the benefit of the audience, since he's talking directly to Bentley's camera and goes on to share a scripted introduction to our adventure:

"We've just landed deep in Australia's Blue Mountains National Park, which stretches more than a thousand square miles—that's the size of New York City, London, and Paris *combined*—over perilous slot canyons, jagged peaks, sandstone gorges, secluded rainforests, and breathtaking waterfalls."

I blink, having not realized the area was so large.

"The park itself is a World Heritage Site," Hawke continues narrating, "and home to hundreds of species of endangered flora and fauna, many of which are deadly to humans."

I *told* Summer that everything in this country would want to kill me.

"It also has a rich cultural history, being the traditional homeland to numerous Indigenous communities," Hawke says, his eyes still trained on the camera. "All of that, along with its natural beauty, makes it one of the most popular tourist destinations in the country. But it's also one of the most dangerous."

Here we go. I consider covering my ears to block out whatever he's about to say next.

"Every year, hundreds of hikers wander off the path and get lost in these treacherous mountains, learning for themselves just how lethal the Australian wilds can be." Hawke's lips curve into a wicked grin. "For the next four days, we'll be trekking through one of the most extreme environments in the world, where a single misplaced footstep could spell our doom. It's safe to say that if my special guests can survive this, then they can survive anything."

Hawke indicates to Bentley that he's done, and the cameraman pivots to film the dramatic view off the side of the cliff. I glance at Charlie and find her chewing her lip, making me wonder which part of Hawke's spiel has her the most anxious. Or perhaps, like me, it was all of it.

"Sorry about that," Hawke apologizes, moving toward us. "Usually those kinds of speeches are recorded during post-production and added as a voiceover, but since this episode is being rushed to air, there may be a handful of narrated moments in the days ahead. Not many—we'll keep things mostly candid from here on out, and my editing team will decide what to use and what to toss." He then adds, "So aside from the rare scripted line, try to forget about the cameras and act as you would without them."

That is an impossible ask, for both Charlie and me, but we nod our false agreement regardless.

"Excellent. Now, let's swap out your harnesses and strap on your packs," Hawke says, dragging over the larger bag that Bentley wore on his chest during the skydive.

Inside are four black climbing harnesses, their simple leg loops and waistbelts making them look harmless enough, but I see Charlie gulp as she's handed hers and shown how to put it on. I want to reassure her that Hawke has been doing these trips for years and won't let anything bad happen, but I don't think my words will make her feel better. So instead, I focus on removing my bulkier skydiving harness and replace it with the more compact mountaineering one, adjusting the buckles until it sits comfortably over my clothes.

After exchanging his own gear, Hawke withdraws a long coil of rope and secures it diagonally across his torso. He then pulls out three smaller backpacks—making me think the designers of the *Wild World* apparel must have discovered the secret to Mary Poppins' magical bag—and hands one each to Charlie and me, keeping the third for himself. Lastly, he shoves our parachutes into Bentley's pack, where they join a myriad of filming equipment, all of which the cameraman hauls onto his shoulders with ease.

"Our extraction point is roughly forty miles northwest of here," Hawke reveals, gesturing over the cliff in that direction.

From this height, all I can see is the landscape dipping down into a forested ravine toward what might be a river or a canyon, then rising again into more peaks all around us. I can't help realizing how isolated we are out here, so far from any trace of civilization, and relying entirely on Hawke's skills to survive.

"So needless to say," he continues, "we have a lot of ground to cover if we want to make it there by Friday afternoon."

"I suppose it's too much to hope that we'll be walking the whole way, and this is just for decoration?" Charlie asks, fiddling with her harness.

Hawke grins. "It's always good to have hope. It can be the difference between life and death in a place like this."

Charlie waits a beat, then says, "You didn't answer my question."

Bentley snickers from behind his camera, and Hawke's grin widens as he hoists his pack onto his back, his only reply being to say, "We're wasting daylight."

I have to choke back a laugh at the look on Charlie's face, and again resist the urge to comfort her as we follow Hawke away from the cliff and into the trees, beginning a gentle ascent up the mountain, with Bentley—and his camera—bringing up the rear.

"What are some of the most important things you need to prioritize when you find yourself in a survival situation?" Hawke asks as we walk. "Zander?"

I've watched enough of his show to confidently answer, "Water, food, and shelter."

"Correct." He sends an approving smile over his shoulder. "But while we can last some time without food and shelter if needed, the one thing we absolutely will need—and soon—is water."

Under her breath, Charlie pleads, "Oh God, please don't let him say we have to drink our own pee."

I grimace, fully agreeing with her.

"That means we need to find a water source," Hawke continues, leading us around a fallen tree trunk as he searches for a clear path forward, "and the best hope for us to do that is to travel downward and look for a creek or stream."

"Not to state the obvious," Charlie says, "but we're hiking up, not down."

"Not everything is as it seems when you're in the wild, Charlie."

There's a pause, before she replies, "Maybe so, but I'm pretty sure my thighs are telling me we're on an incline."

Hawke chuckles. "Keep that sense of humor. You'll need it in the coming days."

"Sense of humor?" she mutters, low enough that I doubt Hawke can hear. If he can, he ignores her to share more about our environment, but whether it's for us or the audience, I'm unsure.

"An interesting fact about this national park is that it's made up of different kinds of forests—rainforests, wetlands, woodlands, heathlands—but over eighty-five percent is covered in what's called a 'dry sclerophyll forest,' which is a group of tall trees growing close together, mostly of the eucalyptus variety." He pats one as we walk past. "These eucalyptus trees are widely considered the reason behind the 'Blue Mountains' name, because the high levels of oil they emit create a blue haze when looking at the mountains from a distance."

"That's great and all," Charlie says, her voice as dry as the forest we're walking through, "but what does it have to do with us finding water?"

"Forests need water to grow," Hawke answers, "so we just need to listen to nature and it will show us where to go."

Listen to nature? I repeat the words in my mind, before reminding myself that I have two tasks over the next four days: to show the world I'm not the reprobate they've come to believe, and to survive this trip so I can reap the rewards. Both of those things rely on me yielding to Hawke's wisdom, even when he says things that would normally make me raise a skeptical eyebrow.

Charlie, it seems, is having similar doubts. "And, um, if nature doesn't want to . . . talk to us?"

"She always does, to those who pay attention," Hawke says sagely, his dark eyes amused as he swivels his neck and notes the looks on our faces. "And speaking of, watch your step."

Right as he says it, a lizard as long as my arm ambles coolly across our path. I jerk to a stop, half expecting Hawke to pull out his iconic hunting knife and say we've found lunch.

Instead, he crouches down to watch as the reptile slowly disappears into the scrub. "I was hoping we'd see one of these," he says, clearly pleased. "It's a monitor lizard—also known as a goanna. There are around thirty different species of them in Australia alone, with the largest reaching over eight feet in length."

I peer into the bushes, wondering if we've just seen a baby and its giant-sized parents will be appearing next. I almost say I didn't sign up for *Jurassic Park*, but Charlie speaks before I can.

"I've seen a lot of goannas in my life," she says, sounding dubious, "but none have been anywhere close to eight feet."

My gaze remains fixed on the bushes. "Let's hope it stays that way."

She doesn't disagree, though she does add, "Fun fact for you non-Aussies: goannas have been known to accidentally mistake humans for trees."

I try—and fail—to envision that. "What happens if they do?"

She shrugs. "What do all lizards do with trees? They climb."

I consider the size of the massive-but-nowhere-near-eight-feet reptile we just saw and shudder at the idea of it even *attempting* to climb a human.

"So if a goanna ever runs at you," Charlie continues, "act like it's a bear and lie on the ground."

"That doesn't work with all bears," Hawke warns. "Only grizzlies."

I jump in as if I know what I'm talking about. "Haven't you heard the saying? 'If it's brown, lay down. If it's black, fight back.'"

"Don't forget the last part—'If it's white, goodnight,'" Bentley calls from behind his camera. He's been keeping mostly silent, maintaining his role of invisible cameraman. "Pray you never come across a polar bear in the wild."

Charlie glances uneasily between us all. "The fact that you have a rhyme for how to react to different bears is alarming. How many attacks *do* you have in your respective countries each year?"

"Not a lot," Hawke answers, "but plenty of close calls, especially where I grew up in Western Canada. That said, it helps to think of bears like you would sharks—we're the ones invading their homes. They mostly want to leave us alone." He returns to his feet, gesturing to where the lizard vanished. "It's a shame to let that monitor go since it'd make a good meal, but goannas are a protected species in Australia, so they're off limits outside of life-and-death circumstances. And besides, we don't want to be carrying the extra weight for what's coming next."

I watch as Charlie swallows and repeats, "What's coming . . . next?"

Hawke dusts soil from his pants, then continues forging a path for us through the brush, calling over his shoulder, "I already told you we have to go down to find water. Remember: nature speaks, we listen."

We hike upward for half an hour through the dense forest, until we find ourselves on another ledge similar to the one we landed on, just narrower—and ending at an even steeper cliff face. Last time, the drop was intimidating, but this time it's a near-vertical edge that Hawke cautions us to keep our distance from. Not that we need the warning.

"Do you want the good news or the bad news?" he asks, opening his backpack and withdrawing an assortment of items that cause a spike of adrenaline in me, and prompt the paling of Charlie's features.

"How about we stick with the good news only?" she says weakly.

Hawke unfolds a map and lays it on the rocky ground. "The good news is, according to this, there should be a small stream a short distance from the base of this cliff." He presses a finger to the paper. It has so many topographical details that it might as well be drawn in hieroglyphs for how well I can read it. "That means water is in our sights."

I hold my breath as I wait for the other shoe to drop, already knowing what he's about to say.

"The bad news," Hawke goes on, "is that the quickest way down is *over.*" He indicates the rope he carries. "Have either of you rappelled before?"

I raise my hand. "I have. It's been a while, though." My stunt double handled the more extreme action scenes in all of the *Lost Heirs* movies, but I still did as many as I was allowed, purely for the thrill of it.

"We rappelled at school camp," Charlie says. Her eyes go to the cliff and her throat bobs. "But that was fifteen meters down a man-made tower with all the safety equipment you can imagine. This is . . . not that."

"Fifteen meters, four hundred feet, they're about the same," Hawke says cheerfully.

Charlie sends him a flat look. "I don't know who taught you math but they absolutely *are not*."

"Give or take a few hundred feet," I murmur. Even *I'm* daunted by the task before us.

"You'll both be fine," Hawke says in a coaxing voice. "In fact, I bet by the time you reach the bottom, you'll want to climb back up and do it all over again."

Judging by Charlie's expression, she doesn't agree. But then she glances at me and holds my gaze, a storm of emotion behind her eyes, before she finally slumps her shoulders with resignation. I feel a pang of guilt over the bargain I elicited from her, and decide that once this trip is over, I'll find a way to thank her outside of what I've already offered for Ember. It's the least I can do, given all that's likely ahead.

Hawke begins to uncoil his rope, gesturing for us to follow him to a nearby eucalyptus tree. "For obvious reasons, it's important to anchor yourself around something strong, and, where possible, rooted deep into the earth. Something like this is perfect." He raps his knuckles against the solid tree trunk and proceeds to wind the rope around the base, showing us how to knot it before tossing the rest over the side of the cliff.

Charlie makes a moaning sound as it falls out of sight, prompting Bentley to peek out from behind his camera and offer her quiet reassurance. She whispers her thanks, but her face remains pinched with dread.

"In your packs you'll find helmets and gloves, so grab those and put them on," Hawke instructs, doing the same himself. Once we're geared up, he clips carabiners to our harnesses and tightens all our straps, before asking, "Who wants to go first?"

A squeak leaves Charlie, so I take one for the team and say, "I will."

At my offer, Hawke hooks the rope into my carabiner and maneuvers us all closer to the side of the mountain.

"You said you've done this before, but it doesn't hurt to have a refresher." He curls my fingers around the rope. "This is your brake hand. It never leaves the rope—that's the most important thing to remember. You let go, you fall." He waits for me to nod, then looks over to Charlie until she does the same, before he continues, "You're in control of your own descent, so go as slow as you need. Lean back, keep a nice wide stance, trust the rope to hold you. Even if you slip, as long as your brake hand stays tight, you'll be fine. Just take your time, don't panic, and find your way back to your feet."

I nod again, my heart beginning to pick up speed.

Hawke goes over a few more safety details, making me recite everything back to him, and Charlie as well, before he checks all our gear one last time and finally indicates for me to approach the edge. He and Charlie are now clipped onto the rope as well, though I know they'll wait until I'm at the bottom before starting their own descents. Bentley, too, is secured, and currently wriggling forward on his stomach until he's half over the edge, angling for the best way to film my rappel from above.

"Ready when you are," Hawke tells me. "Remember: trust the rope."

Given how many times I've skydived, and even how many times I've rappelled before, this shouldn't be as nerve-racking as it is. But still, as I turn my back to the view and lean out over the edge of the mountain, carefully transferring my weight onto the rope, I can't keep my insides from roiling. Fifteen meters or four hundred feet, it really doesn't make a difference when you have to rely on a nylon cord to keep you alive.

"That's it, Zander, you're doing great," Hawke says as I ease my way backward into a horizontal position, my pulse thrumming in my veins. "Relax that brake hand a little so you don't get caught up. There you go."

Hawke continues to offer directions and praise as I begin to work my way down the side of the mountain, the hardest part passing once I leave the edge and fully commit to the descent.

"Awesome work," Hawke calls to me. "Keep it up. Slow and steady."

I gain confidence with every downward step, and soon feel bold enough to cast my gaze around, marveling at the close-up view of the rocky cliff and how it meets the forest spread out beneath me, the contrasting colors indescribable. I think about the last time I rappelled with a similar outlook, and with some surprise, I realize it wasn't for a scene in *The Lost Heirs*, but to celebrate Maddox's seventeenth birthday.

Suddenly, I'm no longer on the side of the cliff, but instead in southern Mexico, vividly recalling the weekend when Maddox flew in to join Summer and me on location in Chiapa de Corzo. She and I were filming the final movie of the series, but we had some rare time off, so the three of us used it to explore the city before venturing out to the Selva El Ocote biosphere reserve, where we rappelled straight down into the forested sinkhole of Sima de las Cotorras.

Nostalgia floods me as I remember how much fun those two days were, but it quickly sours when I think of all that came next. Because a week later, the film wrapped, and then it was only a few months until Summer's world imploded, with mine following soon after that.

And as for Maddox . . .

"Everything all right, Zander? Why have you stopped?"

I'm so lost in my memories that I barely hear Hawke calling to me. But the longer I dangle midair on the rope, the more I realize it's because I can't move.

Something is happening to me.

Something is wrong.

Pins and needles prickle all over my body, my pulse is deafening in my ears, and my vision is dotting in and out of focus. Hawke yells my name again, his tone full of urgency, but I can't respond. I'm having trouble breathing, the air leaving my lungs in short, sharp puffs. It's all I can do to keep gripping the rope, hanging on for dear life.

Maddox's face flashes across my mind again, his caramel eyes bright with mirth, his copper hair messy from running his fingers through it. He used to laugh all the time, bringing joy to everyone around him, even during the darkest days of our lives. But it was all a lie. And on the darkest day of *his* life, when I tried to be there for him, when I gave *everything* to be there for him—

"Zander! *Zander!*"

The voice comes from right beside me, but it doesn't belong to Hawke.

It belongs to Charlie.

She's clinging to a second rope, her violet eyes brimming with concern.

"I need you to take a deep breath, okay?" she says, removing one shaking hand from her rope and reaching out to clasp my arm.

With her words, I realize I'm still having trouble breathing, my vision now blackening worryingly around the edges.

"One big, deep breath in, like this." She inhales loudly.

I try to do the same, but it gets caught in my throat.

"Let's do it again, together," she encourages.

This time I manage a full, wheezing breath.

"That's it," she says in a soothing voice, her eyes holding mine. I know I must look as panicked as I feel, but she doesn't flinch away from whatever she sees in my gaze. "Now let's keep doing that, but I also need a favor. I'm going to ask a few questions, and I want you to say the first thing that comes to your mind. I'll answer, too. Ready?" She doesn't wait for my confirmation before continuing, "What's one thing you can hear right now? I can hear birds chirping in the trees beneath us. Can you hear them?"

Slowly, I nod.

"Your turn," she says.

I think for a moment—it takes everything in me to focus my mind—and I barely recognize my own voice when I rasp out, "Rocks. Clattering down the mountain."

"Nice one," she says, her gaze still locked on mine. "This time I want to know what you can see. I'm not brave enough to look around, but you jump out of helicopters for fun, so I'm guessing you have no problem enjoying the scenery. Is it pretty? Can you tell me about it?"

I keep breathing deeply, trying to stop my attention from spiraling all over again, and glance around before I haltingly answer, "It's—It's beautiful. Blue sky. Fluffy white clouds. Green forests. You should try to look."

"Maybe in a minute," she lies. "What about something you can touch or feel? Even with these gloves, I bet I'm going to have rope burn from how tight I'm holding on. How about you?"

"The wind," I say, my answer coming quicker this time as my pulse begins to settle and my breathing finally eases. I close my eyes as the breeze caresses my face, drying the clammy sweat on my skin.

"And how does the wind feel?"

"Peaceful," I say automatically.

"Focus on that feeling," Charlie tells me. "Do you think you can take a step down now? If we go together?"

I reopen my eyes and, seeing the steadiness in her expression, I nod again.

"We'll go slowly," she says. "Nice and easy."

The moment we begin moving, it's as if my body recalibrates. My mind, too. I'm suddenly overcome with embarrassment, not just for having what I assume was a panic attack—something I've never experienced before, though I've seen Summer hit by them too many times to count—but also that I had it at the worst possible time. I open my mouth to apologize, mortified that Charlie had to come and literally save me from myself, but she doesn't give me the chance.

"Don't," she says, her voice soft but firm.

I look to my side, where she's keeping pace with me as we descend together.

"Don't what?" I croak.

"I used to have anxiety attacks all the time," she says, instead of answering. "Especially when Ember first got sick. And then again more . . .

recently." She clears her throat. "There's absolutely nothing to be embarrassed about."

"I bet you were never hanging hundreds of feet in the air when you had one." My voice is full of all the embarrassment she told me not to feel.

"No," she concedes. "But I did have one when I was merging onto a highway once, soon after I got my license. It was raining so hard I could barely see, and the other cars weren't letting me in because there were two huge trucks taking up so much space. I remember numbness starting at my lips and spreading from there, along with a ringing in my ears as everything started to get hazy. I was sure I was going to die. It was—it was terrifying."

I shudder as she shares her experience, having just felt most of those physical symptoms myself. "What did you do?"

"One of the cars finally made room for me, but the panic didn't leave, so I knew I needed to pull over. Only, there wasn't anywhere safe to stop," she says as we continue lowering ourselves down the cliff. "So I turned my music up until it overwhelmed my senses, and I dug my fingernails into my palms until they hurt, and when that wasn't enough, I visualized the lyrics of the songs as words streaming across my mind, seeing them appear letter by letter. Doing all of that took my attention off what was happening inside me for long enough to bring me back into the present."

"Hearing, touch, sight," I say, noting the senses she used for herself, and how they were the same ones that delivered me from my own mind.

"It's the five-four-three-two-one grounding technique," she explains. "Name five things you can see, four things you can touch, three things you can hear, two things you can smell, and one thing you can taste." She pauses. "I improvised with you and skipped a few steps, but the point is to bring you back to yourself by making you more mindful of what's happening around you. As the name says, it grounds you, and helps distract you from whatever triggered the attack long enough for you to regain control."

"I wish I'd known about it last year," I say. "Summer has really bad panic attacks and I always feel so helpless when they happen to her, just holding her and saying everything will be all right."

There's a weighty silence, before Charlie says, somewhat hoarsely, "If it's any consolation, I would have given anything to have someone do that for me. So don't be too hard on yourself. That kind of comfort . . . there's power in not being alone, especially when you feel like your world is crashing around you."

I glance at her, alarmed by her admission, and wonder what happened to make her feel that way. I'm also painfully aware that her words echo the thoughts that triggered my attack in the first place—how my world had come crashing down, and in the process, I lost my best friend and greatest source of comfort. But before I can figure out how to ask about her own history, I realize with a start that we've reached the bottom of the mountain.

Relief slams into me—along with a wave of exhaustion, both physical and mental.

"That wasn't as bad as I feared," Charlie says, unclipping her carabiner and helmet, then shaking out her hands.

"Speak for yourself," I mutter, causing her to grin at me. It's the most lighthearted expression I've seen from her since we first met, offering a small but undeniable silver lining to what just happened.

Her smile fades as she tucks a strand of blue-purple hair behind her ear and asks, "Now that we're safely on the ground, do you . . . want to talk about it?"

Warmth hits my chest, the feeling pleasant compared to the humiliation I anticipated. Even so, I'm aware that while Bentley may have only captured footage from above, the nano drones would have caught my entire panic attack in high definition, and I'd rather not share what was going on *inside* my mind as the whole world listens. Summer speaks openly about her mental health, otherwise I would have been more careful with what I said about her. But I've never experienced anything like that before, and even if I did want to reveal what prompted my attack, there are other factors to consider—namely, Maddox, and the secrets I won't risk exposing, both his and mine. So I shake my head and say, "Thanks for the offer, but it's still a bit fresh. Maybe later?"

She searches my expression, seeing more than I would like, before she drops her gaze and says, "I'm guessing Hawke and Bentley will be down in about two seconds flat, but while we wait, should we check out what goodies are in our backpacks? What's the chance they packed us chocolate? Or toilet paper?"

A grateful smile touches my lips. "Pretty slim for both, I'd say."

"Figures." She sighs dramatically. "But a girl can dream."

Charlie

Even after Hawke and Bentley join us at the base of the mountain, I'm still trembling from what happened with Zander up on the cliff. I've been acting as nonchalant about it as possible, since I sense that's what he needs, but inwardly, I'm baffled. He jumped out of a helicopter without blinking, for goodness' sake. And he barely hesitated before backing out over the top of the ledge, so I doubt it was the four-hundred-foot drop that triggered his panic attack. All I know is, what happened could have had a *very* different ending if he'd lost control enough to release the rope. No matter how I feel toward him, the what-ifs of that are going to torment me for years.

On my end, I don't know what I was thinking when Hawke was about to rush to Zander's aid and I volunteered to go instead. I further don't know why Hawke *let* me. But regardless of how it came about, the important thing is that our whole group is now off the mountain and safe on the forest floor.

Physically, I amend. We're safe *physically*. I feel like I've fought my way through a mental warzone, and that's *without* me being the one who had the anxiety attack. I can only imagine how shattered Zander must feel, my empathy growing as I realize he won't have a proper chance to recover until we make camp tonight—and that's still at least half a day's journey away.

God, this is the never-ending trip, and we've barely even started.

"I think we could all use a break after that bit of excitement," Hawke says, slinging an arm around Zander's shoulders. "Let's go find that stream and we'll have some lunch and a rest."

I'm not eager for Hawke's version of "lunch," but I could certainly use a rest—as I'm sure Zander could—so I lift my backpack and follow as he leads us from the cliff base into the forest. It's denser and greener than what we hiked through earlier, the air almost humid despite the cool spring temperature, making me think we must now be in one of the rainforest areas of the national park. Hawke confirms as much, then begins to point out different plants as we continue, most of them inedible.

"If we can't find anything else to eat, we'll grab some of this," he says, scraping moss from the side of a tree. "It's pretty tasteless and won't do much to restore our energy, but it'll fill us up and keep any hunger pains away."

I soon hear the trickling sound of gently flowing water, and a few steps later, the trees clear enough to reveal a shallow, bubbling stream.

For a moment, I just stand there and soak in its beauty, but then I glance up and see Zander's pale face, his eyes haunted as he stares at the water. An image flicks across my mind, a photo that has surfaced in the media multiple times over the years showing Zander fishing in a creek like this one, beaming widely between two people—close relatives, I presume, given their features, though not his parents, who I've seen pictured with him at various events. All three fishing companions appeared happy and carefree, so I can't understand the reason for the look on his face right now. But maybe that's not where his mind is; I don't know him well enough to make assumptions, and I try to convince myself that I don't care enough to comfort him.

Thankfully, before I can acknowledge how much that is beginning to feel like a lie, he blinks, and his expression returns to normal once more.

"This looks nice and clear, doesn't it?" Hawke says, opening his backpack and pulling out a stainless-steel water bottle.

"I'm guessing that's a trick question," I say, eyeing the stream distrustfully.

Zander nods his agreement. "Clear doesn't mean clean."

"Top marks to you both," Hawke says. "You're right—no matter how clear or clean water seems, there's usually all kinds of bacteria and parasites living in it that can make you sick, or even kill you." He balances on a boulder and crouches down to scoop water into his bottle. "There are different techniques we can use to filter out those nasties, but the most foolproof way is by applying heat." He shakes his full bottle. "We'll give this a good boil and it should be okay."

"Should?" I repeat, wanting more assurance than that.

"Just be thankful that it's not covered in algae and dead bugs," Zander murmurs, causing me to shudder with revulsion.

Five minutes later, Zander, Bentley, and I have all finished slipping and sliding over the mossy rocks to fill our own bottles, and retreated to a clear spot a few feet away from the water's edge, where Hawke has already gathered a small pile of kindling.

"There are plenty of ways to start a fire in the wild," the survivalist says, "especially in an environment like this where it's mostly dry and out of the wind. But since we still have some distance to cover before we make camp tonight, we're going to cheat." He pulls a fire steel from his pocket and holds it out to me. "Want to have a crack at it?"

I take it from him eagerly and follow his instructions to strike the flint.

Nothing happens, not even a spark.

"That was anticlimactic," I say, frowning.

"Try again, but apply more pressure." Hawke repositions my hands. "It's not about speed, though that helps. It's the pressure that's most important."

Concentrating, I strike again, pressing hard against the flint this time. Sparks instantly leap from the steel onto the kindling, causing me to raise my hands triumphantly and cry, "I'm the fire queen!"

"Hey, fire queen, you might want to make sure it doesn't blow out before you get too excited," Zander drawls.

I curse when I see he's right, and I quickly fan the sparks until the kindling is covered in healthy flames.

"Well done," Hawke praises, holding his palm up for a high-five, before he moves all of our water bottles into the center of the fire. "These are specially designed to withstand heat, so let's leave them here to boil while we go find some lunch. Just stay in sight of the flames—the last thing we want is to accidentally start a forest fire."

As hungry as I am after everything we've done in the last few hours, I'm still dreading what kind of food we might have to stomach, so I drag my feet as Hawke directs us to keep an eye out for worms and ants and other insects. I'm secretly grateful when we only manage to find snails and slugs, both of which are too dangerous to eat.

"Some people make the mistake of thinking wild snails are the same as escargot at a restaurant," Hawke says, shaking his head. "They only make that mistake once."

On that grim note, we continue our search, until Zander makes a pleased sound and says, "Look what I found," while revealing a bunch of orange berries cupped in his hands.

I instinctively slap them to the ground. "Are you *crazy*? Haven't you read *The Hunger Games*?" Remembering who I'm talking to, I amend, "Or seen the movies?"

He crosses his arms. "I did both."

I ignore my surprise and point to the scattered berries. "Then you should know better."

"Actually," Hawke interjects, kneeling to retrieve the small fruits, "these are *Eustrephus latifolius*—wombat berries—and they're safe to eat. Nice spotting, Zander."

A blush rises to my cheeks, and I don't dare look in Zander's direction.

"These, however, are even better," Hawke goes on, moving a few steps deeper into the forest and stopping before a lush green bush full of dark pink berries. "Lilly pillies—common Indigenous bush tucker food. They're high in nutrients, and they also have antibacterial properties, which is helpful when you don't have any salve handy." He pops a few in his mouth. "Mmm. We'll save these for dessert. But *that*"—he indicates another bush, smaller and tucked away behind the lilly pilly shrub—"is something we'll avoid all costs."

I take a closer look, seeing green leaves, purple flowers, and a cluster of what appear to be blueberries.

"*Atropa belladonna*—deadly nightshade," Hawke says. "Also known as 'devil's berries' or 'death cherries.' If you want to go the way of *The Hunger Games*, that's how you do it."

I move an automatic step away and keep my distance from the lethal bush as we gather a bunch of lilly pillies and a handful of wombat berries, using a large leaf Bentley finds as a collection plate. It's looking like I might actually enjoy our lunch, until we start back toward the fire and Hawke sees something further along the bank of the river.

Something furry.

And very much dead.

"It's our lucky day," he says when we get close enough to see what it is.

Nausea crawls up my throat as I recognize the animal.

"What *is* that?" Zander asks, squinting down at the small gray creature.

"A brushtail possum," Hawke answers. I have to turn away when he picks it up and gives it a whiff. "And it's fresh." He grins at us both. "I hope you're not vegetarians."

I look from the possum to him and back again, before rasping out, "I am today."

He has the audacity to laugh. "Possums are protected, just like goannas, but since this one is already dead, it's free game. Let's clean it up and get cooking."

My gag reflex won't allow me to watch as Hawke skins and guts the possum, and I want to cover my ears like a child as he explains every part of the process for the sake of the audience. He even passes his hunting knife to Zander at one point, and while I can tell Zander is almost as disgusted as I am, he's still able to follow Hawke's instructions until the marsupial is roasting on the fire.

All too soon Hawke declares it's done, and he slices a strip of meat off, holding it out to me. When I hesitate, he says, "Survival is about opportunity, Charlie. If you don't want to starve to death, then you need to eat what you can find."

I nearly tell him that I had a large dinner last night and, hungry or not, I'm hardly going to starve within a few hours. But then I see Bentley's camera trained on me and remember that this is all part of the drama of the show, and for Zander's sake, I agreed to be all in. I try to find comfort in thinking about some of the other animals I've seen Hawke feed his guests—maggots, scorpions, and spiders—and the various organs they've had to consume—brains, eyeballs, and testicles—and I know that in comparison, this really isn't too awful. In some places, possum is even considered a delicacy.

Gritting my teeth, I pull the meat from his blade and slam my eyes shut before shoving it in my mouth.

"It's very . . . gamey," Zander says, sampling his own slice.

"I've definitely eaten worse," Hawke says between bites. "More, Charlie?"

I reach pointedly for the berries. "I'm ready for dessert, thanks."

We make quick work of the food, drinking from our now-cooled water bottles and then refilling and re-boiling them before smothering the fire and preparing to leave.

"If you need to relieve yourself, now's the time," Hawke says, ripping some leaves off a nearby tree. "These are great for wiping." He then points to a smaller weed-like bush near his feet. "That, not so much. Stinging nettle."

I cringe, then take off into the forest to see to my business. It's unpleasant, not having access to toilet paper or a flush—or a *door*—but I make do with what I have, knowing it's only for a few days.

When I return to the group, Hawke is in the middle of telling Zander about the "luxury" restrooms at some of his wilderness camps—none of which sound *remotely* luxurious—and sharing the various squatting techniques the attendees are taught. I clear my throat loudly to save my ears from bleeding, and Hawke thankfully wraps things up and moves closer to Bentley to ask him something.

Zander's face is comically horrified as he whispers to me, "I'm going to need a brain transplant to get rid of all the images he just put in there. Note to self: never visit one of his survival camps."

A snort leaves me, but I quickly turn it into a cough when Hawke finishes with Bentley and brings me my backpack.

"Which direction are we heading in, Charlie?" he asks.

"Um." My brain blanks, until I remember that our extraction point is northwest. I check the compass on my watch, and pivot to the right. "This way."

Hawke nods his approval, and we set out again through the forest, following the stream as it trickles slowly downward.

This time we hike for longer, taking regular breaks to sip our water and swallow more berries. It's easy at first, but as the hours pass, the gradual descent makes the muscles in my legs scream their objection. The worst discomfort comes, however, when Hawke begins to grill us for personal information.

It starts out innocently, with him inquiring about my job, then asking about the town I live in and my favorite places to visit; if I love the beach—"I'd be kicked out of the country if I didn't"—if I ever go on local bushwalks—"As long as there are snacks involved"—if I have any pets—"Does helping my best friend 'borrow' our neighbor's dog count?"—and about my family.

At the last question, I clam up enough that he turns his attention to Zander. The actor gives token responses, all things I've heard in interviews from him over the years—that he was raised in Montana and moved to California when he was seven, that he'd love to have a dog but he would feel guilty being away from it for work, that his favorite indulgent treat is peanut M&M's, and that the best thing he ever did was audition for *The Lost Heirs*, since it made all his previously unknown dreams come true.

It's difficult to resist rolling my eyes, but I play my part and school my expression into starstruck adoration as I say, "It made your fans' dreams come true, too. Where would we be without you?"

I realize my mistake immediately, since Hawke's focus returns to me, and I can tell he's about to ask a slew of fan-related questions that I'll have to channel Ember's energy to answer. But before he can utter a word, we step out of the trees to find a rock wall rising high above our heads, continuing to the left and right as far as we can see. It's covered in forest growth—moss and lichen and sprouting ferns—with the rock itself sculpted in a combination of jagged edges and smooth waves.

My insides knot as I wait for Hawke to pull another rope from his pack and say it's time for us to climb, but he doesn't do that, just continues following the stream parallel to the rock face.

"Did you know that the Blue Mountains boast Australia's largest known number of slot canyons? There are around one thousand in this park alone," Hawke tells us—or perhaps tells the audience, since his gaze flicks to Bentley's camera. "Some are dry, some are wet, many of them travel deep into underground caves, and all were carved over eons from rivers cutting through the sandstone, limestone, and even metamorphosed quartz." He trails his hand along the mossy wall. "They're as beautiful as they are deadly, claiming the lives of numerous people each year." His eyes shift to Zander and me. "Any guesses why?"

"Flash floods," I answer as we reach a fissure in the rock and the water turns on an angle to enter the narrow, dark space.

We halt there and look inside the opening, finding the boulder-strewn riverbed dappled with shadows from the sun peeking through the top of the canyon. The stream remains shallow as it curves in deeper and out of sight, barely flowing, but I've seen too many tragic headlines to believe it always stays that way.

"If you've never experienced a flash flood for yourself, then it's impossible to fathom how dangerous they are," Hawke says. "But in a place like this"—he indicates the otherworldly view before us—"once it starts to rain, the rock acts like a funnel and the water rises at an impossible speed. You can be swept away in a matter of minutes, never to be seen again. Even on the sunniest of days, it's best not to linger in slot canyons, since there are other dangers as well: falling rocks, unstable ground, labyrinthine passages, and that's not factoring in the local wildlife." He makes sure we're paying attention before he adds, "Keep an eye out for snakes in here, since these damp, sheltered environments create the perfect habitat for them."

"Snakes?" Zander repeats warily as he squints into the shadows. "Are we talking harmless tree snakes or . . . something else?"

Hawke adjusts his backpack. "How about I answer that once we're out the other side?"

Zander sighs. "Guess there's no need to now."

Like any sane person, I'd also like to avoid a venomous encounter, so I make loud splashing noises as I follow Hawke and Zander into the fissure with Bentley behind me, the path through the canyon small enough that we can only traverse it by walking along the stream. My boots are weatherproof so they keep my feet dry, but the rocks are slippery, and it takes all of my concentration to avoid tumbling into the water.

"This is obviously one of the wet canyons," Hawke says as we navigate our way through the fissure, "but it's nothing compared to some of the others in the park, where there are tiered waterfalls cascading into them year-round, and pools deep enough that it's almost impossible to find the bottom."

I shiver at the thought, since I've always had an irrational fear of what might be swimming beneath me in water where I can't touch the ground.

"Tourists actually visit the Blue Mountains specifically to go on canyoning expeditions," Hawke continues. "They rappel down waterfalls and explore the cave systems, all under the watchful eyes of professional guides." He throws a grin over his shoulder. "You're getting your own advanced class, free of charge."

"I would have been happy starting as a beginner," I mutter, slipping yet again, and saved only by Bentley reaching forward to steady me—for the hundredth time. "Or preferably, watching someone else do it on Netflix."

We're deep in the canyon now, having turned around enough bends that the entrance is well out of sight. The walls keep shifting inward and outward, sometimes becoming scarily narrow, soon reaching the point where the rock tapers in so close that it appears we've hit a dead end.

Hawke, however, has a different opinion.

"Backpacks off," he says. "Are either of you claustrophobic?"

Zander shakes his head while I peer into the alarmingly small gap, my pulse kicking up speed as I try to imagine how any of us will fit through there. "If I say yes, will we turn around and go back to the hotel?"

Hawke chuckles. "There's no time for that, I'm afraid. It'll be sunset soon—we need to get out of here and set up camp somewhere safe."

The idea of night falling while we're in the canyon has goose bumps breaking out on my skin. "Then I guess I'll suck it up," I say. Eyeing the gap again, I amend, "Or suck it in."

It's a good thing I'm not actually claustrophobic, or I wouldn't make it more than one inch into the ant-sized space without following in Zander's earlier footsteps by having my own panic attack. I keep a close watch on him as we all scramble sideways through the minuscule gap, but he doesn't show any signs of anxiety, supporting my theory that it wasn't the adrenaline-inducing task that triggered him last time. My curiosity is piqued, but since I doubt he'll ever reveal what set him off, I resign myself to letting it go.

We continue shuffling through the hairline fracture between the rock walls, my hand beginning to ache from holding my pack, my legs cramping from the uncoordinated crab-walk. I'm the smallest in our group, and I hate every second, so I can't imagine how the others are feeling. Especially Zander with his broad shoulders and lean muscles and—

Stop, I scold myself, my face flushing in the shadowed gloom.

"How're we all doing?" Hawke asks from up ahead. We're in the same order as earlier, with Zander directly behind him, then me, then Bentley and his camera bringing up the rear, as always. "Charlie, you okay?"

"Loving every second," I say through gritted teeth as I bang my elbow on the rock for the third time in as many minutes.

"There's a crawl space coming," Hawke informs us, "so we'll have to get down on all fours to pass through. It might be a tight squeeze, but it should open again quickly, and we'll be able to move freely after that."

Hawke's warning causes my stomach to flip-flop, since it's *already* a tight squeeze. It's one thing to shuffle sideways through the canyon, but another entirely to have such limited room that we can't remain upright. I try to peer past Zander for a glimpse of what we'll be facing, but the sunlight is barely penetrating this narrow crevice, and it's difficult to see more than a few feet ahead. I can't even witness Hawke lower himself into the crawl space, but I do watch when it's Zander's turn, my blood freezing as he folds his six-foot-something body into a crack hardly large enough for a toddler.

"Oh, hell no," I whisper, moving instinctively away, nearly crashing into Bentley.

"You're doing great, Zander," Hawke encourages from somewhere beyond the nightmarish hole in the rock wall, his voice echoing back to us.

"I think I'm stuck," Zander says around his panting breaths. He doesn't sound concerned, just stating the fact. Meanwhile, I'm beginning to hyperventilate.

"Wiggle your shoulders," Hawke tells him. "And rotate your hips. It'll feel strange, but relax your body and worm your way through. There you go, you've got it. Excellent worming—you're a natural."

When Zander's feet disappear from view and Hawke calls out that it's my turn, I find myself rooted to the spot.

"Charlie?" Hawke's voice comes again.

Still, I'm pinned in place.

"Hey, you're all right," Bentley says reassuringly, breaking his unspoken rule of being as cameraman-ghostlike as possible. "They're both much larger than you. If they could squeeze through, you'll have no trouble."

I want to believe him, but I can't stop the trembles racking my frame as I lower myself onto my knees and shove my backpack into the hole in front of me. I try to be grateful that the stream dried up before the canyon narrowed, so at least my clothes aren't getting soaked, but I can barely think beyond the walls pressing in on me.

"That's it, Charlie," Hawke calls as I ease my way through the impossibly tight gap, nudging my pack forward inch by inch ahead of me. "You've got this."

For a moment, I think that maybe I do, and I start to breathe a little easier. But then I reach a point where the crawl space is no longer wide enough for me to remain on all fours, and I have to drop down on my stomach. I want to go back—I *desperately* want to go back—but when I try to—

I can't move.

"Hey—Charlie—*hey*, listen to my voice," Hawke orders after realizing I've stopped. "You're absolutely safe. I wouldn't have made you do this if I didn't think you could. Do you hear me?"

"But I'm—I'm stuck." Unlike when Zander said it, my words come out breathy and afraid. "I don't know how—I can't—*I can't*—"

I'm unable to finish, my heaving gasps making the space around me feel even smaller. But then my backpack moves forward of its own accord, sliding along the crawl space and out of sight, and a moment later, Zander's face appears right in front of me.

"What's a nice girl like you doing in a place like this?"

A strangled sound leaves me, part incredulous laugh, part terrified moan.

"What do you say we get out of here?" he asks, his voice soft, his blue eyes steady on mine.

"I don't know h-how," I say shakily. "I c-can't move."

"That's okay, I'll help you," Zander says, his confidence a balm to my nerves. "If I can ass my way backward to freedom, then you can worm your way forward. You've got the easy job, trust me."

He takes my hands in his, offering a squeeze of encouragement, before he begins to shuffle on his stomach in reverse, drawing me slowly with him.

"I don't think 'ass' is grammatically correct in that sentence," I say between panted breaths, wiggling my shoulders and hips awkwardly as we advance through the narrow space.

"What would you have said?" he asks.

I know he's trying to distract me, but since it's working, I answer, "Maybe something like 'slither ass-first backward.'"

"Ugh." He pulls a face. "Let's not use the word 'slither' when we're surrounded by snakes. I beg you."

My lips curl up at the edges. "Surrounded? We haven't seen a single one."

"They're watching us. I can feel their eyes."

My smile grows. I can't believe he's managed to turn my panic into mirth so effortlessly. "As long as you don't feel their fangs."

He doesn't have a chance to respond before the crawl space opens up into a cavern large enough for him to rise to his feet, pulling me out with him. I stumble slightly once I'm vertical, my head spinning and my feet unsteady, but he keeps holding my hands, not letting me go until I've found my balance.

"That wasn't so bad, was it?" he asks, his eyes dancing.

I brush canyon dirt and damp moss from my clothes as I answer, "I can one hundred percent guarantee that I'm going to have nightmares about this for the rest of my life."

"You were amazing, Charlie," Hawke says, looking me over to make sure I'm not hurt. "Have a rest while we wait for Ben to come through."

My legs are like jelly, so I sit on a nearby boulder, intending to take a moment to clear my mind of all that just happened. But when Zander crouches in front of me and quietly asks if I'm okay, there's only one thing I can say:

"Thank you. You came back for me, and I—" I clear my throat and look down at the ground. "Just—thank you."

When I peek up at him again, his features are gentle with understanding. "Don't mention it," he says. "And besides, it's not like I scrambled down a four-hundred-foot cliff to keep you from plunging to your death. We're a long way off calling it even."

Before I can disagree, Bentley appears out of the crawl space, swaps his GoPro for a larger camera, and indicates he's good to go. My shoulders twinge in protest when I collect my backpack, but as Hawke promised, the worst of the canyoning is behind us, and it's only a short journey through a cave-like hollow before we finally exit the fissure into yet more dense forest. It's notably darker now, the sun moving swiftly behind the mountains, and Hawke urges us to pick up our pace, claiming that we're nearing our designated camping spot.

I hear it before I see it—the sound of gurgling water, louder than the stream we followed earlier. When the trees part, I'm once again awed by the beauty in front of me, this time a river, perhaps twenty meters wide, with what looks like a shallow, slow-moving current.

"Five-star accommodation, right on the water," Hawke says with a satisfied expression. "Who can complain about this?"

It's a rhetorical question, so I don't bother saying I'd still prefer to have a bed—and a shower.

Hawke drops his pack onto the ground before turning to Zander and me. "There are three things you want to prioritize when looking for shelter: a flat surface, protection from the elements, and enough room for a fire. We have all those here, plus something else: dinner."

I look worriedly around, expecting to see another dead animal washed up at the water's edge. There's nothing, though. Not even any berry bushes in sight. But then I follow Hawke's finger as he points to the river, and a moment later I gasp as a fish leaps high into the air before plunging back down beneath the surface.

"The Blue Mountains are known for their freshwater fish," Hawke says. "So let's set up camp and see what we can catch."

It takes less than five minutes to retrieve the parachutes from Bentley's pack and position them around some low-lying tree branches and bush scrub, resulting in two makeshift tents. We follow Hawke's instructions until they're almost fully enclosed—something he says is important to offer insulation from the cold that's beginning to creep in as the sunlight fades. What he *doesn't* mention is that there are only two tents for the four of us, and since he and Bentley are married, the odds aren't in my favor for who I have to share mine with. But I refuse to worry about that just yet, and instead focus on everything that needs to be done before night falls completely.

Given the clock ticking down on us, Hawke asks me to start a fire while he and Zander go fishing. I don't object; the temperature is dropping fast and I'm keen to avoid getting my clothes wet.

It's only after I've collected enough firewood to last the night and used Hawke's flint to get some impressive flames going that I finally glance up and see why Zander didn't have the same concerns—that being because he and Hawke have both stripped down to their black boxer briefs. The two of them are standing in the knee-deep river like Greek gods on display, complete with a picturesque mountain sunset behind them. I can barely keep my mouth from falling open, and I certainly can't keep my eyes off Zander, with his tanned skin and chiseled abs. I'm hardly even aware of Hawke at his side, though I have a vague appreciation for his dark, muscled physique.

But Zander . . .

I've seen him shirtless before—the whole world has. So for the life of me, I can't figure out why this is any different. But regardless, it *feels* different. More personal. More . . . *intimate.*

My cheeks heat up and I try to tear my gaze away, but before I can manage that herculean task, Zander moves blindingly fast, his muscles rippling as he reaches into the water and rises again with a large fish squirming in his hands.

I can't hear what he and Hawke are saying, the gurgling river and crackling fire drowning out their voices, but I can see the proud look on Hawke's face, and the exultant grin Zander wears. Only—there's something else in Zander's expression. Something he's trying to hide, just like when we arrived at the smaller stream earlier today. Something that becomes much clearer when he leaves the river and approaches the fire, dripping all the way.

There's grief in his eyes.

And pain—so much pain.

It's like staring into a mirror.

But then he notices my concern, and I can actually *see* his walls fall back into place. There's a plea in his gaze now, begging me not to ask anything while the cameras are on us.

So I do the only thing I can think of: I arch one eyebrow and say, "I'm surprised it took you this long to take your shirt off, given how much your fans love seeing you without clothes on."

Zander's shoulders slump with relief, the only indication of his gratitude. Outwardly, his features turn mischievous, which is all the warning I have before he replies, "As my biggest fan, I guess you'd know."

I walked right into that one.

But thankfully, I'm saved from replying when Hawke leaves the river to join us, a second large fish wriggling in his hands as he grins at Zander, Bentley, and me, and asks, "Who's hungry?"

Zander

I'm not sure if it's because I'm starving, or because the fish are as fresh as they can possibly be, but our dinner ends up being one of the tastiest meals I've eaten in a long time. It wasn't even awful having to descale and debone them beforehand, following Hawke's easy instructions, just like with the possum—though much less nausea-inducing. If there's one thing I've learned today, it's that I don't have the stomach to live in the wild indefinitely. Neither does Charlie, if the gagging noises she made with both animals are any indication.

After we finish eating, we all sit back on our logs and relax around the fire. Bentley has put his cameras away for the night, so even though the nano drones are still recording us from some hidden place, it's easier not being able to see them, and my guard drops the longer we unwind after our arduous day. I should have expected Hawke's sneak attack given that he already launched his subtle interrogation earlier, but I still startle when he begins questioning me again.

"So, Zander, you've done a lot of interviews in your life, but you're usually focused on promoting movies, and there's always a kind of . . . I guess a *mask* that you're wearing. Would you say that's true?"

My mask, as he calls it, is carefully in place as I answer, "I try to be as genuine as possible, but yes, when I'm promoting a film, there's a level of professionalism I like to keep. I'm not chatting casually with friends—I'm sharing about my work, so that remains at the forefront of my mind."

"I'm the same when people interview me, especially when it's to talk about my camps," Hawke agrees, watching Bentley throw more kindling into the fire. "But right now, you *are* among friends, so I want to know the real Zander Rune. What made you *you*? We've all heard the rags-to-riches story, how you accepted a dare for an audition and it skyrocketed you to fame, but what about before that? And even after that? What was your childhood like? Did you get along with your family? Your friends? How much did your rise to stardom change your life? Tell us everything."

I can practically hear Gabe in these questions, and I'm certain he must have had a hand in them being asked. I shift on my log as I consider my answers, aware of Charlie watching me, her small smirk indicating she can see right through the charade.

"My childhood was . . ." I search for the right word, and settle on, "challenging. I took it pretty hard when my parents died, and then my whole life was uprooted when I had to move across the country."

I'm about to hurry on, wanting to keep Hawke from probing deeper into my most difficult years, but I'm surprised when it's Charlie who stops me from continuing.

"Wait, your parents—" She cuts herself off, like she's unsure how to ask what she wants to know. "It's just . . . I thought I saw photos of you at all four *Lost Heirs* premieres with . . . with your parents?"

"Adoptive parents," I tell her, understanding her confusion, since they've been in my life for so long now that I refer to them simply as "my parents." I try not to advertise my tragic past—I don't hide it, but I also don't go out of my way to use the orphan card, and I always decline any interviews that want to focus on my time in foster care and the whole adoption process. "My birth parents died when I was seven."

Her face floods with too many emotions for me to catch them all—though I do see shock, empathy, and sorrow before she turns to stare into the fire, a muscle ticking in her jaw.

"That's why you moved to California?" Hawke asks.

"Yeah." I look away from Charlie and back to him. "It was hard to adjust at first, but my parents—my adoptive parents—have always been my biggest supporters, even when they took on the mammoth task of caring for a lonely, grieving boy."

I cast my mind back to those dark days, everything I felt back then rising swiftly to the surface: the pain, the isolation, the devastation. It's not surprising that I can feel it so acutely now—it's been bubbling away at me all day, ever since we arrived at the first stream for lunch, and then this very river before us, gleaming under the moonlight. I know Charlie saw it in my expression earlier; I couldn't hide it fast enough, and in turn, she didn't hide her concern. But she didn't press me, and for that, I'm grateful, since there are some things I don't want the world to know—things that are private and should stay that way.

Like how the very last day I saw my parents alive was the day we went camping, and the very last photograph ever taken of us is the one I carry with me everywhere I go—the same photo that has been used by the media for years, and everyone thinks is just a cute anecdote from my childhood, when really, it's the day my life changed forever.

I knew coming on this trip was going to be difficult, because I knew it would dredge up these memories. Summer knew, too, which was why she was so worried about me. She and Maddox are two of the only people who know the full truth of what happened that mournful day, though there are others like Gabe who are aware that my birth parents died sometime around then. Since I'm not eager to share the details with whoever might be watching this episode when it airs, I quickly, and pointedly, move on.

"It took some time for me to get used to California. LA is so different from the small town I grew up in, and everything seemed so big, and so . . . busy," I say, recalling the difficult transition from forests and mountains to traffic and skyscrapers. "It didn't help that I was a scrawny kid, and new to school, so I got picked on a lot. I was nerdy, too, and even though I enjoyed sports, I preferred to be reading books or playing video games." I shrug. "It's a cliché, but all that made me a target."

"You were bullied?" Bentley asks softly, beating Hawke to the question.

"Relentlessly."

Compassion fills Bentley's features, while Hawke's expression turns thoughtful as he notes, "You don't seem too torn up about that."

I take a sip of the eucalyptus tea Charlie made us using leaves from the surrounding trees. It's bitter, but has a fresh, almost minty aftertaste. "Don't get me wrong, it wasn't pleasant," I say. "But compared to the grief I was dealing with, it didn't really penetrate. My demons were bigger than any school kids. When I didn't react, they lost interest in trying to torment me. And then I met Maddox and—"

I cut myself off, but it's too late.

"Maddox?" Hawke asks.

I'm careful, so very careful, when I answer, "My best friend." I don't mention how I'm unsure if that title still holds true. "We were paired up for a homework project when we were ten—I don't think we'd spoken to each other before then, but we became fast friends and were soon inseparable." I look at Charlie. "Much like you and Ember, without the next-door-neighbors part." I swirl my tea and continue, "He's actually the one who dared me to audition for *The Lost Heirs*, since we were both obsessed with the books, and he thought it would be a laugh if we went to try out, him for Sir Archer and me for Prince Tyron."

Hawke tilts his head to the side. "Was he upset that you were cast and he wasn't?"

"No—he didn't even audition in the end." My lips quirk upward in memory. "He got so nervous that he ran straight for the bathroom when they called his name, but when I told him we should just go home, he refused to let me 'chicken out'—the little hypocrite." I smile as I think about my best friend, but despair quickly follows, so I clear my throat and hurry to finish, "You know what happened next, so I guess you could say I have him to thank for where I am today."

It's not a lie—in so many more ways than I would ever publicly say. Not even my mission to improve my image would have me throwing my best friend under the bus, regardless of all the reasons why that would help me. It's a line I can't—and won't—cross.

"What about your other childhood friends?" Hawke asks. "I hear you're close with your co-stars, especially Summer West. Have you two ever been more than—"

A startled laugh leaves me, and I interrupt, "No, absolutely not. I love Summer like a sister, but the key word there is *sister*. We met when we were twelve, so we basically grew up together, through all those awkward puberty years and everything that came with them. It's weird to think of her in any way that's not platonic, and I know she feels the same about me."

"But you have so much on-screen chemistry," Charlie says, sounding shocked.

"She's a phenomenal actress," I say. "She makes it easy."

Charlie opens her mouth before snapping it shut again, a blush rising to her cheeks. I'm curious what she was going to say, whether she was going to insult my acting skills again—or perhaps the opposite, given her embarrassment—but Hawke speaks before I can coax it out of her.

"It must have been hard, everything that happened with Summer last year. But you stood by her side and even defended her, at great cost to your own career. Can you tell us about that from your perspective?"

The fish I ate turns sour in my stomach. I wonder if Gabe put Hawke up to this line of questioning as well, before realizing that of course he did. Anything to help warm the viewers—and the studio—toward me.

I swallow the last of my tea to stall as I think of a way to answer. Summer won't care if I speak about it, since she's encouraged me to do so, many times. But in my mind, it's her story, and I never want to misrepresent what happened based on my own limited viewpoint. Because of that, my words are hesitant when I reply, "You're right, it was hard, but that's because my friend was hurting and no one was listening to her. It was her word against one of the biggest directors in the industry. No one wanted to believe the things she claimed he did to her, so they brushed it off, saying she was exaggerating, that he was just 'having some fun,' that she should be 'grateful' he paid her that kind of attention."

My voice turns as dark as my mood. "It was her first lead role outside of *The Lost Heirs* and it should have been something special. Instead, it broke her. *He* broke her. And now, because she had the courage to stand up to him and warn others about his nature, she's been blacklisted. She hasn't even been able to get an audition since she went public, let alone an actual role."

"And you?" Hawke asks, making me jolt. "You went to bat for Summer when the industry turned on her. You shared loudly how she's not a liar and she would never risk damaging someone else's career for the sake of attention, as many were claiming at the time. Have you had any blowback from defending her?"

"Nothing like what she's faced." I choose not to reveal how hard it's also been for me to get an audition, since there are other factors that led to my own difficulties. "But, yes, it's been challenging. We've both been labeled problematic, even by those who believe her but won't risk supporting her. Regardless of our success with *The Lost Heirs*, we're tainted by association now."

"That hardly seems fair," Charlie says, holding her camping mug in a white-knuckled grip.

"Hollywood is anything but fair," I say, before remembering the nano drones and cursing inwardly. But I spoke the truth, and I'm unsure if I would take it back even if I could.

"Do you regret it?" she asks, her eyes locked on mine. "Standing up for her?"

"I didn't stand up for her—she stood up for herself, I just stood beside her," I correct. "And no, not for one minute. I could never regret that. No matter the cost."

Charlie leans backward, seemingly surprised. Then again, she knows all about my public image problem—and she's smart enough to realize it began with Summer's so-called scandal and only grew from there.

I lift my hands toward the fire, relishing the warmth as I say, leaving no room for doubt, "If my options are to support one of my closest friends when she needs me the most, or abandon her in order to protect my own career, then it's a no-brainer for me. I love what I do, my career is everything, but the people I care about will always come first. *Always.*"

Charlie holds my gaze for a long moment, emotions swirling across her features. She doesn't seem to know how to respond, but I don't expect her to. I also desperately want everyone's focus to leave me, since I feel as if I've given enough of myself tonight—*more* than enough—so I turn back to Hawke and look between him and Bentley as I ask, "Speaking of people we care about, I'd love to hear how you two met."

It's Bentley who answers, "I saved his life."

My eyebrows shoot upward. Even Charlie is visibly stunned.

"What happened?" she asks.

Bentley pulls his glasses off to clean them as he shares in his lulling English accent, "I was visiting a rural village in Somalia while filming a documentary for the British Red Cross, when this one"—he bumps Hawke affectionately with his shoulder—"comes crawling out of nowhere, covered in blood, and rambling feverishly about how he'd found 'the perfect place' to open a new camp for troubled youths. I had some field medic training, so while all the doctors were busy helping the locals with a viral outbreak, I was stuck nursing him back to health." Bentley grins and shakes his head. "He was a terrible patient, kept saying he was perfectly fine despite having his insides nearly ripped out by a lion. Such a fool."

The fondness in Bentley's expression is returned by Hawke, who chuckles and says, "I *was* perfectly fine. Fully stitched up and ready to go."

He raises the hem of his thermal shirt to reveal four scarred claw marks slashed across his lower abdomen. I noticed them when we were fishing in the river, but I wince now that I know how he got them.

"You were attacked by a lion?" Charlie breathes, her violet eyes wide.

"A lioness. And it was a freak accident." Hawke waves it away like it was nothing. "I was scouting the area for my next camp location, and I made the rookie mistake of not paying attention to my surroundings. She was with her cubs, so she perceived me as a threat and acted to protect them."

Charlie grimaces, and I do the same.

"It worked out for the best, since I never would have met this one otherwise," Hawke says, returning Bentley's earlier shoulder bump. "I remained at the Red Cross camp with him until I was fully healed, and by then, he was done with his documentary, so I asked if he wanted to come with me to finish exploring the area, then continue on to see more of East Africa. He said yes, and he had all his camera gear with him, so he filmed a lot of what we did and saw—and the rest is, as they say, history."

"That was the start of *Hawke's Wild World*, even if we didn't know it at the time." Bentley smiles tenderly at his husband before finishing, "Everything that's happened since then is all thanks to that lion."

A gentle silence descends upon us in the wake of his words.

"That's such a beautiful story," Charlie says quietly. "I've never heard it before."

"Your mother didn't tell you?" Hawke asks, before adding, "You mentioned before we left that she's a big fan of the show."

The look on Charlie's face—I can't describe it, but it has me sitting up straighter, my forehead creasing with concern.

"No," Charlie says slowly, hoarsely, as if that word is dredged from somewhere deep within her. "She—She didn't tell me."

Hawke seems to be waiting for her to say more, but her face is pale and her lips are pressed tightly together. She's avoided almost all questions about her family today, even during the promo clips, so I jump in to change the topic, asking, "Do we want to know what's ahead for us tomorrow, or is it better for our chances of sleep if we're kept in the dark?"

The survivalist barks out a laugh. "You'll have to wait and see." He empties the dregs of his tea on the ground, before standing up and stretching. "I know it's early, but we had a long day, and tomorrow will be even longer, so it's a good idea to turn in soon." With a playful grin, he warns, "We have a big ravine to cross in the morning, so rest up, because you'll need all your energy."

So much for him not telling us what's ahead.

"When you say 'cross,' you mean we're walking it, right?" Charlie asks. Silence meets her question, so she presses, "*Right?*"

Hawke stokes the fire, placing a few more thick logs on it before stepping back again. "Whatever you need to hear to help you sleep tonight, Charlie."

"Like that's going to happen now," she mumbles.

I repress a smile, and watch as Hawke and Bentley pack up and say goodnight to us, retreating into their parachute.

The air between Charlie and me becomes uneasy, and it takes me a moment to realize why, but when I do, I quickly say, "You can have the tent. I'll sleep out here tonight."

She frowns. "That's not—I mean—We can . . . we can share."

Despite her words, she's clearly uncomfortable, her eyes darting to the second parachute and back again, her features pinched. She's already done so much for me just by being here; the last thing I want is to make it even harder on her.

"You can't get a view like this back where I'm from," I say, indicating the moonlit river, then pointing upward at the cloudless sky with its unending starry expanse. The timing is perfect, because she follows my finger right as a meteor streaks across the horizon. "It's been a long time since I've slept under the stars," I continue, "so I'm looking forward to this. Go, the shelter is all yours."

She still hesitates, and I know why. The air is cold enough that our breaths are visible, even with the fire, and the ground is rough and pebbled. It won't be the most pleasant sleeping experience, but this way Charlie doesn't have to worry about us waking up tangled in each other's arms.

That image sends an unexpected bolt of warmth through me. I can't deny that I'm attracted to her—not just physically, but what I'm coming to know on a deeper level as well. However, I'm also aware those thoughts aren't reciprocated, and the smartest thing I can do is ignore whatever I feel growing toward her. We have three days left together, and then we'll part ways, hopefully not as enemies, but we also won't be friends. She's made that perfectly clear, and I'll respect her wishes, even if I still don't understand them.

"Well, I guess goodnight, then," she says, rubbing her arms self-consciously.

I make sure my smile is genuine as I return the words. "Goodnight, Charlie. Don't let the forest bugs bite." My smile falls. "No, but seriously, don't. They'll probably kill you."

She chuckles lightly—filling me with yet more warmth that I ignore—and then repeats, "'Night, Zander. I'll see you in the morning. Assuming we're both still alive."

On that special note of dark humor, she disappears inside the parachute, leaving me with the crackling fire, gurgling river, and chirping crickets. The unfamiliar sounds of nature are so loud that I'm sure it'll take me hours to fall asleep, but I couldn't be more wrong.

Because as soon as I close my eyes, the day catches up to me—and I'm out like a light.

The first thing I hear when I wake in the morning is a female voice—but it's not Charlie's.

I crack my eyes open to see Scarlett and a group of black-clothed crew members bustling around our campsite, the former talking with Hawke while the latter help Bentley swap out his camera equipment.

A groan leaves me as I sit up, my body one big ache after the physical challenges of yesterday combined with sleeping like the dead on the hard earth. I work the kinks out of my neck and stretch my muscles before slowly rising to my feet.

"Morning, Zander," Scarlett says when I stumble over to her and Hawke. "Sleep well?"

The cracking sounds my joints make as I approach give her all the answer she needs. "Please tell me you brought some of that for the rest of us?" I beg, looking longingly at her insulated travel mug while inhaling the heavenly scent of coffee.

"There's some waiting for you back at the hotel." Her hazel eyes shine devilishly as she takes a long sip. "You can have it when you return on Friday."

"Cruel," I tell her, though I hardly expected a different answer.

She laughs. "Charlie said the same thing."

"She's up already?" I peer through the dawn light toward her parachute-tent.

"You're the only one who managed to sleep through this racket," Hawke says, indicating the *Hawke's Wild World* team all around us. Before I can ask, he adds, "She's downstream, taking a quick bath. Hopefully emphasizing the 'quick,' or she'll end up with hypothermia."

As someone who was in the river up to my knees yesterday, I know Hawke isn't exaggerating. It's only a few weeks past winter, so the water isn't just cold, it's *cold*. But like Charlie, I'm eager to freshen up, so I ask Hawke which direction she went in, and I head the other way. I'm not daring enough to wade all the way in, but I use a spare sock as a washcloth and clean as much of my body as I can.

When I return to camp, Charlie is already back, and she slides over on her log to make room for me while holding out a bunch of pink lilly pilly berries and saying, "Breakfast."

It's not coffee, but it's also not another dead animal, so I thank her and toss them in my mouth. The fire is low, almost out, but we sit in front of it munching quietly together, until I glance around and ask, "Do you know why the support team is here?"

She follows my gaze to where Scarlett is still standing with Hawke, but now Bentley has joined them, along with another woman. All four of them are examining the map Hawke showed us yesterday, their faces thoughtful as they murmur among themselves.

"Apparently they planned to meet us last night after dinner, but their vehicles had a harder time with the terrain than they expected," Charlie answers. "From what I gather, they're meant to check in throughout the day to make sure we don't have any injuries or equipment issues, plus they do things like resupply the rope that we had to leave on the mountain yesterday. Ropes," she amends, with neither of us mentioning *why* a second rope was needed. "All stuff that's never included on-screen when the show airs, since they want it to look as survival-y as possible. Keep the magic alive, and all that."

I eye her closely. "You don't seem surprised."

She shrugs. "It's no secret that reality television is fake. It's more about drama than any real truth." She stretches her shoulders and winces. "That said, there's nothing fake about how much I'm hurting today. I'd kill for some anti-inflammatories and a hot water bottle."

"Same here," I agree. "I feel like I aged fifty years overnight."

Hawke and Scarlett approach as I'm saying the words, and both of them try—and fail—to hide their amusement.

"Buck up, Prince Charming," Hawke says, his lips twitching. "You'll both feel better once we get moving."

"I have serious doubts about that," Charlie grumbles under her breath.

"You're all doing so well," Scarlett jumps in. "One day down, three to go. Are you enjoying yourselves so far?" Both Charlie and I look at her flatly until she clears her throat and continues, "We'll get out of your hair now so you can continue on, but we'll check in again later today. Our location scouts didn't realize how tricky it would be to get our wheels through the scrub—they did the journey on foot, same as you—so we're having some trouble finding safe routes, but you're in good hands with Hawke here, regardless."

A huge bald man walks over to us before she can say more, his eyes on Hawke as he reports, "The rope is set on the ravine and we've done a full safety check, so you're all sorted there. I've also told Erik and his crew to drive on ahead of us to secure the bridge near your extraction point, even if you won't reach it until Friday. It's early, but

I want it done today, in case the weather turns so bad that we don't get another chance."

Without context, I only understand part of what he said, but all of it has Charlie and me sharing nervous looks.

"Thanks, Hux," Hawke says. To Scarlett, he asks, "What's this about weather?"

"Nothing to worry about yet," she replies, though the bald man, Hux, raises his eyebrows. "There's some rain developing off the coast that we're keeping an eye on, but it'll hopefully stay offshore. If it begins to track inland, I'll let you know."

I glance upward and see nothing but clear blue sky above our heads.

"What happens if it rains?" Charlie asks, peering up as well.

"We get wet," Hawke says, straight-faced.

Scarlett elbows him, before answering Charlie, "Nothing happens, it just means you might have to change your route to avoid flash floods. Or if it becomes too dangerous for us to navigate with the vehicles, we might need to pull our crew back until it passes. But as I said, right now, there's nothing to worry about, so put it from your mind."

With that, Scarlett whistles to her team and makes a circling motion with her hand, indicating for them to get moving. They disperse impressively fast into the trees and, after telling us to take care and reminding us she'll see us later, Scarlett vanishes with them.

I'm still blinking at how swiftly they all managed to leave when I realize it's just Hawke, Bentley, Charlie, and me again.

"Can you two be ready in five minutes?" Hawke asks, glancing at his watch. "We have a big hiking day, so the sooner we go, the better."

It's not a question, more an order, so we quickly finish our berries before helping dismantle the parachute-tents and grabbing our gear. I hiss out a curse when I lift my backpack, but once we leave the camp and start moving, my muscles warm up and the pain eases, as Hawke said it would.

We hike through the forest for hours on an upward trajectory, the ground mostly keeping to a slight incline, with some steeper sections that leave us panting and needing regular breaks. None of us talk much, aside from Hawke occasionally sharing about the native flora and fauna we see—a blue-tongued lizard that crosses our path, different kinds of poisonous fungi, the nine-hundred-odd species of gum trees, a web-covered hole that houses a deadly funnel-web spider—but thankfully there are no deeper conversations. I'm guessing he's leaving those for when we're unguarded, so there's likely a round two coming for me tonight. I already know what it will be about, since I'm certain Gabe will have asked Hawke to make sure I share one important thing with the world:

My DUI and rehab experience.

I'm not looking forward to talking about it, mostly because I'm going to have to lie through my teeth, and yet still somehow come across as repentant.

But that's a worry for later. Right now, I need to get through this endless hike.

Just as I have that thought, the incline finally levels out, and the trees we're zigzagging through begin to thin. A few steps later, we arrive atop a rocky slab similar to the cliff we had to rappel down yesterday. But instead of us being partway up a mountain, there's a massive crack in the ground before us, like an ancient giant came and cleaved the land in two. The far side has to be over a hundred feet away, and the vertical drop between us at least triple that, full of jutting boulders and lethal, jagged edges.

This must be the ravine Hawke mentioned.

And at the sight of the rope stretching across the daunting gap, I know we won't be finding our way around it.

We'll be going straight across it.

Charlie

Prior to this moment, I knew I hated Zander Rune, but staring at the death chasm stretching out before us, I *really* hate him.

Worse, after everything he shared beside the fire last night—how his birth parents died when he was a child, how he was bullied in school, how he stood by Summer when the world turned on her—I hate that I've started to *not* hate him. I can't afford to begin liking him, but he's making that impossible the more I come to know him. And yet . . . I also have no way of knowing how much of what he said is genuinely true. He acts for a living, and the whole point of this survival trip is for him to make people love him again.

But even so, I can't help thinking it's not *all* an act. Because there are things he's still keeping secret, like how he gave only the barest details about his birth parents and about his best friend Maddox before moving on—just enough to make it seem like he's opening up, when really, he's also withholding. I'm unsure why . . . and I'm unsure why I care.

What I'm *not* unsure about is how I feel looking at the ravine we're stepping dangerously close to, since every survival instinct I have is blaring at me to back away, fast.

"Unfortunately for us," Hawke says, "if we want to reach our extraction point on time, we have to cross this."

He might have used the word "unfortunately," but there's nothing apologetic about his expression. He needs to take some acting lessons from Zander.

"Can't we find a way around it?" I ask, looking to the right and left, my view limited by the trees on either side of us.

"There's no way to tell how long that would take," Hawke says, which I'm sure is a lie. His scouts undoubtedly gave him options, but this crossing offers the most entertainment value for viewers. No one wants to see us walking through the forest all day without some kind of death-defying task to contend with.

Then again . . .

A quick glance at Zander has me amending my thoughts. His silver hair is like a halo in the bright sunshine, his flawless physique better than any Michelangelo sculpture, noticeable even beneath his blue and navy outerwear. It's not hard to believe his fans *would* actually be happy to watch him hike through the bush for hours on end. As long as his face and body were on the screen, they'd watch him do anything. He could sit and stare at drying paint and they would ogle him while he did so.

"Charlie?"

I blink back to myself at Zander's confused, questioning tone, realizing *I'm* the one currently staring at him. I fight my embarrassment and swiftly return my attention to Hawke.

"As you can see, my safety team has secured a line over the ravine." Hawke indicates the thick rope stretching from one side of the gap to the other. "So using this, we're going to do something called a Tyrolean traverse—a popular mountaineering technique for traveling from one point to another across open air. Have either of you done anything like this before?"

I shake my head woodenly. Zander also responds in the negative, though his expression is eager and at odds with the dread I feel bubbling within me.

"This will be a fun new experience for you both, then," Hawke says with an easy smile. "There are a few different methods you can use, but since you're beginners, it's probably best if you go upside down and backward, pulling your weight along that way."

Upside down and backward? I feel the blood drain from my face, but I make myself take a deep, steadying breath, recalling everything I overcame yesterday—skydiving, cliff rappelling, canyon squeezing—and I try to shake off my trepidation.

Hawke goes on to explain in more detail how we'll be crossing, and also shares the distance: one hundred and sixty feet. It's less than the length of an Olympic swimming pool—or so he says—but that doesn't make me feel much better about it.

"I'll head over first so I can get a clearer view of everyone crossing," Bentley says, packing away his larger camera and strapping his GoPro to his shoulder. To Zander and me, he adds, "I'll also be able to help you off the rope once you reach the other side—it can be tricky if you've never done it before."

Tricky is likely an understatement, but I'm grateful I won't have to heave myself up onto the ledge without assistance.

It takes mere seconds before Bentley is clipped onto the rope and making his way across the ravine, his movements seemingly effortless. My tension eases a fraction as I watch him—at least until he reaches the far side and I realize the rest of us now have to follow.

"See? It's as simple as that," Hawke says once Bentley waves to indicate he's clear. "Who wants to go next?"

"Not it," I blurt out.

"Charlie, how good of you to volunteer." Hawke's dark eyes are dancing. "Let's get you clipped in."

I scowl at him, before turning my frown on Zander when he coughs to cover a laugh. But then I sigh, knowing I have to cross one way or another, and the longer I wait, the more time my anxiety will have to grow. Might as well get it over with.

I make the mistake of looking down into the jagged gorge as Hawke hooks my harness onto the rope, the view making my head spin. It's not as high as the mountain descent yesterday, but falling would still mean instant death. My palms are sweating as I don my gloves and helmet, and I have to force myself to listen as Hawke starts to narrate information for the sake of the audience, with him relying on the impossible-to-spot nano drones now that Bentley and his cameras are out of range.

"They say the 'Tyrolean' part of the Tyrolean traverse is because this technique originated in the Austrian Alps—specifically in Tyrol—and was used by hikers to cross the numerous rivers and gorges between the mountains," Hawke says as he double-checks my harness. "But interestingly, the longest Tyrolean traverse on record was actually in Bulgaria, not Austria, and it reached one thousand five hundred and fifty meters in length. That's over five thousand feet, which means . . . How's your math, Charlie?"

"Right now, it's nonexistent," I mutter, my sole focus on trying not to hyperventilate.

Hawke chuckles. "I'll help you out, then. It means you'd be looking at this"—he taps the rope crossing the ravine—"and multiplying it by thirty, and you'd *still* be coming in short. Imagine that."

I gulp. "I'd really rather not."

Hawke continues sharing about other significant Tyrolean traverses in history, but I drown him out, concentrating on keeping as calm as I can. I'm unsure if I'm relieved or even more terrified when he finally declares I'm ready to go.

"The first step is always the hardest," he says sagely. "In this case, that means getting you onto the rope and into position. You saw how Ben did it—once you're over the edge, you'll flip upside down and be able to move freely from there. Ready?"

My mouth is too dry for me to answer, so I just do a half nod, half head shake.

"See you on the other side, Charlie," Zander says quietly, and my eyes flick to his, the reassurance in his blue gaze reminding me again of everything we conquered yesterday.

I can do this, I tell myself. I *can*.

"That's it, nice and slow," Hawke says as I repeat Bentley's actions and stretch my body along the rope, trying to keep my trembling at bay. "Slide forward now. You're nearly there."

I have to loosen my grip since I'm only hindering myself, but finally I manage to inch out into open air.

"Good, Charlie, now drop upside down," Hawke says. "Think of a sloth hanging from a branch. Trust your harness to hold you—you're not going anywhere."

That's easy for him to say; it's not his heart that wants to crash through his ribcage right now. But I grit my teeth and yield to gravity until I'm dangling upside down, my hands clasping the rope, my harness holding my lower body in place and keeping me relatively horizontal.

"Excellent," Hawke praises. "Now hook one leg up over the rope for stabilization, and start pulling yourself across. The first half will be easier since your body weight will work in your favor, so give in to it and conserve your energy for the second half. Got it?"

"Got it," I grunt out, eager to move now that I'm hanging like a monkey.

"Then off you go," Hawke says. "Show Zander and me how it's done."

I don't need that added pressure, *thank you very much*, so I ignore the challenge and begin a hand-over-hand method to pull myself backward, trying to mimic Bentley's moves. I don't look down—I'm not foolish enough to do that again, especially as I venture further across the gap, and therefore further away from safety.

I'm about a quarter of the way over when Hawke calls out, "How're you doing, Charlie?"

"So far so good," I call back, surprisingly telling the truth. Aside from some low-level discomfort where the rope is digging into my hooked leg, and the growing fatigue in my arms, it's not as difficult as I feared. It's certainly not as effortless as Bentley made it seem, but it's also not the worst thing I've experienced on this trip.

But then I reach the middle, passing the center of gravity, and I have to fight my way back upward, all while battling the wind that's slamming into me now that I'm far enough out to be unprotected by the forest's barrier. My jaw is clenched tight as I drag myself along the rope, my chest, shoulders, and hands all burning fiercely.

"Stop and rest for a moment," Hawke calls, his voice nearly stolen by the wind. "Shake some feeling back into your fingers."

The exertion has me breathing so heavily that I can't reply, but I follow his advice, hissing at the painful tingling of my nerves. My right leg is aching so much from the rope that I decide to swap it with my left, resulting in me having to adjust to a new coordination when I start to move again. Worse, in doing so, I accidentally cast my eyes downward, and a bout of dizziness hits me so strongly that nausea crawls up my throat.

"You're nearly there, Charlie," Zander calls, as if he can sense my distress. "Only a few more feet. You can make it."

I wish his voice didn't ground me so much. I wish his encouragement didn't make me feel so reassured. I wish—I wish—

I wish he wasn't who he was.

Or rather, I wish he hadn't done what he did.

Because then maybe—

No.

I won't let my mind go there, since there's no point. I can't wish any of that true—he is who he is, and he did what he did. I can't forget that. I *won't* forget that.

My arms are screaming when I finally reach the far edge of the ravine and find Bentley lowering his camera to help pull me up onto the rock. Every muscle in my body is on fire, but I'm safe now—and I did it.

"Well done," Bentley says, giving my shoulder a squeeze, then reclaiming his camera to focus it back toward the other side of the crossing.

I can't deny the pride I feel as I look properly into the gap, appreciating what I accomplished. As much as I'm hurting, there's a larger part of me that recognizes how alive I feel right now. Like yesterday, I realize it's something I haven't felt in a long time—too long. But unlike yesterday, I don't feel as guilty about it today. Just . . . sad. Like I've missed out on something vital, something I didn't even know I needed in my life, because I stifled it.

I had my reasons—God knows I did. But now . . .

I'm not sure if those reasons hold true anymore.

Or if they even should.

But I also know it's not the time to think about it, so I focus on massaging my fingers, arms, and legs as I watch Zander carry out his own Tyrolean traverse across the ravine. He makes it look almost as easy as Bentley did—damn him—and reaches us in record time, his cheeks flushed and eyes bright from the thrill.

"I'll be feeling that tomorrow," he says, shaking out his limbs.

"I'm feeling it now," I return. Despite how proud I am, I'm still one big bruise all over.

Zander doesn't reply other than to give a low, awed whistle as we watch Hawke begin to pull himself across the line, but not in the sloth-like hanging method we used. Instead, the survivalist's torso remains draped over the top of the rope as he pulls himself along, his speed making it seem like the rest of us took months in comparison.

Before I know what's happening, Hawke is safely on our side, telling us to enjoy a well-deserved water and berry break. We don't linger—within minutes we're up and hiking again, like we didn't just drag ourselves over a massive crack in the earth.

I have to remind myself that this isn't anything new to Hawke and Bentley—they do things like this every other week for *Hawke's Wild World*, and Hawke did it for years before that during his park ranger and camp founder days. I wonder what that must be like, living so much of their lives among nature and experiencing such adventures. My heart soars at the idea, but I don't understand why—or maybe I just don't want to consider it. Fear has held me back for so long that it's habit now to yield to it, to stay firmly in my comfort zone.

Or . . . that's what I thought. But after what I've overcome in the last thirty-six hours . . . I'm not so sure anymore. All I know is that, once this trip is over, there are things I'll need to reflect on, things I'll need to face. My own personal Pandora's box is waiting, the key already in the lock, urging me to turn it.

The problem is, I have no idea what will happen if I do—and I'm not yet convinced that I want to find out.

So for now, I ignore it, and concentrate only on putting one foot in front of the other as I trail after Hawke, telling myself that anything—and everything—else can wait.

Our hike continues through the forest, the trees denser here than they were earlier, with the earth covered in raised roots, innumerable plants, and bush scrub—all of which snag around our ankles and make the simple act of walking difficult. Finally, the ground clears again, but only because we reach a cluster of large boulders blocking our path.

"Let me guess, we can't go around these, either?" I ask Hawke on a sigh.

"Up and over," he confirms. "But watch your step—the moss will be slippery, and some of them may not be as stable as they look."

He leads the way, moving easily from rock to rock, his footwork sure. I tread more carefully as I follow directly behind him, then Zander behind me, and Bentley at the rear. My legs are cramping by the time I step off the final boulder back onto the forest floor, and I'm so focused on shaking them out that I'm not paying attention to the path before me.

Or what just slithered across it.

The moment I see the massive brown snake—startling it as much as it startles me—it's too late to do anything other than freeze, my fight-or-flight response nonexistent.

But then, just as it hisses and strikes out at me, Zander's arms wrap around my waist like steel bands, hauling me backward, right as Hawke's hunting knife flies through the air.

I'm still frozen as the survivalist unpins the now-dead snake from his blade and quickly drags it away. "That was close," he says. "Nice reflexes, Zander."

"You okay, Charlie?" Bentley asks, his brown eyes concerned behind his glasses, though his camera remains trained on me.

I am absolutely not okay, so much so that I don't even care that I'm still held tight in Zander's arms, trembling like a leaf.

I press back into him when Hawke picks the snake up by its tail, letting it dangle like a six-foot rope. My pulse is thundering so loudly that I can hardly hear him as he goes into narrator-mode, sharing, "This is one of the deadliest snakes in existence: the eastern brown snake. It's said to have the quickest-killing venom in the world, and an untreated bite can cause death in as little as thirty minutes."

A whimper leaves me without my permission, my legs so wobbly that I can barely hold myself up. Zander notices and pulls me closer, all while Hawke explains how snakes are more afraid of us than we are of them, and generally only attack when threatened or startled—which is unfortunately what just happened.

"It's illegal to kill snakes in Australia, unless they pose a threat to human life," he continues, lowering the snake back to the ground. "So while I can see this has shaken you, Charlie, and while it's a shame to have ended the life of such a noble creature, this encounter is also fortuitous, since it means we've found our lunch."

Before I can process his words, there's another flash of his hunting knife, a quick, downward swipe, and then—

I gag and shove my face to the side, unconsciously turning into Zander's chest. His arms wrap even tighter around me, one hand cupping my head to keep my cheek pressed against him so I don't have to see the grisly scene before us.

"Hawke," he snaps, his voice sharper than I've ever heard it. "A little warning wouldn't hurt."

"I've said it before, and I'll say it again: survival is about opportunity," Hawke states unapologetically.

"I get that," Zander grinds out. "But you could have—"

"It's fine," I rasp, finally pulling away from him. "I'm fine." My words are shaky and I likely look as ill as I feel, but I inhale deeply and keep my eyes on Hawke and *not* the beheaded snake at his feet as I repeat, "Really, I'm fine."

"Snake meat is an excellent source of lean protein," Hawke says. "So as much as it might turn your stomach, this is one meal that's just too good to pass up."

I don't need an explanation. I don't even *want* an explanation. What I want is for us to leave the area in case the snake has friends or family nearby.

Thankfully, Hawke reads that in my eyes, and we move out again, but only until we find a flat, clear space where we can safely light a fire.

For the sake of self-preservation, I tune out everything Hawke says as he prepares the snake for cooking, keeping my focus entirely on Bentley as he replaces his camera battery with a fresh one. It's only when the "meal" is roasted nearly to charcoal that both Zander and I are willing to move anywhere near it, and even then, that's because Hawke threatens to force-feed it to us otherwise. I would rather attempt the world's longest Tyrolean traverse than put the snake meat anywhere near my mouth, but I watch as Zander reluctantly does so, and somehow summon the courage to try it myself.

The first thing I notice is how bony it is. And the second—

"I thought it would taste like chicken," Zander says, stealing the words from me.

"It's almost . . . fishy," I add.

Hawke smiles at us. "See, it's not so terrible, is it?"

It might not be terrible, but it's absolutely not enjoyable—partly due to the taste, but mostly because of the psychological factor.

"Of all the things we've eaten on this trip, it's right down there with the possum," I say, the bony texture alone making it an unpleasant experience. But I make myself take a second bite, knowing I'll need the energy, especially when Hawke tells us that it's all uphill for the rest of the day.

What I don't realize is that he means that literally, which I discover only after we finish our lunch and continue on our hike, soon reaching a sheer cliff—but this one stretches upward, not downward.

"Time for some mountain climbing," Hawke declares, pulling a grappling hook from his pack. "Those extra snake calories are about to save your lives."

Zander

Charlie nearly died today.

That's the only thought screaming across my mind as Hawke continues pulling climbing gear out of his pack, telling us about the task ahead.

If I hadn't seen the snake in time, if I hadn't moved fast enough to haul her backward, if she'd taken one more step—

Thirty minutes, Hawke said. That's how long she would have had if it had struck her. There's no way we would have been able to get her anywhere for treatment in that time. She would have died—and it would have been my fault.

Maybe not directly. But I'm the reason she's here. And feeling her trembling in my arms afterward, knowing how close she'd come to death—

"Zander, are you listening?"

A shuddering breath leaves me and I force myself back into the present, knowing better than to travel down the what-if path. Charlie is unharmed. The snake is dead. We're all safe. That's what I need to focus on now, rather than dwelling on what might have been.

"Sorry, yes," I answer Hawke.

He eyes me suspiciously, and I know I've been caught in my distraction, but he only says, "I was just explaining how we need to make it up this cliff before we can keep hiking, but it should be the last of the strenuous obstacles we have to tackle today." He gestures for Charlie, Bentley, and me to step back, and once we're far enough away, he swings the grappling hook a few times before letting it fly. It takes him three attempts before it locks onto something at the top of the rock face, and he tests it with his weight, nodding in satisfaction.

"I'll go first this time," Hawke says. "Make sure you pay attention to what I'm doing so you can repeat these actions for yourselves."

I assume the warning is for my benefit, given that I spaced out only moments ago, so I concentrate when Hawke shows us how to clip our carabiners to the rope, and how to adjust the foot loop.

"You'll also need a jumar—an ascender," he says, holding up a metal, clamp-like device. "Grip it with your dominant hand, and when you use the foot loop to step upward, slide the jumar along the rope. It locks in place to make it easier for you to pull yourself up without slipping back down. See?"

He demonstrates again, then says, "Helmets on, in case I dislodge any rocks on my way up. And remember: there's no rush. This kind of climbing will really work your core muscles, so don't be afraid to stop and rest."

Just as he says it, the sun disappears, and I look up in surprise to see that the blue sky from earlier is now covered in clouds. They're still high and fluffy enough not to be threatening, but in the distance they're much darker and heavier. Charlie, Hawke, and Bentley are glancing in that direction as well, all with varying expressions of concern.

"It's not raining yet," Hawke says, "so what I said holds true: take your time." He pauses. "That said, we don't want to be halfway up this in a downpour, so let's not linger longer than we have to."

I don't love the way he frowns at the clouds again, but he quickly clears his features and steps into the foot loop, using the jumar to pull himself up the rope and his free leg to grip hollows in the rock, explaining what he's doing as he goes. He makes it seem easy, and is soon up and over the lip of the cliff, out of sight for only a few seconds before his head reappears and he calls down to us, "Who's next?"

Charlie looks grimly at me. "Rock, paper, scissors?"

We play best of three and I end up winning, but I don't know if that means I'm climbing next or she is until she nudges me forward—making me wonder if she would have done the same even if she'd won.

My first few attempts to climb are unsuccessful, leaving me swinging wildly and struggling to move the jumar upward, but I eventually get into a somewhat coordinated rhythm. It's difficult work, my abdominal muscles burning and legs cramping, while my fingers turn numb from gripping the jumar and rope. I think my personal trainer must be lying about what good shape I'm in, since I'm a sweating, aching mess when I finally heave myself over the top and lay panting on the ledge, unable to move.

Charlie is the same when she arrives, hissing a colorful array of curse words around her gasping breaths as she rubs feeling back into her hands, glaring daggers at Hawke the whole time. But there's also a spark in her violet eyes that wasn't there when I first met her, something I've noticed growing over the last two days. It's like she's coming alive the longer we're out here; like every challenge we overcome is transforming something inside of her, making her open up more with each new task we face.

When Bentley joins us—his ascent much faster than Charlie's and mine—we take a few minutes to rest properly, rehydrating ourselves and snacking on some sandpaper figs Hawke found when we were hiking earlier. As I enjoy the sweet, juicy fruit, I find myself grateful that so many plants in the park are edible, and we don't have to survive solely on dead animals. I've already had enough of those to last a lifetime.

We're just getting ready to continue on our way when the bushes rustle and Scarlett emerges with the big, bald Hux by her side. They're both carrying climbing gear, indicating that they, too, had to scale the mountain, since their vehicles would have been unable to navigate the vertical cliff face. Hux moves straight to Hawke and starts checking the rope we used, satisfied when he finds no evidence of tearing. But it's not Hux I'm watching—it's Scarlett. Because the look on her face . . .

"We have a problem," she says, causing all of us to straighten.

"The weather?" Hawke guesses, his dark eyes flicking toward the now menacing-looking clouds coming ever closer.

"The wind changed direction, so we're going to be hit head-on," Scarlett reveals. "They're saying it'll be heavy, but it'll also be fast. It should be clear again by morning."

"That's something, at least," Hawke murmurs, his arms crossed, his gaze thoughtful. "We'll be fine on our end—we're only hiking for the rest of the afternoon, and once we're further up the mountain, we'll find a cave or an overhang for shelter. But I assume you need to pull the crew back?"

"If we don't, we're likely to get flooded in," Scarlett confirms. "We'd be all right if the vehicles were handling the terrain better, but adding in the amount of water the forecast is predicting?" She shakes her auburn head. "We need to backtrack to find somewhere safe to wait it out. But that also means we'll need extra time to reach you tomorrow once it clears, so you'll be on your own for a while. Probably until late afternoon, maybe early evening. Worst case and the rain is heavier than expected, or it circles back, or the flooding doesn't recede fast enough—if any of that happens, we might not be able to meet you until you reach your extraction point on Friday. If that's the case, can you manage alone for the next two days?"

She's looking at Hawke intently, as if communicating something silently to him, but all he says is, "We have everything we need, so focus on keeping the crew safe and don't worry about us." He wipes fig juice from his beard before adding, "You know we plan these trips so the support team is only there for emergencies—we'll just make sure we don't have any of those."

Hearing his confidence, I wonder what constitutes an "emergency," and whether nearly being bitten by one of the most venomous snakes in the world counts. Apparently not, since he doesn't even mention it to Scarlett.

"Just take care of our guests," the producer says, sending strained smiles to Charlie and me. "You two doing okay?"

Even with Charlie aware of the cameras on us, I'm a little worried about how she might respond, so I jump in first. "We're tired and sore, but it's also exhilarating. Right, Charlie?"

Her lips stretch into a bright—and painfully fake—smile as she chirps out, "*Super* exhilarating. We're having the *time* of our *lives*."

I have to look at the ground to keep from laughing—or grimacing—but I glance up again when a freckled young man appears out of the trees, panting and red-faced and carrying his own climbing gear. But he's also carting more than that, since he moves first to Bentley to hand him a new set of camera equipment—weatherproof, I assume—and then to Scarlett to give her a familiar silver box.

The man disappears again, leaving Scarlett to explain, "We've had to take the nano drones out of commission." She indicates the box. "Remember how I said they're prototypes? Well, they're not waterproof yet, so with the coming weather, we can't risk damaging them. But that's fine—we'll reactivate them when we meet up again after the rain clears. Until then, Ben will capture all the footage we need."

"I haven't seen the nano drones since we left," Charlie muses, and I nod my agreement.

"Perfect—that means they're doing their job." Scarlett pockets the box, then looks at her watch and frowns. "We need to get back down the mountain. All set, Hux?"

"Good to go," the safety checker confirms, returning Hawke's pack after having examined its contents. "Everything important can get wet if needed."

"And you've got your sat phone if there are any problems," Scarlett reminds Hawke.

"There won't be," he says, making a shooing motion. "Now go find somewhere safe and dry. We'll see you tomorrow."

Scarlett and Hawke share a long look, one I can't read, before the producer turns to Charlie and me, her smile still strained as she says,

"A little bit of rain never hurt anyone. It's all part of the experience, so live it up, and embrace the adventure."

My brow furrows as she and Hux give us parting waves and disappear back into the trees. It's a strange thing for her to have said, given that we're already nearly halfway through our "adventure." But I shake off my apprehension and hoist my pack over my shoulders in preparation to leave, trying not to think about how much rain might be heading our way—or how difficult it's going to make our journey ahead.

Charlie

About an hour after Scarlett and Hux leave, gentle sprinkles start dusting my heated skin. It's not unpleasant at first, since our hike up the mountain is arduous, so the wet offers a cool relief. But then the rain starts coming down in earnest, and while my outerwear and backpack are waterproof, they still have their limits. I'm soon soaked to the bone and feeling twenty kilos heavier, battling for every upward step.

Hawke finally calls a halt to our waterlogged hike when the downpour becomes so torrential that our visibility is nonexistent, increasing the risk that one of us—likely me—will slip straight off the side of the mountain. I nearly sob with relief when he finds a small cave cut into the rock and declares it's safe enough for us to camp in for the night.

The first thing we do is change into the spare clothes our backpacks miraculously kept dry. Privacy is limited, but I'm shaking so hard that even if Zander, Hawke, and Bentley didn't all turn around while I dressed, I wouldn't have been able to care. I make quick work of it, then busy myself while they do the same, wringing out my clothes and searching for a place to drape them.

The cave is small and dark—darker still because of the rainstorm and the approaching dusk. I worry about how we're going to see anything once night falls, forgetting that I'm with Rykon Hawke, who has plenty of experience starting fires even when everything is saturated. Indeed, he soon has roaring flames heating up the space around us.

"You're my f-favorite person in the w-world," I say through chattering teeth as I collapse in front of the delicious warmth, my hands stretched out in an attempt to coax some feeling back into them.

"Normally I would have had you or Zander light it, but given that you're turning into an icicle, speed was of the essence," Hawke says wryly.

It only takes a few minutes before the fire begins to work its way through me, and soon my trembles ease and I'm feeling much more human again. Even so, every part of me hurts after what we've endured in the last two days, and I'm exhausted beyond belief. If I were home right now, I'd curl up in my bed and sleep for the next twelve years—but only *after* enjoying a steaming hot bubble bath.

Zander takes a seat beside me on the ground, his wet hair sticking up all over the place, making him look more anime-like than ever. I don't have the energy to laugh, but my lips quirk, drawing a curious glance from him. I shake my head, too embarrassed to share my thoughts aloud.

"I collected this on our walk," Hawke says, revealing a bunch of flowered weeds. "Wood sorrel. It's not much, but we're in short supply of any heartier food up here, so dinner is this, berries, and figs."

I try not to show my delight that we don't have to eat another native animal, but at Zander's quiet chuckle, I know I failed.

Hawke just rolls his eyes at me and hands out bunches of sorrel, saying, "It's a versatile weed—you can eat the flowers, stalks, and leaves, cooked or raw, and all of it will provide good roughage and an excellent source of Vitamin C. It also has a fresh, lemony flavor." He winks. "It'll make you feel like you're eating a hundred-dollar salad at your favorite Michelin-star restaurant."

Zander lifts his bunch to eye level and stares pointedly at the clumps of dirt still attached to the roots. "I would want my money back."

I secretly agree with him, but I follow Hawke's lead and toss the weed into my mouth. It's not as awful as I expect; in fact, the taste is familiar enough that I say, "When we were kids, Ember and I used to snack on something similar that we picked from gardens on our way to school." I strain my mind for the name. "We called it soursob, I think. Or maybe sour grass. Or . . . sour something."

Hawke waves the stalks in his hand. "All different names for wood sorrel." To Zander, he asks, "What do you think?"

The actor forces himself to swallow, then pulls a face. "My mouth tastes like a forest."

I bite my cheek to keep from laughing.

"A rave review," Hawke says, his dark eyes full of mirth. He then tosses Zander some sandpaper figs. "Those will go down better."

Unlike last night when we were eating around the fire, Bentley has to keep his camera rolling, being the only source of filming now that the nano drones are gone. After a while, though, he swaps his larger device for his GoPro, attaching it to a head strap to leave his hands free. The moment he does, I relax unconsciously, and Zander also becomes less stiff at my side. It makes no sense, since we're still being recorded, but not having a lens pointed so obviously in our direction makes things easier, psychologically.

I should have recognized it as a warning, because a few minutes later, once we've all finished dinner, Hawke stretches out his legs and renews the probing conversation he began last night. I squirm in sympathy as his eyes home in on Zander, grateful he has no reason to put me in the spotlight with the same kind of interrogation since the world doesn't care about my life, nor do I have a public image problem that I'm trying to improve.

But then Hawke asks his first question, and any sympathy I feel swiftly begins to dissolve.

"We've talked about your childhood, and touched on what happened with your co-star Summer last year, but I'd love to hear more about your last few months," Hawke says.

The words are innocent enough, but there's an uncomfortable feeling in the air now. I'm unsure if it's coming more from Zander—or from me.

"You've made some recent headlines labeling you as 'Hollywood's Bad Boy,'" Hawke continues, "and you even had a court-mandated stint in rehab after a car accident revealed you'd been driving under the influence of an illicit substance. Up until then, your life was squeaky clean. But now . . ." He trails off pointedly, before finishing, "Any chance you're willing to share about what happened?"

I'm stunned Hawke went straight in for the kill with his line of questioning, though I assume Gabe put him up to it, just as I assume Zander has a publicist-approved answer ready. Regardless, I'm as tense as the mountain around us as I wait for his response, struggling to beat back memories that are screaming for my attention.

Zander shifts beside me, and for a long moment, the only sounds I hear are the crackling flames and the rain sheeting down outside. It's too dark to see beyond the cave now that night has fallen, so there's only this small, firelit space to hold our focus, until finally, he speaks.

"You mentioned Summer before, and what happened last year, so that was really when the 'bad boy' label began for me," he says, fiddling with a thread on his thermal shirt. Quickly, he adds, "Not that there's any blame on her—what I meant was, timeline-wise, that's when the industry began to consider me problematic."

Hawke nods in gentle encouragement, and I again feel the stirring of sympathy as I recall everything he shared last night. But I stamp it down, bracing for what I know is coming.

Zander doesn't meet any of our eyes as he goes on, "After Summer spoke her truth and was met with censure, she took some time away from LA, waiting for everything to die down. But she returned for her birthday a few months ago, wanting to have a quiet dinner out with me and—and Maddox—" He stumbles over his best friend's name for some reason, but then continues, "and a few other close friends. The paparazzi found us, and soon co-stars and acquaintances from her life started appearing to celebrate with her. Dinner turned into a raging party, with drinking and dancing"—his throat bobs as he stares at the fire—"and drugs."

My heart begins to pound as I picture the night he's describing, already aware of what comes next, and how much I don't want to hear about it. But also, how much I *need* to hear about it, if only to remind me of who he is, and the stupid, selfish, *hateful* decisions he's capable of making.

When Zander doesn't continue, Hawke presses, "So you were partying with your friends, and you took some drugs . . ."

Zander flinches.

It's a slight movement, but I catch it, my brow furrowing at its strangeness. But then I realize it must be a reaction to the guilt he's feeling. He knows what he did was wrong. I just wonder if he knows how much worse it could have been.

"I was—I was called away from the party," Zander says, and there's a deliberation to his words now, enough that I narrow my gaze, certain he's hiding something. Or perhaps he's trying to remember the script he's had to memorize to make himself seem less culpable. Anger swirls within me at the thought, burning in its intensity. "It was an emergency, and I didn't—" He clears his throat. "I didn't think before getting in my car. All I knew was that I needed to leave, and it couldn't wait."

My blood is roaring in my ears now, as loud as the rain pouring down outside.

"I know I was lucky," Zander says quietly. "When I hit that tree, I could have died. Or—Or—"

"Or someone else could have," I rasp out, the words torn from a deep, broken place inside me.

At the pain in my voice, Zander's eyes shoot from the fire to me, and he searches my face with concern in his gaze. But I can't stand to look at him right now, so I stare down at my hands, clenching them in my lap, my fingernails digging into my palms.

"I know I was lucky," he repeats slowly.

I can barely hear him over the shrieking in my mind.

"And I know I was let off lightly. It was—It was stupid, what happened. What I did. It's the kind of regret I'll have forever, even if I'm grateful there was no lasting physical damage. For me, or for anyone else."

He stops talking, and Hawke asks him another question, but I don't hear what it is.

Regret.

He used the word *regret.*

He doesn't have the first clue what true regret is. He can't possibly.

But I do.

I live with it every day, the searing, relentless agony of wishing I could go back in time and change something—*anything*—about the night my life imploded.

Regret—I have that in spades.

And Zander . . .

Maybe he's telling the truth about how he feels. But that doesn't excuse what he did.

Because while his actions might not have ended in tragedy, they could have.

God, do I know that.

I close my eyes against the sudden sting of tears. My ears are ringing, my lungs constricting as I fight back everything I'm feeling, but it's useless. Try as I might, I'm no longer able to ignore what has been building in me, not just over the last few days, but over the last six months. Hearing Zander's story firsthand, hearing his so-called *regret,* I feel betrayed in ways he'll never understand. I made the mistake of letting my walls start to crumble around him, and now . . .

Now what he did hurts more than ever.

Because of that—because of *everything*—I can't stop the words from spewing out of me, the filter I normally keep firmly in place bursting like a balloon.

"You're right, you were lucky," I cut Zander off from whatever new answer he's giving Hawke. My voice is hoarse, my emotions spilling over as I share with biting candor, "My mum wasn't so fortunate. She was killed by a drunk driver six months ago. Hit and run." Zander's eyes widen in horror, but I'm not done, the words continuing to tumble from me without restraint. "They found her killer three blocks away, but only because he smashed his car into a tree after he ran hers off the road and left her choking to death on her own blood. If he'd stayed with her—if he'd just waited and called for help—"

I snap my mouth shut, blinking fast to keep my tears from falling as I shove my grief deep down, knowing that if I release it fully, it will consume me.

"Charlie . . ."

I recoil when Zander reaches for me, not wanting his touch. Not wanting him anywhere *near* me. His face is drained of color, but I don't think it's because of Bentley's camera. I couldn't care less about our bargain right now, and if Zander does, he doesn't show it. Instead, I see the realization in his eyes as he suddenly understands why I hate him:

Because six months ago, I lost my beloved mother. And three months later, he was arrested for the same crime that killed her.

He might not have been the driver who hit her, and he might not have injured anyone the night of his accident, but to use his own word, that was pure luck.

My mum wasn't so lucky.

Neither was I.

Because the night she died, my world fell apart.

And nothing I do will ever change that.

She's gone—forever.

Zander opens his mouth to say something, but I'm barely holding myself together, my defenses weakened after two days of getting to know him, of actually beginning to *like* him, coupled with the exhaustion I feel deep in my bones. I can't take any more tonight, so I rise swiftly to my feet, not looking at anyone as I say, "I'm tired. I'll—I'll see you all in the morning."

And without waiting for any of them to try to stop me, I grab my bag and retreat to the furthest wall of the cave, turning my back and allowing a single tear to roll down my cheek as I pray for the peaceful oblivion of sleep.

Zander

I don't sleep a wink that night.

Every time I close my eyes, all I can see is Charlie's pale, broken expression as she shared about her mother's tragic accident, and the accusation in her eyes, as if I were the one who killed her.

I understand now—this is why she hates me. Because in her mind, I'm just like the man who mowed down her mom; in her mind, I made the same stupid, selfish, *hateful* decision that he did.

The thing is . . .

That's not what happened.

Not entirely, at least.

And I need to find a way to explain that to her.

It won't change what befell her mom, and she may not even believe me, but I need her to know the truth about the night of Summer's birthday. No—I *want* her to know the truth. But I can't do that with Bentley's cameras rolling, since it's not only my truth to share, and I won't risk the rest of the world hearing it. Charlie, however . . . she needs to know. And maybe, just maybe, she'll stop hating me once she understands.

I'm not sure if that's possible, though, considering I can't stop hating myself.

Just not for the reasons she might think.

Memories play across my mind as I toss and turn for hours, the pouring rain offering a perfect soundtrack to my stormy thoughts. I recall Summer's birthday dinner and how the arrival of so many others turned our quiet evening into a boisterous party, something that Summer despised. But she'd been gone from LA for so long that she felt bad turning anyone away, so she—and we—put up with the added company. Maddox alone managed to sneak off before things became too wild. But his reason for doing so—

My thoughts are interrupted when I hear a rustling sound from Charlie's direction, and I listen hard as she rises from her makeshift bed. I realize with some surprise that the rain has stopped—I have no idea when that happened—and there's a faint golden light bathing the cave as the rising sun breaks through the dispersing clouds.

Charlie yawns quietly as she stretches and stumbles outside, and my pulse kicks up speed knowing this is the perfect time to catch her alone. Hawke and Bentley are slowly beginning to stir, so now might be the only chance I have to speak to her without my words being caught on film.

I give her a few minutes of privacy before I hurry out of the cave, shielding my eyes against the early-morning sun. It's amazing how clear the sky is after the deluge we had, even if there are more heavy-looking clouds looming in the distance.

Glancing left and right, I consider which way Charlie may have gone, then decide she would have headed where the trees are the thickest. I venture after her, trying to take in the view over the mountain, but fog covers the valley beneath us, making it impossible to see how far up we made it before seeking refuge. I feel safer knowing there's no sheer cliff nearby, which means no imminent need to climb up or rappel down anything. Maybe Hawke will give us a reprieve today, given how soaked everything is around us.

The ground beneath me squelches as I move deeper into the trees, calling Charlie's name so as to not catch her in a compromising position. When she appears, her face is both surprised and guarded.

"Is everything . . . all right?" she asks hesitantly.

I wonder if she's hoping I'll ignore what she revealed about her mom so she doesn't have to think about it, and so nothing between us changes. At any other time, I would follow her lead and respect her wishes, but this is too important for me to let it lie.

Despite my resolve, the words get stuck in my throat when I try to speak them, so instead I say, "I wanted to check on you. After—After last night."

If anything, that raises her defenses more, and I curse myself for not just speaking my mind.

"I'm fine," she says coolly, crossing her arms and peering down the steep slope of the mountain. It's still impossible to see anything beyond the heavy fog. "If you're worried about what I said and how it made you look—"

"No, no." I raise my palms. "That's not what I—" I shut my mouth and run a hand through my hair, knowing I need to just get it over with. "There's something I want to tell you while the cameras aren't on us. Something about my DUI."

She steps back automatically, mud sloshing under her boots. I can hear running water nearby, falling somewhere off the mountain, and some distant part of my mind recognizes that as odd, given that I can't see the source. But I think nothing of it, my focus entirely on Charlie.

"I don't want to hear about it," she says, her voice hard. "I'm sure you have a million excuses, and a million more from your PR team, but nothing you say can make me overlook what you did."

I shake my head and step toward her, stopping only when she takes another step away, since I don't want either of us to end up too close to where the mountain angles sharply downward.

"I'm not expecting you to overlook it. I just want you to understand why I did it."

She laughs bitterly. "You really think that will do you any favors?"

I move forward quickly, taking her hands in mine before she can retreat again. "*Please*, Charlie. Let me explain. If you don't like what I have to say, you can keep on hating me. I just—I want you to know the full story. That's all I ask."

Something about my begging reaches her, and she tilts her head to the side, her violet eyes holding mine. I have her attention now, and since this is the only opening she may ever give me, I take a deep, steadying breath, and say, "The night of my DUI, when I was at Summer's birthday, I—"

"There you two are."

Damn it.

I close my eyes and clench my jaw at Hawke's interruption, my opportunity lost. Charlie tugs at my hands, so I release her and turn toward the survivalist, noting that, like us, he's fully dressed, though he also has a rope slung around his shoulders and his hunting knife at his belt. Bentley is yawning beside him, holding one of the larger, handheld cameras and aiming it in our direction.

I try to catch Charlie's gaze, hoping she can read the frustration in my expression, along with the promise that I'll find a way to explain everything when we're alone. But she shows no reaction; if anything, she looks like she has to work even harder to hide how much she loathes me. All the progress I made with her over the last two days has vanished—we might as well be right back where we started.

"It looks like there's more rain coming, so we should take advantage of this break in the weather while we can," Hawke says, closing the distance between us. "I also think we should—" He stops suddenly and glances down at the ground, frowning at the mud. "Can anyone else hear that?"

All I can hear is the squelching of Bentley's boots as he moves closer, along with the earlier sound of rushing water, only louder now. It's almost as if it's flowing directly under our feet, but that can't be right. I assume there must be a runoff somewhere nearby, a creek that's turned into a waterfall or—

Hawke's eyes round with panic, and he shoves Bentley backward, before lunging for Charlie and me and yanking us with him.

But it's too late.

Because whatever Hawke heard, whatever warning the water sound revealed to him, there wasn't enough time to pull us clear of the earth before it erodes beneath us, crumbling away into nothing.

And then we're falling.

Charlie

A scream leaves me as the forest floor gives way, sending me plummeting down the steep slope of the mountain on the world's muddiest waterslide. I was closest to the edge, so I'm leading the fall, but I can hear Zander, Hawke, and Bentley all tumbling with me, none of us having realized that the deluge from last night must have carved a channel for the rain to flow through—a channel that was *beneath* us. We're entirely at the mercy of Mother Nature as we plunge downward, zigzagging around roots and boulders and trees and shrubs, having no control over the direction we move or the speed at which we fall.

I expect to break my neck any second now, my life flashing before my eyes. There's so much more I want to do, so much more I want to see, so much more I want to experience, all of which I've only just begun to acknowledge over the last few days. But now—

Another scream leaves me as I suddenly lift off the ground and fly through the air. It feels like I'm suspended for years before I land unceremoniously in a pool of deep, muddy water. The sole thought in my mind—other than to marvel that I'm still alive—is that I need to get out of the way before three large male bodies crush me, so I half-swim, half-scramble through the sludge, barely making it a few feet before the others splash into the pool behind me.

I'm covered in so much mud that it takes three swipes at my face before I can clear my eyes enough to see properly. I'm also trembling fiercely and struggling to believe I'm not dead, but I force my incredulity aside to do a quick inventory of all my new aches and pains. Miraculously, apart from some light grazes and numerous bruises, I'm unharmed.

"Is everyone all right?" Hawke asks from the middle of the pool, swiping mud from his own face.

Zander is equally filthy and only manages to nod along with me, both of us too shaken for words.

Bentley's glasses are gone, his camera has disappeared, and he's pressing a hand to his head while looking dazed, but he also confirms he's fine.

Hawke glances up at the chute we all just slid down—which is still flowing in a sludgy cascade—and there's a thoughtful look on his face as he murmurs, "That wasn't supposed to happen."

I have to bite my cheek to keep from screaming, *WELL, OBVIOUSLY!* and instead lead the way toward the edge of the pool, slushing into the shallows and crawling on my hands and knees until I'm free of the squelching mud. It's almost worse to be back on solid land, because now sodden leaves and forest gunk stick to the grime covering us, making us look like swamp creatures straight out of a low-budget horror film.

I clean myself as best as I can, wiping my clothes and skin and grimacing at how much muck is wedged in places that will make hiking a special kind of unpleasant. But then I realize we have bigger problems than my physical discomfort.

Zander, also wiping away mud, comes to the same realization, his eyes widening in alarm as he says, "All our gear is back in the cave."

There's not so much as a backpack between us, and given how rain-soaked the slope is, there's no immediate means for us to hike back upward, especially without any proper climbing equipment other than Hawke's rope.

"That's actually the least of our worries," Hawke says, his voice uncharacteristically strained.

I belatedly notice that he hasn't risen to his feet like the rest of us. Instead, he's sitting against a tree, holding his leg.

No—not holding it.

Cradling it.

"You're hurt!" I cry in dismay, squelching my way over to him.

Bentley curses under his breath and reaches Hawke first, kneeling down to check the damage. They share a loaded look, and I instinctively know I'm not going to like whatever they say next.

"Your ankle?" Bentley asks, carefully rotating the muddy boot.

Hawke nods. "I landed badly when we fell—I'm pretty sure it's broken." His voice is still strained, but it's also level enough to hide the extent of the pain he's undoubtedly feeling. He's clearly in survivor-mode, his mind jumping to solutions rather than dwelling on problems. A broken bone is nothing compared to a lion attack, but even so, I'm amazed by his composure—at least until he adds, "But that's still not our biggest concern."

"*How* is that not our biggest concern?" I demand, panic welling in me as I wonder what could possibly be worse than him—our leader and guide—having a broken foot.

There's a look of apology on Hawke's face, as if he's dreading what he's about to share. "I'm not sure if you were paying attention during our unscheduled mudslide, but we . . . got tossed around quite a bit."

That's the understatement of the century.

"And we're now way off course," Hawke continues. "As in, *way* off course." My stomach hollows out at the grim look in his eyes, a feeling that grows exponentially when he adds, his voice full of regret, "And I can't walk."

I swallow back my fear and say, "We'll take turns carrying you. And we'll get back on course."

It seems like an easy answer to me, and I'm the least survival-y of us all, so I'm certain Hawke will agree. Carrying him will be difficult—he's not a small man—but between Zander, Bentley, and me, we'll make it work.

Hawke, however, *doesn't* agree. Instead, he shakes his head, his apologetic look returning. "You're not understanding me. When I say we're off course, what I mean is that we're at the base of the mountain, but on the *wrong side* of the mountain. No one knows where we are, and even if they did, you heard Scarlett last night—the support team has to wait for any flooding to clear before they can return. Not to mention, more rain is coming, which will only lengthen the delay." He points up through the tree canopy to the approaching clouds. "I wouldn't be surprised if they call off any attempt—but even if they *do* risk it later today, they're still not going to know where to find us."

My throat turns dry. "What are you saying?"

"I'm saying we're on our own." Hawke glances down at his leg, before amending, "Or rather, *you're* on your own."

Zander squelches up beside me, his voice tight. "What do you mean by that?"

Hawke shares another loaded look with Bentley, then pulls his park map from his pocket and lays the waterlogged paper over his lap.

"We're due at our extraction point tomorrow afternoon at five o'clock." He points to a circle marked in black ink. "There's a chopper arriving then, and you two"—he eyes Zander and me—"will need to be there in time so you can tell them where we are and have them send a rescue."

I turn solid as the words repeat in my mind.

Zander, too, is frozen beside me, and he slowly says, "*Us* two?"

"I can't walk," Hawke states again, matter-of-factly. "And to reach the extraction point, there are obstacles on the path that you won't be able to carry me over."

I'm about to ask what kind of obstacles, though I'm guessing they're similar to those we've already navigated—climbing and rappelling and God knows what other horrors, all of which would be impossible with a broken ankle. But Zander speaks before I can find out for sure.

"There has to be another way," he says, his muddy brow furrowed. He wipes gunk from his watch and holds out his wrist. "What about the GPS trackers in these?"

It's Bentley who shakes his head. "They only work when synced up to the nano drones."

"Which Scarlett deactivated last night," Hawke reminds us, unnecessarily. "So they're only good for telling the time, and using as a compass or light."

"All our trackable gear is back in the cave, including my cameras and our sat phone," Bentley says. "So electronically speaking, there's no way for anyone to find us."

If there's one upside to all this, it's that we're no longer being filmed, so we can be as candid as we want without having to worry about a global audience. But I would take all the cameras in the world if it meant we weren't facing an *actual* survival situation.

"You both look scared," Hawke observes.

An incredulous laugh leaves me. "What do you expect after you just told us we have to leave you here and—" I stop, my eyes flicking to Bentley, then back to Hawke. "Wait, why did you say only Zander and I need to head to the extraction point?"

"Someone has to stay with Rykon," Bentley answers for him. I'm about to point out that perhaps it shouldn't be the only other person who has any real survival experience, but he continues before I can, "And I'm not leaving my husband behind."

My shoulders fall at the unyielding set of his features.

Zander must see it too, because he sighs from beside me and asks, "What do we need to do?"

Hawke motions for us to come closer, then presses his finger to the map. "At my guess, I think we're about here. You'll need to share this location with the rescue team, so take a good look."

Peering down at the paper, I notice a dotted line marked from where I assume we started, leading directly to the circled extraction point. To my untrained eye, the place Hawke is now pointing to doesn't seem as off course as he implied, only a slight distance away from the inked route.

When I mention this, he nods and says, "That's my hope, since you'll need to get back on track as quickly as possible if you're to have any chance of reaching the extraction point in time."

I wonder why he made such a fuss about us being "way off course" earlier, but then I recall that the support team won't be returning if it's too wet, so it ultimately doesn't matter how close—or not—we are to where we should be. We're still lost, Hawke still has a broken ankle, and even if we find our way back onto the prearranged route, there's no guarantee anyone will come for us. The only guarantee we do have is the helicopter arriving at five o'clock tomorrow.

"What happens if we don't make it there in time?" Zander asks.

"The chopper will leave, and when they can't get in touch with us, they'll send out a search party," Hawke answers.

Relief hits me. "Why don't we all just wait together, then? It's only one more day. Better safety in numbers than us splitting up—isn't that the first rule of survival?"

But again, Hawke shakes his head. "Do you remember when I told you how big the park is? The Greater Blue Mountains Area is over one million hectares. Even if they narrow that down based on the route we're supposed to take, it could still take days for them to find us without any of our tracking gear. Weeks, maybe. Possibly months."

"But you're a *survivalist*," I say. "You can keep us alive out here."

"Ignoring my current injured state, yes, you're right," Hawke says. His eyes are serious as he adds, "But if you have the choice of going home tomorrow, or staying out here living off whatever food and water we can find—bearing in mind that we no longer have access to our water bottles or sleeping bags or clothes or shelter or *anything*—then would you really choose not to be rescued at the first possible opportunity?"

I clench my jaw, conceding his point. He didn't even have to bring up how much I hate eating the wildlife, and how I definitely don't want to do that for days, weeks, or months on end.

Months—*God*, the thought of being stuck out here for that long . . .

I'm sure it wouldn't be months. Hawke's team are professionals; they would use every available resource to find us as quickly as possible. And Zander is an international celebrity—his entire fanbase would come searching for him if they learned he was missing. Millions of people would descend upon the park.

But still . . . it would take longer than tomorrow.

Hawke sees the resignation in my eyes, and his own features soften as he says, in a voice full of wisdom, "It doesn't matter how well planned your journey might be, things can still go wrong. Things often *do* go wrong. That's what survival is about—being able to adapt when the ground falls out from beneath you. *Literally*, in our case." He holds my gaze, then looks to Zander. "You two need to adapt now. You need to survive. Because we're counting on you."

I hate everything about this, but I make myself nod, seeing Zander do the same from the corner of my eye.

Hawke sends us both approving looks, before gesturing to the map once more. "The main thing you need to remember is to keep heading northwest. Even if I'm wrong about where we are now, that will eventually get you back to where you need to be. You'll know for sure that you're on the right track when you reach here"—he taps a spot on the paper—"and with any luck, you'll manage that around mid-to-late afternoon today."

Outside of the route marked in black ink, the topographical details are too complicated for me to understand, so I squint at where he's pointing and ask, "What's there?"

"Prior to last night, I would have told you it's a small creek leading to a narrow waterfall," Hawke says. "But after all the rain we had . . . it might not be so small anymore."

Zander's face is pinched in concentration. "Do we have to cross it?"

"Ah, no. You're going to need this." Being mindful of his injured foot, Hawke shifts against the tree and carefully removes the rope from around his shoulders.

The hollow feeling in my stomach returns as dread ices my veins.

"To stay on course, you'll need to rappel down the side of the waterfall," Hawke tells us. I have a full-body reaction to those words, but he isn't done. "Our scouts who chose the path said there's plenty of room on the vertical rock face, so even if the creek is swollen from the rain, you should still be able to stay perfectly dry during your descent. And you've both rappelled now, so you know what you're doing. This is nothing new."

"But—But we don't have our harnesses," I stammer, feeling light-headed at the mere thought of what we'll have to do.

"It's not ideal," Hawke says, his tone deliberately calming, "but you can still rappel safely without being clipped onto anything. Ben?"

Bentley takes the rope and winds it between his legs, across his hip, and up over one shoulder, explaining his actions and showing us how the resistance works.

Hawke catches Zander's eyes and says, "Fair warning, it's a real nut cracker, but it'll keep you secure."

"You just may never be able to reproduce," Bentley murmurs, untangling himself from the rope once his demonstration is complete. Seeing the look on Zander's face, the cameraman flashes a grin. "Kidding. It's not that bad, promise."

At any other time, I might laugh at Zander's expression. But the last thing I feel right now is amusement.

"The waterfall is about three hundred feet high, so it's a big one, but it's also less than what we rappelled on our first day. You're both more than capable of handling it," Hawke says, trying to reassure us. He then clears his throat. "There's just one slight problem."

Something in his tone has me bracing. Zander, too, is brimming with tension beside me.

"All my longer ropes are back with our gear," Hawke reveals, before nodding to the coil Bentley is holding out for Zander to take. "This one is better than nothing, but it's still a little short."

When he doesn't elaborate, I press, "*How* short?"

Hawke looks like he'd rather slide down the mountain again than answer my question. "About two hundred feet."

A wave of dizziness hits me, and I half-wheeze, half-shriek, "*What?*"

"Breathe, Charlie," Hawke says, raising his muddy palms in the air. "I know it sounds bad, but the geography of that area should be mostly sandstone. That means there will be plenty of hand- and footholds for you to use to climb down the remaining distance. Take your time and be careful, and before you know it, you'll be safely back on the ground."

I wish I had his confidence. I wish I had *any* confidence about what's ahead. But before I can properly sink into my ever-growing fears, Hawke continues his instructions.

"After the waterfall, find some shelter for the night. A cave would be best, especially if the weather remains unpredictable, but make sure it's clear of snakes and bats first. And here, take this." He pulls his flint from his pocket and hands it to me.

I turn it in my fingers. "Won't you need it?"

Bentley jumps in to answer, "There are plenty of ways we can light a fire without it. You'll need it more."

Since I don't want to waste time arguing, I shove it into my mud-encrusted pocket, struggling with the grubby zipper before it finally seals.

"Take this as well, just in case," Hawke says, holding out his hunting knife.

I balk, having last seen it used to decapitate the snake, but Zander doesn't hesitate to strap it onto his belt as he asks, "What happens tomorrow? I assume it's not a straight shot to the extraction point?"

"Your morning will be pretty easy," Hawke says, his finger back on the map, tracing the dotted line. "Keep going northwest, and you'll find another slot canyon. It's a dry one this time—part of an abandoned mining route." He pauses. "I mean, it *should* be dry. After all the rain . . ." His brow furrows, before it smooths again. "It's naturally eroded for quick drainage, so as long as there have been a few hours since the last downpour, you'll be able to pass through it without problem. Just remember what

I said about flash floods, and if it starts raining while you're in there, get out, fast." He looks at me and adds, "There are no crawl spaces this time. Some small caves and narrow walls, but nothing that'll traumatize you."

"I'm holding you to that," I mumble.

His mouth quirks, but then he goes on, "After the canyon, you'll have another few hours of hiking before you reach this: your last obstacle."

Zander and I both lean in, and despite my inability to read the map, not even I can miss the line squiggling across the land.

"Is that a river?" Zander asks, frowning.

"Sort of," Hawke says cagily. He doesn't expand, though, only says, "There's a suspension bridge already in place, but it's old—*really* old. There's no telling how long ago it was used. So to be safe, my team has gone ahead of us and rigged some ropes into place that'll keep you secure while crossing it."

I remember Hux mentioning something about that yesterday. At least one of our upcoming tasks will be safe—relatively speaking.

"Once you're free of the bridge, head straight through the trees and you'll see a small clearing where the chopper will land." Hawke taps the map one final time, right where the circle is. "And that's it, adventure over."

Silence falls as everything he told us settles and processes. I can't believe we're going to do this—I can't believe we *have* to do this. I want to argue that we can wait for the earth to dry out and then find a way back up to the cave without risking another mudslide, but the weak spring sunshine isn't going to make quick work of that, and with more rain coming, there's no way to know how many days it would take. I also can't forget how we had to climb a sheer cliff during our hike up the mountain yesterday, and we no longer have long enough ropes to do that again, let alone a grappling hook and jumar. The cave simply isn't a feasible option. But that leaves us having to do *this*—Zander and me taking off on our own in search of a rescue.

My eyes unconsciously slide to him only to find him already looking at me. After what he said last night, and what he now knows about my own tragic past, he's the last person in the world who I want to be stuck with while Hawke and Bentley rely on us to get help. I don't care that he sought me out this morning, that he has some explanation for his decision to drive while intoxicated—there's nothing he can say that will justify what he did. But even though the cameras are gone and I no longer have to keep up a pleasant charade for the sake of our bargain, our new circumstances mean that I *still* have to set my resentment aside, if only so we can survive what's ahead.

I did *not* sign up for this.

Not even Ember in all her fangirling excitement would have signed up for this.

And yet, here I am.

Here *we* are.

All I can do is make the most of it and try my hardest to avoid dying. If that means I have to grit my teeth and partner with Zander for the next thirty-four hours, then so be it.

My face is hard as our eyes remain locked, and I wonder if he can read what I'm thinking in my expression—and how much he's experiencing for himself. Is he as frustrated as I am? As nervous? As determined to survive so we can get the hell out of here and never see each other again? I can't tell. All I know is that this rescue mission is resting squarely on our shoulders, and no matter what, we can't fail.

On that thought, I turn back to Hawke and Bentley, offering my quiet but firm vow: "We won't let you down."

Equally solemn, Bentley says, "We know you won't."

Hawke refolds his map and hands it to me. "Remember, five o'clock tomorrow. If you're not there in time—"

"We'll be there," Zander says, his voice so full of confidence that even I believe him.

Hawke looks proudly at us both. "You have everything you need within you to make it through all that's ahead. Believe in yourselves. *Trust* yourselves." He pauses. "And trust each other. You're stronger together than you are apart. Don't forget that."

Neither Zander nor I look directly at each other, though we both nod our agreement.

And then, with a final promise that they can count on us, we leave Hawke and Bentley behind as we wander off into the wild, with nothing but uncertainty ahead.

Zander

It's been hours since Charlie last spoke to me.

At first, the silence was natural while we processed the unexpected change in plans, but as we squelched our way through the forest, it grew to the point that it's no longer comfortable.

I've tried to engage her in conversation, but there might as well be a gaping chasm between us. I desperately want to clear the air by sharing my full story, but her defenses are so solidly built right now that I can tell she won't be receptive to anything I say. My only consolation is that there's no rush anymore—the cameras are gone, so there's plenty of time for me to explain what really happened the night of my DUI. Until she's ready to listen, I can deal with the tension between us, even if it does mean there's nothing to distract me as we head toward the route marked on Hawke's map.

When we finally stop for lunch, I'm tired, hungry, and aching not only from the physical strain of the last few days, but also from all the bumps and scrapes I received as we slid down the mountain. I'm also itchy as heck and chafing in places that should never be chafed, thanks to the dried mud covering every inch of my body. Charlie must be feeling the same, because when we halt upon reaching a small, clean stream, she immediately kneels on the bank and begins scrubbing her flesh. I join her, both of us washing as best as we can without risking hypothermia. We're not particularly successful, but when we stand, shivering, we can at least see each other's faces again.

"I think I spotted a lilly pilly bush back there." I point in the direction we came from. "Berries for lunch?"

Charlie nods, then utters her first words in what feels like years: "I saw some wood sorrel as well."

I grimace at the thought of having to choke down more of the bitter weed, but since beggars can't be choosers, I say, "Lead the way."

Together we scavenge as much food as we can carry, and we're just about to sit and eat it when Charlie reaches deeper into the lilly pilly bush for some riper berries hiding at the back. The next thing I know, she's yelping and cradling her hand to her chest, hopping up and down with her eyes squeezed shut.

"What? *What?*" I cry, dropping my pile and lunging for her. I frantically search the area for danger—a snake or spider or anything else that might have bitten or stung her—but there's nothing.

"No—it's—I'm okay," Charlie hisses through her teeth.

She opens her palm, and relief hits me when I see the source of her pain, though I also wince at the thorn sticking out of her skin.

"I didn't notice the vine until it was too late." She scowls down at the prickly weed next to the lilly pilly bush that must have spread into the berries. "Stupid thing."

"Here, let me see." I reach for her hand, and she reflexively curls it tighter against her body. I step closer, gentling my voice. "Please, Charlie. Let me have a look."

She bites her lip, uncertain, but I just hold her eyes—and my breath—as I wait.

Finally, she lowers her hand, allowing me to take it in my own. I try not to show how elated I am that she's granting me this small amount of trust. I only wish I didn't have to do what has to come next.

"We need to remove this," I say, examining the thorn. It's not deep, at least, more like a splinter than anything else, but it'll hurt like hell until it's pulled out. "You ready?"

"Just do it quick," Charlie says, turning her face away.

"On three," I warn, bracing her hand with my left, while I clasp the thorn with my right. "One—"

I yank the barb from her flesh.

Charlie curses and tries to jerk free of my grip, but I hold firm.

"You said on three!" she accuses, her eyes like lightning.

"And you said to do it quick," I return. "Now stop tugging and let me clean it."

Before she can argue, I smush some lilly pillies and smear the juice over the shallow puncture wound.

"Um, what are you doing?" Her tone tells me exactly what she thinks about me gooping up her hand, but I don't stop.

"Hawke said they have antibacterial properties, remember?" I use his hunting knife to cut a strip from my thermal shirt, then wrap it around her palm. "You don't want this to get infected."

"I can barely feel it now. It's not even bleeding, so this really isn't necess—"

"Better safe than sorry," I murmur, concentrating on my task. Once I'm satisfied that I can do no more, I release her and finally glance up to see her watching me, her face unguarded for the first time all day.

"Thank you," she says quietly, examining her freshly bandaged hand. It's overkill, given how superficial the wound is, but I meant what I said about being cautious.

"Don't mention it," I reply, then realize how close we're standing and step back quickly, running my fingers through my tangled, mud-dried hair.

We gather our fallen lunch and return to the stream, finding a damp log to sit on as we eat. I hate this awkwardness between us, and I hate that I don't know what to do about it. I also hate that it's forcing me to wonder if every interaction between us over the last couple of days has been fake. I know our bargain is the reason Charlie agreed to play nice for the sake of the cameras—and I now understand why that was such a sacrifice for her—but I thought . . .

I guess I hoped it wasn't all an act. That maybe there was something growing between us. Now, however . . . I have no idea where we stand.

Glancing at the stream, memories of my birth parents unconsciously flood my mind. I wonder if this is what it's been like for Charlie the whole time we've been together—if, in the same way that I see a creek and think of what happened to my family on the day of our ill-fated camping trip, she's triggered to think of her mother whenever she looks at me. The idea that I might be causing her emotional distress makes my heart ache, and I long for a way to help soothe her pain. My parents died over a decade ago, and while I will never stop missing them, time has dulled my grief. Her mom has only been gone for six months—I don't know how she's even functioning right now.

All of this keeps rattling around in my head as we finish our lunch and continue onward, pausing every so often to lick raindrops off eucalyptus leaves in an effort to stay hydrated. Around mid-afternoon, the clouds that have been threatening all day finally begin sprinkling lightly down on us. It's nothing like the deluge from yesterday, though it's steady enough to make our hike more arduous. The only benefit is that it helps clean more of the muck from our bodies without us having to risk washing in the icy mountain water, so if nothing else, I'm grateful to have some relief from the chafing mud.

But my relief slowly turns to anxiety as the hours pass without any sign of the creek Hawke said we need to find. I know there's plenty of time before tomorrow's extraction, but there's still a lot of ground to cover between now and then, and we can't risk falling behind. Because if we do—

No, I won't let myself consider it. Hawke and Bentley are relying on us, and we won't fail them. We *can't* fail them.

"Should we check the map again?" I ask Charlie, despite it being less than ten minutes since she last pulled it from her pocket.

"What's the point, when neither of us can read it?" she returns.

I almost correct her, since technically, we *can* read the map—or at least, we can follow the dotted line, even if we can't decipher the landmarks—but there's enough of a bite to her voice that I sigh and let it go.

When the rain grows heavier, I start to become genuinely nervous. It's still nothing like yesterday's downpour, but the drizzles are now weighty droplets, and the sky is darkening, warning us that we're running out of daylight. I check my watch and realize with some alarm that sunset is just over an hour away, and if we don't look for shelter before then, we'll be stuck searching after nightfall.

But then—

"Do you hear that?"

Charlie and I ask the question at the same time, and we hurry forward through the trees toward the sound of flowing water. I should be relieved, since it has to be the creek Hawke mentioned, but the noise keeps getting louder and louder until we step out of the forest to find the source, and any excitement I feel swiftly turns to dismay.

"Small?" Charlie splutters, staring at the raging torrent before us. "*Small?*"

My voice is strangled when I reply, "Hawke did say the rain might have swollen it."

Charlie is too horrified to respond, her face as pale as the gurgling rapids.

"Hey, we don't have to cross it, remember?" I say, trying to ease her dread. "It doesn't matter that it's larger than expected—this changes nothing for us."

Her gaze finally leaves the water only to focus incredulously on me. "If this is what it looks like here, what do you think the 'narrow waterfall' is going to look like? Do you really think it's going to be the trickle Hawke implied?"

I blanch, acknowledging her point. But the waterfall isn't visible yet, and with any luck, the river—definitely *not* a creek—will shrink before then.

"Let's just wait and see," I tell her. "It might not be so bad."

Turns out, I'm right.

It's not bad.

It's whatever comes *after* bad.

Because when we follow the river around a bend, the roaring grows ever louder until we finally stagger to a halt at the view of the immense waterfall plunging out of sight.

This time, it's Charlie who sounds strangled. "You were saying?"

I'm lost for a reply, unable to do anything but gape at the colossal amount of water streaming over the cliff. At any other time, it would be beautiful, one of nature's hidden wonders, but knowing we have to find a way down it makes me feel like there are ants crawling around in my stomach.

I try to muster some reassurance for us both, and I settle on saying, loud enough to be heard over the roaring falls, "Hawke seemed confident there'd be enough rock for us to rappel down without getting wet, so let's move closer and see what we have to work with."

On the plus side, the rain has paused, almost like the heavens have decided to give us a break for a change. Either that, or they're laughing because they know we're about to get soaked in a different, much more thorough way. My apprehension is at an all-time high as Charlie and I carefully approach the cliff, but I exhale in relief when I see that Hawke spoke true about the spacious rock face. The torrent is strong enough that we won't be able to avoid the spray—I can see the sandstone we'll be descending is darkened by water—but we won't have to battle the deluge itself.

"Ugh, that's high," Charlie moans, placing a hand over her eyes. "I was never afraid of heights before this trip."

I don't think she's afraid of heights now—it's more that everything about our situation has us both brimming with unease. Even I feel a wave of dizziness as I look toward the base of the waterfall, where the river continues raging on a white-water current around a bend and out of sight.

"There's about an hour left of usable light, so I figure we have two options," I say, still having to speak loudly to be heard. "We can follow Hawke's instructions and rappel down this now, then find shelter for the night once we reach the bottom. Or we can backtrack and search for a place to sleep up here, and tackle this"—I jut a finger out over the edge—"tomorrow."

"I don't like either of those options," Charlie states. "But if it rains more in the night, there will only be more water in the morning, and we'll also have to make up the time we lost. So let's just get it over with."

That's my thinking as well, so I nod and unwind the rope from around my shoulders. "Help me find somewhere to tie this."

We seek out a thick tree trunk as close to the edge of the cliff as possible, neither of us forgetting Hawke's warning about the rope's limited length.

"You first, or me?" I ask Charlie once we've both double-checked the knot is secure.

She glances over the edge, her voice shaking as she answers, "I don't mind."

The lie is clear to see—as is her fear—so I wrap the rope around myself the way Bentley demonstrated, and say, "I'll shout once I'm as far as I can go, but keep an eye out in case the water is too loud for you to hear me."

"Are you—Will you—" She swallows, then tries again. "You'll wait for me before you continue climbing down?"

I wish I could give her a comforting hug without her wanting to shove me away. Instead, all I can do is say, "Of course I'll wait for you. We're in this together, Charlie."

She swallows again, and this time it looks painful. But then she nods and says, "See you soon."

I truly hope that's the case, since it will mean Bentley's no-harness rappelling technique has worked and neither of us has plummeted to a watery grave. I don't say what I'm thinking, though, and only offer a slight smile—the best I can manage—before I shuffle in reverse toward the cliff, then slowly lean my weight out over the edge.

It's an entirely new kind of terror, relying on the rope to hold me while knowing I'm not clipped onto anything. But I force my breathing to remain steady and my mind to stay clear as I work my way into a horizontal position perpendicular to the rock face, not allowing myself to think of the panic attack I had during our last rappel, since one here would be disastrous. The water is gushing only a few feet away from where I'm hanging, the spray like little icy daggers spearing my skin, but that's not my only concern. I didn't anticipate how hard it would be to keep my hands from slipping on the rope and my feet from sliding on the wet, mossy sandstone. It takes all of my concentration just to keep lowering myself safely, my muscles straining and body screeching as the rope digs into my flesh. Hawke wasn't wrong about his "nut cracker" warning, and when I finally reach the end of the rope and find a narrow ledge to rest on, I grimace and wonder if I'll ever be able to walk properly again.

"I'm clear!" I shout up the waterfall. "Your turn!"

I don't think Charlie hears me over the roaring, but I can see her head peeking out at the top of the rock, and I wave my arms to indicate I'm free of the rope. She disappears, and the next thing I see is her tangled up like I was and leaning backward over the edge of the cliff.

My heart is in my throat as I watch her, more nervous now than when I was navigating the descent myself. If she loses her grip—if she slips—if anything happens to her—

Every part of me is tense as I wait for something awful to happen, but Charlie is rappelling like a pro, and she soon sets her feet down on the ledge, trembling but safe.

"Let's never do that again," she says, freeing herself from the rope and pressing her back against the sandstone, moaning when she sees how far we still have to go.

"Hawke was right about the hand- and footholds," I say, trying to keep positive. "See? There are heaps of places we can use to climb down."

What I don't mention is how little confidence I have in those hand- and footholds, given the crumbly nature of the sandstone. And that's ignoring the slippery moss and lichen covering the rock, the water spray making everything more perilous.

I realize we're both stalling as we glance down at what's ahead, so I stand taller and say, "We're committed now. As you said before, let's just get it over with." Her throat bobs, but she doesn't argue when I add, "I'll go first again; stay close enough to watch what I grab onto."

With that, I lower myself down from the ledge, searching with my boot for a hollow in the rock wall, then a place to grip with my hands. Carefully, ever so carefully, I begin the downward climb, uttering a warning to Charlie whenever I encounter a crumbly or slippery hold. It's slow going, and my shoulders feel like they're tearing out of their sockets, but I finally land on another ledge that's large enough for us to pause and rest, with her joining me a moment later. We're both panting and sweating despite the frigid spray hitting us, and I take a second to massage my arms and neck, seeing Charlie do the same.

When our breathing returns to normal, I peer out over the ledge in search of the next foothold, my stomach sinking when I see that the nearest one is going to be a stretch for me, and there's no way Charlie will be able to reach it with her shorter legs. I keep looking for something else that might work, but there's nothing in range. There's only one solution I can think of, and I already know she's not going to like it.

"I'll have to lower you down," I tell her, showing her how far away the foothold is. "It's our only choice."

Her eyes widen and she backs away from me, before stopping quickly as she remembers how narrow the shelf is that we're standing on. "Nuh-uh."

I knew that would be her response, but her lack of faith in me still stings.

"You can trust me," I tell her encouragingly.

"No, I can't." The words are instant, like she didn't even have to think about them.

They feel like a slap in the face.

"Charlie," I begin slowly, "I—"

I'm unsure what I'm going to say, but she interrupts me before I can figure it out.

"I can't trust you, Zander. I don't. I *won't*," she declares, her voice unyielding. "I know you want me to, not just with this"—she waves a grime-covered hand toward the rock wall beneath us—"but also with everything else, and it's just not going to happen."

All day, I've been trying to find the right time for this conversation, and if ever there was a *wrong* time, it would be while we're resting precariously halfway down a waterfall. But even so, I can't help the response that leaves me. "Maybe if you'd give me a chance to explain—"

"No, we're not doing this." Charlie gives a sharp shake of her head. "I know there's some big secret you think will help make everything magically better between us, but I don't want to hear it. As I said, I don't trust you. And more, I don't *want* to trust you. Not after what you did."

I jerk backward, stunned—and hurt—by her candor. But she's not done, everything she's bottled up until now streaming out in its own toxic waterfall.

"You made a selfish decision, and you could have killed someone," she states, her expression as hard as her words. "That's inexcusable. Any explanation you have for it won't change anything—and it certainly won't absolve you. And while some people might be able to ignore it or forgive it, I'm not one of them. So let's just do what we must to get down this cliff and make it to that helicopter tomorrow, and then we can be done with each other. Agreed?"

Her words are ringing in my ears, even louder than the water cascading around us. I know I should let this go, that I should retreat and lick my wounds. She's unwilling to hear anything I have to say—and I'm no longer sure I want to tell her. But there's something rising within me, a need to defend myself against the injustice of her accusations, and I don't have the strength to fight it back anymore.

"I know you're hurting because of what happened to your mom, and I understand why it's making you feel the way you do about me," I say, trying to keep my temper in check. "But there are things you don't know, Charlie."

Her eyes flash with warning. "Don't talk about my mum. Not when it could just as easily have been *you* who killed her."

Hearing that, my remaining thread of patience dissolves completely, and I snap, "You aren't the only one who lost a parent to a drunk driver. I was seven years old when both of mine were taken from me, and there's no way—*no way*—I would ever willfully risk doing that to someone else. So stop acting like you know anything about me and my so-called choices, because if you'd only *listen*, then you'd know I was drugged without my knowledge the night of my DUI, and I only left the party because my best friend was about to *kill himself*."

My voice breaks on the words as I remember that horrible, *awful* night: how I received a text from Maddox that made me know something was so very wrong; how I raced to my car, having no idea why I felt so disoriented but ignoring my lightheadedness in my desperation to reach my friend. The memory returns to me with excruciating clarity, my panic, my dread, my terror that I wouldn't reach him in time—

And then the crash.

I'm breathing heavily, hating how everything just poured out of me when I'd intended to share it a much different way. But I'm also hating how angry I am—at Charlie. She has every right to be upset after what happened to her mom, but it's unfair of her to misplace the blame onto me without knowing my story. I wanted to tell her this morning. I wanted to tell her every moment since then. But now—

Now I just want to get away from her.

I can't even look at her, my eyes searching for any other possible footholds so we can get off this damn ledge and put some space between us.

But then she calls my name.

"Zander," she whispers, her voice wobbling.

I drag my gaze back to her, only to find confusion and uncertainty in her features. And heartache. But it's not her own pain she's feeling—it's *mine.*

"Zander," she whispers again, and this time she reaches for me, a slow move of her hand, as if to offer comfort. She steps toward me. "I—"

But whatever she was going to say turns into a scream, because the moment her weight transfers to her new position, the sandstone crumbles out from beneath her.

I don't think, I just act, diving onto my stomach and lunging for her as she falls over the edge. I manage to grab her hand a split second before she drops too far, my fingers circling her wrist like a steel clamp.

"Hold on!" I yell, even though I'm doing the holding.

"Don't let go!" she begs, terror in her violet eyes as she dangles into open air.

Adrenaline is zinging through my veins, my pulse is drumming in my ears, but I still take a moment to anchor myself before I carefully begin to pull her upward. "You're okay—I've got you."

And then I haul her back over the ledge, where she tumbles straight into my arms.

I'm not sure which of us is shaking harder as we hold each other tightly.

That was close—way too close.

But she's safe. We both are.

Until—

With an almighty *crack*, the entire ledge gives way beneath us, and for the second time today—

We're falling.

But unlike with the mudslide, there's nothing to slow our descent as we plummet down the waterfall, down, down, *down*, until we smash through the surface of the raging, icy river.

And then—

Pain.

It's the last thing I know.

Because everything goes black.

Charlie

I'm going to die.

That's my only thought as I hit the water, my nerve endings blaring with agony, the cold sinking into the deepest part of my being.

I'm immediately sucked under, tossed and turned by the weight of the deluge falling on top of me. By some miracle, there are no rocks to crash against, but the current is swift and drags me along, making it impossible to gain any control. It's all I can do to fight my way upward, finally breaking through the surface long enough to gasp in a choking breath before I'm sent straight back under again.

Zander—*where is Zander?*

I can't see him anywhere, the rapids tearing at me as they haul my quickly freezing body along the river, around boulders and bends and down even more waterfalls, albeit mere bumps compared to the beast from which we just fell. Every time I manage to suck in more air, I search desperately, but I still can't see any sign of him.

But then—there he is, swimming ahead of me.

No, not swimming.

He's being dragged along as helplessly as I am. Only—there's something wrong. He's not splashing and struggling and battling the rapids like I am. He's eerily still, his limbs floating lifelessly as the river carries him along, his face turned upward and his eyes—

His eyes are shut.

Panic slams into me and I fight harder than ever against the current, swimming with everything I have. I cry out when a sharp turn nearly sends me crashing into a boulder, my lungs burning as I inhale a mouthful of water, but still I swim, harder and harder, until I finally manage to close my fingers around Zander's arm.

He doesn't respond to my touch, not so much as a fluttering of his eyelashes.

I act on instinct, hauling his unresponsive body closer and kicking with all my might toward the riverbank, then somehow find the strength to heave him out onto dry land. No longer burdened by his weight, I'm nearly torn away by the current again, but I grasp hold of a tree root and pull myself up until I'm free, panting and spluttering on the rocky earth, my heart crashing against my ribs.

"Zander?" I choke out, kneeling over him. "*ZANDER!*"

I'm so frozen that I'm physically aching, but I barely notice, because something else much more important has my attention.

Zander isn't breathing.

For one horrifying moment, I'm paralyzed, but then years of first-aid training kick in and I lunge to check his pulse, finding nothing. I don't allow myself to think before shoving my fingers into his mouth to make sure his airways are clear, and then I immediately begin chest compressions, bearing my whole weight down on him.

"Don't you dare die on me," I command, my words breaking. "*D-Don't you dare.*"

I finish my first set of compressions and hurriedly pinch his nose, placing my mouth over his and breathing air down his throat until his chest rises, once, twice, and then I return to my compressions.

"Zander—*please*—" I beg him, tears streaming down my face as a bone-deep fear begins to swallow me.

How long has it been? How long does he have before—

Suddenly, Zander gives a violent jolt, and then river water spews out of him as he coughs and coughs and coughs, the sound as painful as it is beautiful.

Because he's breathing.

He's *alive.*

My relief would bring me to my knees if I wasn't already on the ground. I don't know when I started fully sobbing, but I'm shaking as hard as he is when I wrap my arms around him, holding him close as he gasps in life-saving air. I know I should move him into a recovery position, but I can't bring myself to let him go.

"Y-You're okay," I tell him, rocking him gently. "You're—You're s-safe."

Pulling back slightly, I frame his face with my hands, shifting wet hair away from his eyes. He's dazed and disoriented, and still breathing hard, but he's finally starting to come back to himself.

"Please say something," I whisper, tears continuing to roll down my cheeks. I have no idea how long he was unconscious for—how long he was *dead* for. The cold water will have worked in his favor, but there could still be brain damage if his oxygen supply was cut off for too long. If I was too slow in getting him out of the water—if I didn't move fast enough when I—

"Charlie," he breathes my name, halting my spiraling thoughts. He leans forward until his forehead is resting against mine. "Charlie."

That's all he says, but it causes a new sob to leave me, and I pull him even closer, tightening my embrace.

We hold each other like that for long enough that our breathing settles, but if anything, we're shaking more now, as both shock and cold set in. Dusk is well on its way, and we need to find shelter, preferably somewhere dry enough to light a fire. It's already going to be difficult since it's starting to drizzle again, and a quick look upward tells me there's more rain coming. We can't dally on the riverbank, and we should take advantage of our adrenaline while it's still coursing through us.

Yielding to wisdom, I reluctantly draw back and ask, "If I help you, do you think you can walk?"

Zander nods weakly, but it still takes two attempts before I can get him to his feet. Even then, he has to sling his arm around my shoulders to keep from stumbling, his heavy weight like a sack of potatoes pressing down on me.

But he's alive, I remind myself. If I have to carry him through the entire forest in order to make sure he stays that way, then that's what I'll do.

My determination isn't motivated by what he confessed before we fell into the river—though I do feel ashamed after what he shared. I have questions, so many questions, but even if he hadn't revealed what he did, I would still be helping him now. I'm not a monster—I might have loathed him, but I never, *ever* wanted to see him hurt, let alone dead. And the idea of him drowning because I couldn't save him in time . . .

I already know I'm going to be haunted by memories of him being swept away with his eyes closed, then of his motionless chest when he failed to breathe.

"Hey, you okay?" Zander asks me, his voice raspy from coughing so hard.

I realize I'm full-body trembling against him, making our task of stumbling through the trees more challenging, but I'm still incredulous enough to say, "That's my line."

"I'm not the one shaking like an earthquake right now."

"Give it time," I murmur, looking for any sign of a shelter.

The sprinkling rain soon grows heavier, fueling my urgency to find protection from it. It's getting later and darker and—

"Over there," Zander says, pointing through the trees. "I think I see some rocks. There might be a cave."

I move us in that direction, hardly daring to hope, and then nearly sobbing all over again when I see he's right. The cave is mostly buried by the forest and smaller than the one our group slept in last night, but it's out of the elements, which is all we need.

"Sit," I tell Zander, not giving him a choice as I lower him to rest against the inner rock wall. "Stay."

Hurrying back outside, I search until I find a downed tree that still has some dry wood deep within the hollowed trunk. I gather as much as I can and run back to the cave, dumping it on the floor. Belatedly, I realize we didn't check for any native animals, but I'm past caring now—if they're here, they can mind their own business and let us share the space in peace.

I must say that last part aloud, because Zander rasps out a quiet chuckle and says, "Here's hoping they agree with you."

I ignore him and get to work, stacking the kindling among the larger chunks of wood, my hands so frozen that it takes me three tries to unzip my pocket and retrieve Hawke's flint, then another four tries to strike a spark from it. But finally—

"Ahh," Zander moans as the flames lick the wood and warmth starts filling the cave.

It's not enough, though.

The river was too cold and our outerwear is too wet for us to get the heat we need as fast as we need it. Practicality has me crouching beside Zander and tugging at his sleeves as I say, "We need to get your clothes off."

His eyebrows shoot upward. "First you hate me, and then you try to get me naked? I might need a moment to catch up."

My cheeks flush, but I keep yanking until he's free of his sodden coat. "I'm not trying to get you naked. Just strip down to your thermals—they're moisture-wicking so they'll dry quickly, and then they'll help you retain warmth."

I don't address the hating-him part of his comment, since I'm still confused about what he shared earlier. Instead, I leave him to remove the rest of his outerwear while I brave the rain and run back into the forest one last time, heading straight to the sandpaper fig tree I saw when I was searching for firewood. I wrestle off an entire branch full of fruit before sprinting back to the cave, then toss it on the ground and immediately get to work stripping my own clothes. I stop when I'm down to my long-sleeved top and thermal pants, and then I collapse beside Zander and wrap my arms around him once more.

His entire body tenses.

"Body heat," I explain.

Slowly, his arms circle me, as if he expects me to pull away—or to push him away—but if anything, I press deeper into him.

I wasn't lying; we'll warm up faster this way. But that's not the only reason I want to be close to him right now.

I need to feel his chest moving.

I need to hear his heart beating.

I need to feel him *alive*.

And somehow, he senses that, because instead of me offering him comfort after what happened to him, he tucks me in closer and begins to run his hand up and down my arm, a gentle, soothing motion intended to bring me calm. To make me feel safe. All things I should be giving to him.

We sit like that for a long time; long enough for the fire to dry our clothes and burrow into our skin, chasing away the frost of the river, both of us holding each other in silence. Until, finally, I can't keep quiet any longer.

"You stopped breathing."

The words leave me in a whisper.

"I'm sorry," Zander says.

It's the most outrageous thing I've ever heard, and it's enough to have me jerking in his arms and tilting my head back to look at him. Sure enough, his face is full of remorse.

"You can't apologize for *dying*," I state, incredulous.

His eyes hold mine as he replies, "I can apologize for scaring you, though."

I stifle my automatic urge to tell him he's wrong, that I wasn't scared. Because we both know the truth—I was *petrified*.

Softly, Zander goes on, "Thank you for saving my life, Charlie."

I have to shut my eyes at the tenderness in his voice. It doesn't feel right to wave his gratitude aside with a trite response like "You're welcome," so instead I ask, "How are you feeling? Are you in much pain?"

He grimaces, which is answer enough. "Nothing I can't handle."

I touch my hand lightly to his chest, right over where I did my compressions. The bandage he so diligently wrapped around my palm earlier is gone, stolen by the river, but I meant what I told him about it being unnecessary. I can't feel the wound at all now that the thorn is out. Zander, though . . .

"Seriously, did I hurt you?" I press. I wouldn't take it back, but I'll still feel bad if I cracked any of his ribs.

Zander curls his hand around my fingers, trapping them in place. "I'm a little bruised, but it's my throat and lungs that are hurting the most. I must have coughed up the entire river."

"And then some," I say, remembering how much liquid came out of him. I reach for the fig branch, plucking off some fruit and holding it out. "The juice should help."

He doesn't look eager to eat, but when he notices my concern, he forces some figs down. Relief touches his features almost instantly, and his voice is much stronger when he speaks again. "Where did you learn CPR?"

His question is innocent enough, but there are two answers I can give him, one easy, one . . . less so. I start with the easy one. "My boss, Sandy, makes all of their employees take an annual first-aid course because we work with children. There's no harm in being prepared, as Sandy always says."

Zander makes a humming sound of agreement and leans his head back against the wall, his hand resuming its path up and down my arm. I wonder if he knows he's doing it—or if he's realized we're warm enough now that we no longer need to share body heat to stave off the cold. I could move away from him. I *should* move away from him.

I don't move away from him.

Instead, I take a risk, and share, haltingly, "But that's not where I learned it. My—My mum taught me. She was an ER nurse, and since I grew up in a coastal town, she saw so many drownings that she refused to let me go to the beach with my friends until we all learned how to do it."

Zander's hand freezes at the mention of my mother. But then he relaxes again, as if trying to keep me at ease.

Unable to stop myself, I ask, "What you said earlier, about—about your parents . . . is it true?"

For a long moment, Zander doesn't answer. I wonder if I lost my chance to hear his truth by not being willing to listen when he wanted to share it with me, and my heart shrivels in my chest. But then he leans across to where his coat is drying beside the fire and unzips a pocket to retrieve something, before resting against the wall once more.

I recognize what's in his hand: it's the photograph I've seen in the media, the one of Zander fishing with the man and woman who I always assumed were his relatives but not his parents, given that I thought his mum and dad were pictured with him at his movie premieres. But now that I know more about his history . . .

"Are they your birth parents?" I ask quietly, touching the picture. It's laminated, but it has enough wear that I can tell Zander carries it with him at all times.

"It's the last photo I have of them—taken the last day I saw them alive," Zander says, his eyes on the image. "We were on our way home from a camping trip when we collided head-on with a car that swerved into our lane. The driver was seven times over the legal limit, and she still managed to walk away mostly unscathed. But my parents—" His throat bobs. "My parents died on impact."

I suck in a breath. "Zander," I whisper, but I say no more. There's nothing more I *can* say, my own grief hitting me anew. It was the worst experience of my life to have one parent stolen from me—I can't imagine how he survived losing both of his, and at such a young age.

He lifts the hem of his thermal shirt, and at first all I can see is the bruising that's already forming from my compressions, but my guilt is diverted when he runs a finger along a scar traveling vertically down his side. It's long—about the length of my hand—but faded enough that I've never noticed it during the times I've seen him shirtless, both in person and on-screen. Then again, I've also never been this close to his bare torso before.

"Glass from the passenger window," Zander explains. "Thirty stitches." I flinch, even as he goes on, "I don't remember the pain—I just remember being told my mom and dad were gone, and then all I felt was numb."

I know all about that.

It's how I've felt for the last six months, ever since that policeman showed up on our doorstep.

I open my mouth, then close it again, unable to summon any words.

But Zander doesn't need me to. "I meant what I said on the waterfall. I would never knowingly endanger someone else's life, not after what I lost." He lowers his shirt again, unable to hold my gaze as he admits, "But saying that, what happened the night of my DUI was still my fault. I was—I was reckless. I was stupid. Even if I didn't realize just how much."

"I don't understand," I say hoarsely.

"I knew there was something wrong with me." Zander's brow is furrowed in memory. "I didn't know what—I was dizzy and disoriented and nauseous, but I also wasn't thinking clearly, so there's no way I could have guessed I'd been roofied. That was—" He shakes his head. "I still can't believe it, to be honest. But even though I only drank soda that night, I knew I wasn't feeling right, and that should have been enough to stop me from getting in my car."

The self-loathing in his tone indicates this is something he's been struggling with for a while. Normally, I would be agreeing with him—he *shouldn't* have driven off if he was feeling that unwell, despite not knowing the cause—but I also remember what else he said earlier.

"What happened with Maddox? You said he was going to—going to—" I can't bring myself to finish the sentence.

Zander shudders against me, his voice hollow as he answers, "He left the party early—said he had a headache and didn't feel like being around people. I offered to leave with him, but he laughed and told me he didn't need a babysitter, while also reminding me that Summer could use the backup after being away from the city for so long." His gaze turns distant. "There was nothing strange about how he was acting. I've gone back over that night so many times in the last three months, and there was nothing to indicate he was even *thinking* of—"

He cuts himself off, slamming his eyes shut.

I don't press him, giving him the time he needs to gather himself.

Finally, he opens his eyes again, staring into the fire as he says, in a voice full of pain, "Even leading up to it, there was nothing. He's my best friend, and I had no idea what was going on in his head. I *still* have no idea. I just wish—I wish I understood. I wish he'd *told* me. I wish I'd known what to look for."

Now I'm the one rubbing my hand up and down his arm, offering any comfort I can.

A tremulous breath leaves him, and he continues, "I got a text from him while I was at the party, a few hours after he left. I'll never forget what it said. Just six words: 'Love you, man. Don't miss me.'" Zander's face is haunted. "I figured he must have taken some pain meds for his headache and they'd scrambled his words around, or they were making him sentimental or whatever. But then came one more text: 'Take care of Wookiee for me.' That's when I knew something was really wrong."

Seeing my confusion, Zander explains, "Wookiee is his dog. He rescued him as a puppy and loves him more than most people. He also hates being away from him, and since he didn't have any trips planned at the time, his text set off alarm bells, making me read his first one in a new light and realize—realize—"

He stops talking, and this time I do press, "So you left the party?"

A terse, ashamed nod. "All I knew was that I had to get to him. I couldn't think beyond my panic."

I lick my lips. "And—And did you? Get to him?"

"Yes and no," Zander answers. "I crashed right near his house. It was the dead of night, and the sound of crunching metal—" He winces in memory. "Whatever Maddox was intending to do, hearing that stopped him in time. And then pulling me from the wreckage seemed to give him a wake-up call."

I latch onto one word: "Seemed?"

"I haven't seen or spoken to him since it happened." Zander's expression shows how much that upsets him. "I've called him a thousand times, even gone around to his house, both before and after my time in rehab, but he refuses to talk to me. He's my best friend and I—"

Zander's voice breaks, and my heart breaks with it.

With another tremulous breath, he steadies himself enough to say, "I feel like I failed him. He was always smiling and laughing and I had no idea it was covering what he was really feeling. And now that I know, he won't let me be there for him." Zander rubs a hand down his face. "He hasn't stopped talking to Summer, at least. So I know from her that he's been getting professional help, and he's doing better. But he still won't speak to me. Summer says he's ashamed—that he blames himself for me rushing to him that night and getting the DUI, which then caused problems with my career. But I don't think that's the reason. It's more likely he feels guilty because he's one of the few people who knows what I just told you about my parents, so he's also aware that I'd never get behind a wheel while intoxicated—which means he thinks I made that choice deliberately, for *him*. He doesn't know I was clueless about having been drugged, and I don't have a way to tell him and ease his guilt until he's finally willing to speak with me again."

"Can't Summer tell him?" I ask.

Zander shakes his head. "She doesn't know I was roofied."

I blink, surprised. "Why not?"

"Summer already blames herself for my career troubles after I supported her last year," Zander answers, swatting at an insect drawn to the flames. "If she knew I'd been drugged at her own birthday party, and everything that's led to—the 'bad boy' label, the difficulty getting auditions, potentially losing the role of a lifetime—how much more guilt do you think she'd feel? It's absolutely not her fault, but Summer has always felt a lot more than most people. Something like this would devastate her, and that's the last thing she needs while she's still dealing with all her other industry heartache."

I understand his point. "Is that why you wouldn't tell me anything until the cameras were gone?" I don't need him to confirm, since I already know it's true. Well, that, plus his sensitivity toward Maddox's mental health, which I can tell Zander would never want splashed across headlines, even if it could save his own reputation. I gasp as that realization hits me, and I quickly add, "Everything you just said—it's the reason you took the blame for the DUI even though it wasn't your fault, isn't it? You kept quiet about what really happened to protect your friends."

"It *was* my fault," Zander says firmly. "I take full responsibility for getting in that car."

"That's a credit to you," I say, just as firmly, "but it doesn't mean you're not a victim in all of this."

Zander turns toward the fire again. "Nobody likes being called a victim, Charlie."

"That doesn't make it any less true."

We're at a stalemate, until Zander sighs and says, "My two closest friends both blame themselves for everything happening in my life right now. I hate that they feel that way—and that I don't know how to make them stop. One of them won't even *talk* to me." His voice turns impossibly sad as he finishes, "I miss my best friend. Maddox has always had my back, and now that he needs me, I wish he'd let me return the favor. Do you have any idea how much it hurts, not being there for him?"

The words echo in my mind—and in my heart. I think about Ember and all we've been through, how for years I held her hands as she underwent her medical treatments, and then how in the last six months, she's been the one holding me together through my grief. I can't imagine how I would survive if she suddenly vanished from my life.

I curl into Zander, offering the only words I can find. "I'm so sorry. I wish I knew what to say to help make it better." Something comes to me then. "It's not the same, but—" My throat tightens, making it difficult to speak. "My stepdad hasn't been able to look at me properly since Mum died. She was young when she had me, and as I grew older, people always marveled over how similar our faces were. I used to love that, knowing I looked like her. But now that she's gone, I guess—I guess it's too painful for him, seeing her in me. So even though we live in the same house, and we go through the motions, I might as well be a ghost to him."

"Charlie," Zander whispers, before repeating my own words. "I'm so sorry."

I try to shrug, as if that will make the pain any less. "Ember says I need to give him time. And while I don't know Maddox, it sounds like that's what you need to do, too." Quieter, I add, "That doesn't make it any easier, though."

"I've never been great at waiting," Zander says with another sigh.

We trail off into silence, but it's not uncomfortable. I stare into the fire, feeling ashamed all over again for the resentment I've been keeping toward him, especially now that I know the full story. He's right that he's not blameless—he *did* choose to get into his car that night. But if I put myself in his shoes and imagine Ember texting me the way Maddox did, I would have acted exactly like Zander. I would do anything to keep her alive. Hell, I'd do anything just to make sure she's *happy*—as evidenced by me being on this hellish survival trip in the first place.

I want to find a way to tell Zander that I understand what he did. I also want to apologize for how I've been acting toward him since we met. And as hard as it will be, I want to explain *why*—or rather, why *him*—since it's not as if I lash out at every person who has ever driven a vehicle while intoxicated. I think they're stupid and risking so much more than they'll ever understand, and I wish they knew how devastating their choices can be, but I don't take personal offense to their actions like I did Zander's.

However, before I can figure out how to do any of that, the events of the day catch up to me, the flames hypnotizing enough that my head drops onto Zander's shoulder. I don't even realize I'm falling asleep until my eyelids flutter shut, and by then it's too late for me to fight it, or to even think about putting some space between us.

So I don't.

"Charlie, wake up."

Zander's soft voice lulls me from sleep, making me sit up and rub my eyes as I slur around a yawn, "'S time t'go alre'dy?"

But when I blink into awareness, it's still dark beyond the cave entrance, though there's a white glow of moonlight bathing the forest floor, indicating the rain has finally cleared.

"Not yet," Zander says, his voice still soft. "There's something you have to see."

I groan and shove weakly at him. "Sleep now. See later."

Zander chuckles, then takes my hand and drags me to my feet. He gives a grunt of pain, reminding me that only hours ago he was quite literally *dead*, and that sends a bolt of recollected fear through me enough to quicken my waking.

"You should be resting," I say sternly.

"I will in a minute. I just went to get us more firewood."

I glance at the freshly stoked flames. "You should have woken me. I would have—"

"I'm bruised, not broken," he interrupts, squeezing my hand and making me realize our fingers are still entwined. "And I needed to stretch anyway. Who knew falling off so many things in so few days would make every part of me ache?"

His words are lighthearted, but they still make me grimace, because we *have* done a lot of falling on this trip—and we both have the marks to show for it.

I follow reluctantly as he pulls me out of the cave and into the crisp night air. Our thicker clothes are still drying, and I step unconsciously closer to him when goose bumps break out on my flesh.

"It's not far," he promises, leading me into the moonlit forest. The earth squelches beneath our boots, making me wonder how long it's been since the rain stopped—and how long I was asleep on Zander before his midnight wake-up call. Of all the outrageous thoughts to cross my mind, I really hope I wasn't drooling on him when he rose to get firewood.

"Just up here," Zander says, indicating a small incline, at the top of which sits a layered rock formation rising above us.

"Very nice," I say once we reach it, having no clue why he dragged me out of our warm cave for the sake of some stacked boulders dappled in moonlight. "Can we go back to bed now?"

I cringe at my wording, but Zander laughs quietly and says, "We're not there yet."

He points a finger upward, and I balk, realizing he intends for us to *climb* the rocks in front of us.

"Don't you think we've defied death enough times today?" I ask. "Let's not tempt fate."

Zander rolls his eyes and tugs me forward. "Come on, Charlie, where's your sense of adventure?"

Flatly, I say, "It's back at the hotel, where I left it on Tuesday."

"Liar." He shoots me a grin that makes my toes curl. "Ignoring the aforementioned death-defying hiccups—"

"You call those *hiccups*?"

"—there have been moments of this trip that you've loved," he finishes. "Admit it."

I will do no such thing, and only keep tugging against his grip as I say, "We're going to fall and kill ourselves. For real this time."

Zander stops trying to get me to climb, and turns to face me. He's so close that our boots are touching. "Do you remember what I told you when we were about to jump out of the helicopter?"

"I think you mean when you pushed us out," I correct. "There was no jumping. That was a decidedly involuntary move on my part."

His lips twitch, but he says nothing as he waits for my answer, so

I lower my gaze as I shyly recall, "You said you wouldn't let anything happen to me."

He squeezes my hand again. "I meant it then, and I mean it now. I won't let you fall, Charlie. I promise." He pauses, before taking a breath and asking, so quietly that I barely hear him, "Do you trust me?"

I have to close my eyes at the emotion in his voice, remembering what happened the last time he said I could trust him, and how I bit his head off, telling him not only that I didn't, but that I never would. I'd had my reasons, but still . . . he didn't deserve how I treated him.

"I'm sorry for what I said earlier," I whisper, meeting his eyes again.

There's nothing but understanding and forgiveness in his expression. "I know you are." His solemn features turn more playful as he adds, "You can make it up to me now."

I glance apprehensively at the boulders. "If we break our necks—"

"—then it'll be a bonding experience," Zander finishes for me, not taking this seriously *at all*. "Come on, Charlie. Before we miss it."

That sparks my curiosity enough that I hesitantly follow him up the rocks, taking care on their mossy surfaces as we climb higher than our heads, then higher still. Soon we're above the canopy of the trees, and only then do we reach the top, where we come to rest upon a large, flat boulder.

Standing there and staring out over the crown of the forest glittering in the moonlight, with the mountains surrounding us on all sides, I can admit that it's a beautiful sight. But when I turn to Zander, he's not looking at the view.

He's looking up.

I follow his gaze, and a gasp leaves me at the starry expanse stretching above our heads. I've never seen the night sky so clear, the Milky Way so close that I could almost reach out and touch it.

I'm stunned speechless by the magnificence before me. Zander, too, is silent, as if we both fear that uttering a sound will break the magic of what we're seeing. Instead, we sit down on the edge of the boulder, our legs dangling out over nothing but air, our heads still tilted upward as we marvel at nature's most spectacular offering.

I don't know how long we sit like that—long enough for me to begin shivering from the cold, long enough for Zander to pull me closer to his body, long enough for me to not even question it when his arms wrap around me and I curl into his warmth again. I can't remember the last time I felt this safe, and because of that, I take a risk—and open my heart.

"My mum and I used to stargaze," I say quietly. Zander's head turns toward me, but I can't look at him and still share what I want to, so I keep my eyes upward. "There's a lookout near where I live, and she used to take me there on clear nights. We'd bring blankets and snacks and cuddle together as we tried to find different constellations." A sad laugh leaves me. "We weren't very good at it. Though there were a few we could always find." I raise my hand to point them out as I list, "The Seven Sisters"—I move my fingers to the right—"Emu in the Sky"—I move again—"Orion's Belt"—I then stop at four bright stars, with a fifth, smaller one between them—"and the Southern Cross. That one was always the easiest to find. Mum used to say—" My voice is suddenly hoarse, but I make myself go on, "She used to say that as long as I could see the Southern Cross, then I'd always know she was with me, somewhere under the same sky. She said I'd never be alone, as long as I remembered that." I swallow, and it feels like there are knives in my throat. "But then she left me, and—and—"

I can't bring myself to finish. I don't even realize I'm crying until Zander wipes a tear from my cheek. Then another.

It takes me a full minute to pull myself together, and when I do, I inhale shakily and share, my voice barely a whisper, "The first few weeks after she died were like a black hole. I don't remember anything. Ember didn't leave my side, forcing me to eat and drink and sleep. I'd never known grief like that—I didn't know how to process it, physically, mentally, or emotionally. How could I go on when Mum was gone? How could I live knowing I'd never see her again?"

I still have trouble thinking back to those early days when my pain was raw and unrelenting. Even now, I don't want to linger there, so I continue, "But then I found something that helped pull me out of the darkness. Not completely—just enough that I could breathe again. It was a distraction, but at the time, a distraction was exactly what I needed."

When I don't go on, Zander asks, his voice full of all the pain he feels for me, "What was it?"

There's no way for me not to be embarrassed as I admit, "You." I feel him startle beside me.

I quickly explain, "Not *you*-you, though I guess it was, uh, kind of you. I just mean—" I cut myself off before I can ramble too far, and start over. "I told you how Ember was with me constantly, and you already know she's obsessed with you, so unsurprisingly, she was streaming all of the *Lost Heirs* movies on repeat in the hope that it would take my mind off—off everything. And somehow, it worked. Instead of me visualizing Mum's death over and over, I began to daydream about being in the Enchanted Vale with Prince Tyron, and how we would slay dragons together and overthrow the corrupt kings and queens of the Five Realms. It was a pure fantasy playing out in my mind, nothing but escapism from the pain of my real life, but front and center to it all was, well, *you*."

My face heats with my confession, and I keep my gaze firmly on the stars as I continue, "You were my safety net, Zander. I know it sounds mad, and even a bit stalkerish, but you kept me sane during that time. Not just as Prince Tyron, but as *you*." I'm not about to expand on my stalkerish admission by sharing how I watched every interview I could find as a way to feel connected to him. He can fill in those mortifying details himself. "And I know it's not fair of me, but that's the reason why what you did impacted me so strongly. Because I'd finally found something solid to anchor me in the wake of my mum's death, and then, only three months later, your DUI was all over the headlines, and I thought—I thought—" I rasp out the words, "Suddenly, my hero turned out to be no better than the man who killed her."

Zander's arms tighten around me, almost painfully. "God, Charlie, I'm so sorry. I—"

"No, please don't," I say, finally turning to him and placing a finger over his lips. "I understand now, I do. I just—I wanted *you* to understand.

That's why I was so angry at you. Not because of what you did—or at least, what I *thought* you did—but because in my mind, you betrayed me. My escape was no longer an escape. And that meant I had to actually face my grief head-on. It made me feel like I'd lost my mum all over again, and this time, I didn't have a prince in a fantasy world to distract me on my darkest days."

It's humiliating, admitting all of this to him. But it's also liberating. Not even Ember knows how deeply I retreated into my own mind during those early weeks of grief, or about the solace I found there. And she certainly doesn't know what I'm about to share next.

"My whole world fell apart when my mum died, Zander," I say quietly. "I eventually learned how to function again, took myself to work, kept myself alive, remembered how to laugh despite the gaping hole inside of me. And I know all of that will get easier as time passes—as you know yourself. But what I didn't realize until coming on this trip is how I've let my life just *stop.* All the dreams I used to have, all the plans I had for my future . . ." I shake my head. "It's like they died along with her. And I didn't notice. Or maybe—maybe I didn't *want* to notice. Ember told me. Even Sandy told me. I know they've been worried, but I just—it's taken everything for me to survive day to day, let alone beyond that."

Life isn't about survival—life is beautiful, and it's meant to be lived.

More tears well in my eyes as Ember's words return to me, words I gave little thought to when she said them, but now they're burning in my chest.

"I forgot, you know," I whisper in a choked voice. "About this—how big the world is." I gesture to the forest, the mountains, the stars. "Being here these last few days, jumping out of helicopters and crawling through canyons and falling down waterfalls . . . you were right when you said there are parts I've enjoyed." I scrunch my nose and quickly amend, "Not the waterfall part. *That* I could have done without." A shudder leaves me, before I continue, "I used to dream about doing those kinds of things. When I was a kid, I always imagined going on adventures to discover the secret places of the world. My bedroom walls were covered in photos of far-off destinations, my bucket list pages long. Ember was the same—we spent hours making up stories of our escapades, the people we'd meet, the things we'd see, the dragons we'd slay."

There's a hint of amusement in Zander's tone when he says, "More dragon slaying? I'm sensing a running theme here."

My lips curl up at the edges. "So I might have had an overactive imagination *before* daydreaming about being with you in the Enchanted Vale. But I had to start somewhere, and in my defense, Ember and I did mostly stick with the real world, planning all the places we would one day visit: the pyramids of Egypt, the lost city of Petra, the ancient ruins of Machu Picchu and Mesa Verde and Khara-Khoto . . . the list went on and on."

Melancholy hits me, and my voice turns quiet again. "Then Ember got sick, and we stopped dreaming about any of those places and focused only on getting her better. By the time that happened, we were older, and she'd found her love of acting and had new dreams for her future—and I was just so grateful that she was still alive to *have* a future that I didn't take the time to figure out what my own new dreams were. And then—and then Mum died, and after that . . ." I trail off, needing a moment to pull myself together all over again.

In a whisper, I repeat my earlier words, "My life stopped, Zander. I didn't even realize how much I've been missing until everything from the last few days reminded me that there's so much more to living than just being alive." A strained laugh leaves me. "Isn't that crazy? This ridiculous nightmare of a trip, where we've nearly died too many times to count—and you *have* died—is what made me remember how important it is to live. How did *that* happen?"

It's a rhetorical question, so I'm unsurprised when Zander doesn't have an answer.

Sobering again, I say, my voice sad but thoughtful, "I know my mum would have wanted more for me. She'd want me to live my life, and to embrace every moment of it. She'd want me to go on all those adventures I once imagined. She'd want me to see the world and find my place in it, to learn and to love and most of all—" I swallow. "She'd want me to dream again. More than anything, she'd want that for me."

Quietly, oh so quietly, Zander asks, "What do *you* want?"

My answer is just as soft, as if I'm afraid to say the words and what they will mean. But I find my courage and say, "I want that, too. I want to dream again. I want to *live* again."

His arms around me give a squeeze, his voice rough as he says, "I'm glad."

It's only two words, but there's enough emotion in them that I know he's feeling them deeply. Almost as deeply as I am.

Silence falls upon us again, but it's more peaceful than any we've yet shared. More than that, I feel *hopeful* for the first time in a long time. A few days ago I could barely think further ahead than next week, but now, ideas and thoughts are sparking in my mind, memories of long-forgotten dreams being reawakened. My plan had always been to move away with Ember to study once we finished high school, but I realize that's not something I want anymore. Not yet, at least. What I want is everything I just told Zander—I want to see the world, I want to find my place in it, I want to *live*.

I have no idea how I'm going to do any of that, but right now, wanting it is enough. I'm excited about something for the first time in months—*years*, even—and it's such a welcome change from my heartache that I nearly start crying all over again.

Instead, I lean further into Zander, staring up at the stars and letting everything we shared tonight settle deep within me.

It's only when we're both so cold that not even our combined body heat can keep us warm that we finally admit defeat and return to the cave. I don't think twice before wrapping myself around him again, and for the second time tonight, I fall asleep on him. But this time I do it with a lighter heart . . .

And a smile on my lips.

Zander

I wake up with the rising sun—and with Charlie tangled in my arms.

For a moment, I just lie there, holding her, and thinking over everything she told me under the star-strewn sky. I'm both humbled and honored by how much she trusted me with the deepest, most painful parts of herself. I also feel as if a weight has lifted from my own shoulders after everything I shared in this cave, almost as if I can suddenly breathe again. I didn't realize how much guilt I was carrying until I was finally able to speak about what happened with Maddox, and even with Summer. But now Charlie knows everything—and she doesn't hate me. Not anymore. If anything, the way she clung to me last night, and the way she's snuggling into me even now . . .

My heart skips a beat as I look at her, her features soft with sleep. She's always been beautiful, but now that she's lowered her defenses and allowed me to see who she truly is, I have no way to describe everything I feel as I hold her close.

Try not to fall in love with your stalker-fan, or I'll never let you live it down.

I smile as I remember Summer's threat, and how ridiculous I thought her words were at the time. Now, however . . .

As if sensing my gaze, Charlie stirs in my arms, her eyelids fluttering open. For a moment, she's disoriented, blinking around the dawn-lit cave until she finally manages to focus on me.

"Hey," she whispers.

"Hey," I whisper back.

A soft, contented sound leaves her, and she presses deeper into me. Her next words come out muffled against my shirt, so I have to ask her to repeat them.

She pulls away slightly to ask, "Did I drool on you?"

I bite back a laugh, since she absolutely did. Like a lake. "No."

She drops her head onto my chest again. "Phew."

My grin is wide, but only because I know she can't see it. I run my fingers through her hair, enjoying this sleepy, cuddly version of her, and I musingly ask, "What color is this? Purple? Blue? I can't figure it out."

"It's called 'galaxy,'" Charlie answers. She goes on to tell me about a pact she made with Ember years ago when Ember first started her medical treatments and her hair fell out, making my heart warm all the more toward Charlie and the depth of care she has for her friend. She finishes by muttering, "We can't *all* have interesting natural hair, Mister Anime Character."

A startled laugh leaves me. "Mister what?"

Charlie freezes, as if she didn't intend to say that out loud, and she quickly covers, "Ember has a good eye with picking colors for me, but I like this one the most since it makes my eyes look violet."

"Mmm, I've noticed that," I say, pushing her hair back from her face to look into those ethereal eyes.

"They're normally a much more boring bluish-gray," Charlie states, her breathing picking up speed as she stares right back at me, a blush staining her cheeks as she notes how close we are. But she doesn't pull away.

My voice is husky as I say, "I have trouble believing anything about you could be boring, Charlie Hart."

She sucks in a quick, surprised breath, and her blush deepens. Her gaze flicks to my lips, and I shift ever so slowly toward her, waiting to see how she'll react. But again, she doesn't pull away. Instead, she moves closer.

Until—

A loud, gurgling sound rumbles from her stomach, and she slams her eyes shut, her blush becoming red paint splashed across her face. "That's embarrassing," she mumbles.

I try to hold back my mirth, but it's impossible, especially when she cracks one eyelid open to shoot a glare at me.

Our intimate moment is effectively—and regrettably—broken, so I rise to my feet and pull her up with me, saying, "Let's get you fed."

There are a few sandpaper figs left on the branch she brought in for us last night, so we finish those off, before checking the status of our clothes. My hiking pants and fleece pullover are dry enough for me to tug them on over my thermals, but my coat is still soaked from the river. When I peek out of the cave, the sky is clear, just like when we were stargazing, so both Charlie and I decide to risk leaving our heavier outerwear behind. If all goes to plan, we'll be back in civilization before the temperature drops again tonight anyway.

My stomach swoops at the thought of our imminent rescue, anticipation swirling within me—not just for us, but for Hawke and Bentley, too. I know they have plenty of experience surviving in the wild and there's no logical reason to be concerned about them, but I can't help wondering how they fared overnight, stranded at the base of the mountain. Hawke's injury means they have no choice but to sit and wait for us, which only heightens my sense of urgency to get them help. And we will, later today. Because if we don't . . .

No. Positive thoughts only.

I turn my mind to Charlie, pondering what our rescue will mean for the two of us beyond getting the hell out of this forest. We haven't had a chance to talk about what will happen once we're no longer relying on each other to survive, and until last night, she made it clear she was eager to be rid of me. But now . . . I'm hoping that's changed, even if it does create a whole new set of problems, given how vastly different our worlds are—not to mention that we live on opposite sides of the globe. The thought of flying back to LA tomorrow and leaving her behind prompts a tight feeling in my chest, but it eases slightly when I remember what she said about how she's ready to dream again, to see the world, to *live*. Because that more than anything gives me hope that we'll be able to work something out—assuming she feels the same way.

"Ready to go?" Charlie asks, breaking into my thoughts.

I smother the dying embers of the fire. "Ready."

Together we leave the cave, blinking against the early-morning sunlight filtering through the trees. I'm thankful we won't have to deal with the rain again today—especially since Hawke warned about another slot canyon coming up—but even without having to battle the elements, we still have hours of hiking ahead, plus two more of his aptly named "obstacles."

I wince as I consider how much more damage my body will sustain before we're done with this trip. As it is, I feel as if I've been trampled by a herd of elephants, and while my pain isn't as severe as when I first coughed up all the river water, my chest, lungs, and throat are still sore from my near-drowning. Or actual drowning, really. I'm going to need time to process what happened—how I stopped breathing, how Charlie brought me back to life. It hasn't sunk in yet, how close I came to dying. All I know is that I'm immensely grateful to still be here, even if we have a long way to go until we can be considered safe.

Fortunately—or unfortunately, given how it came about—our trip down the river yesterday worked in our favor, since the twists and turns of the rapids sent us roughly in a northwestern direction. According to the map, it hasn't shaved much time off our hike, but it also hasn't added to it, so we consider that a win as we head back to the river and follow the bank, squelching through mud and jumping over roots and saplings the whole way.

The water eventually narrows enough that we're able to use a fallen tree trunk to cross over to the other side—a harrowing experience, and yet nothing compared to what we've faced during the last few days. Charlie even grins as she balances her way along the log, loving every second of her rediscovered thirst for adventure.

Onward we hike, and unlike the discomforting silence of yesterday, today we converse freely. Charlie tells me more about her childhood, both before and after Ember came into her life, giving me deeper insight into her family and her world. I learn how she never knew her biological father but she doesn't feel like she missed out on anything because her stepfather, Jerry, is amazing—when he's not struggling with grief over her mother, that is. I hear how she and Ember wanted to take a gap year after school to go backpacking, but that was derailed by Ember's sickness and then, later, Charlie's sorrow. I also discover that their original plan included them returning from their travels only to move away to university, but when I ask Charlie what she'd intended to study, she admits that she was never able to decide on anything, and she was going to wait to see what course she was accepted into.

To me, it's even more evidence that what she realized last night is what she needs the most right now—to explore the world and find her place in it. When I tentatively mention as much, I'm worried about her response, but she only agrees, shyly at first, before a steely, even excited, determination comes over her.

Back and forth we talk, learning more about each other. She asks about my early years in Montana and California, curious about my life before stardom. I tell her things she'll never find in any online interview, anecdotes I prefer to keep private because of how impacting they were in shaping who I am today—like how my third-grade teacher heard I was getting bullied so she gave me the first book in the *Lost Heirs* series, along with a note that said: *Whenever you need an escape—the Enchanted Vale awaits.*

"In hindsight, she really should have done more about the bullying," I say with a thoughtful frown as I help Charlie over a rotten log. "But I guess she didn't want to inflame the situation, especially since I was so lost in my grief that I wasn't reacting to it anyway."

We continue talking about anything and everything, the floodgates opening when Charlie realizes I don't mind her asking about the movies, at which point she unleashes her inner fangirl. It's cute, something I didn't expect from her, especially given how much she was holding back from me before. I love that she's comfortable being herself now, because that makes it easier for me to be the same in return.

The hours pass quickly as we press on toward our extraction point, both of us aware of the time ticking down, though we're still careful to stop regularly to rest our tired legs and munch on whatever we can forage to keep up our strength.

"As grateful as I am that they've kept us alive, I never want to see another lilly pilly in my life," Charlie declares, glaring at a bush full of pink berries as if they've personally offended her.

Eventually, the trees begin to thin and the ground turns more gravelly and less muddy, before the foliage gives way to a rising rock wall stretching out before us.

"Here we go," Charlie says with a resigned exhale.

"Hawke did say it's a dry canyon," I remind her. "And he promised no crawling this time."

"Hawke also said the river yesterday would be 'small' and the waterfall 'narrow,'" Charlie returns, scowling at the sandstone structure before us, "so forgive me if I have trust issues toward him now."

I turn away to hide my grin, even though I wholeheartedly agree with her.

We have to walk for some time before our map leads us to a crack in the rock large enough to step through, but then we both sigh with relief upon discovering Hawke was right about it being a quick-draining canyon—the ground is damp but nothing worse than that. I'm a little concerned about us getting lost when I see how high the sandstone walls rise above us, creating an open-roofed labyrinth, but the deeper we move into the canyon, there's only one obvious path to take. It almost seems *too* easy, considering the other tasks Hawke made us suffer through.

"I don't like it," Charlie murmurs suspiciously as we wind our way through the yellow-hued stone. "There's a distinct lack of danger. Are you sure this is the correct route?"

"You're the one holding the map," I point out, though I'm also on edge. "And to be fair, there was no real danger with the first slot canyon Hawke made us go through—aside from falling rocks and flash floods and snakes and all the rest."

"Excuse me, but did you somehow forget how we *both* got stuck in that crawl space?" Charlie states incredulously. "How was that not 'real danger'?"

"Come to think of it, I do remember risking my life to come back for you." I send her a wide smile. "You're still welcome for that."

Charlie scoffs. "Risking your life? Hardly. And if we're keeping score, I think there's a firm winner on the scale of who's been saving whom the most."

"'Whom'?" I chuckle. "What are we, the grammar police?"

She opens her mouth to respond, then snaps it shut, before narrowing her eyes and saying, "I know what you're doing. It won't work."

I look at her innocently as we turn around another bend, moving deeper into the canyon. "I have no idea what you're talking about."

"You're trying to distract me," Charlie says, kicking a rock out of her way. "But the joke's on you, because *clearly* there's some kind of Indiana Jones–style mortal peril coming up, and when it appears—"

We both come to an abrupt halt at the sight before us.

Charlie groans. "I *hate* it when I'm right."

In this case, I hate it when she's right, too. Because it looks like we've reached a dead end, the sandstone rising up above us—and that would be okay, if it were true. But there's a narrow opening at the base of the rock near our feet, a swift descent into a hollowed-out tunnel, belatedly reminding me that Hawke said this was an old mining route. What he *didn't* say was how all the rain might have collected in the tunnel, siphoning down the canyon walls to fill the dark, narrow space with water.

"Hard pass," Charlie says, her voice sounding strained. There's a rustle of paper as she pulls the map from her pocket, followed by a quiet curse that tells me what I already know: there's no other way around the canyon if we want to reach the extraction point on time.

I crouch down to get a closer look at where the ground drops away, wondering how deep and long the tunnel is. There's a small gap between the surface of the water and its jagged, rocky ceiling, offering a reasonable breathing space, but I can't tell if it continues the whole way through, since the canyon's limited light only allows me to see a few feet ahead before everything is swallowed by darkness.

I'm not ashamed to admit how much I don't want to swim through an underground tunnel of indeterminate length and depth, with limited room to keep our heads above water, all while being unable to see anything. But then I catch sight of Charlie's watch and remember that it has a built-in light. Mine, too. They're not bright, but since our only other option is to make a torch and somehow keep it dry—while also avoiding smoke inhalation in the restricted breathing space—then I can accept that weak light is better than no light.

"That's not your best argument," Charlie says warily as I press the button on my watch to show her the blueish glow it creates. "You can't seriously be considering this."

It's a statement, not a question, but I still reply, "We have less than four hours until the helicopter arrives, and the map doesn't offer any alternative routes. I don't see another choice."

"But it's—it's—" Charlie gives up mid-sentence and glances fearfully at the black water, holding her elbows. Finally, she says, her voice grumbling but only to hide how tremulous it is, "We only just got our clothes dry."

I can't believe I have to fight a laugh right now. But I *do* fight it, since I can see the terror on her face. I step closer and take her hands in mine. "We'll be quick, in and out," I say, having no idea if that's true, but needing to believe it as much as she does. "It'll be like we're walking, just . . . wet."

She gapes at me. "That's the most ridiculous thing you've said—and you've said a lot of ridiculous things." She shakes her head disbelievingly.

"Wet walking? Are you kidding me with that?" Tugging one hand free, she jabs a finger toward the submerged tunnel. "We have to *swim* through a *canyon*, Zander! Swim! Canyon! Dark! Deep!" She leans into me, her hysteria clear. "Did I mention *dark* and *deep*?"

"There was heavy emphasis on both, yes," I reply mildly, having to repress my laughter all over again, and wondering if she knows how adorable she is. "But just to say, it might not be deep. We won't know until we get in it."

"It's deep," she says with grim certainty. "*Of course* it's deep. It'd be too simple if it wasn't."

I don't utter my agreement, and instead say, "Where's your unfailing optimism, Charlie Hart?"

Her tone is deadpan when she answers, "It's back at the hotel with my sense of adventure. They're vacationing together, having a grand old time without me."

This time, I can't repress my chuckle, but my humor flees when I see her trembling. I draw her close, wrapping her tight in my arms as I say, "I know it's scary—I'm scared, too. But we'll do it together, like everything else. We've made it this far, haven't we? Nothing can stop us now."

Instead of being emboldened, she groans against my chest. "Don't jinx us! Couldn't you have said that *after* we're out the other side?"

I pull back so I can grin down at her. "Don't worry, I'll say it again then, along with 'I told you so.'"

She wrinkles her nose and makes a huffing sound. "No one likes a smug know-it-all, *especially* before they have a reason to be smug."

"Then let's give me a reason," I say, turning her toward the tunnel and moving us both closer to it.

She doesn't resist, though I know every part of her wants to. Instead, she declares, "You're going first. I don't care if I have to push you—I'll do it. Consider it payback for the skydiving."

I was planning to go first regardless, if only so I can help Charlie if she freezes up again like she did during our first slot canyon experience. This one is different, since we won't be wedged between any rock walls—*hopefully*. But it's a new kind of claustrophobia we'll be dealing with, having the added element of water. I'm trying not to think about what happened with the river yesterday, since I know my mind will run away from me if I do. As it is, my heart is beginning to hammer behind my bruised ribcage, a painful reminder that no matter how careful we are, things can always go wrong.

But there's nothing for it, and I need to keep outwardly calm for Charlie's sake, so I draw on my acting skills to appear as unruffled as I can while I lower myself into the water.

A hiss leaves me at the cool temperature, but I can at least say, "It's not as icy as the river." That's one of the benefits of it being rainwater, rather than mountain runoff. A small mercy.

"Oh, good," Charlie mutters, "we can scratch hypothermia off the list. Just three million other things for us to worry about."

I don't respond since I'm concentrating on easing myself down, while silently praying I'll be able to reach the bottom. But the water keeps rising above my hips, my waist, my chest and then to my neck before I resign myself to not knowing the depth.

"Please tell me you can touch the ground?" Charlie begs, watching me with an anxious expression.

I tread water, deciding honesty is best—with a dash of hope. "Not quite, but we'll likely be able to once we're further along." It makes sense, since the tunnel surely has to slant upward again for us to exit it on the other side.

Charlie isn't reassured, but she gathers her courage and crouches on the canyon floor before sliding into the water, yelping quietly at the cold.

"You good?" I ask.

"Far from it," she grits out. "Just go before I change my mind."

Heeding her request, I turn toward the darkness and swim slowly into it, careful to keep my head above the surface. All too soon the sunlight trickling into the canyon fades, leaving us surrounded by blackness, with only the faint glow from our wristwatches offering any reprieve.

"For the record, I hate this," Charlie whimpers behind me, her words hoarse around her panted breaths. Our paddling isn't overly strenuous, so I know it's terror that's constricting her lungs.

"You're doing great," I say, before wincing at how much I sound like Hawke. I try to take her mind off her fear by asking something I've wondered since I first met her. "Why Charlie Bear?"

I sense her confusion even in the darkness. "Why what?"

"Charlie Bear," I repeat. "Ember's nickname for you—where did it come from?"

"Oh." Charlie releases an embarrassed laugh. The sound eases something in me, since it means my diversion is working. I continue swimming forward, listening as she begins her explanation, and hoping she'll remain distracted enough not to notice that the tunnel ceiling seems to be lowering.

"You remember last night when I said I used to dream about going on adventures and exploring the world?" she asks.

I make a sound of confirmation.

"Well, I went through an arctic stage," Charlie admits, still sounding embarrassed. "And during it, I was maybe a *little* obsessed with polar bears."

I smile even though she can't see it. "How obsessed?"

"Obsessed enough to want one for a pet," she answers. "And obsessed enough to cry for days when I kept being told it would never happen. Something about the whole slice-your-throat-open savagery was apparently a red flag. Go figure."

"Shocker," I say dryly.

"Anyway," Charlie continues, "Ember thought the whole thing was hilarious, and somewhere in there she started calling me Charlie Bear as a joke, but it ended up sticking. Just for her, though—no one else calls me that." I hear a splashing sound before she asks, "Did you have any nicknames when you were a kid?"

"Maddox used to try out different names for me," I answer, casting my mind back. "He was big on rhyming, so things like Commander Zander and Zander Panda stuck for a while. But the one that lasted the longest came when we went through our wizards stage—much like your arctic stage, but instead of me daydreaming about a pet polar bear, I daydreamed about having magic."

"We all did that," Charlie says, so matter-of-factly that I snort.

"True," I agree, before continuing, "Maddox was still doing his rhyming thing, and he was testing out Zander Salamander, but somehow it morphed into Salazander. We both thought it sounded epic, so it became my official wizard name." As an aside, I add, "Maddox's was Magic Maddox, shortened to Magidox. So together, we were—"

"Salazander and Magidox." Charlie snickers. "What nerds."

"And proud of it." I grin into the dark. "There's no shame in loving what you love."

Before I can say more, or think of a new distraction, Charlie makes a startled noise that tells me she's finally realized the space between our heads and the tunnel ceiling is considerably less than when we entered the water. However, what she can't yet see is the shadow of something up ahead that has my insides twisting with apprehension.

A few more swim strokes bring us right to it, revealing a sudden drop in the rocky ceiling, effectively blocking our path—or at least, blocking the empty space where our heads are bobbing. When I reach out with my hands, I can feel that the new tunnel ceiling is only a few inches beneath the surface of the water, but it might as well be miles given that no space means no air, and no air means—

"Please tell me that's not what I think it is," Charlie breathes, paddling up beside me.

"Don't panic," I tell her—and myself. "Just . . . wait here, and let me check it out."

"*What?*" she cries, grabbing my arm, and nearly pulling us both under. "*No*, Zander. You—"

"We can't tread water forever," I interrupt, gently but firmly. I'm already feeling fatigued, and I know she must be as well. Soon enough our muscles will start protesting in a way we can't ignore. "I'll swim a little ahead, see where the ceiling rises again, and come straight back. That's all."

"Need I remind you that you *drowned* yesterday?" Her fingers are like a vice. "Tell me honestly that your lungs aren't still sore from that, and you're happy to dive full-body into a dark passage with no air?" She shakes her head wildly, her face as blue as her hair thanks to the glow of our watches. "You're crazy if you want to do this."

"I don't *want* to do it," I state. "But sometimes you have to do things in life that you don't want, so that you can achieve the things you *do* want."

She blinks and stutters, "Did you—Did you just Hallmark-quote me?"

My lips twitch despite myself. "No, I made it up on the fly." I pause. "Or maybe I read it in a fortune cookie. Either way, it's good advice." I hold her gaze and say quietly, and with meaning, "I'll be back before you know it."

I can see she wants to keep fighting me on this, that she's concerned after what happened to me yesterday, and because of that, I know she's about to insist she goes instead, regardless of her own fear. So before she can make that offer, I unlatch her fingers from my arm, take a deep breath, and dive beneath the surface.

I've always been a strong swimmer—aside from yesterday, but that doesn't count since I was unconscious—so I propel my body through the passage with ease, using the glow of my watch to light the way. I keep reaching above my head for any hint of air, but there's nothing beyond solid rock, making my blood pressure skyrocket. If we can't find a way through this tunnel, then we'll have to go back to the canyon, and then . . . what? Search for a way around it? That could take hours. *Days*. There's no way we'd make it to our extraction point on time. This is the path Hawke told us to take, and we *need* to take it. For his and Bentley's sakes as much as ours.

I'm about to admit defeat and turn around when I finally feel a gap above me, and I shoot upward, sucking in a lungful of oxygen. The space is small, only a few feet of somewhat-stale air before the rock dips down again, but it'll work as a place to rest and catch our breath before we continue on.

I debate swimming ahead to find the end of the tunnel, but I know Charlie will worry if I don't return soon, so I inhale deeply again and swim back to her, coughing slightly upon my arrival thanks to my decidedly tender lungs.

I'm barely above the surface when she lunges for me, touching my face, my arms, my chest, as if to make sure I'm truly all right.

"I think I hate you again," she says shakily. "God, you scared me."

"Sorry," I croak out, trapping her still-frantic hand against my heart. "I'm okay. And I found us an air pocket."

"An air pocket?" she repeats dubiously. "Not an exit?"

"I'm sure that's close as well," I lie.

Her lips tighten, but she only nods and says, "Lead the way."

I don't need any more encouragement than that, so I tell her, "Deep breath," and dive under yet again, making sure she's at my heels as I guide her through the tunnel.

Three times we do this, with me swimming ahead to find new air pockets, then returning to lead Charlie to them, moving us ever-deeper into the tunnel. Each time we surface again, Charlie is a little paler, and a lot more shaken—and I am, too. We still can't touch the bottom, but our legs are now cramping enough that we have to rest them by gripping the rock with our fingertips, making our arms ache all the more. I'm increasingly aware that we can't keep this up for much longer.

Finally—*finally*—I see a hint of light ahead during my next scouting swim, and I push myself further than ever to reach it, coughing and spluttering when my head breaks through the surface. I'm so winded that it takes me a moment to get my bearings, but when I do, I find myself in a large pool beneath an open-roofed cavern, the sun beaming down from the gaping hole in the rock, like light from heaven. It's unimaginably beautiful, but my attention is on something much better: the dry ground at the edge of the water, and how it meets a fissure in the canyon wall—one that leads straight outside.

Euphoria fills me, but I only let myself enjoy it for long enough to catch my breath before I dive back under and return to Charlie.

Once again, I have to cough when I reach her in the air pocket, this final leg of the swim so much further than any of the others.

"What happened? Are you okay?" she asks anxiously, while trying to help keep me above the waterline. "You were gone a lot longer this time. Did you—"

"I found the end of the tunnel," I rasp out around my coughs.

The look on her face—I can't tell if she's about to cry with relief, or kiss me. As much as I want the latter, what I want more is for us to be free of this underwater prison.

"Are you sure?" she asks, as if she can't believe it.

"I'm sure." My chest is on fire and my muscles are screaming, but at least now I know the end is in sight. "It's an uncomfortable distance, so you'll need to take your deepest breath yet and swim as fast as you can. And be careful—there are rocks or stalagmites or something rising up from the ground partway along, so don't swim too low or you could hurt yourself."

There's worry in her eyes, but resolve as well. "I'll keep a close watch. Now let's get the hell out of here."

I draw in as much air as I can while Charlie follows my lead, and when we're both ready, I dive under the surface one last time.

My fatigue and pain are becoming an increasing worry the further I propel myself through the tunnel, but I'm more concerned about Charlie. There are no more air pockets between us and the end of the passage, and if she can't hold her breath for long enough, or if she can't swim fast enough . . .

She's fine, I tell myself as I hurtle through the water. *She's right at my heels.*

But when I finally reach the end of the tunnel for the second time, gasping in lungfuls of air, I know within seconds that something is wrong.

Because there's no sign of Charlie behind me.

Charlie

I'm running out of air.

I can feel it, the searing in my chest, the desperation to draw in a breath, the need for fresh oxygen to pump through my veins, but there's nothing I can do, no way to relieve the agony building and building and *building* in me.

Because I'm trapped.

My foot is stuck, the laces of my left hiking boot caught between the rocks Zander warned me about.

I saw them as I was swimming, the glow of my wristwatch illuminating them rising from the unknown depths below, and I gave them a high berth, not even thinking about my trailing bootlaces. But now . . .

Panic grips me as I attempt to yank myself free. When that doesn't work, I reach down to tear my shoe off, willing to sacrifice it to save my life, only to realize all my tugging has pulled the laces so tight that I can't slip my foot out.

A bubble of air leaves me as my terror grows, and I brace my right leg against the rock, heaving my weight against it. I feel like I'm about to snap my own ankle off, but no matter how hard I try, it doesn't give.

I tug and yank and pull and do everything I can to wrench myself loose, but it's no use.

My vision begins dotting, my blood is pounding in my ears, my body shrieks for relief, and I realize I'm out of time. There's no air left in my lungs and my strength is quickly fading; all I can do is kick helplessly at the rock, but I might as well be kicking a mountain.

The last of my precious air leaves me, and I know this is it. I want to cry and scream and rage because I only just found the courage to dream again, to see a future, to *want* a future, and now it's being stolen from me. I'll never get to explore the world and go on more adventures. I'll never get to laugh with Ember again, or make sure my stepdad knows how much I love him, or tell Zander that I—

Hands grab me, shocking me enough that I would gasp if I had any air left. But there's nothing; it's taking all of my remaining strength to keep my mouth shut and not inhale the water, though I know I only have seconds before I lose even that small control and my body surrenders against my will.

But seconds might be all I need.

Because Zander is here.

He sees the problem immediately, gives one firm tug to my leg, and when that yields no results, he pulls Hawke's hunting knife from his belt. Without hesitating, he slices it straight through my bootlaces, then wraps an arm around my waist and hauls me backward through the water.

I'm all but limp in his arms as I fight to remain conscious, to ignore the stabbing torment I feel in every part of me.

I can't hold on any longer.

I can't—

My head breaks through the surface and I'm choking and choking and *choking* as Zander holds me against his body, keeping me from dropping back beneath the water, telling me to *Breathe, Charlie. Just breathe.* I barely hear him, unable to do anything but suck in burning, wheezing, painful breaths. Zander is panting with me, holding me so close that I can feel his heartbeat galloping in his chest, echoing my own, as he keeps saying those same words over and over.

Gradually, my agony begins to fade, and my breaths start to slow. I feel as if I've been in a battle, and it's a struggle to open my eyes, but when I finally manage to do so, I want to slam them shut again straight away.

Because we're still in the tunnel.

Back in the air pocket.

No, I think, unable to say the word aloud.

Zander must see it written on my face, because he rasps out, "I'm sorry—this was closer than the other end, and I didn't know if—" He shudders against me. "I wasn't sure how long you had."

He's still holding me, treading water for us both, and the enormity of what he just did hits me.

"You came back for me." My voice is hoarse from both emotion and strain.

"Of course I did," he whispers. He keeps one arm around my waist but moves the other up to frame my face, pushing my hair away before pressing his hand to my cheek. "At the risk of sounding like another Hallmark-quoted fortune cookie, I'll always come back for you."

A half laugh, half sob leaves me, and I lean forward until our foreheads touch. My words are tremulous when I say, "I d-don't think I can do that again."

"We'll wait a minute, catch our breaths." His voice is soft, encouraging. "We're so close, Charlie."

"I n-nearly drowned, Zander," I say, the shock hitting me, causing me to shake all over. "I *would* have, if you hadn't arrived when you did."

His arm at my waist tightens. But when he speaks, he just says, "Don't go stealing my thunder, Charlie Hart. Only one of us gets to drown on this trip. Those are the rules."

His playful tone has me shifting back enough to see the teasing glint in his eyes, though I can also see the depth of fear it's covering—fear for *me*.

He holds my gaze, his playfulness fading as he turns sober and says, "I won't let anything happen to you—I promised, remember? And something to know about me: I never break my promises." His eyes are locked on mine. "We'll go together this time. I'll be right beside you the whole way. You can do this, Charlie. *We* can do this." He pauses. "Are you with me?"

I'm still trembling violently and every part of me wants to say no, but seeing the assurance in his gaze, the confidence, the *promise*, all I can do is whisper, "I'm with you, Zander."

A weighty breath leaves him and, as if he can't help himself, he presses his lips to my forehead, the move so quick that I would wonder if I imagined it if not for the tingling it leaves behind.

"Ready, then?" Zander asks, not giving me time to dwell on his tender action. "One last deep breath."

I follow his lead and fill my lungs with as much air as possible, doing everything I can to ignore my fear of what we're about to do—*again*.

But then Zander is releasing his hold on my waist, only to grab my hand, entwining our fingers as we dive under the surface and shoot forward through the water. It's harder, joined as we are, but I'm not about to let him go, needing to feel him beside me, needing to know I'm not alone.

I see the rocks approaching, glowing blue under the light of our watches, and my stomach clenches as I think about what would have happened if Zander hadn't returned for me. But he did, I remind myself. He came back for me, he *saved* me.

And now the rocks are behind us, our swim strokes steady and sure as we pass right over them.

There's light up ahead, and seeing it makes me want to weep. My lungs are burning all over again, but we're nearly there—nearly there—

Nearly—

—*there.*

We break through the surface, coughing hard and sucking in fresh, clean air for the first time in what feels like years. I'm not sure if it's water streaming down my face or tears, but when Zander guides me toward the shallows of the underground pool we've arrived in and I can finally touch the bottom, it's definitely a sob of relief that leaves me.

"We did it," I say disbelievingly, as I glance around the beautiful, open-roofed cavern. "We actually made it."

The next second, I'm swept up in Zander's arms, water flying all around us.

"Told you so," he says into my ear.

A surprised laugh leaves me as I recall what he said earlier. "Guess you have an excuse to be a smug know-it-all after all."

He draws away again so he can grin at me, his eyes dancing. "I'm only smug when I know I'm right." He winks. "And for the record, I usually am."

"Humble, too," I say, grinning back at him. My relief that we're clear of the tunnel, that we're *safe*, has me feeling as light as a feather, like I could conquer anything. I shake my head and look in the direction from which we appeared, saying with awe clear in my voice, "That was incredible."

Zander stares at me like I've lost my mind. "If by incredible, you mean the opposite, then sure."

"Don't get me wrong," I say, still looking toward the tunnel entrance. "I'm going to wake up with night sweats about this for the rest of my life, but . . ." I bite my lip and admit in a quiet voice, "It's kind of amazing, what we did. Don't you think?"

Zander just keeps staring at me, before pressing his hand to my brow, checking my temperature. "What I think is that you must have swallowed some of the bacteria-laced water and now you're running a fever. The delirium has already set in."

I shove his arm away, unsure whether to laugh or scowl. I settle on rolling my eyes. "You know what I mean. We'll look back on this one day and be proud of ourselves for how we survived. For *what* we survived."

"That's not a 'one day' thing—I'm proud of us now," Zander says. "But we're not in the clear yet. We still have one of Hawke's obstacles left, and we're down to"—he checks his watch—"less than three hours to go."

A whole new kind of fear fills me.

"We need to hustle."

"We need to hustle," he confirms.

Part of me wishes we could stay in the shallows of this ethereal cavern for longer, just to revel in its beauty. Another part of me—admittedly, a much larger part—wishes Zander would wrap me in his arms again, this time closing the distance between us in a way that I so desperately yearn for. From the looks he keeps giving me, I know he wants the same, even if I understand why he's holding back: because if all goes to plan, in three hours we'll be on our way back to civilization, and tomorrow we'll be returning to our lives—*separately*. Starting anything now would only end in heartbreak.

But watching him as he exits the water and holds out his hand for me, I can't help wondering if maybe it would be worth it.

"You coming?"

I startle at Zander's question, realizing I haven't moved, and he's still waiting with his hand outstretched. At his arched eyebrow, I quickly wade forward to join him on dry land. I'm tempted to kiss the ground for how grateful I am to be standing upright again, but I resist the urge and instead hurry with him across the cavern, following the sunbeam spearing down from the open roof until it leads us through a gaping chasm in the rock wall. And then, suddenly, we're outside again, the canyon behind us as if it never existed.

Zander halts as we're about to step back into the encroaching forest and checks the compass on his watch. "Northwest is this way," he says, gesturing to the left.

I pull the waterlogged map from my drenched pocket, grateful that its wax coating has kept it from becoming a pulpy mess after everything it's endured over the last few days.

"I think we're here." I indicate the dotted line leading out of what I assume is the topographical mark for the canyon, before tapping the black circle. "And here's where we need to be by five o'clock."

Zander peers over my shoulder. "If the scale is right, we still have a few miles to go." He squints at the map. "I can't tell for sure, but it *looks* like we only have forest between us and the final river Hawke said we have to cross"—he presses his finger to the meandering waterway—"so hopefully it'll be smooth sailing from here to—"

I slap my hand over his mouth to stop him from finishing. "What did I say about not jinxing us?"

He smiles beneath my fingers, his eyes bright with mirth. "Sorry," he says, the word muffled against my hand.

Feeling his lips move on my skin, electricity sparks all the way up my arm, causing me to shiver. Zander notes my reaction and his eyes change, a different, more heated light entering them as he looks knowingly back at me. I remain suspended for a moment, trapped in his gaze, until I remember where we are and how far we still need to go. I quickly—albeit reluctantly—lower my hand and clear my throat, before refolding the map and zipping it back into my pocket.

"Let's hope you're right and it's just forest—and let's also hope it's all downhill," I say, my voice slightly hoarse. I hate the effect he has on me, almost as much as I love it. It's becoming impossible to deny how much I want to explore what's building between us, but we're on a rescue mission with the clock ticking down, and if ever there was a bad time to consider anything, it'd be now. Zander seems to realize this as well, since the heat leaves his eyes and his face turns serious as he glances in the direction we need to travel.

Together we venture back into the forest, our pace as quick as we can manage without risking tripping over rocks and roots, or slipping on moss and lichen. We're so near to the end of our journey now, and neither of us can afford an injury. If we don't get to the extraction point in time . . . if we miss the helicopter's arrival . . . if we can't tell anyone what happened and send help to Hawke and Bentley . . .

The fears spiral around in my mind as we hurry through the trees, our steps swift enough that we're soon panting, sweaty messes and mutually agree to take a short break. We haven't eaten anything since before we entered the slot canyon, and now that the adrenaline from the underwater tunnel has faded, I'm growing weak from hunger, so it comes as a relief when we find a small clearing with a fallen log we can sit on to catch our breath.

"Choose your poison," Zander says, pointing to a lilly pilly bush and a vine full of wombat berries.

I go straight for the wombat berries, causing him to chuckle. I meant what I said earlier—as grateful as I am for the lilly pillies keeping us alive, I'll be happy to never see another one after today.

We're side by side on the log and munching in silence when Zander asks, "Do you remember when Ollie was filming his promo questions and he asked what we're most looking forward to once we get back?"

I swallow my mouthful and nod, even though I can't recall what answers we gave, just that we were in fake-it mode for the sake of the cameras. How far we've come since then.

Zander continues, "What would you say now, if Ollie were here and asking again?"

I think about it for a moment, unable to decide between clean clothes, a hot shower, washing my hair, a flushing toilet, a warm bed, food that we don't have to forage or kill, and all the other basic comforts that I'll never take for granted again. But I don't think that's what Zander's really asking, so I give it deeper consideration, before finally answering, somewhat hesitantly, "I guess I'm most looking forward to figuring out what's next for me, especially after everything I've come to realize about myself while on this trip."

Zander pops another berry into his mouth. There's a gravity to his expression that I don't understand—or maybe I'm just too afraid to read into—when he asks, "Any thoughts on that yet?"

I offer a wry grin. "I'm still baby-stepping it here. All I know is that I want to see more of the world. I suppose that's where I'll start."

"So you'll travel?" Zander asks, reaching across to pull more fruit from the vine.

"I think so." Nerves bubble in me at the idea, along with an excited thrill. "That was always the plan for this year before everything . . . happened. I doubt Ember will come now since she's busy chasing her acting dreams, but as much as I'll miss her, I'm not going to let that stop me. No more excuses or delays." A thought hits me and I frown. "My passport is expired, though. I'll have to get that renewed, or I won't be going anywhere."

"Well, look at that: you now have step one on your baby-stepping to-do list," Zander says, smiling. "That means you're one step closer to getting where you're going." He cocks his head to the side. "Where is that, by the way?"

"Where is what?" I ask, wiping sticky fingers on my hiking pants.

"Where you're going," Zander clarifies. "First stop is . . . ?"

My mouth opens but no words come out, because I suddenly realize I don't have an answer. All I know is the longing in my heart to explore the beauty this world has to offer, but nothing *specific*. Worry hits me, since how am I supposed to figure out my next steps if I can't even settle on a starting destination?

Seeing my deer-in-the-headlights uncertainty, Zander senses my growing panic and says in a calming voice, "Do me a favor and close your eyes."

My brow furrows. "What?"

"Just trust me."

At his open, encouraging look, I follow his request.

"Good," he says. "Now, I want you to imagine you're at an airport. You've checked yourself in. You're walking onto the plane. You're flying through the sky. Hours pass, and you're ready to climb the walls if they don't let you out soon. But then, finally, the pilot says you're beginning your descent, so you peek out the window and see—"

"Iceland."

The word leaves my lips without thought, and my eyes shoot back open.

"Iceland?" Zander asks, with gentle curiosity.

I'm unsure why I feel so shy as I answer, "Vatnajökull National Park. It's about five hours from Reykjavík. I used to have photos on my walls of the blue ice caves—they're like something straight out of a fairytale, and I promised myself I'd visit them in person one day. And the northern lights . . . . I used to dream of seeing those as well. And of course

Diamond Beach and the Blue Lagoon and the Strokkur Geyser and all the waterfalls and—" I cut myself off, before finishing, sheepishly, "Iceland is where I want to go first."

"It sounds perfect," Zander says softly.

"Have you ever been?"

He shakes his head. "No. We nearly filmed some of the second *Lost Heirs* movie there, but they decided on New Zealand instead."

"Also on my list," I murmur, remembering just how large the world is, and wondering how I'll be able to see it all. Money, at least, isn't a concern, since I've been saving ever since I was old enough to get a job, and I also have my mother's life insurance payout. I haven't wanted to touch it, hating that it even existed, but I know down to my bones that this is something she would want for me.

"What about you?" I ask Zander. "If Ollie re-asked what you're looking forward to, what would you say? What are *your* next steps?"

Zander twists the now-fruitless vine between his fingers. "It all depends on whether the studio lets me stay on for *Titan's War*. If this trip does what it was supposed to and the limited footage we got helps boost my public image enough that I get to keep my role, then it shouldn't be long before shooting begins, so that'll be what's next for me. On the other hand, if the producers aren't satisfied and they decide to terminate my contract . . ." He shrugs, his gaze on his fiddling fingers. "I'm not sure what I'll do, to be honest."

"You won't have to find out," I say with as much confidence as I can. When he looks at me with doubt, even a little fear, I lower my voice and assure him, "Truly, Zander. If you could make me, your harshest critic, come to—to stop hating you"—I can't believe the word that nearly slipped through my lips, and I quickly cover my stumble by continuing—"then you'll have no trouble making the world fall back in love with you. We had entire days of footage before we lost the cameras; that'll be more than enough for them to see who you really are." My mouth curls upward as I add, "And don't forget, you caught a fish with your bare hands, while shirtless. Emphasis on the *shirtless*. That alone will do the job of making sure no one cares about any perceived indiscretions of yours. Trust me, you have nothing to worry about."

Zander's lips twitch. "Are you objectifying me, Charlie Hart?"

I stand up from the log to stretch, tossing over my shoulder, "Have you *seen* your abs?"

A choked laugh leaves him and he rises to join me, both of us preparing to set out again now that we've recharged.

I'm not sure what comes over me, but before we can resume our journey, I turn serious and say, "You're gorgeous, Zander—that's no secret. But I hope you know it goes beyond your looks. What's inside you here"—I press a finger to his chest, right over his heart—"is more beautiful than what's here"—I move my hand up to his cheek, offering the gentlest of touches before lowering my arm again—"and if I can see that after just a few short days, then anyone who can't is an idiot." I hold his gaze as I finish, with quiet solemnity, "And they don't deserve you."

My breath hitches at the look on his face. There's such raw emotion in his expression: gratitude, hope, and a storm of feelings that make me want to throw myself into his arms and never let go. It takes everything in me to resist the impulse, my self-control hanging by a thread.

"Thank you," he finally says, his voice raspy. "That's the nicest thing anyone has said to me in a long time. Maybe ever."

I try to come up with something light and witty to offer in return, if only to bring some levity to the moment, but my mind blanks on anything other than to reply with a heartfelt, "You're welcome."

There's a long beat of silence between us, the air charged, but then a branch snaps off a distant tree and crashes to the ground, reminding us of where we are—and where we need to be.

"We should probably go," I say, with reluctance.

"Yeah." Despite his agreement, Zander only shuffles his feet, before asking, "Is it weird that part of me doesn't want to return home? That I'm nervous about going back to reality? It's not just Titan—everything with Maddox is still so up in the air, and I . . ." He trails off, blowing out a weighty breath.

"Maddox will come back to you," I tell him, full of reassurance. "He's your Ember. That kind of friendship can never stay broken for long. He just needs—"

"—time," Zander finishes for me, sighing. "I know. You're right."

Eager to pull him from the darkness that has gripped him, I offer a jaunty grin and say, "I'm always right. Haven't you figured that out yet?"

His mouth tips upward and some of the heaviness leaves his shoulders. "Now who's being a smug know-it-all?"

"I learned from the best," I say, my grin still in place as I link my arm through his and drag him back into the forest. "For the record, I'll be ready to say 'I told you so' once you've made up and your bromance is back on track."

"Do people still say 'bromance'?" Zander muses.

"Since I am people, and I just said it, the answer is yes," I return.

And so we continue through the trees, conversing freely and living in the moment, while knowing that soon enough, everything will change. We steer clear of discussing what we'll be to each other after today, or even if we'll ever see each other again. It's clear we're both tiptoeing around it, wanting the other to say something first, but neither of us does, and then neither of us *can*, because we soon realize how quickly the time is passing, with less than an hour to go now until we're due at the extraction point—and still one obstacle left between us and rescue.

By mutual agreement, we stop talking and start jogging, then running, then sprinting through the forest, throwing caution to the wind and praying we don't trip over anything. I'm concerned that the land seems to be on an incline instead of traveling downward to meet the river, but when I point this out to Zander around my heaving breaths, he checks his compass and confirms we're still going in the right direction.

Up and up we run, skirting trees and boulders and shrubs, the slope continuing ever higher until finally we reach the top and the ground plateaus. I can hear a distant roaring over the sound of my rapid heartbeat, and a bolt of giddy anticipation hits me as I recognize it as fast-moving water.

"The river," I pant to Zander. "We must be close."

But aside from the trees beginning to thin, there's nothing in sight.

It's only when they clear entirely that Zander and I stumble to a shocked halt, my stomach turning to mush at the view before us.

In an instant, I'm pulled back to our final conversation with Hawke before we left him and Bentley, how he pointed to the squiggle on the map that made Zander ask, *Is that a river?* and Hawke respond, *Sort of.*

In hindsight, I should have questioned his cagey tone.

Because it's *sort of* a river all right, but it just happens to be raging far below us, at the bottom of a jagged, unscalable gorge. And in front of us—

There's a suspension bridge already in place, Hawke's voice returns to me, *but it's old*—really *old. There's no telling how long ago it was used.*

"Sonofabitch," I breathe as I stare at the dilapidated wooden bridge stretching from one side of the gorge to the other.

Fear slams into me, but then I remember how Hawke also said his team had already secured ropes for us, and I peer frantically around for them. I see nothing aside from the ancient, frayed ropes barely keeping the rotted planks aloft, so I ask Zander, "Can you see the safety ro—"

I choke on my words, because I finally spot them.

It takes half a second for me to know we have a real problem.

Because they're dangling uselessly down the opposite side of the gorge.

It takes me another half second to realize what that means:

If we want to make it to the extraction point, then we have to cross the decaying bridge without a safety net—and one wrong step will be the last we ever take.

Zander

Taking in the danger of the task before us, every swear word I've ever known screams across my mind. They only grow louder as I stare at the safety ropes hanging from the far side of the bridge, swaying in the breeze as if to taunt us.

"The rain must have unraveled them from this end," I say, cursing yet more rotten luck.

Charlie glares at them. "So much for being secure."

I shudder at the thought of what might have happened if we'd been using the ropes when they came undone. And then I shudder again when I realize the enormity of what we now have to face.

"We have fifteen minutes," I say grimly, checking my watch. "Hawke said that once we cross this, all that's left is for us to head straight through those trees over there"—I indicate the small thicket beyond the far side of the bridge—"and we should find the clearing for the helicopter."

"That's all well and good," Charlie returns, her voice tight with fear, "but we have to live through this in order to make it to that clearing. And I'm not super confident that's going to happen."

I have doubts as well. "It's your call. If you're happy for us to try crossing it, then we will. But if you're not, we won't."

Charlie makes a frustrated sound. "Don't give me that responsibility! If we die, you'll haunt me forever, blaming me for your untimely death."

Despite my growing dread, my lips still curl upward. "I don't think ghosts can haunt other ghosts."

"You'll find a way." Charlie's face is dead serious. "You're stubborn like that." But then she repeats her frustrated sound and says, "We have to cross it. There's no way in hell I'm going back into that underwater tunnel to retrace our steps to Hawke and Bentley, and we still don't know how long a search party might take to find us. This is our best chance at a rescue. In fifteen minutes, we could be on our way home."

Or on our way to the bottom of the gorge, I think but don't say, because as much as I don't want to do this, I agree that crossing the bridge is our best course of action.

With our decision made, there's no point in delaying the inevitable, so I step forward. "I'll go fir—"

"No." Charlie grabs my arm to hold me back. "I'll go first this time." Her face is pale but determined as she explains, "Some of those wood planks look like the slightest touch will make them disintegrate, and you're heavier than I am. If one breaks beneath me and I fall, you can catch me. It won't work as well the other way around."

"I knew I should have skipped that burger in Katoomba," I mutter, rubbing my flat stomach.

Charlie groans. "Don't make me want to laugh right now. I need all my concentration not to pass out."

"Is this where I remind you that you're the one who wants to go on grand adventures all around the world?" I ask dryly.

Through gritted teeth, Charlie clips out, "No. It is not."

Now I'm the one who has to bite back laughter. But any humor I feel vanishes the moment Charlie moves to the entrance of the bridge, her hands reaching for the tattered ropes strung along the sides and grabbing onto them like her life depends on it—because it *does.*

"I'm right behind you," I tell her, staying close.

I see her shoulders rise and fall as she breathes in deeply to steady her nerves, and I do the same. It does little to calm my racing heartbeat, which only speeds up more when she takes her first step onto the bridge.

Every muscle in my body is tense as I prepare to lunge for her and drag her back to safety, but there's no need, because the wood holds under her feet. She tosses me a relieved smile over her shoulder, and then steps forward again, pausing to make sure I'm following.

My mind blares a warning as I set foot on the ancient wood, my survival instincts screeching for me to back away, but I ignore them and press onward, praying the timber will be strong enough to bear our weight the whole way across.

Step after step we venture over the bridge, balancing our weight on the sturdier outer edges of the planks where they connect to the rope rather than the weaker middle sections that bow worryingly downward.

"You doing okay back there?" Charlie asks.

"I've got the easy job," I say, all of my focus on making sure she doesn't fall. It helps distract me from the gaping holes that have started to gather between the planks the further out we walk, and how the wind is making the bridge swing in an alarming way.

Step.

Step.

Step.

We're halfway across the gorge when the first plank cracks beneath Charlie's boot.

A gasp leaves her and I react without thinking, dropping one hand from the rope to snake it around her waist, hauling her back against my body.

"We might skip that one," she says shakily, patting my hand at her stomach. "Thanks for the quick reflexes."

While the wood didn't snap completely beneath her, the warning crack is still ringing in my ears enough that I don't want to let her go. But we're at the most dangerous point in the bridge and we need to press on, so I hesitantly release her and watch even more closely as she steps over the now-broken plank to settle on the next one along.

"It's solid," she reports, testing it with a small bounce.

"Don't do that," I say sternly, since I know she's only checking to make sure it can hold my weight.

A violent gust of wind steals her reply, causing us both to latch onto the threadbare ropes with white-knuckled grips as the whole bridge sways around us.

"Find a happy place, find a happy place," Charlie chants under her breath once the wind eases enough for us to continue.

When we reach the three-quarter mark, I start to feel tentatively hopeful that we might actually survive this without anything traumatic happening. But just as I have that thought, the gaps between the wood begin to spread even further apart, with some planks missing entirely, while others are broken and dangling vertically into the empty space beneath us. We're left with no choice but to leap the ever-growing distances, placing all our trust in the decaying rope-railing to bear our weight as we do so.

"A safety line would be a *real* comfort right about now," Charlie grits out as she jumps a two-foot gap that offers a view straight down to the churning river below.

My hands are stinging from rope burn, causing me to hiss when I leap after her and say, "If Hawke were here, he might have made us do it without the safety line anyway. What's the point if we're not risking death? There's no fun in that."

Charlie utters a strained chuckle. "Especially when the cameras are rolling. Gotta entertain the viewers."

"Reality television is nothing if not dramatic," I agree, flinching when the wood groans angrily under my feet. I jump to the next plank just as my previous one crumples and falls, the sight of it plunging down into the rapids prompting a wave of nausea in me.

"You okay?" Charlie asks, having heard the noise.

I don't want to worry her, so I answer, somewhat weakly, "All good."

But then—

"Do you feel that?" Charlie whispers.

I don't merely feel it—I *hear* it. A mix of tearing, squeaking, and snapping that accompanies everything around us shaking.

This time, it's not the wind.

I spin around and find the cause immediately, dread filling me at the sight of the worn-out ropes unraveling behind us, our combined weight causing too much strain on the connections.

The bridge is falling apart.

And we're still too far away from safety.

"GO!" I bellow. "Go, go, *go*!"

Charlie's eyes widen as she turns and sees the danger. The next second, she's leaping forward, with me right on her heels. We're reckless now, unable to take the care we need while the bridge begins collapsing around us.

We leap from plank to plank, the wood cracking beneath our feet. My boot goes straight through one board that splinters on impact, and I only keep from falling with it because of my grip on the railing—but the railing is starting to loosen as the ropes continue tearing, taking any security we have with them.

"Hurry!" I urge Charlie.

A quick glance over my shoulder reveals the entire bridge is buckling now, like a giant wave, the ropes snapping free of their connections, the wood falling and crashing into the river beneath us.

"Watch out!" Charlie cries, and I face forward again just in time to see the plank she's on crumble. My heart lodges in my throat, but she manages to get clear in time, and I use my momentum to soar the extra distance to the next safe plank, staying as close to her as I can as we sprint dangerously fast across the last remaining length of the bridge.

We're so near to the end now that hope surges in me once more—only a few more steps until we're safe—but then the loudest *SNAP!* of them all has the entire bridge losing its suspension as the ropes give way completely.

"JUMP!" I yell.

Charlie is one plank ahead of me and she pushes off the wood in the split second before the bridge loses all tension, using her velocity to fly through the air and land in a tumbling, rolling heap atop the side of the gorge.

I'm not so lucky.

The wood beneath me gives way before I can attempt a powerful enough jump, and I realize mid-leap that I'm not going to make it. There's a weightless feeling for all of two seconds before I slam painfully into the rocky escarpment, my hands scrambling for purchase as gravity tries to pull me down the jagged slope and into the raging river far below.

I'm hanging on by my fingertips, and for one optimistic moment, I think I'll be okay as I start to pull myself up. But then the rock crumbles beneath my hands, turning to dust in my grip, and suddenly, I'm falling.

My life doesn't flash before my eyes. I almost wish it would, if only to distract me from the overwhelming grief I feel at everything I'm about to lose. I'll never get to make up with Maddox, never see Summer or my adoptive parents or Gabe again, never know what might have happened with *Titan's War*, never get to tell Charlie how I—

"Got you!"

With two words, my grief evaporates—and my fall stops before it even begins.

Because Charlie is leaning over the edge of the gorge, her face white and her fingers clasped around my wrists in a bruising monkey grip.

"Hold on!" she says, grunting from the effort of bearing my weight.

I snap back to myself and try to use my legs to take the strain off her, but the rock only crumbles more from my efforts. "I can't get any leverage!"

She tightens her hold, her features resolute as she uses all of her strength to haul me upward while rasping out, "We didn't"—*grunt*—"come this far"—*heave*—"for you"—*another grunt*—"to die!"

I finally get my left boot into a solid foothold, and with a mighty push from me and another heave from Charlie, I lurch up and over the edge of the gorge, the force of our efforts sending her flying backward with me landing on top of her.

For a moment, all I can do is lie there, panting and shaking, shock setting in now that I'm no longer about to plummet to my death. Charlie holds me close and rubs my back in comfort, until finally I'm able to pull away slightly. I don't draw back completely, just hover above her, looking down in wonder.

"You saved me," I say, not hiding the emotion in my voice. "*Again.*"

"You saved me in the tunnel," she reminds me softly. "It was my turn to balance the scoreboard."

I think back over everything she's done for me on this trip, from the very first day when I had my panic attack on the mountain. "You're still leading the tally."

"It's not a competition." Her voice is breathy now as she realizes I haven't moved. "But if it was, I'd be winning."

My lips hitch up. Her gaze flicks to them—and stays there. Heat pools in me at the look in her eyes, and I'm helpless to resist the longing on her face. I don't let myself consider all the reasons why this is a bad idea before I lower my head toward hers, moving slowly to gauge her reaction. Everything about her is saying she wants this as much as I do, her hands tugging me closer as one of mine moves to cup her face.

"Charlie," I whisper her name, needing to know that she's real, that she's in my arms—and that she needs me like I need her.

Her lips are so close that I feel her breath on my skin, causing a shiver to roll down my spine even as warmth envelops me, the sensation sending sparks of awareness through my blood. I can't wait any longer to close the distance between us—

But then I hear it.

My head shoots up at the distant *whup-whup-whup* sound of rotor blades slicing through the air.

Charlie's violet eyes turn fearful as she gasps, "The helicopter."

Our heated moment is shattered in an instant, reality crashing over us as we realize what will happen if we don't make it to the clearing in the next few minutes.

I stare back at Charlie as dread floods us both, before I scramble to my feet and pull her up with me, uttering a single word:

"Run."

Charlie

We sprint through the trees as if there's a pack of wild animals snapping at our heels, pushing our bodies faster and faster toward the clearing. I wish I could say all my attention is on the approaching helicopter and making sure we reach it in time, but as I race through the forest, there are only two things bouncing around in my mind:

Zander nearly kissed me.

And I wanted him to.

Desperately.

His lips were *right there*, barely a whisper away from my own. If the interruption had only come a few minutes later, even a few *seconds* later . . .

I shake my head at myself, unable to believe my thoughts. For days, all I've wanted was to reach the extraction point and fly away to safety. And now that our rescue is imminent, all I feel is hormone-driven disappointment. But at least I'm not alone—I saw the look on Zander's face when we first heard the sound of the blades, his frustration as strong as mine. I would snort at our mutual absurdity if I wasn't so focused on not tripping over my own feet as we dash through the last of the remaining trees.

And then, finally, they end, causing us to skid to a halt at the edge of a small, grassy clearing covered in native wildflowers. As stunning as the sight is, there's something even more beautiful before us, something that makes me stop thinking about our almost-kiss and instead stifle a sob of relief.

The helicopter is here, dropping down from the sky to land softly among the flowers.

I turn to Zander, unable to keep the tears from my eyes, and equally unable to resist throwing my arms around him and laughing into his neck.

"We made it," I breathe. "We actually *made* it."

He picks me up and spins me around, laughing incredulously with me, our jubilation like a drug.

But then I sober as I remember—

"Hawke and Bentley! We need to tell Scarlett!"

Zander releases my waist only to grab my hand, leading me in a crouched jog toward the helicopter, where the pilot is sliding open the rear door. I raise my free arm to protect my face from all the dirt and leaves the wind is kicking up, the space around us turning snowy from dandelions losing their fluffy white seeds. I'm sure I must look like a yeti by the time I reach the landing skids and hoist myself into the cabin—mostly because that's what Zander looks like—but I'm too elated to do anything other than dust myself off quickly as I lean toward the front passenger seat, preparing to tell Scarlett everything that happened to us.

Only, she's not there.

No one is.

I frown at Zander as the pilot slides our door shut and returns to the cockpit.

"Excuse me," I shout over the engine, tapping the man's shoulder to get his attention.

He turns and says something I can't hear, so I cup my ear pointedly, prompting him to grab two pairs of familiar aviation headsets and pass them back to us.

Zander and I don them, and Zander instantly asks, "Where's Scarlett?"

"Back at base, waiting for you," the pilot answers around a mouth full of chewing gum. He fiddles with his controls, and a moment later we're lifting off the ground. "I'll have you to her in no time."

"No, wait." I unzip my pocket and pull out the map. "There was an accident. Hawke broke his ankle—he and Bentley need to be rescued."

"I'm not authorized for a rescue," the pilot says, popping a bubble. "I was hired with clear instructions to collect whoever was waiting in the clearing and bring you straight back. No detours."

"But—" I halt my protest when Zander squeezes my hand.

"A few more minutes won't make much of a difference," he says in a calming voice. "And assuming Hawke and Bentley haven't moved far from where we left them, it's going to be tricky for a helicopter to reach them without proper planning. The forest is so dense that they'll need to be winched out—and that'll require a team of professionals who know what they're doing."

I blow out a breath, conceding his point. "It just feels wrong that we're safe and they're still out there."

"I know," Zander agrees, his brow furrowed with concern. "But we only need to be patient for a little longer, and then once we speak with Scarlett, she'll send help straight away. They'll be back with us soon, I'm sure of it."

His confidence is a balm to me, and when he wraps his arm around my shoulders, I don't hesitate to lean into him, finding comfort in his warm, steadying presence. A wave of exhaustion hits me as I rest my weight against him, all of the adrenaline that kept me alive over the last few hours—and days—fading now that it's no longer needed, making it hard to keep my eyes open as I stare out the window at the passing scenery.

"You know what I just realized?" Zander murmurs into his microphone, sounding as tired as I feel.

"What?" I ask.

He's looking out the same window as me when he answers, "We didn't see a single koala. Or a kangaroo. I thought they'd be everywhere." A small pout touches his lips. "Your country has false advertising."

At the disappointed look on his face, a weary chuckle leaves me. "Be thankful we didn't see one when we were with Hawke, or he probably would have made us eat it."

Zander shudders against me, and I echo the motion. But then we both fall silent as we watch the trees and mountains and canyons and rivers sail by beneath us with hushed reverence. I can't believe we were just down there, nor can I believe how many dangers we faced in the last four days. There were so many times we could have been killed, and yet, we survived. I wouldn't wish what we went through on my worst enemy, but I can't ignore the sense of pride and accomplishment I feel now that it's over.

Or, *almost* over. We still need to get Hawke and Bentley to safety before I'll be able to truly relax and consider our adventure complete.

"We're making our final approach," the pilot's voice breaks into my thoughts as the mountains grow smaller and the forest thins out, with patches of civilization starting to become visible. I soon spot a road winding between the trees and wonder if it's the one we drove along to reach the airfield on Tuesday morning.

"There's a strong headwind," the pilot goes on, "so buckle up and brace for a bumpy landing."

I groan as I draw away from Zander to secure myself. "If we made it through four days of hell only to perish in a fiery helicopter crash, I'll be *really* annoyed."

"You and me both," Zander murmurs, tightening the belt around his waist.

But aside from a few jerking dips of the aircraft when we reach the familiar grassy clearing, our landing is otherwise uneventful, enough that I can't help asking, "Is that it?"

The pilot shrugs and pops another bubble. "Tell your people to give me a five-star review. I need the business."

I'm unsure what to say to that, so I just unbuckle my seatbelt, remove my headset, and grit my teeth against the deafening sound of the engine as I wait impatiently for him to open our door. Once he does, I jump down onto the grass with Zander beside me, and only then do I look around properly, becoming instantly confused by what I see.

Or rather, what I *don't* see.

The flurry of activity from Tuesday morning is gone; there are no black-clad crew members moving gear or looking at maps or inspecting equipment. And while that makes sense, since all of that was in preparation for the trip, I still expected there to be *some* of Hawke's team milling about the now-empty hangars, ready to welcome their fearless leader back. Instead, the only thing in sight is a single dark vehicle with tinted windows and the same driver who delivered us here from the hotel four days ago.

"I thought you said Scarlett was waiting for us?" I shout to the pilot over the whirling blades.

I don't think he hears me, because all he does is point toward the vehicle, before sliding the helicopter's door shut and returning to the cockpit.

When it becomes clear that he intends to take off again, Zander and I hurry out of the way, keeping low as we run toward the hangars.

My stomach twists with apprehension as the helicopter leaves, and a million questions are on my lips when we reach the driver, but Zander gets in first.

"What is this? Where's Scarlett? Gabe? Ember? *Anyone?*"

I hadn't even thought of Gabe and Ember, my mind too distracted by everything else. But Zander's right—they knew we were returning today, so why aren't they here to greet us?

"Miss Hart, Mister Rune, if you please," the driver says calmly, opening the rear door and gesturing for us to enter. When we don't move, he straightens his suit jacket and explains, "Ms. Quinn intended to be here in person, but something came up last-minute. She's waiting for you at the hotel. I assume your friends are with her."

It takes me a moment to remember that Scarlett's surname is Quinn, and when I do, I'm even more confused. What could possibly keep Hawke's executive producer from meeting him upon his return?

"I don't like this," Zander mutters beside me, and I nod my agreement.

"We can remain here as long as you wish," the driver says. "However, I don't have the information you seek, so might I suggest . . ." He gestures to the open door again.

Zander and I look uneasily at each other, aware that we have little choice unless we want to walk however far it is back to the hotel.

Warily, we enter the car, and the driver closes the door behind us. My eyes need a second to adjust to the darker interior, but when they do, the first things I see are the bottles of water in the center console, along with the protein bars. Zander notices them at the same time, and we snatch them up, him cracking open a water and tossing back its contents, while I shove a whole protein bar into my mouth, barely chewing before swallowing.

Only when we're well on our way to Katoomba and have finished gorging and hydrating ourselves do we finally sit back and rub our satisfied stomachs. It might not have been a three-course meal, but it'll keep us going long enough to reach Scarlett and share our news about Hawke and Bentley—news I'd hoped she would already know by now.

"This is weird, right?" I ask Zander quietly. "It's not just me?"

"Definitely not just you," he says, peering out the window. There's a frown on his face as he watches the forest-lined road start to reveal houses at the outskirts of town, but it clears when he asks the driver, "Do you have a cell phone we can borrow?"

The man glances at us through his rearview mirror. "I'm afraid not."

I share a look with Zander, before I clarify, "As in, you don't have a phone, or we can't borrow it?"

I get my answer when a ringing sound fills the car. I look at Zander again, both of us even edgier now, and I wonder if we're going to end up on another kind of television show—the true crime kind. But the driver only answers his call politely and a moment later says, "Yes, I have them, Ms. Quinn." Then, "No, no problems." Followed by, "Uh-huh," and "Mm-hmm," and then finally, "We're about five minutes away." There's one last long pause before he says, "Understood. I'll deliver them as close to the entrance as I can get." He then disconnects the call, his eyes returning to his rearview mirror as he tells us, "Ms. Quinn is waiting for you in the lobby along with your friends, Miss Ember Ashley and Mister Gabriel King. They're all very eager for your reunion."

My growing fears about being abducted vanish and I turn to Zander in relief, seeing the same expression on his face. But then I look through the window beyond him to see that the sun is beginning to set, and I nervously ask, "Do you think they'll still send out a rescue in the dark?"

"It's Hawke and Bentley," Zander says, as if that's answer enough. And maybe it is. He reaches for my hand, entwining our fingers as he adds, "They're going to be fine. I promise."

He has no authority to make such a promise, but once again, the reassurance in his tone soothes me and I allow myself to relax slightly, knowing we're doing everything we can, and anything else is beyond our control right now.

But any peace I feel vanishes as we pass through the center of Katoomba and approach the hotel only to see what's awaiting us.

No—*who's* awaiting us.

Because it looks like the entire population of Australia is lining the street and the long driveway all the way up to the front doors of the hotel. The crowd is screaming and waving, most with their phone cameras pointed our way, many with painted signs that they're holding above their heads saying things like MARRY ME, ZANDER! and I ♥ PRINCE TYRON! and I'LL BE YOUR QUEEN! among numerous other messages and requests.

"What on earth?" I breathe as I stare out the tinted windows.

Zander groans. "Hawke's team must have started their early promo for our episode and revealed the location to build hype."

Hype is one word for it.

I gape at the sight of so many people—so many fans. They're all here for a glimpse of Zander, the enormity of his celebrity hitting me like a bucket of ice water. This is his life, his *world*. I can't imagine what it must be like, living this reality day in and day out.

"Now we know why Scarlett couldn't come to us," Zander mutters, his lips pressing together as if he's angry at himself.

But this isn't his fault—he didn't ask all these overzealous fans to come here, nor did he ask them to block the driveway, making us crawl forward at a snail's pace to keep from mowing them down. My patience is growing thin, but our slow speed lets me read more of their signs, surprise hitting me when I see my name.

WE LOVE YOU, CHARLIE!

CHARLIE & ZANDER 4 EVA!

#ZARLIE HAS MY HEART!

"Zarlie?" I wonder aloud, before a quiet snort from Zander has me realizing, with no small amount of embarrassment, that we've been allocated a ship name. Our episode hasn't even *aired* yet, and they're already rabid for us.

"At least they didn't go with Chander," he says, chuckling. "That sounds like something a cat might vomit up."

I send him an incredulous look. "How can you laugh at this? They're *shipping* us, Zander. As in, *romantically*."

His eyes are dancing as he replies, with unmissable meaning, "They're not the only ones."

My cheeks flame as I hold his gaze, our near-kiss blasting to the forefront of my memory. But before I can replay the moment properly—or return us to it in real time, now that there's no incoming helicopter to interrupt us—the car rolls to a stop.

Zander glances past me out my window, his face turning serious. "Quick paparazzi lesson: head down, eyes ahead, don't panic. In a different situation, I'd say you can answer any questions you're comfortable with, or use 'no comment' for anything else, but since we're in a rush to get to Scarlett, best to ignore them today. Okay?"

I barely get a chance to nod before my door is opened by a muscled hulk of a man, one of his hands indicating for me and Zander to exit the vehicle, while the other is stretched out to hold the crowd back. Another equally large man is doing the same just beyond the first.

The screaming reaches fever pitch as I leave the car, and it becomes impossibly louder when Zander slides out beside me. There are only a few feet between us and the front doors of the hotel, but the shrieking horde makes it seem like miles. Bright flashes go off, blinding me, and there are microphones being shoved in my face with reporters shouting questions. I can't make out anything they're saying, my mind freezing. My body, too. But then Zander's arm curls around my waist and I turn to him, feeling instantly soothed by his presence. He smiles encouragingly at me—prompting even more flashes and squeals from the crowd—and guides me forward while the bodyguards clear our path.

It feels like hours but is really only seconds before we're through the doors, the screams and shouts immediately muted, leaving my ears ringing in their wake.

I'm panting as if I've been running, and I wheeze out to Zander, "Your paparazzi lesson could use a few more warnings."

"Are you all right? I know that was overwhelming—"

"It's fine, I'm okay," I say, surprisingly meaning it. That was intense, but it was nothing I couldn't get used to if we—

My thoughts stumble to a halt when I see Scarlett standing in the center of the empty foyer waiting for us. There's an odd, tentative smile on her face, but I ignore the alarm bells her expression raises in me and grab Zander's arm, hauling him toward her.

Before we can make it two steps, a blur of motion has me looking to the left just in time to be tackled by my best friend. I stagger sideways, only managing to keep from falling because I slam into Zander.

"I'm sorry!" Ember wails, her arms so tight that I'm nearly choking. "I swear I had no idea! You nearly died! And Zander *did* die! I promise, I didn't have *any*—"

"Em, what are you—" I don't get to finish before I'm interrupted by another voice, this one deeper, and nearly as tremulous as my best friend's.

"Charlie."

I pull away from Ember, gaping at the sight of my stepdad standing before me, his green eyes welling with tears behind his glasses, his graying hair looking like he hasn't brushed it in days.

"Jerry?" I'm too shocked to articulate more than his name.

The next second, his arms are around me.

"I'm so sorry, baby girl," he whispers in my ear, holding me close. "I didn't mean to make you feel like you were all alone. I should have dealt with my grief better, not made you think I couldn't stand to look at you. I have a lot to make up for, but you have my word that I'll spend the rest of my life making sure you never feel abandoned like that again."

I'm so stunned by his declaration—and his presence—that it takes a moment for me to realize there is something very wrong with what's happening here. My alarm bells from when I first saw Scarlett are turning into blaring sirens as Ember's words belatedly process, because what she said—

I gasp and draw away from Jerry to ask her, through numb lips, "How do you know Zander died?"

The look on Ember's face . . . for the first time in my life, I can't read her at all. But I feel Zander's hand wrapping around my elbow, feel the waves of shock and confusion emanating from him as he turns me toward the hotel concierge desk behind which a muted television is showing—showing—

Showing *us*.

Right here, right now, standing in this very foyer.

I whip my head around, searching for a camera, but there's nothing. I don't understand what I'm seeing, don't understand *how* I'm seeing it, or *why*, but before I can utter a single question, Zander's grip tightens, his face flooding with disbelief as he looks toward Scarlett once again.

Gabe is beside her now, but he's not the reason for Zander's reaction.

No, it's the two other people who have appeared, both smiling just as tentatively as Scarlett.

My blaring alarms become instant, deafening silence.

Because Hawke and Bentley are here.

And there's not a broken bone in sight.

Zander

"What the hell is going on?" I breathe the words, unable to believe what I'm looking at. *Who* I'm looking at.

I can feel Charlie's stunned shock like it's my own—because it *is* my own—but she pulls herself together before I do and tugs me toward the center of the foyer. Ember and the man who I assume is Charlie's stepdad stick to our sides like glue, but I barely notice them, too distracted by the small group in front of us.

Hawke and Bentley—I can't wrap my head around them being here. They're meant to be awaiting rescue at the bottom of a mountain, not standing before us without crutches or a cast or anything else to show that one of them was ever hurt.

A sinking feeling hits me and I glance suspiciously at my agent, but there's nothing in Gabe's expression to indicate whether or not my growing fears are valid, so I return my focus to the other three, waiting on an explanation.

"Before we answer your questions," Scarlett starts, "do either of you require any urgent medical attention? You had a number of close calls that we didn't anticipate, so let us know if you need to get checked over now, or if you can wait until after we talk."

I become as still as a statue at her words, since they make me recall what Ember cried to Charlie upon our arrival: *You nearly died! And Zander* did *die!*

Dread pools in me as a premonition takes root, and I look to the concierge desk again, my eyes on the television screen that's no longer showing us standing here, but something else entirely.

I hear Charlie's voice as if from far away, asking how Scarlett knows about our close calls. I reach for her numbly, turning her toward the television for the second time so she can see the answer for herself.

A news report is on, the journalist sitting in front of a screen that begins to play a highlight reel of footage taken on the early days of our trip, from us jumping out of the helicopter to rappelling down the cliff, navigating the first slot canyon and its crawl space, the Tyrolean traverse across the ravine, the rock climbing up the mountain, and flashes of everything between.

But it doesn't end there.

Because it then shows the mudslide.

And us landing in the pool at the base of the mountain.

I have only one thought as I watch us scrambling through the muddy shallows: Bentley lost his camera in the fall, so this footage shouldn't exist.

Nor should any of the footage that comes next:

Charlie and me venturing forth on our own.

Our waterfall plummet into the raging river.

Her giving me CPR and saving my life.

Us cuddling under the stars.

The underwater tunnel and her near-drowning.

Our mad dash across the collapsing suspension bridge.

Charlie saving my life—again—and me lying on top of her, our lips moving ever closer.

The footage fades out there, leaving the reporter grinning and saying something through the muted screen, but I don't need to hear their words to understand what happened.

We've been played.

My eyes spear toward Scarlett, Hawke, and Bentley, and I instantly see the familiar silver box in Scarlett's hand—a box that is open, and *empty*.

The nano drones.

They were never deactivated.

Everything we did, every word we said . . .

It was all caught on camera, with the whole world watching—and watching *live*, if the first footage I saw of us here in the foyer is any indication.

Charlie is standing so close to me that I'm unsure which of us is shaking more. I feel violated, knowing my unfiltered words were heard by millions. Everything I shared about the deaths of my birth parents, about Summer, about Maddox, about—*God*, the drugging and DUI . . . I'm going to be sick. Charlie, too, revealed things I know she never would have wanted others to hear, especially her grief and her revelations about her life and future. We shared the deepest parts of ourselves, never once imagining that there might be an audience watching as we did so.

I have to swallow back bile as I stare incredulously at Hawke, Bentley, and Scarlett, ignoring Scarlett's question about our health to instead say, through clenched teeth, "Someone had better start talking. Right now."

"It was my idea," Gabe speaks up. "Mine, and Valentina's."

My stomach drops, my earlier fears proving true, even if I still don't understand.

"Who the hell is Valentina?" Charlie's voice is hoarse, telling me that she, too, has figured out that we've been deceived.

"Valentina Martínez, director of *Titan's War*, and close friends with Rykon here," Gabe says, motioning to Hawke. "She's the one who managed to get him and *Hawke's Wild World* on board to help improve Zander's public image. But early approval projections showed it would take more than just a single episode to get the results we needed in the time we had, so we came up with the idea to stream your whole trip—or your waking hours, at least—in order to generate more interest from the wider public. Reality television, uncut."

He misreads our horrified faces and quickly goes on, "Don't worry, we also provided a recap at the end of each day for viewers who only wanted to watch the more dramatic moments, but the unedited streaming option was the real audience-grabber. You should have seen the reaction once people realized they'd get to have unrestricted, real-time access to your adventure, right from their living rooms."

"Real-time," Charlie repeats weakly. "As in . . . ?"

Scarlett jumps in to confirm what I've already realized, "Since the moment you left on Tuesday, up until you set foot in this foyer a few minutes ago, everything you've said and done has been streaming live." She waves the box in her hand, grimacing slightly as she adds, "I may have told a *tiny* fib about the nano drones—they weren't prototypes, and they were fully waterproof. They stayed with you every step of the way, even in the underwater tunnel. I'm actually surprised you didn't notice them there, given how small the space was. But I suppose you had other things on your minds."

Other things—like *not drowning.*

I can't handle what I'm hearing, my body trembling from disbelief and betrayal.

"In our defense," Gabe says, noting my expression, "it's your own fault things got so carried away." He indicates between me and Charlie. "Viewers clued in quickly about the trip being a publicity stunt, but they were intrigued enough to keep watching because of how strained your early exchanges were. It was obvious Charlie was repressing some pretty strong negativity toward you, Zander, which made everyone hungry to know more. Even when you weren't getting along, your chemistry was off the charts, which led to a social media outcry for more 'Zarlie'—as they so aptly named you. So we decided to give them what they wanted, orchestrating a situation where you would be forced together, alone."

Hawke steps forward then, raising his hands in a placating gesture. "It wasn't meant to go the way it did," he admits. "The viewers may have been on board with it, but I still had a duty of care to you both—not to mention, my own brand to protect. Once Ben and I were told about the change in plans, I did what I could to make sure you were equipped to deal with the rest of the obstacles on your own, using the two days we had together to give you similar tasks to tackle. After you had some experience under your belts, I was going to fake an injury—the public voted for a broken ankle—and Ben would stay with me while you two finished the rest of the trip alone. But we didn't anticipate the mudslide and losing our gear, or all the rain that made the final obstacles much more hazardous than they should have been. If we'd known . . ."

He shakes his head in apology, but all I can think about is what he said after we landed in the mud pool at the base of the mountain, his face thoughtful as he murmured, *That wasn't supposed to happen*. His comment had seemed odd at the time, since *of course* it shouldn't have happened. But now I understand—the mudslide wasn't part of the plan, but he capitalized on it to lessen any suspicion Charlie and I might have had about him and Bentley remaining behind, leaving us alone without any cameras.

Or so we thought.

"This is—This is—" Charlie splutters, unable to finish. Finally, she manages to rasp out, "What you did is *completely* unethical. Never mind how dangerous it was for us—which it *was*—but legally speaking, you had no right to—"

"We did, actually," Scarlett interrupts, pulling her tablet from her vest and swiping at the screen. "You both signed consent forms agreeing to be livestreamed."

"We absolutely did not," I grind out. "I read everything I signed, and—"

I stop, realizing that's not true. I read all the liability waivers I filled in before arriving, but I *didn't* read the unending document on Scarlett's tablet that Charlie and I had to sign on Tuesday morning—the same document Scarlett is now turning around to show us, revealing proof of our own idiocy. I should have trusted my gut and read the damned thing, and the only reason I didn't was because Gabe told me it was fine.

I've already read it all and made the necessary amendments, he said that morning.

Necessary amendments—like us agreeing to be abandoned in a survival situation with hidden cameras streaming our every move.

I glare daggers at my agent, but he only looks back at me calmly, making me realize that deep down, I'm not surprised by his ruthlessness. As much as it pains me to admit it, he was doing what I pay him for, and acting in what he thought were my best interests. I needed to drop my guard and show myself as human to the world, so he created a situation in which that might happen.

He's right—in a roundabout, messed-up way, I have only myself to blame.

But Charlie . . .

She's a casualty in all of this.

And when I turn toward her, seeing her pale, wide-eyed face, I can't think of a single way to express how sorry I am to have ever dragged her into this nightmare.

She, however, isn't looking at me—she's looking at her stepdad.

His remorse is visible as he answers her unspoken question, "I thought you knew it was being livestreamed. Ember said it was a competition, so I figured that was public knowledge. And the terms were sound—there were no red flags in the language or I never would have signed it."

I remember now that he had to co-sign as her guardian, since she's underage. He was her Gabe, offering the assurance she needed to place her own signature on the document.

Her eyes close slowly before reopening again, and I feel as if I'm staring into a mirror when I see the storm of emotion in them. But then a steely look comes over her, and she pins a glare on Hawke. "We could have died. Not once, not twice, but *numerous* times. How can you justify—"

"We can't," he says simply, holding her gaze. "I knew the moment you fell from the waterfall that we'd made a mistake, and I didn't breathe at all as I watched you resuscitate Zander. But by then . . ."

"By then, the world was invested," Gabe jumps in.

"And despite Rykon's name being in the title of the show," Scarlett says, "there's an entire board of executives who call the shots. The streaming numbers were so astronomical that they told us to wait and see how it continued playing out."

"We wanted to come and get you," Bentley says, his first words since we arrived. "And we would have, regardless of our orders, if not for the rain starting back up. It's a miracle Scarlett was able to get Rykon and me out during a gap in the weather, but when more rain came, we had to retreat again to avoid the rising floodwaters, so our next chance to reach you wasn't until partway through today. And by then, you'd already entered the slot canyon."

"It was *meant* to be dry," Hawke states, repeating what he told us when we last saw him. "Even with the extra rain, we truly didn't anticipate you having any problems, so we decided to hold off and keep watching from afar. By the time we realized you'd have to swim through the tunnel, it was too late for us to intervene."

"And then came the suspension bridge, which should have been the easiest obstacle of them all, since our safety crew went ahead to secure it," Bentley says. He winces and adds, "Though, uh, you saw for yourselves that the rain caused yet more unanticipated complications there."

"I'd hardly call the entire bridge decaying beneath us a 'complication,'" Charlie grits out. "What would you have done if any of those tasks ended a different way? If Zander hadn't responded to my CPR? If I'd drowned in the tunnel? If we'd both fallen down the gorge? Did you have a backup plan for us dying on live television?"

Hawke places a hand on her shoulder, his dark features serious. "I'm sorry, Charlie. You have every right to be upset." His gaze flicks to me. "You both do. But if it's any consolation, what you did—what you overcame and survived—was astounding. I'm so proud of you. And you should be proud of yourselves. This trip is something you'll never forget, and unless I'm mistaken, it's already left its mark on you both, in the best possible way." He looks between us and asks, quietly, "Can you honestly tell me you regret it? Any of it?"

I stare down at the floor, unwilling to concede his point. But the truth is, he's right. While I still feel equal parts manipulated and violated, I can't regret the last four days, because they made me realize how capable I am. And more, they brought Charlie into my life.

When neither of us responds, Hawke releases Charlie with a small, knowing smile, then says, "Our medic wants to examine you both, and I'm sure you're eager for hot showers, so take an hour to freshen up and then we'll meet for dinner in the hotel restaurant. We can answer any other questions you have while we enjoy our last night together. Sound like a plan?"

My eyes move to Charlie at the reminder that we'll all be leaving tomorrow, but she doesn't look my way, and I realize she hasn't since we learned the truth about the last four days. I wish I could talk to her privately and find out how she's feeling, whether she wants to rage at the world—or at *me*—for having her words and actions aired live without her consent. But she only nods her agreement to Hawke and allows her stepfather and Ember to pull her away, not glancing back at me once.

I'm still staring after her when Gabe clears his throat and says, "Shall we?"

He's the last person I want to be around, but I give a stiff jerk of my head and tell Hawke, Bentley, and Scarlett that I'll see them soon, before I follow Gabe toward the elevator. As we walk, I notice crowds of people still pressed up against the front doors and windows of the hotel, all trying to get a glimpse of us now that the cameras are off. I wonder what they would think if they heard the conversation we just had, but then a new fear hits me and I ask, "Are the drones gone?"

Gabe is quick to reassure me. "Yes. But if you're worried, give me your watch. It has the GPS and the microphone, so without it, they're useless."

I immediately unfasten the band and hand it over, feeling an odd sense of loss as I remember how the compass kept Charlie and me on track, and how the light gave us visibility in the tunnel.

"You can keep it if you want," Gabe says, noting my hesitation. "I only assumed—"

"No," I cut him off. "You take it." As much as the memories mean to me, I'll feel better knowing there's no chance I'm being recorded from here on out.

We don't speak again as we enter the elevator and ride it up to our floor. The silence is strained, with me still stinging over everything he arranged behind my back, even if I know it was technically for my benefit.

It's as we're walking along the carpeted hallway toward our rooms that he finally says, "Val called earlier today. I know it'll take some time for you to forgive us both for our roles in all of this, but if it helps, what we did worked."

I'm distracted by a mirror we're walking past that shows my silver hair standing on end and dirt smeared across my face, my hiking clothes torn and battered, and every part of me looking worse for wear. Because of that, it takes a second for Gabe's words to process, but when they do, my neck whips toward him and I breathe, "What did you just say?"

Gabe grins wider than I've ever seen. "The producers have agreed to let you stay on as Titan. The decision was unanimous." He claps me on the shoulder, fully beaming now. "Congratulations, Zan. You did it."

An incredulous laugh leaves me, throaty and full of feeling, and my knees wobble from the weight of what this means. The studio isn't terminating my contract. I get to play Titan Wolfe, the role of a lifetime. I can't believe it. I'm desperate to tell someone, wishing I knew Charlie's room number so I could go find her, especially since she helped bring this about. I'm not sure if I can wait a whole hour to see her again, but at least my cell will be back in my hands once I enter my suite, and I'll be able to call my parents and Summer to give them the good news. And Maddox—well, he won't pick up, but I'll still leave him a message, since the best friend I know and love will want to hear about this, even if it's over voicemail.

My euphoria fades as I realize I'll also need to warn him about everything I shared when I believed the cameras were off. He might already know, but if he doesn't . . .

He wasn't talking to me before. Now he may never do so again.

The thought makes my stomach churn, but I force my worries about Maddox aside when Gabe and I reach my door, because he turns to me, his face suddenly grave.

"I need you to know that I never would have agreed to Hawke leaving you alone if I'd thought for one second that it would lead to the dangers it did," Gabe says, his dark eyes solemn. "I'm aware that I'm considered a shark in this industry, but that doesn't mean I don't love you like a son, and seeing you on the bank of the river, not breathing . . ." His big body shudders, before he goes on, quieter, "I wish you'd told me about the DUI. I understand why you didn't, but I still wish you had. Promise me that if anything like that ever happens again, you won't keep it from me. We're a team, kid. You have to tell me these things so I can have your back. Understood?"

I shuffle my feet, my residual anger vanishing in the face of his concern. *This* is why he's been my agent for the last six years—because despite his merciless business decisions, he cares for me deeply. And I care for him, which is why I say, "You still have a lot of groveling ahead, but for my part, I'll try to be more honest in the future." I can't help adding, "I also want it on record that I'm not doing any more reality television. Not even a cooking show. I'm drawing a line."

Gabe chuckles, his solemnity gone. "Noted." Then an unexpected spark enters his eyes. "I have one last surprise for you."

I groan. "I've already had too many of those today. Can we not—"

"You're going to like this one." He opens the door to my suite. "Or rather, these two." My brow furrows, but before I can ask what he's talking about, he finishes, "See you all in an hour."

Then he's pushing me through the door and closing it behind me without an explanation.

But I don't need one.

Because the next thing I know, Summer is tackling me, her blond hair flying as she leaps into my arms, her jade-green eyes full of tears as she cries, "Don't you *ever* do anything as stupid as this trip again, you idiot!"

The wind is knocked out of me from the force of her attack, but even if it wasn't, I'd still have trouble breathing at the sight of the other person standing in my hotel room.

Because Maddox is here, leaning against the wooden post of my bed frame, his copper-colored hair a familiar tousled mess, his caramel eyes locked on mine.

"Thank *God* for Charlie!" Summer continues shrieking into my ear. "I take back everything I said about you falling for a fan—she's the *best*, and she *literally* saved your life. She's also *so* out of your league, but luckily for you—" She trails off when she realizes I'm frozen against her, and slowly pulls away, her eyes darting between me and Maddox. "I'll, uh, give you two a moment."

And then she ducks into the bathroom, leaving me alone with my best friend for the first time in three months.

I have no idea what to do. No idea what to say. My heart races wildly as I stare at him, recalling everything I shared with Charlie about the night of my DUI—my truth, but also his truth. His mental health struggles, his suicide attempt . . . I revealed his most painful secrets to the world, betraying his trust to an audience of millions. It doesn't matter that I did it unknowingly. The footage aired live, the damage instant—and irreversible.

I need to apologize, to beg his forgiveness for exposing his private life so publicly, but my lungs have seized, stealing my breath, and all I can manage is to wheeze out a lame, "Hey."

For a long, agonizing minute, he just looks at me. But then tears fill his eyes and a shuddering breath leaves him, and suddenly, he's marching across the room and yanking me into a rib-cracking embrace.

"God, I'm so sorry, Zan," he rasps out, his normally smooth voice rough with emotion. "For all of it—for everything. That night, and all the weeks since then. I can't—I don't—" He shudders again, this time against me.

I'm a statue in his arms, afraid to move in case I wake up and discover this is a dream.

Maddox's voice remains hoarse as he continues, "I should have returned your calls, but I was so ashamed. You were right when you told Charlie that I hated myself for putting you in that position after what happened to your parents, but it was more than that. I was embarrassed by what I nearly did that night, by you *knowing*, and I—I was worried you would think me weak or—or—hell, I don't even know. I was so lost in my own head that I couldn't see beyond the darkness gripping me. But I should have let you in. I shouldn't have pushed you away. I should have—I should have—"

He stops speaking only to pull me tighter against him. My bruised chest is screaming but I embrace him just as fiercely, tears filling my own eyes at the realization that my best friend flew halfway across the world to see me, that he's not mad at me, that he doesn't hate me for what happened—any of it.

But even realizing all that, I still need to make sure he knows how sorry I am.

"What I said, everything I revealed—" I begin, but he doesn't let me finish.

"Don't," Maddox says, pulling away and swiping at his cheeks, his serious eyes catching mine. "Firstly, you didn't know you were being filmed. And secondly, I'm not hiding anymore. I should have spoken up and gotten help sooner. If my story can make one person do that, or just make them feel less alone, then I'm glad the world knows. I *want* them to know."

Relief slams into me, eclipsed only by my pride in him. But then it hits me anew that he's standing before me, after three long months of radio silence, and I croak out, "I can't believe you're really here."

His face softens with understanding. "As soon as I got your message about doing this trip, I booked a flight. I may have been icing you out, but I still knew how hard this would be after everything with your parents, and I couldn't not be here for you."

Hearing that, fresh tears fill my eyes. But he's not done.

"I was halfway over the Pacific when the show started streaming, so I was already on the ground when it all went to hell. Summer, too, since she decided to cut her Maldives trip short to meet me here, saying it'd be fun to surprise you. She arrived right before you and Charlie fell from the waterfall." Maddox closes his eyes, as if that memory haunts him, but then rallies and continues, "We tried to shake some sense into Hawke's team, and I nearly came to blows with Gabe, but they wouldn't budge about bringing you back in. I don't think Sum or I have slept since you and Charlie had to go off on your own. That was nail-biting television, man."

"Apparently that was the point," I say, recalling everything Hawke, Bentley, Scarlett, and Gabe told us. "And while I hate the way we were manipulated, it paid off. I've officially been given the green light for Titan."

The bathroom door bursts open and Summer flies through it, her screaming words proving she could hear everything we said through the thin walls. "YOU GOT TITAN?"

She leaps into my arms again, pulling Maddox in for a three-way jumping hug.

"I knew it!" she cries. "Charlie totally saved your ass in more ways than one! I *love* that girl!"

But just as quickly, her excitement fades and she steps back, only to punch me in the arm.

"Ow!" I yelp, rubbing my newest bruise. "What was that for?"

"You were freaking *roofied* at my birthday and you didn't tell me." Her glare could slice metal. "I'm not some fainting damsel who you need to protect, Zander. I love that you want to, but please, *stop*." She shoots her narrowed gaze between Maddox and me. "And for the love of everything, both of you need to stop hiding your struggles from each other. There's no shame in having feelings—ever. The good, the bad, and the ugly. That's what friendship is for: warts and all. If either of you forget that again and make me play go-between for so much as a *minute*, let alone three months, I'll kick your asses and make it my life's mission to post embarrassing photos of you across social media." She pauses, wrinkling her nose. "Okay, maybe that last part is going too far, but I'll think of something equally terrible without the public visibility element. Consider yourselves warned."

My lips are twitching by the time she finishes. "Are you done?"

"For now." She tosses her golden locks over her shoulder. "As long as you two are good again?"

I look to Maddox, wanting him to answer. *Needing* him to answer. He doesn't make me wait, only says, his eyes shining with reassurance, "We're good."

"It's about time," Summer mutters. But then she links her arm through mine and starts leading me across the room, saying, "FYI, we wanted to meet you in the foyer with the others, but I was drawing too much attention from the crowd outside, and Maddox is a big baby who was scared to see you without me holding his hand."

Maddox rolls his eyes, but there's a smile tugging at his lips that makes me feel like I'm floating on air. We still have a long way to go to catch up on everything we missed in the last three months—and all the secrets from before that—but seeing him here, hearing he dropped everything to come meet me, I know we're going to be all right.

"So all that's to say," Summer goes on, "before Gabe banished us to your room, he told us about dinner. And I mean this in the kindest possible way, but you're filthy, Zan. So let's pause this little reunion-slash-bonding sesh while you take fifteen showers between now and when we're due down at the restaurant."

"Hawke's medic is coming to check you over as well," Maddox reminds me. "Maybe make it fourteen showers so you don't keep the doc waiting."

As eager as I am to rid myself of my grimy hiking clothes and scrub my skin raw, I hesitate when Summer releases me at the bathroom door.

Maddox reads me like a book, his voice low and steady as he promises, "We're not going anywhere, Zan. We'll be right out here, probably arguing over who gets the chocolate mint sitting on your pillow."

I arch an eyebrow. "It's my pillow. Shouldn't I—"

"Dibs!" Summer declares, shoving me into the bathroom and slamming the door behind me.

I can't keep the smile off my face as I listen to their muffled bickering over the minuscule chocolate, my heart lighter than it's been in months now that I have my best friend back. But my elation fades when my thoughts turn to Charlie, wondering what she's doing and whether she just had her own difficult conversations with her stepdad and Ember. I wish I knew how she's processing everything that's happened since we returned, my insides knotting as I remember how she didn't look at me once after we arrived in the foyer. Dread claws at me, but I tell myself there's no point worrying before I have a chance to speak with her. Instead, I clear my mind as I undress and step under the blissfully hot spray, sighing in contentment as I relax for the first time in days.

That contentment doesn't last, however, because after the medic clears me with a warning to be careful until my bruising heals, Gabe knocks on my door to escort us down to the restaurant, where Charlie, Ember, Jerry, Hawke, Bentley, and Scarlett are waiting in a cordoned-off private area—and in an instant, my dread returns, stronger than ever.

Because Charlie still isn't looking at me.

In fact, she seems determined to avoid my gaze entirely.

Like me, she's cleaned up since I last saw her, now wearing a white dress paired with a purple cardigan, while I've donned dark wash jeans and a blue sweater. But when I try to tell her how nice she looks, or say how good it feels to be clean and ask whether she's as relieved as I am, all I get is a tight smile as she looks past my shoulder and nods in agreement.

Unease gnaws at me, making it difficult to concentrate through dinner. I'm vaguely aware that the conversation is strained and the mood is heavy, at least until the charismatic trio of Ember, Summer, and Maddox work their magic to bring about quick smiles and quicker laughter. They clearly bonded while awaiting news of our potential demise, and it warms my heart to see them getting along so well, even if I'm still worried about why Charlie has closed herself off to me.

I barely notice when dinner ends and Hawke, Bentley, and Scarlett all say their goodbyes, claiming they have an early-morning flight to their next filming location and this is the last we'll see of them. But I do manage to snap back to myself when Hawke pulls Charlie and me aside to tell us again how proud he is of the way we handled ourselves, before saying we're welcome to join him on another adventure any time we want.

"Or you can visit one of my survival camps," he offers. "The one in Ecuador is my favorite. Cougars, jaguars, anacondas, piranhas—the Amazon really delivers. Consider this a standing invitation."

At the identical looks of horror on our faces, he bursts out laughing, then draws us in for quick hugs before leaving with Bentley and Scarlett. Soon after, Gabe and Jerry retreat to their rooms as well.

It's Maddox who drags the rest of us back to my suite, his arm slung around Charlie's shoulders to make sure she doesn't escape—likely because he can see, just as I can, that she wants to. I'm desperate to talk to her alone, but I exercise patience as Summer, Maddox, and Ember share about the last few days from their perspectives, and then our conversation morphs into a casual, easy-going hangout, as if we're old friends. It's surreal, purely because it *isn't*. Ignoring the tension surrounding Charlie and me, the dynamic between the five of us is almost unnaturally cohesive, like we've known each other for years rather than days—or in some cases, hours.

Despite how enjoyable it is, and how much I'm beginning to relax again even with Charlie's walls raised sky high, all of that shatters when I step into the bathroom to relieve myself and then return to the suite. Because while Maddox, Summer, and Ember are still chatting merrily among themselves—

Charlie is gone.

Charlie

Zander finds me sitting on the wooden bench in the hotel's fairy garden, staring out at the view of the moonlit mountains.

I knew he would come—I've been waiting for him.

As much fun as I was having spending time with his friends and Ember, and as surreal as it was to discover how well we all get along, I couldn't stay in that room with them a minute longer or I would have screamed.

For hours, my mind has been a battleground, ever since I learned how we were manipulated and deceived. At first, I feared Zander had been in on the ruse, but his pale-faced disbelief was genuine. That made it easier to stomach what happened to us, if only because I wasn't alone in feeling so betrayed. And admittedly, the things he shared when we opened up to each other were much more damning than my own secrets, even if I still wish the world hadn't been privy to my deepest thoughts. As it was, it took most of the hour before dinner to convince my stepdad that I forgive him for descending into his grief after Mum died, all because of what he heard me tell Zander last night. It was a relief when Hawke's medic arrived for my health check, since it gave me a break from Jerry's relentless apologies.

In some small way, part of me is grateful my stepdad was able to witness my heartache and his role in what I'd been bottling up. Ember, too, after the revelations I had about focusing on her for the last few years and forgetting myself in the process. But I still wish I could have told them without millions of strangers watching. I feel so . . . so *violated*, and I'm sure Zander must feel the same, given how much he values his privacy. It's like the world has seen us naked—in an emotional and psychological sense—and it's going to take me some time to come to grips with that.

But that's not why I had to leave our friends in Zander's room, nor is it why I've been avoiding his questioning gaze all night.

I'm not sure when my self-preservation instincts began to kick in, whether it was as soon as the rescue helicopter landed, or when the screaming crowd was pressing in on us, or maybe it was when we learned the truth about our every word and action being streamed live since we left four days ago, but sometime over the last few hours, the inevitable happened:

I came crashing back to reality.

And now I have to make sure Zander crashes with me.

At the guarded look on his face as he approaches me in the garden, I think he might already know. But that doesn't mean this will be any easier.

"May I sit?" he asks.

I close my eyes as the words pull me straight back to Monday evening when he asked the same question. We were both in our pajamas then, while now we're in our dinner clothes, his tight blue sweater hugging his torso in a way that has been tempting me all night. Everything would be much simpler if I wasn't so attracted to him, or if he'd been the troll I'd once hoped for, personality-wise.

But he's not.

He's wonderful, and I—

I halt my own thoughts, not allowing them to continue, and I shuffle over on the cold bench, granting him room.

For a moment, neither of us speaks, but then we both talk at once.

"So I—"

"Are you—"

We look at each other with sheepish smiles.

"You first," Zander offers, nervously rubbing his jeans-clad leg.

The words I need to say get stuck in my throat. Instead, I manage, somewhat lamely, "What a day, huh?"

A half laugh, half moan leaves him and he runs a hand through his hair, ruffling the now-clean silver strands. "You said it. Can you believe that this time last night we were under these very same stars, having no idea that—" He stops himself, wincing.

But he doesn't need to finish for me to know what he was going to say: *. . . having no idea that the world was watching us pour our hearts out to each other.*

"It's pretty unreal," I agree, rasping slightly. I clear my throat and say, my voice soft, "I'm glad you and Maddox have made up. He seems really great. Summer, too."

"We have a lot of work ahead of us," Zander says, looking out at the misted national park. "But yeah, I'm so happy he's here." He turns to me, his lips quirking. "I think you owe me an 'I told you so' now that my bromance is back on track."

My lips quirk in return. "That sounds like something a smug know-it-all would say."

He laughs, the sound full of relief, and I instantly feel awful, wondering why I'm letting this go on.

But I know why.

Because I don't want it to end.

Even if it has to.

I sober, and am about to try once more to say the words, but Zander gets in first, his serious eyes capturing mine. "Thank you, Charlie. You got me Titan, and I'll never be able to—"

"*You* got you Titan," I interrupt firmly, not letting him give me the credit. It took all my willpower to resist throwing my arms around him when he shared the news at dinner, especially when I saw his puzzled, hurt expression at my lack of reaction. "The world fell in love with *you*, Zander. Or re-fell—whatever you want to call it. I was just along for the ride."

"It wouldn't have happened without you," he maintains.

"It might have happened easier or sooner without me," I argue. "Imagine if you'd been out there"—I wave to the shadowed mountains—"with a fan like Ember. You heard what Gabe said about viewers picking up on the animosity between us. You wouldn't have had that if you'd been with someone else, which means you might have won the public back sooner, *and* you wouldn't have been abandoned by Hawke and Bentley."

That realization hits me hard, especially as I recall what Gabe said in the foyer: *It's your own fault things got so carried away.* He's right, even if neither Zander nor I could have known that our early strained interactions might result in us being stranded together.

"That might be so," Zander says slowly, "but it's only *because* we were left on our own that I became unguarded enough to make the public like me again." He pauses, then says, pointedly, "And I believe the word Gabe used was 'chemistry,' not 'animosity.' There's a big difference."

I'm careful not to look at him as I reply, "Whatever he called it, and however things turned out, what I'm saying is, you earned Titan all on your own because of who *you* are. And I'm—I'm really happy for you."

There's a moment of silence before Zander says, quietly, "You could have fooled me."

Hearing his forlorn tone that's full of both awareness and painful understanding, I have to blink fast to keep my tears at bay. I can't stop myself from taking his hand, gripping hard as I angle my body to look straight into his sad blue eyes. The grief in them makes my heart ache as I realize how much this is killing him—and how much it's killing me, too.

But it has to be done. And while I might greedily want to put it off for as long as I can, it'll only hurt us both more if I keep delaying the inevitable.

So I don't.

"You know this will never work," I whisper, holding his mournful gaze. "The last few days we were in our own bubble, but now that we're back, the reality is, our worlds are too different. You *know* that, Zander. Tell me I'm wrong."

His fingers tighten, and his free hand moves to trap mine between both of his palms. "We can make it work."

I'm already shaking my head before he finishes speaking. "We can't—and I'm not sure that we should." That has him turning still, so I rush to explain, "You're about to be locked in a studio filming the movie of the decade, and all your attention needs to be on that. And it *should* be—because you deserve this, and you should be able to enjoy every second of it without distraction." I squeeze his fingers. "And as for me—"

"You need to see the world and find your place in it," Zander says with a sad, knowing sigh, "not stuck in LA waiting for me to finish an eighteen-hour day on set after which I'll be too exhausted to see you, let alone do anything else."

My eyebrows shoot upward at his presumption that I would have gone back to Los Angeles with him, especially since we never once talked about the possibility. But despite my surprise—and my knee-jerk reaction to wonder why it would be *me* who has to uproot my life, before realizing his assumption is based on my desire to travel, which is fair—I have to fight back new tears at the image he's just laid out. Because part of me *wants* that. I *want* to see his home and witness his life. I want to meet his adoptive parents and spend more time with Summer and Maddox. I want to be there waiting for him at the end of a long day, regardless of whether we only have a few minutes together before he needs to crash. I want to be at his side during the highs and lows of everything he experiences in the utterly insane industry he works in. I *want* all of that—desperately.

But I also know the timing isn't right. I need to see to my dreams first before I can support him in his. For once, I need to be selfish, even if that means sacrificing something precious in the process: *him*.

"I'm sorry," I whisper, feeling my heart break at the sight of his eyes gleaming with tears. "I wish things could be different. But my mum used to always tell me that everything happens for a reason, and I have to believe she's right. So let's be grateful for the time we had, knowing it was special for us both, and that we'll never forget it."

"Why are you making this sound like a goodbye?" Zander asks hoarsely.

"Because it *is*," I say. "It has to be."

"We might have to go our separate ways, but we live in a world of technology," he says, not understanding. "We can phone each other and video call and text and email and—"

I pull my hand from his and jump to my feet, unable to remain sitting with so much emotion flooding my veins. I begin to pace on the grass, the fairy lights dappling my white dress with gold splotches. "Do you honestly think you'd be able to handle that?" I ask. "Because to me, staying in touch but not being with each other would be like . . . like cutting off an arm and slowly bleeding to death."

Zander stands as well. "So . . . what? You're saying you want to cauterize the wound? Is that really what you want—a clean break where we never see or talk to each other again? *Ever?*"

"I don't *want* that," I say, throwing my hands out to the side. "I *need* that. Anything else would be too painful. And you need it just as much as I do."

"No, Charlie, what I need is *you*."

At his words, I stop pacing and stare at him. I can't hold in my tears any longer, letting them drip silently down my cheeks.

Zander watches them fall, one after the other, and then he slowly closes his eyes, a look of devastation coming over him, mixed with resignation—and defeat.

He steps forward until he's standing before me, reaching out to gently wipe my tears away as he says, his voice achingly soft, "I'm sorry—you're right. I just—I don't want to let you go." He exhales a trembling breath. "But I'm going to. Because you deserve to be happy, Charlie Hart. And I'd never forgive myself if I became the person who was keeping you from flying free."

God, why does he have to be so *perfect*?

More tears fill my eyes, and I nearly take back everything I said, leaping into his arms and saying I want to go to LA with him to stay by his side forever. But I can see the resolve settling into his features now, and I know without asking that he wouldn't let me even if I begged. He won't allow me to forfeit my dreams, and I—I—

I love him for that.

I *love* him.

And I have to let him go.

Because he has dreams, too. And for the same reason that he won't let me abandon mine, I won't let him surrender his.

A shuddering breath leaves me and I do what I've wanted to do all night, throwing my arms around him. He draws me close, both of us knowing it's the last time we'll get to do this, and neither willing to let go.

But eventually, we have to.

I pull back first, ignoring every part of me that longs to stay wrapped in his embrace.

"I'll never forget you, Zander Rune," I whisper, leaning up to kiss his cheek. "Thank you for helping me dream again." A final tear falls down my cheek as I offer him a tremulous smile and say, "I'll see you on the big screen."

And then, without giving him a chance to respond, I turn on my heel and run back up the cobblestone path into the hotel, my heartbreak so strong that I have to flee in order to tear myself away from him.

Ember is waiting in my room when I stumble inside, and as soon as she sees me, her face crumples with realization, and she opens her arms.

I can't hold in what I'm feeling anymore and I burst into loud, sobbing tears as she envelops me with her body. She tells me over and over that everything will be all right, but for once, I don't believe her.

Because the moment I left Zander, I already knew:

I just made the biggest mistake of my life.

And even if it was the right thing to do, I'm still going to regret it.

Forever.

Zander

I used to love airports.

I loved wondering where people were going, and why. Whether it was a holiday or a business trip or to visit a loved one—the sense of anticipation emanating from travelers always made me feel electric. And the deeper metaphor always spoke to me on a philosophical level, the concept of transition, of departing one place and leaving something behind in order to go forth and step into something new.

I used to love that feeling, that wondrous expectation, that tangible exhilaration.

But today I don't feel anything as I wait in the executive lounge at the Sydney International Terminal, just as I haven't felt anything since Charlie tore out of my arms in the garden on Friday night and ran from me, not looking back.

I don't know how long I stood out in the cold after she left, praying she would return, while also knowing that if she did, I would have to be the one to leave her. Because I meant what I said—I won't keep her from her dreams. Part of me wishes I could be selfish enough to do that, or even self*less* enough to turn down Titan and go with her on her adventures, but she'd never let me give up my role in a million years, and if I tried, I would lose her regardless.

Just as I've lost her now.

I have no memory of returning to my room that night, only that when I did, Summer and Maddox were waiting for me, and seeing my pale, tearstained face, they both ran to embrace me, looking almost as devastated as I felt. They haven't left my side since then, not all through yesterday when we left Katoomba and headed back to Sydney, not when our plane was delayed and we had to spend another night in the city, and not when we rose at the ass crack of dawn today for our rescheduled Sunday morning flight straight through to LAX.

They haven't said much, or if they have, I haven't heard them. I feel like I'm walking through a cloud, part delayed exhaustion, but mostly I'm lost in my heartbreak over having to leave the girl I love behind.

Because I do love her.

I love Charlie Hart.

I don't know when it happened—it might have been from the very first day we met when I asked if she was excited for our trip, and she replied with a sarcastic, *Can't wait.* After years of people falling at my feet, it was refreshing to have someone do the opposite. Humbling, even. But more likely, it came on gradually during our time away together as I got to know her, inside and out. It terrifies me, how much I feel for her, just as it terrifies me that *because* of what I feel for her, I can't be with her. If only our lives weren't so different, if only we could—

"Zander, are you listening?"

I blink out of my despondent thoughts to see Gabe standing in front of where I'm seated. Summer is curled up on my right, and Maddox on my left, all three of us having been staring out the large windows at the early-morning planes coming and going while we wait for our gate to open. I'm not sure how long we've been sitting here in silence. I'm not even sure when Summer took my hand in hers, or when Maddox replaced my cold cup of coffee. They're worried about me, I can tell. And they're heartbroken on my behalf, as only the best of friends are when sad things happen to those they care about.

"Zander?" Gabe calls my name again, and this time he waves his phone in my face. "Have you heard a word I've said?"

I shake my head, both in answer and to clear it. "Sorry, what?"

Gabe sighs, then repeats, "That was Val on the phone. Your shooting schedule has just been finalized, so she's sent through your itinerary."

As hard as I worked to get it, and as much as I'm sacrificing to keep it, Titan is the last thing I want to think about right now.

"Great," I say, lacking enthusiasm. "I'll read it when I get home."

I turn to the window once more, aware of Maddox and Summer sharing a concerned look. But Gabe isn't done.

"I think you're going to want to open it now."

A moment later, I hear a notification on my phone.

I don't pick it up, not ready to return to reality.

Because as soon as I do, that means I'll be leaving Charlie behind for good.

She's probably sleeping now, like most sane people at this hour. She would have returned home with Ember and her stepdad yesterday, probably had a nice dinner with Jerry and then an early night knowing she has to be up in a few hours to supervise a children's birthday party at her work today—something her boss called her about on Friday night, begging her to take the shift. We were all hanging out as a group in my suite at the time, and Charlie had groaned and said into her phone, "I swear, Sandy, if I survived the last four days only to be torn apart by a bunch of sugar-high eight-year-olds, I'll be writing you a *very* stern letter from the afterlife."

Remembering that now brings a smile to my lips, even if it makes the pain in my heart grow ever stronger.

"Zander!"

This time Gabe snaps his fingers together, frowning as he points to my phone.

That breaks through to me enough that I narrow my eyes and say,

"We're about to be stuck on a fifteen-hour flight, Gabe. It's nothing that can't wait."

He makes a frustrated sound and rubs a hand over his cropped black hair, grumbling about how he needs a vacation. But then he exhales loudly and pulls up a chair, his expression softening. "I know you're hurting, kid. And I know everything with Charlie didn't turn out the way you wanted, but if you'd just—"

I rise from my seat and walk away, unable to have this conversation. I can't talk about this—about *her*. Not yet. It hurts too much.

But I also can't escape it, because Maddox hurries after me, grabbing my arm and halting my retreat.

"Let me go," I say, trying to pull away. But my best friend holds firm.

"No. It's tough love time."

My brow furrows. "It's what?"

"You're miserable." Maddox jabs a finger toward me. "It's been nearly two days and you're not eating, not sleeping, barely speaking—how long does this have to go on before you realize you're making a huge mistake?"

I cross my arms. "I *know* it's a mistake. But there's nothing I can do about it. She wants to travel, and I'm tied down with Titan."

"For what, three months? Six months?" Maddox scoffs. "It's one movie, not a life sentence."

"If it's successful—which it will be—then it'll be another blockbuster franchise," I remind him. "And even if it flops, there will be a different movie after it. Then another. And another. Plus, it's not just the filming—it's the publicity and the tours and the screaming fans and everything else that comes with it. This is my *life*, Maddox. So unless I want to give it up, which I don't—and Charlie wouldn't let me do that for her anyway—then this is my future. Indefinitely."

"So you're saying you'd be the first actor to ever get involved with someone outside the industry?" Maddox rolls his eyes. "Sure, I can see how mind-blowing that idea is."

I clench my jaw at his sarcasm.

We're drawing looks from the other early-morning lounge patrons now, so Maddox lowers his voice and moves closer to say, "I get where you're coming from, Zan. Truly, I do. But what about *her* future? Is she planning to travel forever? What happens when she's finished finding herself or whatever, and she's ready to put down roots? Why can't that be with *you*?"

I swallow and look away, because that's the argument I *should* have made to Charlie on Friday night when she said we couldn't stay in contact. She was right that it would be painful, and I understand her desire for a clean break in an effort to ease some of that, but it also means cutting off any chance of a future when our paths might align better.

"Come on, Zan," Maddox presses when I'm silent for too long. "Why didn't you fight for her?"

It's the disappointment in his tone that has me rasping out, "Because I was afraid she would say no."

Maddox's caramel eyes widen, before his expression falls with sorrow. "Oh, Zander." He hauls me in for a tight embrace. "You're such an idiot. A lovable idiot, but an idiot all the same."

"He's right, you know," Summer says, and I pull away to see her standing beside us. I wonder how long she's been there, and how much she heard, before realizing it was probably everything. "Charlie is crazy about you, Zan. Ember says she's even more heartbroken than you are."

I jerk at that. "You spoke with Ember?"

Summer makes a huffing sound. "Just because *you* didn't get anyone's contact details doesn't mean *I* didn't." She glances at Maddox, a strange, almost sly look entering her eyes. "Or *we*, I should say. Right, Maddox?"

My best friend shuffles his feet, not looking at anyone, and I wonder what that's about. But I don't have a chance to think on it before Gabe steps up to us, frowning at me all over again.

"This is all well and good," he says in a snippy tone, "but if you would only *listen* to me and check your phone, you'd see that the solution to your problem is painfully simple."

"My problem?"

Gabe looks at me as if I'm mad, and says, with emphasis, "*Charlie.*"

"What are you on about?" Maddox asks him.

Gabe finally loses his patience and snaps, "Just read the damn email, Zander." When he sees my eyebrows shoot upward, he sucks in a calming breath and says, in a gentler tone, "Please, trust me. I promise you'll understand in a moment."

I have no idea why this means so much to him, especially *now*, of all times, but I pull my cell from my jeans pocket and bring up my emails. My inbox is a disaster zone after having been neglected for most of the last week, but I ignore the blaring notifications and tap on the most recent arrival, seeing the words *FWD: CONFIDENTIAL—FOR YOUR EYES ONLY* in the subject line. It's redundant, but I don't mention that to Gabe since he's already on edge.

The airport Wi-Fi is so slow that I have to wait for the email to load, then for the attached document to download, but when it does, I'm so shocked that I need a full minute to process what I'm reading.

When it finally sinks in, I gasp out an incredulous, "Is this for real?"

Hearing the disbelief in my tone, Maddox and Summer peer over my shoulder and read the words for themselves. Maddox barks out a laugh and slaps me on the back, while Summer squeals and throws her hands in the air.

Gabe just smiles, before tapping on his phone, and a second later, I receive another notification.

It's a new plane ticket.

For today.

Only, it's not to Los Angeles.

Summer's phone pings, as does Maddox's, and I know Gabe has sent them both new tickets as well.

Then my agent steps forward and, in a rare display of affection, he pulls me into a hug, saying in my ear, "I'll see you when you get home. Fly safe."

I'm still reeling, so all I can do is squeeze him back and croak out, "Thank you."

His arms tighten around me as he hears the depth of meaning in my words, since I know—I *know*—he had a hand in the email I just read, even if I don't know how he did it. But then he releases me quickly again, straightening his suit jacket as he warns, "You're leaving from a different terminal. I suggest you run."

I don't need to be told twice, and after one last grateful look, I take off in a mad dash across the airport with Maddox and Summer sprinting beside me.

Fear is screaming at me to stop. Doubt is begging me to turn around.

But I ignore them both, because something else is urging me onward, something much more powerful:

Hope.

Charlie

I'm running late.

I was meant to be at work twenty minutes ago, but Jerry is taking pains to make up for his distance over the last few months, and that meant he wanted us to enjoy a home-cooked breakfast together this morning. Since he can't boil water without setting the house on fire, I had to step in to save us both from his good intentions, which delayed my preparation for *The Little Mermaid*–themed birthday party I'm supervising today, and left me rushing around last-minute to get my costume ready.

Sandy so owes me for taking this shift, since the last thing I want to be doing right now is driving through our sleepy coastal town dressed as Sebastian the crab, complete with googly eyes, antennae, and pincers. If I had my choice, I'd be curled up in bed and crying my heart out—which, outside of making breakfast, is all I've done since we flew home from Sydney yesterday.

It's ridiculous that I miss Zander so much, when a week ago, I didn't even know him—and what I did know, or *thought* I knew, I despised. But I can't deny what I'm feeling, or the depth of my pain knowing I'll never see him again.

Ember stayed with me last night, holding me as I sobbed until I had no tears left, just like she did the night before in Katoomba. When I woke this morning, she was gone, but there was a note on my pillow saying she'll see me at work later today. I hate that I've been such an emotional mess over the last two days, especially since I'm the one who pushed Zander away—and have regretted it ever since—but I also don't know how to stop the ache that's like a dagger buried in my chest.

While I might not feel like supervising this birthday, I'm grateful for the distraction it will provide. For three hours, I won't have time to feel sorry for myself, since I'll be too busy helping a bunch of mermaids and princes concoct gaudy ice-cream creations. If nothing else, it'll offer a reprieve from my relentless heartache. Not even the exhilaration of having figured out what I want to do next in life has helped ease my pain—though at least it's kept me from dwelling on the fact that I'm currently driving down Main Street dressed as a bright red crustacean. I always have to leave my dignity at the door on party days, but today is next-level commitment.

Upon arriving at Sandy's Scoops and Sprinkles, I glance around the parking lot, relieved to find no trace of the paparazzi I feared would follow me home from Katoomba. I was certain they would hound me for days after the trip, begging for interviews and media appearances, but aside from a small group waiting at the hotel yesterday morning and another cluster at the Sydney airport, I've mostly been left alone. I can only assume that with Zander gone, they've already moved on to the next big scoop, and I'm immensely thankful for that—especially since it means there's no one around to witness me in all my crabified glory as I struggle to get out of my car. The padded legs attached to my sides are particularly unruly, making me so frustrated that I almost tear them off.

When I'm finally free, I hurry to the front glass door, nearly tripping twice because of the cumbersome outfit. If I hadn't felt so wretched this morning, I might have donned my much simpler seashell bikini and sequin skirt instead, but I didn't feel up to wearing anything sparkly today. The kids, at least, will get a kick out of the crab costume—kids that I can see have already started arriving, since there are numerous Ariels and Prince Erics and Ursulas and King Tritons bouncing with excitement on the other side of the glass.

I take a moment to brace myself before entering, belatedly wondering why Ember's car is here. I didn't expect her to appear until after my shift, but it's not unusual for her to hang out with Sandy while I'm looking after the children, so I don't dwell on it. Instead, I take a breath and prepare to get through the next few hours without thinking about Zander, praying it will begin to feel easier after that. I know deep down that it will never fully stop hurting, and that I'll always be haunted by my decision, wondering if we could have found a way for it to work despite his career commitments and my newfound wanderlust. But I also know I can't live like that, forever chained by my regret, buried in doubts and crippled by what-ifs—nor could I have lived knowing he was on one side of the world, locked in studio after studio, while I was somewhere else entirely, our hearts entwined but our lives separated. That would destroy me, just as it would destroy him.

Then again, I could be wrong—he might have already moved on from our time together. His flight will be landing in LA sometime today, and he'll go back to his life and—and—

And forget about me.

God, that hurts. I almost buckle from the weight of it, and I press my clawed hand to my chest, fighting back tears, before I give myself a mental kick and pull myself together. I can return to sobbing once I get home; for now, I need to summon my mediocre acting skills and get through this party.

Despite my best efforts, it's a struggle to paint a friendly smile on my face as I open the door and step into the familiar pink-and-cream-colored parlor. I immediately spot Sandy in front of the counter, talking to a group of young mermaids who are staring at the ice-creams behind the glass, pointing out their favorites. Seeing the twinkle in Sandy's brown eyes as they share animatedly about all the flavors makes me realize with a pang of sadness that I'm going to miss this place when I leave. But I can't chase my dreams while staying where I am—that's not how dreams work.

"Miss Hart!" calls a familiar young girl who has been to numerous parties here since we started offering them. "Look at me—I'm Ariel!"

"So you are," I say as she runs over with her friends, my smile not so forced now as I take in all their excited faces. I gesture to the silver fork tied around her neck. "I like your necklace."

"It's so I can brush my hair, just like Ariel does!" she says with unmitigated glee.

"Very practical," I tell her, before clapping my clawed hands together. "Who's ready to make some ice-cream?"

My ears ring with their shouts of "ME! ME! ME!" and "I AMMMM!" and I raise my arms for calm, before saying, "Into the party room, then."

They squeal with delight and sprint off toward the rainbow-painted annex, while I start to follow at a much more human pace. But then Sandy clears their throat loudly and says, "Hold up a moment, cherub."

I look at them in question, seeing the bright grin on their purple-glittered lips as they nod pointedly toward the corner of the parlor behind me. Puzzled, I turn around, then come to a jarring halt, unable to believe what I'm seeing.

Because Ember is seated at a table with Maddox and Summer, all three of them beaming at me. And standing next to them, leaning against the wall—

Is Zander.

I gape at them, at *him*, certain this must be some kind of heartbroken fever dream and my alarm will wake me up any second now. But the longer I stare at them—at *him*—the more real they become.

It hits me that I'm not imagining this when Zander straightens and walks slowly toward me, meeting me in the middle of the now-empty parlor. I can hear the kids laughing in the next room, and I'm aware of Sandy still grinning hugely from the glass counter, but I have eyes only for Zander as he comes to a stop before me.

"What are you doing here?" I breathe, afraid one wrong blink will reveal this is a fantasy after all. "Why aren't you on your way home?"

Zander cocks his head to the side, a smile quirking his lips. But his blue eyes are guarded. Afraid, even. Considering the last time he saw me was when I told him I didn't want to see or speak to him again, before I *literally* ran away from him, I understand his hesitation—though it still breaks my heart into a thousand new pieces.

"Our flight was delayed until this morning," he replies, not quite answering my question, since if that were the case, he'd be on it right now. "We were waiting at the airport for it, but then I got an email, and our plans . . . changed."

He pulls his phone from his jeans pocket and begins swiping at the screen. If I could summon any words beyond my shock at seeing him, I would be pleading for an explanation, but all I can do is wait, frozen in place, as he finds what he's looking for.

When he glances up at me again, there's a nervous look on his face, but he blows out a breath and squares his shoulders before meeting my eyes and saying, "I need you to know that I heard everything you said on Friday night, and if you truly believe our worlds are so different that we can't be together, or if you don't feel the same way about me as I do about you, then—then—" He stumbles slightly, before recovering, "Then I'll respect that, and you'll never hear from me again. But before you make that call, I have a proposition for you."

He holds his phone out for me to take.

My hand is shaking as I reach for it, the claw covering my fingers making it difficult for me to get a good grip. At Zander's urging, I glance down at the screen, noting the big *CONFIDENTIAL* warning at the top, frowning slightly as I wonder what it is I'm looking at.

But then I realize.

And my heart stops.

Before it starts again, beating double-time in my chest.

My eyes shoot up to Zander. The nervous look has returned to his face, only it's much more amplified now.

"Is this—Is this—" My voice is little more than a croak.

"It's my filming itinerary for *Titan's War*," he tells me. "It's all locked in."

I read the document again, the words all but screaming at me through the screen.

Reykjavík.

Vatnajökull National Park.

Diamond Beach.

The Blue Lagoon.

Stokkur Geyser.

It's a list of all the places I told Zander I wanted to travel to first, and seeing them, I realize—

Titan's War is being filmed in Iceland.

Tears start brimming in my eyes as I understand what this means, what Zander is asking me.

"I know there will be a million challenges ahead," he says quietly, stepping closer. "I know this is only for a few months, and there's no certainty beyond that. We could be right back to being two worlds apart. Or maybe—" He moves another step closer. "Maybe it'll give us a chance to figure out how to make this work. To make *us* work."

He's right in front of me now, near enough that I can feel his body heat.

"I want you to come with me, Charlie," he whispers. "I want to explore Iceland with you, and whatever comes after that. Because I think we're worth fighting for." His words are shaky now as he asks, with everything he's feeling clear in his voice, "The question is, do you?"

My tears are falling steadily now, but I don't wipe them away. I just hold his gaze, seeing his heart laid bare before me, seeing how much he wants this, wants *me*, as well as his fear that I'm going to say no. He doesn't realize I spent the last two days wishing for this—wishing for a way we could be together and yet still follow our own paths. But now . . .

I truly must be dreaming.

And it's the best dream I've ever had.

So I decide to embrace it, my voice husky with emotion as I say, "I guess I should ask for a rush order when I renew my passport."

It takes him a moment to understand my reply, but when he does, his eyes widen, before a relieved, incredulous laugh leaves him, and the next second, I'm being swept up into his arms.

Ember, Maddox, and Summer are whooping from the corner, and Sandy is cheering from the front counter, with the kids peeking their heads out of the party room to see what's going on. But all I can think about is Zander holding me—and this time, I don't have to let him go.

Only, there's one thing I want more than his arms around me—and that's his lips on mine. So I pull back to make that happen, but he speaks again before I can follow through.

"I had a longer speech prepared," he says, the joy on his face like pure sunshine. "Maddox and Summer helped me come up with it on the plane here, but once I saw you, every word fled my mind."

I lean into him, feeling warmth spread through me at his admission, realizing I affect him as much as he does me.

But then he goes on, "Seriously, it was nearly impossible to keep a straight face and not ask what the hell you're wearing. It's a miracle I was able to focus at all." He flicks one of my antennae. "Do you normally dress up like this? Because if so, I might need to—"

I cut him off by tugging him close and ordering, "Just shut up and kiss me, Zander."

He doesn't need any further encouragement, his lips twitching with humor before they finally—*finally*—meet mine.

Our friends are hooting even louder now, as is Sandy, all over a chorus of "Eww, Miss Hart!" from the watching children.

But I don't care, because I feel Zander's mouth smiling against mine, and nothing else matters in our world, just that I'm in his arms, and he's kissing me.

Our future may be uncertain, but I do know this:

We're going to step into it, one day at a time.

Chasing our dreams.

Together.

AUTHOR'S NOTE

Firstly—and most importantly—thank you for reading this book! (Also, was that not the cutest ending *ever*?!? Oh my heart!)

If you've made it this far, then you'll probably know I took some *teeny-tiny* liberties with certain parts of the story, and I figure I should mention a few of them here.

For example, while I'm sure there are a number of lovely hotels, motels, Airbnbs, and whatnot in Katoomba, maybe even some with their very own tea gardens and fairy lights and postcard-perfect views of the mountains, the one featured in this novel is *most definitely* made up.

Similarly, I have no idea if there was ever any mining done in the area of the Blue Mountains National Park that my characters visit, so the claim of an "old mining route" is, again, made up.

Ditto to the existence of the dilapidated bridge.

And—and—*and*—

Well, let's face it.

This book is a work of *fiction*, so there are loads of things that I added for the sake of—*jazz hands*—*drama*.

Don't get me wrong, I did plenty of research. I learned more about adventure activities like skydiving, rappelling, mountain climbing, canyoning, and free-diving than I ever thought possible. I also learned way too many general survival skills for someone who doesn't even go camping, including—*gags*—how to skin and/or debone various kinds of animals. (Needless to say, I would *not* have lasted as long as Charlie and Zander did out in the wild, or anywhere near close to it!)

Another thing I took *a lot* of liberties with was Zander being a famous Hollywood actor, most notably how he wasn't surrounded by a team of people 24/7. Summer, too, for that matter. Actually, here's a story for you: a few years ago I was signing at a convention where John Travolta was the headlining guest, and no joke, every time I saw him in the green room, he had *at least* five people with him—two bodyguards, a manager, an agent, an assistant . . . the list went on. Given the level of fame that Zander and Summer have, they would likely require the same kind of entourage wherever they go, and they'd *definitely* be hounded by more paparazzi than what I included in this book. (Especially for that end scene at the ice-cream parlor—but, really, how could I give #Zarlie their happily-ever-after if there were cameras flashing and ruining the moment?! Talk about a mood killer!)

And staying on Zander for a second, him being accredited at tandem skydiving is probably a *bit* of a stretch, though it's not impossible with the training he did in Europe. But, either way, remember what I said about drama? That scene would have been nowhere near as much fun if Charlie had been strapped to anyone else! (Admit it, it's true!)

I think you get the point by now that I fudged a few things in order to make the reading experience more pleasurable. The books I write are intended to offer you an escape, and since reality can often get in the way of a good story (annoying!), I had no shame in bending a few truths for entertainment purposes. Despite that—or maybe because of it—I hope you were able to enjoy this (mis)adventure as much as I enjoyed writing it.

And, hey, if nothing else, let's all remember that I'm usually a fantasy author, so it's really quite a miracle that I didn't add in a dragon.

Oh, wait . . .

The Enchanted Vale. Prince Tyron. The Five Realms. Dragon slaying.

I forgot, I totally did that.

I guess what they say is true: old habits die hard.

Laughs awkwardly and slowly closes laptop

ACKNOWLEDGMENTS

You know, it's going to sound strange, but it's almost harder to write acknowledgments than it is to write an entire book. I'd love to consider the psychology behind that, but I fear it might result in the equivalent of the "stop yabbering and get off the stage" music that plays at the Academy Awards, and it would be embarrassing if I got (justifiably) cut off from finishing my own acknowledgments. So, instead, I'll hazard a guess that the reason it's always difficult to write these is because it means a story is really, truly over—and that, in turn, is always a little bittersweet.

But!

It also means I get to thank a whole heap of amazing people, and this time around, the talent level of those who helped make this book happen is off the charts!

I absolutely must start with my agent, Jen Azantian, for taking a broken, burnt-out, barely functioning shell of a human and nurturing me back to life. You showed me moment by moment, day by day, that I could trust you, that you would protect me in this often intimidating and overwhelming industry, that you would have my back and be my fiercest advocate, champion . . . and friend. Thank you, Jen. My life changed for the better the day you entered it, and I will be forever grateful for you.

To magic-working editors, Zoe Walton and Mary Verney, you astounded me over and over again with your thoughtful insights and clever suggestions, all of which transformed this book from a pumpkin into a—well, not a princess. That's the metaphor I'm after, but I'm now remembering that the pumpkin turns into a carriage, and while, sure, that's pretty with all the sparkles and whatnot, but it doesn't sound as good to say my editors helped turn my book into a carriage. What even is that?

ANYWAY.

Mary and Zoe, you were instrumental in making this book an actual *book*, and I learned so much through the process (including a great many things that I'm still cringing about—I'm SO SORRY for all the *just*s, *even*s, *barely*s, and *look*s. *Hides face*). It was an absolute privilege to work with you both, and I can't wait to do it again soon!

I also must send gigantic amounts of gratitude to the entire PRH Aus team for all the care and support and passion you put into my books, including (but not limited to), Julie Burland (aka CEO Extraordinaire), Belinda Conners (aka Publishing Director Genius), Angela Duke (aka Sales Wizard), Adelaide Jensen (aka Accounts Wonder—who, note to self, does *not* live in Adelaide), Hannah Armstrong (aka Another Accounts Wonder), Georgie Martin (aka Campaign Manager Mastermind), Elena Cementon and Benjamin Fairclough (aka Production Savants), and Isabelle Werro and Veronica Eze (aka Audio Producing Marvels)—you're all *the best* and I'll never have enough words for how much I appreciate all that you (and the rest of the team) do for me!

And staying on the PRH side of things for a moment: Bec Diep, I would be lost without you. *Lost*, I tell you! I still get teary when I remember the day you offered to become my publicist, and my gratitude has only grown ever since. You are such a delight to work with, and I'm so thankful to know how safe I am on this wild journey because you're walking it with me.

Jumping across the pond to the US now, I'm so ridiculously grateful to the entire Blackstone team for loving this book enough to take a chance on it—and on me. To my editor, Dan Ehrenhaft, I truly can't thank you enough for everything you did to make this happen, and I'm so, *so* excited to see what comes of it. Ditto to all the other incredible people who have worked so diligently on this book: Lydia Rogue, Jesse Bickford, Sarah Bonamino, Francie Crawford, Isabella Bedoya, Cole Barnes, and so many more. Fingers crossed we get to meet one day so I can thank you all in person!

To Anna Kuptsova and Larissa Ezell, thank you for two of the most stunning covers I've ever seen *in my life*. Your artistic skills are unparalleled, and I will never not be obsessed with how perfectly you captured Charlie and Zander and brought them to life.

There are a million other people I could thank professionally, but to avoid the aforementioned risk of being cut off à la Academy Award music style, I'm going to switch gears to offer shoutouts to those in my closer personal circles.

To the earliest readers of this book, Krystal Gagen-Spriggs, Alison Elzayed, and Bridey Morris, thank you for your copious amounts of enthusiasm and encouragement, especially with my "BUT IT'S NOT FANTASY, SO WILL PEOPLE EVEN READ IT?!?!" freak-outs. I hope one day you all get to meet so you can know how much you mean to me (but I also hope you know that anyway).

To my author pals who offered wisdom while I was writing this book: Richard Swan for the legal advice about DUIs and contracts, and Luke Arnold for all the acting-related questions and a peek into that side of your world, thank youuuu! You both rock, and I can't wait for the next time we all get to hang at an event together again!

To my teenage bestie, Jodie Coffey, thank you for sharing your skydiving experiences and helping make that scene as real as possible. (I had no idea about the quiet!) And to all my friends, near and far—*thank you*. Big love to Teeshie Peffer, Jackie Davison, Renee Chopping, Rachel Griffiths, Kylie Trendell, and Mellie Bos for always being just a message away, and also to Debbie and Tom Conwell for upholding me through some really tough times.

Speaking of tough times, ooof, the last few years have been a doozy, and I would have been in real trouble without my faith, so as gimmicky as it sounds, thank you to God for always being there, through the good times and (especially) the bad. I also wouldn't have survived those times without the gentle love and unending support of my family, so to Mum, Dad, Steve, Reesh, Noah, Caleb, and Aunty Noni—I love you all.

Right! I'm sure I've missed a thousand people (eeek, sorry if that's you!), but I'm going to wrap this up here by saying how grateful I am to every single person reading this. I've said it before and I'll say it again (forever), but you're the reason I get to write, and keep writing. Thank you for loving my books, for sharing them over socials, for telling your friends and family and neighbors and strangers (be safe, folks!), and for simply being the best readers in the world. I couldn't do this without you. (No, but seriously. And I wouldn't want to, either. *Biggest hugs *ever**)

Here's to our next adventure together, but until then, I'll leave you with some encouragement from Rykon Hawke himself:

Live now, not later.

ABOUT THE AUTHOR

Australian author **Lynette Noni** studied journalism, academic writing, and human behavior at university before venturing into the world of fiction. She is the #1 bestselling and award-winning author of the Prison Healer series, the Medoran Chronicles, and the Whisper duology. To date, her books have sold more than one million copies in over twenty countries across the globe.

LYNETTENONI.COM

Instagram, Tiktok, and Facebook:
@LYNETTENONI